GROWING UP

GROWING UP

Frances Paige

Severn House Large Print
London & New York

This first large print edition published in Great Britain 2006 by
SEVERN HOUSE LARGE PRINT BOOKS LTD of
9-15 High Street, Sutton, Surrey, SM1 1DF.
First world regular print edition published 2005 by
Severn House Publishers, London and New York.
This first large print edition published in the USA 2006 by
SEVERN HOUSE PUBLISHERS INC., of
595 Madison Avenue, New York, NY 10022.

British Library Cataloguing in Publication Data

Paige, Frances
  Growing up. - Large print ed.
  1. Glasgow (Scotland) - Social life and customs - 20th century - Fiction
  2. Love stories
  3. Large type books
  I. Title
  823.9'14 [F]

  ISBN-10: 0-7278-7514-0

       ted and bound in Great Britain by
        Books Ltd, Bodmin, Cornwall.

Book 1

Chapter 1

1939

'Race you to the foot, Dad,' Mirren said, and they set off from the mahogany door of their flat with the impressive brass furniture, down the stone stairs. He's all right, she thought, he's quite all right, what I was imagining isn't there, he's got over Mother dying at last, he's all right...

Behind her thoughts, there was the ring of footsteps, his and hers, filling her head, stretching back in time, how often had she run down these stairs, listening to the clatter, boots made a dull, solid sound, but best of all were Cuban heels which struck the stone and rang staccato.

Years ago, when she was small, she remembered being helped by Mother down these stairs, 'That's right, Mirren, try it, Mum's holding you, one, two, three, four. Mary's at the back door.' We're at Mrs Crail's now and there's Mrs Baxter's. You know them, they sometimes give you sweets, now we're on the last flight, not far to go now. 'Five, six, seven, eight, eating cherries off a plate.' It was only a two-storey tenement building, select, so that although their flat was on the top storey it wasn't too high up. 'Nice and airy,' that's what Mother had said of it, as she opened the sash windows, and let the air come rushing over from the park. 'Nice and airy and green. All those trees...'

'Now, we're down,' Father said. 'You can't beat me yet.' The ringing footsteps were still in her head, as they stood at the kerb, waiting to cross the street to the park gates.

'Ages since we did this,' she said, looking at him, her dad, so handsome with his leonine head and profile. She remembered when she had been at school she had been reading a book about the Plantagenet Chronicles, and she had imagined him as a crusader, because of the way he held his head.

They entered the park and their feet followed the path which climbed above the fountain to the equestrian statue at the top, rearing in front of Park Terrace. She remembered long ago being taken by mother there to see a specialist recommended by Dr Clark, their family GP, because she was having abnormal pelvic pain, and she had been enchanted by the views of the park from the long windows and beyond that the outspread city. There had been a long mirror hanging between the windows with a vase of white lilies reflected in it. The whole effect had entranced her, and she had compared it with the view from the windows in their flat at the foot of the park. It had represented to her the difference between those who could afford to live up amongst the clouds, and those at the foot. Even the large entrance gates shutting them from the park had a symbolism.

She ought to see Dr Clark about Dad, she thought. She knew he wouldn't be persuaded to go to his surgery. The footsteps were still ringing in her head, and she was panting. Was it because of the steep incline? She looked for a bench. 'Shall we sit down?' she asked. 'I'm all puffed.'

'Right.'

They chose a bench in a little clearing ahead, and sat down. He was smiling at her. 'Fancy you being puffed, and I'm all right. Do you remember we once met a man here?'

'A man. When? What was he like?'

'It was when Aunt Meg came to take charge of the house after ... Jane died. Somehow I never forgot him. It was the contrast. Smart city suit, rolled umbrella, bowler hat – and the worn shoes, the toecaps were scuffed, although well-polished, and I noticed the heels were worn down at the back, as if he did a lot of walking.'

'Yes, it's coming back to me. I was still at Jordanhill, and you're right, Aunt Meg was with us. She said to us, "You two should go for a walk in the park."' Her eyes had met Mirren's across the room. '"The rain's stopped." There was something pathetic about him, the bent shoulders.'

'Pathetic?'

'Yes, like a dog who had been whipped. It was the bowler. The contrast. He was eating a sandwich, and when we sat down he stuffed it in his briefcase. And as if he felt he had to apologise to us, he said that on good days, he couldn't bear going into the restaurant near his office, so he came here to get some fresh air.'

'That's right. You've got a good memory.'

'And you said you agreed with him about fresh air, and that you and Mum had enjoyed walking in the park so much because you both came from Waterside and missed the countryside...' The man's image was rearing up in her memory, the general impression he gave of someone who had been beaten by circumstances, haunted, or hunted ... 'And you began to talk to him.' But he always spoke to people, she thought. Perhaps it was a country habit.

'Well, I thought we couldn't just sit there and not talk. He looked so sad, as if he was running away from something or somebody.'

8

'You gave him your whole history.' She saw his shamefaced look, and felt mean that she should pull him up. He had told the man about his father having a farm, but that his wife didn't like cows, and they had decided to move to Glasgow. The bit about cows had been put in to make the man laugh. She knew him, and how much more sociable than her he was, but there was no doubt about it, the man had been pathetic.

And then, one rainy day after that, she had seen him at the Mitchell Library, the very same man. He was looking up and their glances met, and he smiled across the desks, a tentative smile. With his bowler off he had looked older than she remembered, grey hair, wispy about the ears, white face, the same pathetic look, haunted, hunted. 'He never told us anything about himself, did he?' she said to her father.

'No, I don't know why we're talking about him so much, or why we remembered him. Come on, lazy-bones! You're just putting off walking down that hill.'

'Who says?' He was smiling, almost care-free, and she thought, what a difference from this morning. I'll ask Dr Clark to call, and perhaps we'll visit Aunt Meg at Waterside and I'll ask her if she notices any change in him since she last saw him.

'Come on, then, it's good of you to take the old man a walk when you've so many young ones hanging around.' Yes, it was the old Dad. The crusader.

'I should be so lucky.' When she was at the university and later Jordanhill College, she had dashed home every night worried about his grieving, and had somehow missed belonging to societies or going to dances where she could have met other students. But now she was finished studying and had a teaching post, starting after the summer holidays, and she would be able to look after him. She knew he didn't sleep very well, she had heard him padding about during the night, but that had started after her mother had died of cancer. He had now rejoined all his societies, and had started going to Cranston's Coffee Room to meet all his old pals – she teased him about it because women weren't allowed there, except Maggie, the waitress, who treated them all like naughty boys. She often teased him about going, and asked him if they were all afraid of women. Perhaps, she thought, he didn't want any involvement with them since her mother's death.

To be honest, she thought now, I haven't missed Mother as much as he does. I know when he's thinking about her, he goes silent. There was her graduation day, when he had said, 'Jane would have liked this.' She wondered. Mother would have preferred me to be more like her, fond of clothes and make-up, and, she supposed, flirtatious. There had always been the feeling that mother would have preferred her to get married with all the fuss that went on nowadays about 'a white wedding', than become a teacher, and losing, as she had said, her 'chances'. Teachers were regarded as old maids at Waterside. Of course, she knew she should have left home and shared a flat with some of her friends when she went to university, but there had been Dad, and Mother ill, and then the diagnosis and her death. What he had missed, she thought, as well as the sex – she allowed herself to think like that although she had no experience at twenty-five of it – was the direction Mother had given to his life. She had ruled the roost, advised him, pushed him around, which had puzzled Mirren because he didn't look hen-pecked, and she had never encouraged him to exercise his taste in the house.

When Mirren had gone to visit Jessie Baxter, her close friend since schooldays, she had been surprised how the whole family were ruled by Mr Baxter, a presence which she thought Mrs Baxter had created, whether he was there or not. Someone had to run and get father's slippers ready for him coming home, and put them at the fire to warm, someone had to be on hand to hang up his coat, pull out his chair, give him his evening paper ... 'Let Daddy talk...' Mrs

Baxter was for ever shushing the children.

Next morning, when she was preparing breakfast, her father said, 'I have an appointment with McBain this morning.'

'What for?'

'God knows. I've imagined he was rather funny with me recently. I asked some of the other chaps if they had noticed anything and they said no.'

'Well, you'll soon know. Are you ready? You're going to miss the tram.'

'Are *you* ready? You're going to be late too. What class have you this morning?'

She looked at him in surprise. Her graduation photograph hung in the sitting room. 'I don't go to Jordanhill now, Dad. Have you forgotten? I start teaching at Pollokshields after the holidays, September.'

She saw he was looking confused. 'How can I remember everything?' he said, turning away.

'But this is a momentous time in my life, Dad,' she smiled, 'studies over...'

He suddenly got to his feet. 'You're full of yourself, aren't you?' She felt her jaw drop with surprise.

'I've never complained about the work I've had to do to reach this...' She stopped herself. 'You'll miss your tram.'

He left the table without a word and she could hear him stopping in the hall to get his coat, then the outside door banged. She sat transfixed, blaming herself. You knew you were worried, that you had decided to go and see Dr Clark, then you forget and answer him back. She reprimanded herself. There was the feeling at the back of her mind that the present situation was a repetition of some incident or incidents which had happened before. 'Stupid,' she said aloud and, grabbing the door keys, went dashing into the hall and to the door, which she opened. She could hear his footsteps, ringing, ringing, and looking over the banister, saw that he was passing Mrs Crail's and Mrs Baxter's doors on the landing below. Then fainter, there were the ringing steps again, and he was gone.

She was mortified. He had been worried about this appointment with Mr McBain, she knew, and she had turned the conversation to herself. She should have remembered how this morning he had called her from his bedroom, and when she had gone in, he'd said, 'Mirren, where's my blue striped shirt?' He hadn't liked it when she had told him it was in the ironing basket. 'But I particularly wanted it for this morning,' he had said, and she had replied, 'Wear that white one you like. With the blue tie. It matches your eyes,' but he had been angry, and she had thought, tough luck, and gone to cook the breakfast.

She ran along the street, and turned the

corner where his tram stopped. No one there. She saw the tram for Partick disappearing in the distance. He was away. Mother's approach had been much better on any occasion, the goodbye kiss, the flattery, 'You're looking smart this morning, Cameron,' the special breakfast, 'Two eggs this morning for you,' the putting down of the plate in front of him, her hand on his shoulder, her cheek brushing his.

She felt unsettled as she returned to the flat, sitting down again at the table in the kitchen. She got up and took the teapot from where she had placed it at the side of the range to keep warm, poured herself a cup of tea. 'Stewed,' she said aloud, putting down the cup again. She tidied up, deciding that she would have a look round the shops in Sauchiehall Street. When she got to the street she saw it was a pleasant morning. The leaves of the trees in the park were turning now, shaking in the wind, she heard the rustle, and she was tempted to cross the road and have a walk there but, deciding against it, she started walking along Sauchiehall Street, passing Sandyford Place towards Charing Cross, busy with traffic. When she was looking in Lyon's windows at their display of compendiums – who used that word now? she thought – she changed her mind and turned the corner into Elmbank Street. Dr Clark's surgery was in Bath

Street, the first corner.

She'd try to make an appointment. The receptionist told her to wait and she would 'see if she could squeeze her in.' She was successful, and after half an hour she was shown into the doctor's surgery. 'Come away, Mirren,' he said. He had known her for a long time. 'What can I do for you?'

'I thought I'd report to you about Dad, Dr Clark. You said I was to come and see you if I were worried.'

'And are you?'

'Yes. Well, as you said, he's gradually got over Mother's death, and he's taken up his outside interests again, but he's changed. He never had a temper, but lately he's lost it with me, and his memory is bad.'

'Suppose you tell me the details?'

She told him about the episode with the shirt this morning. 'It's so unlike him.'

'Is he aggressive?'

'No, it's not in his nature.'

'Do you get the feeling he's absent-minded?'

'Yes, I suppose I do. And then there's this irascibility. I thought of asking Aunt Meg if she had noticed anything different about him ... She's stayed with us several times, but she never said anything.'

'How is he getting on at the yard?'

'He never mentions it. He used to tell us little snippets, jokes, about the other men,

15

but not now. And we would know when there was a rush on in the drawing office, because Mr McBain harried them, but he never mentions the yard now, or what's being built. We were quite *au fait* with what was going on. He was upset this morning, as I told you, and I wondered if it was because of this appointment he had with Mr McBain, who's head of the drawing office. Dad always imagined he would get that job. Mother used to ask him questions about his day, but I don't seem to draw him out as she did.'

'You're not Jane. He's still missing her.'

'But why take it out on me?'

'You look like her, the same fair hair, and mannerisms, you press your lips together they way she used to when she had finished talking, and your shape is the same. And you're there.'

'But my temperament isn't the same. I'm not good at humouring him.'

'I don't think you have any cause for worry. Try to understand how he's feeling. They were a very devoted couple, they came together to a strange place, Glasgow, they depended on each other, and he's probably labouring under a sense of grievance at her being taken away from him. And he's getting old.'

'I can understand that, and I don't feel adequate enough to fill her place.'

'Don't try to, but be gentle with him. Remember you're the stronger character. I'm not making light of your loss, but it can never be the same as the loss when one member of a loving couple dies prematurely. Does he sleep well?'

'No, I don't think so. I often waken with the sound of the tap running in the kitchen and know that he's making tea. And another thing, he suddenly gets up when we're sitting together at night, and goes out for a walk. He never asks me to go with him, and I didn't mind because I was studying, but that's finished now, and I'm due to start teaching in another month.'

'Things will settle down, I'm sure. Encourage him to ask his friends in for a meal...'

'They've all been very kind, and couples whom they both knew drop in and ask us to visit them, but I can see he doesn't like the two of us going out together – he feels it should be Mother, I suppose. They never seemed to need anyone else when Mother was alive.' She heard her voice thicken with tears ... 'I wanted him to have a holiday with me after my graduation and before I start teaching, but he keeps avoiding the subject.'

'Why not try to get him to visit your aunt with you? Does she live near?'

'Yes, where they come from. Waterside, in Lanarkshire. I could try that, or maybe go to the farm. Roger, his brother, runs it. Mother

17

and Father turned their backs on that sort of life.'

'Still, family ties are strong. You try that, Mirren, and if you're worried again, don't hesitate to come and see me. It wouldn't do if I called in...'

'Yes, I see that.' He wanted her to go. There wasn't anything he could cure, it was all too nebulous. She would have to get on with her own life. There were her friends whom she'd dropped when she was studying, knowing that they were all in the same boat, but maybe if she confided in some of them, Jessie, for instance, it would help. She got up. 'Thanks very much, Dr Clark. I can see that it will sort itself out.'

'Maybe he'll start planning for himself. He's been used to Jane planning for him. He's getting on, though. Sixty, isn't he?'

'Yes. She always made all the decisions.'

When she reached Sauchiehall Street again, she had no wish to shop, and began walking home. At Charing Cross she went into a café and ordered a coffee. Sipping it, her eyes on the imposing frontage of the Charing Cross Hotel across the street, she saw the stir of people round it, and then a bride and groom appeared on the steps. There was a photographer fussing about, and he must have asked them, because the groom bent his head over the bride's upheld face, and kissed her, a long kiss. Mirren was

18

touched, and damped the feeling down by telling herself that they didn't know what was ahead of them. It could have been her parents, she thought, on their wedding day. Or it could have been her with an unknown man? She had never thought like that before, but she certainly didn't want to go on teaching all her life.

She reviewed her life so far. A loved child, and loving parents. But now that she was an adult, and her father depended on her, she mustn't allow herself to be at his beck and call. She should contact her friends and ask them to drop in. They all liked him, praised his good looks, and his 'jokiness'. Their lives didn't have to shut down because Mother had died. Life had to go on, as everybody said.

When she got back to the flat in the afternoon, to her surprise her father was sitting at the table in the kitchen, his back to her.

Chapter 2

'Dad!' she said. 'You're never in at this time. Is there anything wrong?'

He looked round at her and she saw his face.

'I've been given the push.'

'From the yard? Oh, no...!' She went to him and put her arm round his shoulders. If she was shocked, how must he feel? 'Did Mr McBain give you a reason?'

'Cutting down, he says, but we've got some good contracts in at the moment. Unless it's Chamberlain and his treaty with Hitler that's the cause of it! I'm just over sixty and not due for retiral for another five years. Says he knows I'll understand that things are changing and they have to move on, make room for the youngsters!'

'What an excuse!' she said. And then, to distract him, 'What's in the envelope?' McBain obviously wanted rid of him, although he'd always been regarded as a good employee and had steadily ridden up through the department.

He held out the manila envelope to her

without speaking.

She took what looked like a certificate out of it, and saw the writing on it was in a flowing script. She muttered the words as she read them.

'Laidlaw and Company, Shipbuilders, Partick, place on record their sincere appreciation of the services of Cameron James Stewart, who retired today after twenty-three years with the company.'

'Well,' she said, 'succinct. There's nothing about dismissal there.'

'I've been retired on full pension. The retiral age is sixty-five.'

'You don't think it's a generous gesture, Dad?'

'If it is it's creating a precedent.'

'Can you think of any other reason?' She couldn't say it, that his work had been steadily falling away since Mother's death.

'Only if McBain felt my work wasn't up to scratch.' He looked at her, his chin up.

'I'm sure that's not the reason, Dad.' But if he had been as forgetful at work as he was at home ... She handed him back the certificate. 'I should try and take it as it's meant. You've given them all those years, and no one has been more devoted to their work than you. Remember how Mother used to say that the Queen Mary could never have sailed if it hadn't been for you.' She stopped speaking because she saw his eyes fill up with tears.

'Aye, I've been involved in many a ship that sailed the high seas...'

'And you've seen the Queen Mary launched by the Queen.'

'It won the Blue Riband, too.'

She smiled at him. 'You sound like the Ancient Mariner. Don't distress yourself too much, Dad. I tell you what. Why don't we visit Waterside? You'd enjoy seeing your old home again, wouldn't you? We could stay at Uncle Roger's and visit Aunt Meg. She wouldn't have room for us. What do you say?'

'And take my certificate with me?' His smile was bitter. 'All right. I'll go along to the kiosk at the corner and phone Roger tonight and see if he can have us. I'd like to see the old place before I fall into senility.'

'You're far from that. You can be the city bloke paying a visit to the old home ... just like a film star.'

'That's an idea.'

'And while we're talking, I have another idea. When you come back, you could start on a project. You're always reading books about ships. We're near the Mitchell. You could read about the development of them from Captain Cook onwards. That would fill up your mornings. And you have your various societies. Now that you have more time you could offer yourself for office. You always said you hadn't time when they asked you.'

'Don't plan my life for me, Mirren.' His tone was bitter.

'I'm not doing that. Just try to remember that you will have more time on your hands, and you'll not be any worse off. Now, you choose what you'd like for supper.'

'Let me see,' he was looking more cheerful. 'There's nothing wrong with ham and eggs, is there?'

'And some chips on the side?'

'Jane didn't like doing chips because of the smell. We never had them.'

'Well, I'll open the window, and the air from the park will blow it away.'

She got up from the table. 'I'll go and get started. I brought you the *Citizen*. Sit at the window and have a read.'

'Right. I'll have a wash first.' His smile was forced. 'We'll have to see about getting that certificate framed.' He was joking again.

'Hang it up above the mantelpiece?'

'Impress the neighbours.' One side of his mouth was up, but she saw that the hurt in his eyes was still there.

Chapter 3

They set off for Waterside a week later. There had been a dinner given for her father by the drawing office, and there had been various friends calling at the house. She noticed everyone avoided making any comments about him leaving the firm earlier than had been expected and she took the same line. She guessed he was putting a brave face on it. He started getting up again during the night, and she was often wakened by the noise of the tap being turned on in the kitchen. After a long time she would hear him going back to his room.

His enthusiasm had gone for Waterside, she thought. He was silent in the train. To make matters worse, it was raining, and the countryside looked drenched and bleak. Cows sheltered under trees. On days like this Mirren preferred the city with its bustle – she was a city girl, with a liking for the countryside provided it conformed to her idea of the countryside, where the sun perpetually shone, and front gardens were a riot of colour, and there were green vistas of fields with sheep and cows grazing. She noticed he cast a critical eye over the terrain from time to time, and wondered if he was disappointed with the reality.

Uncle Roger was at the station to meet them in his old Ford. The two brothers greeted each other warmly, and Mirren was amused to see how they ribbed each other, an old habit from boyhood. 'So your father's a man of leisure now,' he said. 'Maybe he'll take over the housekeeping when you start teaching?'

'I think he's going to be too busy, Uncle Roger. He has other plans.'

'We can always use him at harvest time, if he likes to offer. Eh, Cameron?'

'I might at that. I'm still quite fit, although you wouldn't think so. They're getting rid of me.' She saw her uncle's surprised look.

'You certainly look fit. And so do you, Mirren. You're like Jane. It could have been her stepping out of that train.'

Mirren noticed that her father was quiet after that, but was affable when they got to the farmhouse, where they were greeted enthusiastically by Aunt Margaret who was still black-haired, buxom and jolly. She threw her arms round both of them in turn. 'It's been too long. How the time passes, but now that you've found the way, we'll maybe see more of you.'

'You should come and visit us and have a

25

day's shopping in Glasgow, Aunt,' Mirren said.

'I'm not one for shopping, Mirren. I know Jane enjoyed the shops, but I find that Hamilton has all I want and I can get there easier. On a farm there's precious little chance to take time off, by the time you've fed and milked the beasts, and then there's the chickens ... you were always keen on the animals when you came as a little girl.'

'I actually believed then that the brown hens laid only brown eggs.' She was aware that her cousin, Josh, had appeared in the farm kitchen, bigger and stronger looking than she remembered. He still had his mother's colouring. 'Josh!' she said. 'It can't be Josh! The last time I saw you ... you were this height!' She held out her hand about the level of his chest.

'I might say the same about you! Aye, it's me all right!' he said, enveloping her in a hug and swinging her off her feet. When he put her down she knew she was blushing.

'Mirren's not used to your country ways, Josh,' his mother said. 'She's a city girl. Sit here.' She dusted a chair for Mirren. She always had a duster to hand, Mirren remembered.

'What kind of dances do they go in for there?' he said to Mirren. 'I was going to take you to a barn dance tonight, but maybe you're not used to sitting on bales of hay.'

26

'No, we have chairs in Glasgow,' she laughed, 'but I expect the dances are the same. I don't go to many.'

'You've been working too hard at your books. It'll do you good. Won't it, Mother?'

'Go and say hello to your uncle, Josh,' she said. 'He's sitting chatting to your father in the parlour.' She didn't answer his question.

When he had gone, Mirren offered to help her aunt with the meal, and in the kitchen she talked about Josh with evident pride. 'He's got all the village girls mad about him, that one. There's one next door who would like to catch him. He's like Cameron, who was the same, not like Roger, who would rather have his cows, but Jane came along and charmed him.'

'Yes. Father took some time to get over her death. Even yet, I wonder...'

'Yes, it was a love match that. She wasn't from farming stock, but she captured your father's heart in no time. She had such smart, taking ways, and she dressed differently from us village girls. Even then she always went to Glasgow for her clothes. Of course, her father was a big grocer in these parts, and being the youngest she was spoiled. Meg couldn't be more different.'

Josh's sister, Maggie, came in later with her two children, and the table was loud with noise and laughter. The little boy and girl were the centre of attraction, and Mirren noticed how good her father was with them. Theirs had always been a quiet table, with the three of them, and she and her mother had been soft-spoken, listening for the most part to his jokes and tales of the yard, until Jane would interrupt him with some brisk remark, and start clearing away. Mirren's studies never came up for discussion. She had always had the belief that her mother didn't approve of them, and would have liked a daughter who went shopping with her, and took an interest in clothes. Jane never read, except ladies' magazines, which she devoured, and followed their instructions about caring for her appearance, and what to cook. 'What's this?' Father would ask when she put, say, smoked salmon in front of him, or avocado with prawns, and she would be lofty in her reply, and say, 'Oh, Cameron, you're still at the farm!' But then, she would lean over him, to ask him how he liked her new perfume. Mirren always felt that she was a sore disappointment to her. Politics didn't interest her mother, and so there were few topics of discussion which could be raised which would interest her. Her interest was in people, preferably those in the public eye, but also anyone she came into contact with. She enjoyed dissecting their motives and their opinions. 'Pulling people apart,' her father called it. She knew what was the latest fashion, and if she couldn't follow it, she would regale Mirren and her husband with information about the *dernier cri* in London, or Paris.

At the end of the meal, Josh said, 'Well, Mirren, are you prepared to come to the dance and give the locals a treat?'

'It's too rough for Mirren,' Maggie said.

'You used to enjoy them before you hooked Tom.'

'I didn't bring a dance dress,' Mirren said.

'What you're wearing is a way better than what you'll see there,' Maggie said, cradling one of the children to her breast.

'Right, Josh,' Mirren said, 'you've persuaded me.'

They set off in one of the old cars which were lying about in the farmyard, and when Josh helped her in, he said, 'You'd better be careful with that dress. The last occupant of your seat was a pig.'

She laughed, sniffing. 'You don't have to tell me.'

He said when he was driving, 'I was very sorry when your mother died, Mirren. Has it been difficult for you?' He was sympathetic.

'Not so bad. Of course I miss her, but it's Father. He took it badly, and now he's been paid off by the yard.'

'Paid off? But he's just sixty, isn't he?'

'Yes, the retiral age is sixty-five. It's the shame of it to him. He hasn't said so in so many words, but I know he's hurt.'

'I thought the yards were all doing well with the prospect of war.'

'I would have thought so too. What would you think was their reason for giving him the push, Josh?'

He didn't answer for a second or two, pretending to bend over the wheel. 'This is a bad piece of the road. It's like a tunnel with the trees, light's bad ... if it weren't your father I'd say he's not coming up to scratch. You get those young smart men who know it all ... possibly in his department.'

'That's what I think. He's been very absent-minded lately. I wondered if he hadn't been concentrating on his work, you know, on his drawings.'

He nodded. 'You have to look at it like this. You can make mistakes in some job but not in something like plans. Maybe they got fed up with his mistakes. Always presuming that's the reason. But if he's thinking that too, it'll make him more depressed than ever. Tell you what I'd do. I'd get him to speak to the doctor.'

'But if he doesn't realise there's something wrong?' She told him about the episode with the shirts. 'Things like that, and forgetfulness, and not sleeping ... as a matter of fact I did go to the doctor, but he didn't seem too perturbed, just told me to keep an eye on him. You can see how worrying it is.'

'He'll have told my dad, won't he?'

'Yes, I think he will. But don't say you know until your father or mother talk about it.'

'No, I'll keep mum. But I still feel he's just growing old. It's not as if your mother had just died recently. Here we are.' He pulled on the brake and she saw they were parked opposite two barns, one larger than the other. As they got out she heard the sound of dance music, and the shrieks of girls' laughter and male deeper-toned laughter. Josh put his arm round her. 'Come on! They're having a good time. You should do the same, Mirren, and forget your worries.'

They climbed steps into the larger of the two barns, and although she was expecting to be surprised, it was certainly a unique kind of dance that was taking place.

'Do you know it?' Josh asked. 'Eightsome reel.'

She shook her head, 'I've never done it.'

They took their place amongst the on-lookers, who were sitting on bales of hay, whooping and clapping in time to the music, which was lively. Mirren saw a fiddler sawing away with his bow, foot tapping, red-faced.

A girl of about her age came running up to them. 'Oh Josh,' she said, 'I thought you weren't coming.'

'I told you, Grace,' he looked embarrassed, 'that my cousin was coming to stay. Here she is, Mirren Stewart. Remember her? This is

Grace McFarlane, Mirren. They've got the farm next to ours.'

Mirren held out her hand to the girl, smiling. 'I think I remember you.' She was pretty, with a petulant expression. 'Trust Josh Stewart to be late,' she said. 'And – ' she turned round – 'here's another yin o' the same kind.' A young man had joined them.

'Hi, Josh,' he said. 'Hi, Grace. Are you going to introduce me?' His bold eyes were on Mirren.

'If I have to.'

'You know the wee lassie who used to come wi' her folks to visit?' Grace McFarlane said.

'Oh, aye.' He gave Mirren a bold look. 'Not in your class, Grace.' He looked at Josh, 'Ur ye no' goin' to introduce us properly, Josh?'

'Give me time. Trust Bulldog Drummond to be where the action is. This is my cousin, Mirren Stewart, from Glasgow. Jack Drummond of Calder End Farm.' Mirren smiled at the young man and he held out his hand.

'It's no' often we get a visitor from Glasgow.'

'Look out, Jack,' Josh said, 'she could wind you round her little finger.'

'You better go and dance with Grace, Josh, she's pining for you, and I'll lead the lady from Glasgow round the floor.' He bowed exaggeratedly to Mirren, and said, 'May I have the pleasure? Will that dae?'

She burst out laughing. 'Humour him, Mirren,' Josh said. 'It's no' often Jack gets the chance to meet a real lady.'

'Hey, mind whit you're sayin'?' Grace seemed to be in a state of perpetual annoyance, Mirren thought. She reflected on the difference between town and country, as they joined the dancers. In towns, girls didn't show their feelings like Grace. In fact there was a cloak of pretence; they watched their behaviour; didn't divulge anything about themselves; kept their cards close to their chest. Jack Drummond, she thought, wasn't having any metaphorical soul-searching. She looked up at him, meeting his eyes.

'Whit d'you think o' Waterside, Mirren?' he asked. 'You can pit your arm roon ma neck. It's the fashion here.'

'Like that?' she said, obeying him. 'Waterside? Well, I know it. It's very pretty. We don't have any countryside around us, where we live. Sometimes my father and I take the bus to Balloch.'

'Balloch? Is there nowhere nearer than that?'

'Unless you count Kelvingrove Park. We live opposite it.'

'Your folks came frae here, didn't they? I remember your father, brother of Josh's?'

'Yes, they went to Glasgow when they got married. My mother died...'

'I know her sister, Miss Calder. She's well

thought of in the village. I cut her grass for her sometimes, or one of my lads.'

'Do you? Aunt Meg will be glad of that. We'll be going to see her.'

'You and your faither?'

'Yes.'

They danced without speaking for a few minutes. She felt his arm tighten round her waist. I haven't much experience with men, she thought, although Mother set me a good example. She was flirtatious. She saw some of the girls had their heads tucked in under the men's chins. She had seen that at the university dances, but her partners had never inspired her to do the same.

'Do you like reading, Jack?' she said.

'Here! Ur ye a teacher?'

'As a matter of fact I am. But what has that to do with it? Do you like reading?'

'I'm mad aboot ma fitba' team. I read all aboot them in the local paper.'

'Do you play?'

'Ur ye kiddin?'

She tried hard to think of another topic, but was out of her depth.

'Whit do you read?' She met his eyes. They were tender, not about 'fitba'' she thought. 'Romances? Aw the lasses read romances.'

'I like *Wuthering Heights*,' she said, knowing that she was teasing him.

'Whit's that?'

'Just the greatest love story of them all.'

'Whit's *Wuthering Heights*? Is it a place?'

'Yes, in Yorkshire.'

'Oh, England!' He dismissed England as if it couldn't hold a candle to Waterside.

After a pause he said, whispering into her ear, and holding her closely to him, 'We know all about love, Mirren. Here in the country. A could show you that. We could find a nice bale and—'

She interrupted him. 'I would have to ask Josh.' She was getting the hang of it, the teasing. 'He's in charge of me.'

'Oh, he'll be busy with Grace. She's mad aboot him. He'll gie in. He's a softie.'

The music stopped, everyone clapped, then there was a rush to the buffet, which was in the smaller barn, through an adjoining door. Mirren looked around for Josh, but didn't see him. Perhaps Grace had spirited him away. 'Well, I wouldn't mind sampling your buffet,' she said, thinking that even a stodgy sausage roll would be welcome. She felt decidedly hungry. There were trestle tables in the small barn, and scattered about the floor, bales of hay, some already occupied by couples. 'Lights out!' someone shouted, and immediately some were switched off, making it difficult to see. Jack took hold of her hand, and led her to a vacant bale in a dark corner. He must have cat's eyes, she thought. 'You sit yersel' doon there,' he said, 'and I'll bring the food and drinks. What would you like?'

She had no doubt. 'Two sausage rolls, and lemonade.'

'Lemonade! Will ye no' have some whisky?'

'No, thanks. I never drink whisky.'

She sat, watching, hearing comments from his friends standing at the table. 'Good for you, Jack!' 'Mind how ye go!' Everyone seemed to be turning round and smiling at her, and nodding. Was he the Don Juan of the village?

Jack came back with a tray and settled himself down beside her. 'Oh, good!' she said, lifting a sausage roll, and digging her teeth into it.

'Your lemonade was good for a laugh,' he said, handing her a glass.

'Tough luck.' She gestured with the glass. 'Isn't that dangerous?' The fourth side of the barn was open to the night air. There were doors, pushed back against the wall.

'It's a loading bay,' Jack said. 'The lorry which comes has a lift on it and that's winched up to the level of this floor here, and then the bales are piled on it, and taken down to the lorry.'

'I see. We don't have this in Glasgow!' she laughed. She thought again of the dances at the university hall. 'No barns or bales.'

'Any wenchin'?' He nudged her.

'Some.' They all seemed very tame compared with this, she thought. She knew she

36

was considered to be stand-offish, and certainly she had never been asked to go to the 'Sitooterie', as the dimly lit room had been called there. She hadn't had a steady boyfriend, and most of her partners seemed to prefer to dance. Now she realised it had been her fault. She was more relaxed here. She noticed that Jack was looking round the room, his head up, sniffing.

'What's wrong?' she asked.

'I thought I smelled smoke. Josh and I are officials. Smoking is strictly forbidden.' He shouted. 'Anyone smoking here?'

There were shouts of denials. 'We're too busy, Jack.' 'Whit an idea!'

'You all know it's against the rules. They'd lie through their teeth,' he said to Mirren.

'I don't smell it. Perhaps it was someone walking along the road and it blew in here?'

'Aye,' he said, distractedly. He turned towards her. 'Have you finished? My goodness, you've fairly polished off these sausage rolls.'

'I was hungry.'

'We've got to clear the coast for action.' He took off his jacket, and spread it behind them. 'There, lie back. It's the best way of getting to know each other.' He pushed her back and bent over her, resting his face in his hand, his arm supporting it. She lay, looking up at him. His eyes were laughing at her.

'You haven't learned much in the city,' he

said softly, and, straightening his arm, fell on top of her, nosing her face with his chin.

'What do you think you're doing?' Her heart, beating loudly, seemed to occupy the whole of her body. It strangled her voice.

'Dinna ye ken, or to put it in English fur ye, don't you know? You're the teacher,' he said. 'You haveny read the rule book. It's your move now.'

'What rule book?' Her voice sounded false and ladylike to her, she thought, as she felt his body moving on top of hers. He kissed her, pushing his tongue into her mouth.

She lay. 'Fur goodness sake,' Jack Drummond said, 'pit yur arms roon ma neck, or move, or something.'

'I'm not used to—' He stopped her with another probing kiss.

'Whit ur ye?' he said. 'A bluidy statue?'

She was mortified, fighting this assault, and fighting the steady, loud beating of her heart which was sounding all over her body. He must hear it.

'You must feel something,' he said, whispering in her ear. One hand was gently massaging her breast.

She raised her head towards him and said, 'Kiss me, Jack,' which made her think of a similar saying: 'Kiss me, Hardy.' She smothered a giggle.

'That's better,' he said, smiling down at her. 'You're alive, at least. I can hear your heart beating. Let yourself go, Mirren. You've never done that in your life.' He began caressing her body, and she responded, at first against her will, and then because she liked it. She could hear murmurs and groans all round her. The words 'knocking shop' occurred to her, and she came to her senses. What was she doing, rolling in the hay with this yokel? She freed herself by wriggling from under him and off the hay bale, and got to her feet. She was devoid of anger, and speech. He still lay on it, looking up at her.

'You're a queer lass. It's you who need a teacher. We're a rough lot, here. It's lucky fur you that I'm me. Do you know what I'm goin' to tell you, Mirren Stewart? I'm right sorry fur ye.' He was on his feet himself and was dusting himself down with his hand. 'Ye've got yersel' into a terrible pickle inside yersel. Here, turn roon and let me brush you down. You'll have folks laughin' at you if you go back to the barn wi' lumps of hay hangin' to yer backside.' She felt his hand give her a smart slap. 'Feart, ur ye? Aw right. Only try and not look like a wumman that's been raped. They telt me that Glasgow ladies were different. Now I know what they meant.' He put his arm round her shoulders, 'Come on, then.' He guided her out of the room.

At the entry to the large barn she turned to him and said, 'I'm going to excuse myself.

Ladies.'

He nodded, 'On ye go. I'll be here when you come back.' He leant against the wall where they were standing.

In the ladies' room, she stared at her face in the mirror, dabbing powder on it, putting fresh lipstick on, while she thought about Jack Drummond. He had been trying to humiliate her, but that was partly her fault. She knew how she must have come across to him, an inexperienced girl, even if she came from Glasgow. He had been trying her out, and she had been quite unable to protest. Why? Was it because of the strange sensations running through her body? Curiosity? Anyhow, she had made a fool of herself or been made a fool of, and she didn't want to spend the evening with Jack Drummond, that was for sure. He was smart, indeed sharp. He'd read her like a book, someone who was unable to cope with men, someone who hadn't read the rule book, as he'd said. She could imagine him in the pub with his cronies retailing his evening with her, saying these very things. There was a girl beside her, watching her.

'You're fairly slapping the lipstick on, ur ye no? D'you live aroon here?'

'No,' she said, and to herself, 'thank God.' She went out of the room, letting the door slam behind her.

When she looked about, she saw there was

a ladies' choice dance in progress. A girl whom she didn't know grabbed her arm and said, 'Come on! See if we have any luck...' She found herself whirling round in a circle with all the other girls, and then men revolving in an outer one. When the music stopped, everyone stopped. Josh was opposite her. He stepped forward and whirled her away.

'Where did you get to?' he asked.

'I might as well ask you the same question.' She laughed up at him. One thing you're good at, she told herself, is pretending that nothing's happened. Was it that she had come face to face with herself lying under Jack Drummond's body, and didn't like what she had discovered about herself? 'The men here are all tall, Josh. Is it the country air?'

'Well, Grace...' he said, answering her first question.

'Is she possessive?'

'Well, she's a neighbour, and everybody, my father and mother and hers...' Not for me, she thought, and then again, is Josh like me? Doesn't know how to be assertive? Does it run in the family?

'I'm only teasing,' she said. The music stopped abruptly. Jack Drummond was still on her mind. Had it gone on, she might have asked some questions about him.

'Well, it's cheerio,' Josh said.

41

This time the young man who stopped opposite her was very shy. His hair had been sleeked down, but a tuft had escaped and was lying on his forehead. 'This is my first dance here,' he said. 'A'm no' very good.'

'It's my first here too, so we're both the same.'

'Ur you Josh's cousin? The lass frae Glesca?'

'Aye,' she said, falling into the vernacular, 'that's me.' She winced when the nice young man stood on her instep.

'A went last week wi' some o' ma pals. We went to the pictures. A great big place with padded seats. It was great! And the lights at night! We walked to a park in the West End to see the view.'

'Kelvingrove Park?'

'That's right. How did you know?'

'I live opposite it.'

'And you just have to walk a step or two to get to those great shops and the pictures?'

'That's right.'

'Oh, here we go,' he said as the music stopped again.

'What a shame,' she said, 'just when we were getting into the swing of it.'

She joined hands with the other girls, trying not to limp. When the music stopped again, she found herself opposite Jack Drummond. 'Where did you get to?' he said as they danced away.

'I got pulled into the girls' circle.'

'Well, we meet again. Feeling better?' He smiled, looking down at her. He had a slanting smile and wicked eyes. He was laughing at her. And he was a good dancer, she realised with relief after her experience with the shy young man. What one might call a stylish dancer, she thought, as he whirled her and bent her over his arm, clearing a space as they went round the floor. It was a waltz and they didn't speak much, in her case, because she was trying to follow him, in an effort to redeem herself. His arm was tightly round her waist, in a proprietorial way, and she put her hand on the back of his head and kept it there. 'You're learnin',' he said in her ear. This time the band kept playing for what seemed a long time, and the lights were lowered. The mood of the dancers seemed to have calmed down.

Suddenly the comparative quiet was interrupted by two men running into the barn. 'The wee barn's on fire!' they shouted. 'You lot better get out!'

'Good God!' Jack Drummond said, looking at her. 'Remember, I thought I smelled smoke?'

Everyone had stopped dancing. He took Mirren's hand and began pushing towards the door. 'You heard Tommy and Joe! Come on! Make for the door!' he shouted. He said to her as they were pushing behind the frightened crowd. 'Remember, I told you? I was right!' And raising his voice again, he shouted, 'You at the front. Get on! You're blocking other folks!'

Josh and Grace had come running up to them. Josh said, 'We must get them all out, Jack! I had a word with Tom.' He indicated the door to the smaller barn. 'The loading bay's open in there!'

'The draught ... Aye, I noticed that. You girls better get away out of here. Josh and me will have to keep an eye on things.'

Grace took Mirren by the hand, 'Come on!' she said.

Together they pushed through the crowd which had gathered near the exit – men were shouting, girls were screaming – but they managed to get out. They ran down the stairs and into the street, joining the crowd standing underneath the open loading doors of the smaller barn. Flames were leaping out. 'I hope there's no one in there,' Mirren said to Grace.

'There will be. It's no' called the wencherie for nothing. That's why the doors are left open. To cool the passions!' She gave a sarcastic laugh. 'You were there, were ye no', with Bulldog?'

'Just for a little while.' Why am I apologising to this girl? 'Funnily enough, Jack said he thought he smelled smoke. There must have been something smouldering.'

'They're no' supposed to smoke, but you get fools who don't use their heids.'

They saw Jack and Josh pushing through the crowd, carrying a long ladder between them. People made way for them. They put the ladder up against the stone wall of the barn and Josh began climbing up it. There were two people, a man and a girl, standing at the open doors, waving, and behind them Mirren could see the flames and smoke swirling. 'Where's the fire brigade?' she asked Grace.

'They'll be on their way. They'll have been warned. They two shouldn't go in there,' she said, looking up.

Mirren watched. Josh was first. He was obviously trying to persuade the girl to come on to the ladder, but she seemed to be in no fit state. She was being supported by the man.

'I don't know who that is!' Grace said. 'She's fainted, I think. Oh, I wish the fire brigade would come!'

They both watched. It seemed that Josh at the top of the ladder and Jack further down were trying to persuade the two to come on to it. Mirren could hear Josh saying, 'You'll be all right, Jennie,' but the man was speaking to them and shaking his head.

'My God, I hope Josh doesn't go in!' Grace wailed. 'He's game for anything!'

They could see him, as he went up two or

three steps and launched himself at the opening. He reached it, and he was bending over the girl, who was crouched on the floor, speaking to her. Her companion was looking anxious and waving his arm at the onlookers, who were shouting, 'Come on doon! Save yersel'!'

'A canna!' he was shouting, 'Jennie's fainted.' The smoke billowed over the three of them and when it cleared, Mirren saw the man being helped on to the ladder by Jack. Discretion the better part of valour, she thought. At that moment she heard the warning note of the siren and the crowd parted to let the fire engine draw up underneath the open doors of the barn. Immediately some of the firemen jumped down, and began putting a ladder against the wall, while others detached the hose and directed it at the flaming building.

Mirren saw that the man who had been helped down the ladder by Josh was being supported by two firemen towards an ambulance, while Jack Drummond, at the foot, was speaking to what looked like the foreman.

'The smoke will have gone for they two, whoever they are,' Grace said. 'If Josh doesn't come down he'll be in the same state.'

Mirren looked up. She saw the hose being played on the open doors of the barn, revealing Josh still bending over the girl, who was now stretched out on the floor. Another two men had winched a long ladder with a platform at the end of it against the wall of the barn, guiding it to stop at the open doors. Firemen were shinning up it. The other ladders had been removed.

'That's good,' Grace said, 'they'll get the girl down that way. There's Josh waving to us. He's been told to come down.' Mirren watched him climbing down the ladder, and then the girl being helped by two firemen on to the platform. It was difficult to tell if she had recovered, or not, but Mirren saw she was in a state of collapse. When Josh jumped on to the ground the men were busy with their hoses, sending a stream of water through the open doors, and she saw the foreman speaking to him. The girl was being put on a stretcher and carried away to the ambulance, and Jack had joined Josh. The girls saw them shaking their heads as the foreman spoke to them.

'They're being asked if they want to go to the hospital,' Grace said, 'but they seem to be all right. Come on over and we'll see how they are.'

Mirren followed her, feeling dazed. The quiet countryside, she thought, first Jack Drummond, then this.

They joined Josh and Jack, who seemed to be all right, and watched with them while

47

the hoses continued to spray water into the barn. After a time, several of the firemen shinned up the ladder and clambered inside the barn. 'They're going to see if there's anyone else in there,' Jack said. 'I hope not.' The firemen emerged. They were supporting a man between them, who seemed to be in a bad way. One helped him on to the platform and they were winched down.

'You two get into the car,' Josh said. 'They'll want an estimate of how many were at the dance.'

It seemed a long time before Josh and Jack joined them. Grace had stopped talking and Mirren, welcoming the respite, was sitting beside her in the back seat, glad of the comparative silence.

When the men got in, Mirren said, 'Was anybody else found?' She saw Josh's head nod.

'A girl. She came to the dance with the man who was helped down the ladder. Both from Cambuslang. They've all been taken away in the ambulance.'

'Is she deid?' Grace said from the back.

'Grace!' Jack said. 'No, she's no' deid, but she's got smoke in her lungs like the other two. It was a foursome who came from Cambuslang. They're all in hospital now.'

'You two should have gone and got checked as well,' Grace said. 'What did I tell you? You shouldn't let off-comers in. They

48

don't know how to behave. I bet that four-some were smoking!'

'I hope somebody will tell their parents. They'll be expecting them home,' Mirren said.

'The police will. There was one there, checking everybody. We've to go to the station tomorrow,' Josh said, 'and give them the numbers. We've got the stubs of the tickets. A lot of the dancers had gone home. Their fathers and mothers had arrived to collect them. The news had spread.'

'You two were running the dance, weren't you?' Mirren asked. 'Will you have a note of who the tickets went to?'

'We've never had a fire before.' Grace was still on the one subject. 'I bet it was the Cambuslang folk. They don't know how to behave.'

'Shut up,' Josh said wearily.

'Let's go,' Jack said, who was sitting in the front beside Josh, and they drove off. 'I hope the auld yin hasn't heard the news. She'll be worried sick.' Mirren put her arm round Grace, who was sniffing and wiping her eyes with the back of her hand.

'My father sleeps like a log,' Josh said. 'I doubt if he would know anything about it, nor my mother.'

'My folks will be anxious too,' Grace said. What about my father, Mirren thought, but didn't say it.

'We'll soon be home.' Josh was driving swiftly through the village. When they got on to the road, Mirren could hardly see the branches of the trees on either side, only aware that they made the road darker. He's used to the darkness, of course, she thought, comparing it to the well-lit streets in Glasgow. He drove confidently. Once she saw a fleeing rabbit caught in the headlights. That I wouldn't see in Glasgow, she thought. She remembered when she was a little girl how under the Central Station bridge had seemed like fairyland to her, with all the shops lit up with golden lights.

They stopped at Grace's farm first, and Jack helped her out. 'Cheer up, Grace,' Mirren heard him say. Josh got out of the driving seat and he said, 'Don't be upset, Grace.' There were lights in the farm windows and she saw a woman at the gate waiting for them. She saw her run forward and put an arm round Grace, and heard her say, 'Am I glad to see you! Your father's gone down to the village with your father, Josh, to see what's happening.' She was talking to Josh and Jack, and Mirren saw her peering through the darkness. She waved, and Mirren waved back.

The two men came back to the car. Josh said, 'You come in beside me, Mirren. I'm going to drop off Jack first. You hop in the back, Jack.'

'But oor hoose is past yours,' he protested.

'I'll take you home first. It's no distance.' Jack helped her out, and she moved in beside Josh. The three of them waved to Grace and her mother standing at the gate.

'She's quite right,' Jack said from the back. 'They off-comers don't know the rules.'

'That's spilt milk now,' Josh said. 'We shouldn't have sold them the tickets.'

'You shouldn't jump to conclusions that they have anything to do with it,' Mirren said.

'That's us told off,' Jack said. The men laughed.

'Our lights are on,' Josh said as he drove past his farmhouse. 'We'll get a right royal telling-off for taking you into danger.'

'Just drop me here Josh,' Jack said, 'I'll walk the rest.'

'No, I said we would see you home.'

'There are no lights on.' Mirren could see the dark mass of Jack's farmhouse when they reached it.

'Maybe the auld yin will be asleep and I'll be able to creep in without her knowing. Nice to have met you, Miss Stewart. You'll sleep tonight after all that excitement,' he said. 'I hope we'll meet again.'

He got out, and walked up the path. He had a cocky way of walking, she thought. I wonder if I'll hear from him again.

Josh turned the car in his yard, and pulled

away. He said as he was driving, 'He lives alone with his mother, and runs the farm. His father died last year. She's a bit of a targe.'

'Poor Jack,' she said, thinking of that cocky walk. 'He should get married and move his wife in, and put his mother in a cottage in the village.'

'That's city talk. It's not so easy with the old folks,' Josh said. 'They've had a hard life.' When he was parking outside his door, he turned to Mirren and said, 'I wanted to apologise to you for taking you into that tonight.'

'Oh, was that why you told me to sit here? Be reasonable, Josh, you didn't know what was going to happen.' She bent forward and kissed him. To her surprise, his lips clung to hers. Was that Grace's kiss I got? she wondered. She didn't know why she had kissed him. Was it to reassure herself that all men weren't like Jack Drummond?

When they got in they were greeted by his mother and her father, who were sitting at the table in the kitchen having a cup of tea.

'What did I tell you?' Aunt Margaret said to Mirren's father.

'I hope you weren't too worried, Dad.' Mirren went towards him and put an arm round his shoulders.

'I was trying not to be. Margaret's been cheering me up singing Josh's praises.'

'He's got a sensible head on his shoulders, my Josh,' she said, smiling at him. 'Not like some around here.'

'Your Uncle Roger has driven down to the village. Someone came to the door and they went away together,' Mirren's father said.

'John Nesbitt, from Great Stedding,' Margaret said. Josh nodded.

'They wouldn't let me go,' Mirren's father was plaintive.

'And quite right too. We don't want you coming here to fight fires. Now, you two sit down and have a cup of tea, and then off to bed with you. You've had an exciting time. We'll hear all about it tomorrow.' Mirren thought she gave Josh a meaningful look, and she saw him look towards her father...

Chapter 4

They had paid two or three visits to her mother's sister since they had arrived. They had found Meg hale and hearty, still ensconced in her cottage in the centre of the village, 'where she could keep an eye on things', but Mirren hadn't had the chance to speak to her on her own. Accordingly, one day when her father was working with his brother on the farm, she took her opportunity and walked to her aunt's house.

She found her in the garden. She looked up from her knees to welcome her. 'You've just come at the right time,' she said. 'I'm getting a bit weary and was thinking of stopping to make a cup of tea.'

'Do you want a hand?' Mirren said, and helped her aunt up.

'Getting old,' she said, 'it comes to us all, in one way or another.'

In the neat little parlour where her aunt had insisted they should have their tea, parlours being for 'company', she looked at her niece. 'I've a feeling you've come for a reason, Mirren. Am I right?'

'Yes. I'm worried about Dad, Aunt Meg. Did you notice anything different about him?' Her aunt looked at her.

'I'm glad you've raised the subject. Yes, I did. When I came to you when Jane died, I thought his occasional forgetfulness was the result of losing her, but I've noticed it again. He's different, Mirren, it's something in his eyes, a kind of lost look. As if the old Cameron was in there, imprisoned, begging to get out.'

Mirren held out her hands to her, and her aunt took them. 'I'm worried, Aunt Meg. That's exactly it. Sometimes he isn't with me. I catch him looking at me, as if ... as if he was trying to work out who I was. Does that sound strange to you?'

'Well, he's over sixty. Here in the country we think of that as getting old, which means being unable to tackle manual work, but in the city they don't retire until they're sixty-five, isn't that right?'

'Yes. And that's what he expected to do. I think he's got worse since he was made redundant, was put on the shelf, I'm sure that's how he views it.'

'Well, you can understand him. A man who has worked in the city all his life, worked as an apprentice in that drawing office, and was promoted, he must have had a feeling of pride to have made his way, and my personal opinion for what it's worth is that he expected to be made manager of the drawing office, then a younger man was promoted over his head ... isn't that true?'

'Yes, that's true. McBain, he's called. That happened just about the time Mother died.'

'And there's another thing which I've never dared to say. I don't think Cameron would have left farming, if it hadn't been for my sister. Jane always knew what she wanted, and that was to leave Waterside. And so, when she and Cameron fell in love, I'm pretty sure she changed his mind for him.'

'But they were happy that they had made a life in Glasgow, or so it seemed to me.'

'Cameron was the type who would make

the best of a bad job, but Jane had to have her way. She took him to Glasgow before they were married, introduced him to the idea of dining out, that sort of thing. She always said to me I was too content with life, but to tell you the truth, Mirren, I wasn't interested in boys or marrying when I was young. Somehow I fell into a pattern here, Meg Calder was the one you called upon when someone was having a baby – I was good at that, but never wanted one for myself. I've often wondered about that, thought there was something odd about me.'

'The only thing that's odd about you is your kindness and generosity.' She patted her aunt's hands. 'Everyone speaks well of you.'

'Still, it's a lonely life in some ways, but it's the one I've chosen and I've only followed my bent. And that's what you should always do.'

'I'll remember that, but at the moment no one has touched my heart.' Is that true? she thought. This Jack Drummond has made me wonder what it would be like. She dismissed him from her mind. No, he wouldn't do. They had nothing in common. 'But I've come to talk about Dad, not about me. I think I'll know if and when I meet the man for me. That was the case with Dad and Mother. She gave him the incentive he lacked.'

'Maybe so. He was bright at school and everyone said he'd go far, but his father and mother wanted him in the farm – he was the older of the two boys, and they didn't push him. He could have been anyone, a doctor, or something like that.'

'Well, he was happy in what he did. I never thought he missed the farm until I saw him here. He loves working with Uncle Roger, and I've discovered how knowledgeable he is about the farm. I was always struck in Kelvingrove Park how he could identify birds and trees for me. He it was who was keen that I should go to university, Mother didn't want that road for me, she wanted me to meet someone and get married, she liked me to go shopping with her, her idea of bliss was to sit in Fuller's in Buchanan Street and have China tea and their special walnut cake. She dressed up for that as if she was going to meet the Queen. She would wear her fox fur and her hat with a veil, and look around at the other ladies sipping tea, and push her fur on her shoulders, rearranging it … I can see her now. I thought she was quite beautiful.' Her voice broke.

'That was Jane. The village had never seen a wedding like theirs. Little bridesmaids, train-bearers she called them, Nora Crichton's little ones, and two grown-up ones, and "ushers". Have you heard of those? What a day that was! I was one of the bridesmaids, and the ushers were our partners, mine was Jack Drummond's father, and now his son gives me a hand in the garden. It's strange! I could have been his mother.'

I wonder if Jack's father ever proposed to her? Mirren didn't dare ask. 'Yes, Mum loved dressing up. I think life was a stage to her.'

'That's true. But to get back to Cameron. Have you spoken to your doctor?'

'Yes, he didn't seem to take me seriously. Murmured something about he didn't think it was senility, he was too young for that, but he didn't offer to come and see him.'

'Doctors don't know enough about the mind. They're happier with a broken leg.'

'Oh, Aunt Meg!' Mirren laughed.

'It's true. Their intelligence is limited. They pretend to know everything with their bed-side manners. Believe me, I've seen them in action. Still, we've got to be content with what we've got. If I were you, I'd persuade Cameron to go with you. Seeing's believing.'

'It might make Dr Clark think? Is that what you're saying?' Her aunt nodded.

'You'll soon be starting with your teaching. What does Cameron think about that?'

'He doesn't seem to have taken it in. I've explained that I'll be away during the day, but he's quite capable about the house. Or was. Mother demanded a lot of attention from him. The doctor did talk about getting help in. I doubt if he'd be able to look after himself now.'

'I think you'd feel happier if there was someone coming in to cook his midday meal. Include him in interviewing applicants for the job. And Mirren, if you have any financial difficulties, I can help you out. Our mother left this place to me, and what money there was, but that was, I think, because I tended her in her last illness, and had been running the house for Father. I always felt guilty that they didn't leave Jane anything.'

'It's good of you, Aunt, and I'll remember your kind offer, but I have to try it out first. I'll have the travelling every day, of course, but we'll see. I've even thought of moving to Pollokshields to be near the school. When I try to talk over the changes with Dad, he looks blank, as if I haven't told him before! So I have to start all over again, and he gets angry with me, and says I haven't told him, and so it goes on.'

'Well, it won't be long now. Remember, you can always call on me.'

'Thanks, Aunt, but I think that might alarm him further. But it's good to know you're all here.'

'I know Roger and Margaret see a change in him, and they would gladly have him for a holiday.'

'I feel better already. That was a lovely cup

of tea, and your cake is as good as Fuller's any day of the week!'

'Maybe that should have been my destiny, a cook!'

'No, you're needed here.'

'Anyhow, I've missed the boat now. Just think of me, and don't turn down any offers.'

'Chances', Mother called them.

She and her father travelled back to Glasgow the following day. She saw him peering out of the window of the train as they gradually left the fields behind, and the industrial environs of Glasgow filled the windows. She imagined he looked sad.

Chapter 5

They settled down in the flat when they got back. Mirren was busy preparing to start teaching, buying clothes, and trying to find a woman who would come in while she was away. In the newsagent's on the corner of their street, she asked the owner, Mrs Muir, if she knew of anyone, and explained what she wanted.

'There's a change in Mr Stewart since your mother died,' Mrs Muir said.

'Have you noticed anything?' Mirren asked her.

'Nothing I could put my finger on, but he seems a bit absent-minded, forgets to pick up his change, that sort of thing.'

'Yes, he is,' Mirren agreed. 'That's why I want someone to come in and cook his lunch while I'm teaching at Pollokshields.'

'A bit away. Let me see, there's a youngish woman who comes in here occasionally, Doris Bathgate, her husband left her, and she's got two children, both at school. I think she's a decent enough woman. Would you like me to speak to her? She did mention that she would have to earn some money.'

'Would you, Mrs Muir? And if you would ask her to call and see me if she's interested.'

'I'll do that. The two children are at school all day, so she might be available when you need her.'

Mirren left the shop feeling elated. She decided she must tell her father what she'd done, in case he would be annoyed at her if the woman arrived, unannounced.

That afternoon when they were walking in the park (it had become a habit since they came back from Waterside), she said to him, 'You've taken a liking to walking here every day, haven't you?'

'Aye, it's the nearest to country we have,' he said.

'I thought that might be it. Do you miss

61

Waterside?' They were sitting on a bench by the River Kelvin watching the ducks diving in the water, 'No chicks,' she said. 'It'll soon become too cold to walk here.'

'I'll have to stay in then.'

'And I'll be teaching all day.'

He looked at her astonished, 'Teaching?'

'Yes, hadn't you remembered?'

'I remember for a time, then other things come into my head and blot it out.'

'Would you be able to cook a meal for yourself at lunchtime?'

'I don't fancy that. Your mother spoiled me. If I had still been working, there was the canteen there, but that's finished.'

'Well, try not to worry. Be glad you've got time to yourself. You couldn't be in the park every day for instance, and there are your societies.'

'They don't appeal to me now. I'm not quick enough on the uptake.'

'That's what's called growing old gracefully.'

'If I were at Waterside I could be helping Roger with the harvest. And he said the next time I came he would teach me how to drive the tractor. I'd have plenty to do there.'

'Well, there's no harm in going back. We could see what Aunt Margaret thinks. Meantime – ' she looked at him – 'I heard of a woman near here who might be willing to come in and cook a meal for you during the day. How would you like that?'

'She'd be a stranger.'

'But you'd soon get to know her.'

'I could take the tram down to Argyle Street. There are some good restaurants there. Miss Cranston's—'

'Well, we'll bear that in mind, and also the prospect of you going back to Waterside. But I think you would have to wait a few weeks for that. Meantime, Dad, I start work on Monday.'

'What day is this?'

'Tuesday. I'll ask Mrs Muir if she would ask the woman to come and see us. She's called Doris Bathgate. A young married woman—'

'That's near Edinburgh,' he interrupted her.

'Yes, I know. It's a name as well. Will you meet this Mrs Bathgate if I ask her to come here, and see what you think of her?'

'If she can cook like Jane, that'll be all right.'

'I can't promise that. We'd better get back home, Father.'

'Will Jane be there?' His look was infinitely pathetic.

She shook her head. She couldn't speak. She helped him to stand up, but she felt the weakness was because he wasn't trying, or else his mind was far away.

On their way home, they went into Mrs

Muir's shop.

'Well, well,' she said, 'you haven't been giving us much custom lately, Mr Stewart. Are you feeling well?'

'Quite well, Mrs Muir. We were just taking a little constitutional along by the Kelvin.'

'Some people have all the luck. If I could leave this shop for ten minutes, I'd be joining you,' she said.

'I've been talking to my father about Mrs Bathgate,' Mirren said. 'Do you think you could ask her to call tomorrow morning, maybe after her children have gone to school?'

'I will, Mirren. I think you'd like her, Mr Stewart.'

'I don't intend to marry her, Mrs Muir.' He laughed, and Mirren saw the woman's look.

Doris Bathgate came the following morning. She was a much younger woman than Mrs Muir, dark-haired, and dressed smartly.

Mirren brought her in and introduced her to her father, who was sitting in his usual chair at the window. He turned round when he saw the stranger. He was obviously flummoxed.

'Remember, Father, I told you Mrs Bathgate would be calling.'

He got to his feet and held out a hand. 'Pleased to meet you, Mrs Bathgate,' he said. He showed her a seat, turned and walked to the door.

'Where are you going, Dad?' Mirren called.

'I thought you would want to speak to her alone.'

'No, she's come to see us both. About cooking you a meal every day. Sit down.' He turned, walked back to his seat and sat down.

'Can you cook like my wife, Mrs Bathgate?' he asked.

'Well, I cook an evening meal for my two boys,' she said, 'and if you have an appetite like theirs, yes, I think I could manage.'

'Would you be free between say twelve and three, to come here?' Mirren asked. 'That would give you time to get home and prepare for your boys. You wouldn't mind cooking all day?' She smiled at the woman. She seemed straightforward enough.

'I worked in a restaurant before I got married, so that wouldn't be any trouble to me. I'd like to help you out.' Her eyes seemed to be sympathetic.

'I'll be away all day teaching,' Mirren said.

'I think I could do it. Mr Stewart could tell me what he liked.'

'There are a few things I don't like: cabbage, rice pudding—'

'You sit there, Dad,' Mirren said, rising, 'while Mrs Bathgate comes with me. I'm going to show her round the kitchen.'

65

They sat down at the table waiting for the kettle to boil, and Mirren agreed with Mrs Bathgate the terms of her employment, hours and payment.

'It's just till I find my feet, Miss Stewart,' Doris Bathgate said. 'I'm waiting for my divorce to come through, but this would fill in nicely.'

'Well, it would give me a breathing space too till we see how it works. He might be going to stay with his brother later.'

'If we agree to help one another out, it should be a benefit to us both. I can see you're quite worried about your father.'

'Yes. You'd probably notice his memory is bad. I think it began with grieving for my mother when she died.'

'I know all about grief, and my husband didn't die.' She shook her head. 'You're lucky to have a career. I had to take work where I could find it.'

'Did you? But a career, whatever it is, is very time-consuming.'

'Your parents probably supported you. Ah, well, no point in crying over spilt milk. In our house it was "find a man and get out". So I did.' She smiled at Mirren. She was glad to see that Doris Bathgate wasn't going to unload the story of her life on her and why her husband had left her.

They went back to the sitting room with Doris Bathgate carrying the tray with cups of coffee and biscuits on it – she had been adept at finding her way around while Mirren was making the coffee. She put the tray down on a table near Cameron, smiling at him. 'I'm going to be cooking your lunch for you for a little while, Mr Stewart, before you go to Waterside, isn't it?'

'Yes, my brother took my father's farm over. I could have gone in with him. He misses me and he wants me to help with the harvest.'

'Well, that sounds a good idea. Here's your coffee.' She handed it to him. 'A biscuit?' She held out the plate. She's quite at ease, Mirren thought, watching her.

Cameron smiled at Doris Bathgate, as if it were a game. 'I don't mind if I do,' he said, taking one. She's right for him, Mirren thought, it's going to work. He wouldn't have liked a 'decent body'. This one is just right, pretty, feminine, nice legs. She remembered that Aunt Margaret had implied that he'd had an eye for the girls.

Doris Bathgate came the following morning at twelve o'clock, as agreed with Mirren. They prepared the meal together, and she saw that the woman was adept at cooking, indeed, better than her. She didn't appear to mind peeling and slicing vegetables, a job Mirren hated, and she was glad to hand it over.

The three of them sat down together to

have lunch, and the steak Doris had prepared was succulent, the vegetables tender.

Cameron praised her, and said, 'You did a good job there, Doris.' The two exchanged smiling glances. 'It reminded me of my wife's cooking. Mirren hasn't the touch.'

'Thank you very much,' Mirren said, laughing.

She set off for her new school, reassured. The headteacher, Mr Young, who greeted her, was named appropriately, she thought. She had expected a much older man. He seemed to her to be in his middle thirties and had an unconvincing businesslike air. He gave her the impression of someone who had rehearsed his role insufficiently, resulting in behaviour which was a mixture of authority and flirtatiousness. 'I'm new to this job too, Miss Stewart. You are to take Miss Currie's place – she's leaving soon. At the moment there's Miss Currie and Miss Fyfe, both ladies very much your senior. I'll take you to the common room and introduce you. But first of all I'd better tell you your duties. You'll be teaching class three, that is the one before the eleven plus, which is taken by yours truly. Yours is a responsible job, but you are the only one with a university degree. The other two ladies only have their college certificates, and so couldn't be promoted. The rules were slack up until a year ago but now they're being tightened up,

68

I'm glad to see.' He gave Mirren an appreciative glance. 'Let me see, you're a Glasgow University graduate? Nice. I'm Dundee. My home is St Andrews.'

'I know St Andrews,' Mirren said, feeling he should be put at ease. 'When I was young my parents took me there on holiday. My father insisted on me swimming in the outdoor pool with him, and all I remember of it was the shock when I jumped in. The cold!'

'The people of St Andrews are armour-plated.' He smiled at her. 'Much softer skin in the west coast, eh?' He seemed to Mirren to be doing his best to strike a happy note with her.

'What subjects would I be teaching, Mr Young?'

'The usual, and I'm thinking of increasing their language skills. Are you fluent in one?'

'French up to Higher Certificate. I've never had a chance to go abroad.'

'Neither have I. Well, I'll give you the register, and you'll get an idea of how each of them is doing.' He looked at her. 'Is there anything you want to ask me?'

'No, thanks, Mr Young, but it would be helpful if I could have a chat with Miss Currie so that she could give me the lowdown on the pupils. It will be a test for me and them. I haven't taught before, except at Jordanhill, but I'm looking forward to it.'

'Do you like teaching?' The question didn't

seem to warrant his roving eye.

'Yes, I've always wanted to do it. Nothing else presented itself, although I should have liked to go abroad, but there isn't much choice for girls nowadays.'

'No, it's a man's world. But I'm pretty sure things are going to change.'

'So am I. It's taken the war to prove it.'

'Well,' he said, rising, 'I see you and I are going to get on very well. How could I not believe in feminism when I am hopelessly outnumbered by members of my teaching staff? And it's a lady who comes in to teach the girls sewing. Perhaps we should have had a man to show them how to change a fuse! Shall we go to the common room?'

'Yes.' Mirren got up, feeling that the two women she was going to meet would be more critical than Mr Young.

Miss Currie was a talkative woman, not in her first youth, grey-haired, precise in manner, a typical spinster. When would she be labelled similarly? Mirren thought. Miss Fyfe was leaving to be married. She said to Mirren, when Mr Young had gone away, 'He thinks I should be sorry to give up teaching, but I was never cut out to be a career girl. I'm getting married. My mother will have to live with us, I've been taking care of her, but my fiancé doesn't mind.'

Miss Currie was equally voluble at morning break. 'Have you any one dependent on

70

you, Miss Stewart?'

'Yes,' she told her, 'my father. Not financially, but I've looked after him since my mother died.'

'You're the same as Jessie Fyfe. I feel sorry for her, burdened with her mother in her married life.' Perhaps she doesn't feel sorry for herself, Mirren thought. 'Where do you live?' Miss Currie was curious.

'The West End. It's quite a journey to school.'

'Maybe you'd think of taking over my flat? It's just round the corner from Albert Road, nice and handy, near shops, we've got everything there including the City Bakeries, I love their cream buns, and a good butcher. I have two bedrooms and it's a nice flat, handy for the trams, and there's Pollok Park nearby. 'Why not come back with me from school and see it? It's an area I think your father might like. A good address.'

Mirren felt her future was being arranged for her, but there was no doubt, being near the school would be convenient. She might even be able to go home at lunchtime and cook a meal for her father, but against that there was the tearing him away from the West End where their lives had been centred for so long. To change from one side of Glasgow to another was as bad as uprooting and going to live in the country. But her life was going to be a city one, she thought, and for the first time she looked into the future, and thought that now that she had reached her goal, worked through university and was teaching, the prospect was not inspiring.

'Where do you intend to go, Miss Currie?' she asked her, feeling bleak as she looked at the woman and her future.

'Oh, I've always known that. I'm going to buy a nice wee bungalow in Helensburgh, and try a different kind of life. I have several friends there, retired school teachers, and they have a great time! So many societies to join, and the churches are good. They all tell me they've never regretted going there.'

She mentioned the idea of moving to her father, and he looked askance at her. 'We've never had anything to do with Pollokshields, or the people there.' He looked horrified.

'They're not Zulus. You'd like it. There's a good park near to walk to, and good shops, a newsagents at the corner. But, of course, if you don't like the idea, we won't go. Are you quite happy with Doris?'

She thought he looked sly for a moment. 'She's all right. Tries to please me, goes in for a bit of patting, treats me like one of her boys, Dougal and Iain. She's always boasting about them...'

'That's natural.'

'What I want to know is why her husband left her? There must be some reason?'

'Well, it's none of our concern, is it?'

But it turned out that it was.

A few weeks after Doris had been coming to cook, she dropped her bombshell.

'I'm afraid I'm going to let you down, Miss Stewart.'

'Why?' Mirren's heart began to beat faster.

'Well, I might as well be honest with you. I'm getting married again. My divorce papers came through this week.'

'Oh, well, I'm pleased for you. We both felt our arrangement might not last too long. Will it make any difference immediately to you coming here?'

'I'm afraid so. We're getting married next week.'

'Oh, I was hoping, for Father's sake, it wouldn't be as soon as that. But I quite understand.'

'I'm sorry. I'll miss your father. We got on quite well. I might as well tell you, my husband walked out because I was having an affair with the man I'm going to marry. He's in the Territorials, and we'll be moving away from here.'

'Well, I'm glad that everything has turned out so well for you.'

'I didn't think George would want to get married right away. But he's impatient. It's quite a chance for me, with the two boys...'

'I can see that. Well, of course you must think of yourself first. Dad will be disappointed.' As she said that, she thought what an innocent she was. She didn't know how the other half of the world lived. Anyhow, she must accept the circumstances, and then and there, she made up her mind to move house. It would upset her father to begin with, she knew, but she had to look after her own affairs. She could look after him as well – if she took Miss Currie's flat she would be near the school – and perhaps a change would help him when he was removed from familiar surroundings. But she knew it would upset him.

In bed that night, she decided she wouldn't tell him of her plan to move. She thought of his remark about Doris: 'All men know them.' You have to face up to it, she told herself, you're in your middle twenties and you know nothing about sex. She mouthed the word. It's no good blaming your parents, you aren't a child, you've been shutting your eyes to it all your life. You've felt yourself attracted by some of the young men at the university, and by Jack Drummond – a heightening of feeling, of thrills running up and down your body when you thought of being touched. Living with parents who loved each other should have alerted you, but instead you buried yourself in your studies, and didn't want to know. She had disliked how her friends laughed together in groups, but she had pretended not to be interested. Why were you afraid? Here was this woman, Doris Bathgate, who wasn't afraid of sex, in and out of marriage, had had two children, and still wanted to repeat the process. She's far more honest than you, who thought a degree would make you happy, but it doesn't. You've not been really happy since you became an adult. The move would mean a new stage in her life. When her father realised that she had decided, he would have to fall in with her plans.

Chapter 6

After a week of preparing a meal for her father, and leaving it ready to go into the oven, Mirren saw it was not a solution. Most of the time when she came home, he had forgotten, or he had raided the larder, complaining there was nothing for him to eat. When she compared this with the alert man she'd known, she had to admit that there was a great change in him. If only there was someone to give me advice, she thought, but Dr Clark clearly didn't think there was much wrong.

If she scolded him he looked pathetic, and she immediately felt guilty. 'I went for a walk in the park, you told me to do that, and the time just slipped past...' He laughed. 'It was only when I found myself eating the bread that I had taken for the ducks that I realised it was lunchtime.'

They laughed together, and she said, 'Well, I'll leave you some sandwiches, and I'll cook dinner for us in the evening.'

'I don't know the difference between dinner and lunch,' he said. 'People call it different things. We had "bites" at the farm, then Margaret made a bumper tea, then we had supper before we went to bed. I was never hungry there.'

Why are there no restaurants near us? she would think. There must be hundreds of old people living around here, but no provision is made for them. And then she would realise that the problem had to be solved by herself, and that the obvious thing would be to give up teaching and stay at home to look after him.

After school one day she went with Miss Currie to see her flat. It was on the first floor, an improvement on the West End one, which had been two up, which was a disadvantage in one way, because all refuse had to be carried down to the bin in the backyard; equally, washed clothes had to be taken down the stairs in a basket if she wanted to hang them out. Against that there had been the wonderful feeling of being high up and

76

looking over the park on the other side of the street, with the university buildings rearing up on one side.

'What are the neighbours like?' she asked Miss Currie when they were walking down Albert Road.

'Very nice, although I haven't had much to do with them. Some have children but they're well behaved. Then there's a Miss Cunningham, a retired lady, and in the ground-floor flat Mr and Mrs Campbell, very refined. He always raises his bowler when we meet, and his wife, who doesn't go out much, is quite friendly if I meet her in the shops. They have a young son who's at the university, I think, and naturally he's not interested in an old fogey like me. He's not about much, but of the family I like Mr Campbell best. For a long time I thought he looked ill, but recently he's looking much better. I think he works long hours – I see him from my front window coming back quite late. Oh, you wouldn't have any trouble with the other tenants; indeed your father might fraternise with Mr Campbell.'

The flat had two bedrooms, one larger than the other which her father could have to accommodate all his books. Miss Currie had a few shelves in it, but she could add to those. The kitchen was large, looking on to the grass backyard, but from the oriel window at the front there was an unimpressive view of flats of red stone which looked exactly like the frontage of her own. Of course, it wasn't the West End, with everything near, the best shops in Sauchiehall Street, St Andrews Hall in Berkeley Street for concerts, the university, Kelvingrove Park, all of it familiar territory, and hard to leave. Pollokshields didn't have beautiful buildings, the sign of the type of people who had lived and worked there.

'There's no park near,' she said to Miss Currie. 'We were just across from Kelvingrove Park.'

'We have Pollok Park near here, just a tram ride away. It's an estate, but the public are permitted to use it. You can get all the exercise you want there.'

She told her father that she had seen Miss Currie's flat, and when he said, grudgingly, that he didn't know the district, and she said, 'Well, let's go on Sunday and have a look around,' he reminded her that they had planned to go to the Botanic Gardens, a favourite rendezvous of theirs with its Edwardian air, in Great Western Road.

'Well, we can go again another Sunday,' she said, thinking that's another of the advantages of living here, and wondering how he had remembered. If something appeals to him, he'll remember, but anything which doesn't, he can dismiss it utterly from his mind. But, when she told him that Pollok park had been owned once by a well-known Glasgow family called Maxwell, that their house had been designed by Adam, and they had bequeathed it and their estate to Glasgow Corporation, his look was dismissive.

'But if we left here I would lose the Mitchell Library,' he said, 'I can read the *Herald* there for free. The West End has everything we need.' He didn't suggest going to Pollok park, and seeing his mood, she decided to leave that for another day.

'Of course it has,' she said, 'but I'm working at Pollokshields, and I'm sure there are fine libraries there.'

'Aye, maybe so,' he conceded, and was silent on the way home. He went off to bed early, leaving her feeling as miserable as he looked.

Miss Currie asked her the following week if she had made up her mind about the flat.

'I'd like it,' she told her, but my father baulks at the thought of leaving the West End.'

'Well, I've always been a south-sider myself, there's nothing wrong with it,' Miss Currie almost tossed her head.

'It's quite a decision,' Mirren said. 'In many ways I can sympathise with how he feels.'

'To me it's a question of living in Glasgow, and it doesn't do much good to feel the only place for you is where you live. I daresay when I go to Helensburgh I'll think of the convenience here, but you have to weigh up the pros and cons. Your job and the district you live in go together, and it seems to me the only way to make life easier for you. I'm looking forward to Helensburgh, and to a new life there. You want to look after your father. That's your prime consideration. You have to look ahead.'

'You're right, Miss Currie.' There were advantages in making the changes together, house and job, and who knew, there might be something in Pollokshields for her which she hadn't found in the West End. And perhaps moving away from the house where the three of them had happily lived together would help her father to settle.

After much thought, she told Miss Currie she would have the flat, and then had to face telling her father. She took the opportunity that evening when they were having their meal together.

'I think the Mitchell's going down the nick,' he said. 'They don't buy enough *Heralds*. I couldn't get near it this morning.'

'You shouldn't be so mean, Dad,' she said. 'Your tram fare would pay for the cost of it and besides, Mrs Muir would keep one for you.'

'But I look forward to my trip there in the mornings, and by the time I get back it's time for my sandwich.'

80

'Think of me travelling to and from my school every day. I'm trying to correct papers on the tram, and I'm getting behind with my work.'

'You never put it like that before, Mirren.'

'Perhaps I didn't. Miss Currie says there's a newsagent right beside her flat and they deliver each day. I'd pay for that.'

'But I've got plenty of money!'

'We need that for the rates. Dad, I don't think you ever give a thought to how this house is run. One thing, Pollokshields has a different rating system from here, and remember, when we bought this flat, Mother told me the agent said it was a prime location and we had to pay for that. I remember you used to be annoyed at what it costs to live here, but now you don't think about it.'

'You're right, Mirren, I never give it a thought.'

'Well, don't you think, for my benefit, we should take this opportunity to buy Miss Currie's flat?'

'We'd have to sell this one.'

'Well, supposing we tell the agent to put it up for sale. You would then know if you had enough money to buy Miss Currie's.'

She telephoned the next morning to the agent's office, and he told her he thought he had a client waiting for it. 'It's a customer who has a branch of his firm here. He travels

81

to London to buy his stock. He's waiting for a flat in this district. His shop's at Charing Cross. Furs.'

He brought Mr Abrahams the following evening to see it, and the man, well-dressed, and with a preponderance of male jewellery decorating his person, was pleased with it. He wasn't impressed by the park opposite as much as by the convenient tram service. The offer he made for it astounded her father, and quite won him over. He was a typical Scot. He liked a bargain.

The subsequent visit to Miss Currie to strike a bargain with her became a pleasure, and he shook hands on the transaction, walking away with a sizeable profit. They were moving in at the beginning of October, and Mirren, looking at the beauty of the red and golden foliage across the street, didn't draw her father's attention to it, in case he would regret his decision.

He telephoned his brother at the farm to say they were moving house, and offered his services to him. Mirren overheard him when she accompanied him to the telephone kiosk. 'Mirren says she could make the move while I was at Waterside.'

He pretended to be overjoyed, but she noticed he no longer mentioned his walks in the park, nor the Pollokshields flat. She had the impression that he had shut his mind against that, and all he talked about was

Waterside, and how he would be able to help his brother.

On the Saturday before they left the flat, they had a surprise visit from Josh and Jack Drummond. They were standing on the mat, smiling, when she opened the door.

'You look as if you had seen two ghosts,' Jack Drummond said. She was aware that she must look flushed and surprised, and was immediately ashamed of her reaction. 'Josh had to come to town to shop and see your father, and I took the chance to come along with him.'

'Come in,' she said. 'Father will be pleased to see you.'

'Are you sure it's all right?' Josh said. Of the two he looked the more reluctant, and she wondered if he had been pushed into this visit by Jack.

Her father looked up astonished. 'Goodness gracious me! It's Josh.'

'And Jack Drummond,' she said.

He got up and shook hands with the two young men. 'Have a seat. Mirren, chairs. And what brings you here?' He spoke to Josh.

'We've come to shop in Glasgow,' he said, 'and I've a message for you from Father. He says if you feel up to it he'd be glad of your help.'

'Are you taking me back with you?' His eyes lit up.

'No, Uncle. I can't do that.' Mirren saw his face fall.

'And I wondered, while your father and Josh were talking, if I could take you to a matinee?' Jack said to Mirren.

'Well...' She looked at her father. He was looking downcast. He'd been upset that he wasn't going back with Josh.

'Don't you worry about leaving Uncle,' Josh said. 'He and I will have a fine chat while you're away.'

'On you go,' her father said, surprisingly. 'It'll do you good.'

'Well, only if I can cook a meal for all of us when we come back,' she said.

'No, there's no need,' Josh said. 'We'll just get on home when you get back. Uncle and I will have a talk about the harvest while you're gone.'

While they were all talking, Mirren slipped away to make a cup of tea for them. She was putting cups and saucers on a tray when she realised Jack was at her side.

'This was ma idea, Mirren,' he said. 'I wanted to see you. Ah can't stoap thinkin' about you.'

'It wasn't a good idea,' she said. 'My father was disappointed when Josh said he couldn't go back with him.'

He looked taken aback. 'Oh, the auld yins don't worry for long. In one ear and oot the other. A know by ma mither. But what about

84

you? Ur ye no' glad to see me?'

She turned to him, still annoyed, but trying to disguise her pleasure at seeing him. 'I'm glad of the chance to talk to you about that night at the barn dance.'

'That's why I'm here. Josh is a pal. He made up the excuse about visiting your father. I told him I wanted to apologise to you. I'm really sorry fur ma behaviour that night. I got carried away.' He put his arms round her waist, drew her to him. 'Wull ye forgive me?'

'I think I got carried away too,' she said.

'So everything's all right then?'

'I don't know about that.'

'Does that mean you don't like me?'

'No, it doesn't. But I'm not sure.'

'I've never met a lassie who had such queer notions as you,' he said.

'It's just that...' She was hopelessly tongue-tied. He watched her embarrassment, smiling, and again pulled her to him.

'Ah, come on,' he said, 'forget that night ever happened.' He bent down and kissed her. This time, to her further embarrassment her hands went involuntarily to his shoulders, and she fancied her lips clung to his. She struggled in his arms and pushed him away. 'Puir wee lassie,' he said, 'you need Jack Drummond to sort you out.' He looked down at her, laughing.

Her temper flared, and she said in her

iciest tones, 'What I wanted to tell you was that I was behaving out of character that night.' She turned to the cooker, where the kettle seemed to be going mad, whistling stridently, its lid jumping up and down. 'I must make the tea.'

'We have yin like that at hame. Drives you mad. Behaving out of character? Whit does that mean? Is that some more of your teacher talk?'

'No, it isn't. I meant what I said. I've got to give it more thought.'

'Give it up, Mirren.' He sighed hugely. 'Admit it. You were attracted to me. Do you accept my apology?'

'For what it's worth.' She saw the laughter die out of his face. He seized the tray, with the cups and saucers on it. 'I'll carry this. Pit the teapot on it,' he said, 'and I'll carry it through for you. It'll make a good alibi, show that I was busy making tea in the kitchen and not raping you.' She was speechless, and haughty, as she got some biscuits out of a tin, and put them on a plate.

'On you go,' she said. 'I'll follow you.'

While they were drinking their tea, she talked to Josh, enquiring about Grace, and Aunt Meg, and if there were any developments about the fire in the small barn, and anything about the village which occurred to her. All the time she was aware of Jack's eyes on her.

'Well,' he said, getting up, 'if we're going to get to that picture house, we'd better get going.'

She got up too, reluctantly. 'I'll not be long, Father.'

'There's no rush,' he said. He turned to his nephew. 'You were telling me how the sheep broke through in the far field, Josh.'

When she and Jack Drummond got to the outside door, he said, 'Don't look so worried. Make up your mind that you're going to enjoy yourself.'

She smiled at him. 'I must admit I'm dying to see that film in the Regal. Myrna Loy.'

'Good. So am I. Come on!'

They ran down the stairs together. 'Can you do two at a time?' Jack said.

'Yes, easily.' At the foot, he turned to her, smiling. 'That's put roses in your cheeks. You look really excited.'

'Do I? Well, that's good.'

'Josh is a pal. It's great to see you, Mirren. And you're not offended?'

'Only at myself. Don't give it another thought.'

'Aye, all right.' She saw puzzlement in his eyes.

She was still determined to enjoy herself, as they walked down Sauchiehall Street to the Regal. She stood beside him while he asked for the best seats, and was led by the girl with her torch to the back of the stalls.

Jack sat down beside her, and heaved a sigh. 'Everything's going according to plan,' he said, putting his arm round the back of her seat. She saw other girls snuggling into their partners, and relaxed against him. She felt his arm dropping to her waist, tightening.

Although she had said Myrna Loy was her favourite actress, she was too conscious of Jack Drummond beside her to concentrate on the film. Occasionally he turned and kissed her cheek, and once he turned her face with his hand and kissed her lips. 'Mirren,' he said, 'I've been dreaming about this.'

When they left the cinema, she knew her face was flushed and, keeping it turned away from him, she said, 'We'd better hurry home. Dad gets worried if I'm away too long.'

'Have you tested him?' he said.

'What do you mean?'

'What do you mean? You either are out often, or you're never out, and you don't know what he'd be like.' She hurried on, not replying. 'Have a look at yourself, Mirren,' he said, making up on her. 'You're using the old man as an excuse to hide from men, and you know you enjoy it when it happens, isn't that right?'

'No, it isn't right.' She made up her mind. 'Jack,' she said, 'I'm sorry you came today, but thanks for taking me out. I would like to remain friends with you, but nothing more. I admit I was attracted to you, and if I gave you the wrong impression, well, I'm sorry.'

'I'm glad you were able to say that,' he said. 'At least you're honest. And I'm not hurt. I've had quite a lot of turn downs in my life! I admit I came on too strongly, but that was sheer bravado, the city girl and all that ... but I soon found out I was wrong. That's what worried me, and why I wanted to apologise. Of course I'll remain friends with you, but if you ever change your mind aboot me, and would like to see me again, just let me know. I've fallen for you, Mirren. You're quite different from any girl I've known.'

He put an arm round her and gave her a hug. 'Friends, eh?'

He was like the young man at the dance, amazed at how near the shops and cinemas they were. She teased him. 'You're just a country yokel.'

'Aye, that's me. D'you not see the straw sticking out of my ears?'

When they got back to her flat, they went into the front room, where she found Josh and her father deep in conversation. They both looked up, as if surprised.

Josh said, 'Back already? We were just discussing the price of wheat.'

'That sounds interesting,' she laughed.

'It was a great film,' Jack said. 'Mirren enjoyed it, poor little soul. She hardly ever gets out.'

'This one teases me all the time,' she said to Josh, and to Jack, 'Sit down, and I'll make you two something before you begin on your journey back to Waterside.'

He and Josh looked at each other, 'I think ... we'll just get on our way,' Josh said, 'and I've said to Uncle that I'll drive here to collect him when the date's fixed.'

'Did he tell you that we're moving to Pollokshields?' she said.

'No.' He looked at his uncle, surprise on his face.

'If you could pick him up during the removal, that would be a great help, Josh.'

'It might be a fortnight before I'm able to come again,' he said.

'Well, that's all right. Isn't it, Dad?' He gave her a doubting look but didn't answer.

She saw them to the door, and said, 'Well, there's nothing like surprises to brighten one's life.'

'She's beginning to think there's more to life than teaching,' Jack said, with his one-sided smile.

When she went back to the room, her father was standing at the window, watching them getting into the old Ford.

'They might have taken me back with them,' he said.

'But you're not ready to go yet,' she said. 'I'd have to get your clothes ready and pack

90

your bag.'

He didn't reply. He sat down in his chair and after a time he heaved a sigh. 'What's for supper?' he said.

'I've got some nice pork chops. Would you like that?'

'Aye, and plenty of vegetables, like Margaret. She grows them herself.'

'Well, I don't,' she said, getting up and going towards the kitchen.

The following day he seemed *distrait*, and occasionally when she looked across the table at him, she caught his eyes on her. She felt uneasy, especially as he didn't reply to her when she mentioned the visit of Josh and Jack. After breakfast she was busy in the kitchen, and she heard him in his bedroom moving around, and once or twice, sounds like the wardrobe door shutting. She began to feel uneasy because of the silence. What was he doing? She could imagine him sitting on his bed, thinking. But what about? The clattering of the dishes she was washing filled her ears for perhaps a few minutes, when suddenly a noise from the hall, a clicking of a lock, perhaps, broke through the clatter. She stopped with her hands in the basin, alert. Had it been the front door? She hurriedly dried her hands on the tea towel, and ran through the hall, her heart beating against her ribs.

When she opened the door, she heard the

clattering sound of footsteps. Rushing to the banister, she leant on it and looked over. On the landing below, she saw her father, with a bag in his hand. Terror overtook her, terror at what it might mean.

'Dad!' she shouted. 'Where are you going?'

She saw him hesitate on the flight of stairs and look up. 'Don't follow me,' he shouted. 'I'm going to Waterside!'

'No!' she shouted. 'Come back! You can't go alone!' She began running down the stairs, seeing him go past Mrs Crail's door, then Mrs Baxter's, and make for the second flight of stairs. She was halfway down behind him, when she saw he was swaying dangerously because of the heavy bag, and while she tore down after him, missing steps on the way, it happened. He missed his step and went hurtling down the stone staircase. His voice was a prolonged screech as he fell.

Immediately, as if they had been waiting for this moment, Mrs Crail and Mrs Baxter appeared in their doorways. She didn't know which one it was who first spoke to her. The other one – it was Mrs Crail, she now saw – stepped forward and looked over the banisters. 'Oh! Oh!' She put her hand to her mouth. 'It's Mr Stewart!'

'So it is.' Mrs Baxter had joined her. 'Oh, dear, Mirren, what are we going to do?'

She was halfway down the second flight of stairs to where her father lay, stretched out, one leg buckled under him, and his head, twisted horribly, resting on a step further down. His face was drenched in blood from a wound in his scalp. She found she still had the tea towel in her hand, and she knelt down and mopped his face with it. 'Oh, Dad...' she said. He was alive – she saw his lips moving. She bent over him to hear what he was saying. 'I was going ... to ... Waterside, Mirren...' She stroked his cheek while his voice became fainter and fainter, saying, 'It's all right, Dad ... We'll get you...' His voice was becoming fainter and fainter and then it stopped altogether. His eyes were wide open, fixed on her, she imagined accusingly, and she wailed loudly, aware that someone's hand was on her shoulder.

'Come away, Mirren, come away! Oh, your poor father! Mrs Crail is dialling 999.'

'You go back to your house, Mrs Baxter.' Even in the midst of the shock she was feeling, petrifying her, making it unable to grasp the terrible circumstances which she had to confront, she felt sorry for the old woman. Her mouth and chin were shaking (it had always been a secret about her age, but she was certainly too old for this). Dad said he had once seen her without her wig. 'Not a pretty sight,' he had said. To her surprise Mirren felt a laugh bubbling to her lips, which changed immediately to a loud wail, a kind of keening. She wished she could weep like an ordinary person, but every time she looked down at her father's immobile face, his eyes staring out of the mess of blood, she wailed again. She heard Mrs Baxter say, surprisingly, at her side, 'Damn! A canna kneel! Oh, you poor thing!' Her hand was on Mirren's shoulder. 'I'll stay with you till somebody comes.'

She would never forget, she knew at that moment, the vigil she and Mrs Baxter shared at her father's body. It was endless, purgatory. If only somebody would come, they would be able to mend him – she knew she kept on saying that to Mrs Baxter, who had no words except, 'There, there...' with frequent pats on her shoulder.

Out of the blackness at last there was the stirring of voices and footsteps in the entry, and then two men in uniform with a stretcher appeared at her side. 'Ma Gawd, Jimmy!' she heard one of them breathe to the other, an older man who gave his companion a brisk order. 'Get on with it. Help her up!' She felt strong hands supporting her, and then she was transferred to the frail support of Mrs Baxter, and they both made their way, stumblingly, up the stairs, one supporting the other, towards Mirren's flat.

They passed Mrs Crail, who was standing in her doorway, wringing her hands. 'I did all I could, Mirren. Phoned the Western and all. Oh, you poor soul! And I phoned Dr Clark.

He's my doctor, and they said he was yours.' She joined the procession, still talking. 'The ambulance men will attend to everything. I'll come up too, and help to make you a cup of tea...'

She knew she was ministered to by the two old women who fussed around her with tea, and got her to lie down on her bed, then mercifully Dr Clark appeared, and said, 'I'll send a nurse to look after Miss Stewart. When she comes, you two ladies must get back to your homes.'

The nurse who arrived soon despatched them, still wringing their hands, and saying over and over again, 'Oh dear! Oh dear! What a terrible thing...'

'You get back to your homes, ladies,' Mirren heard her say. 'You've been a great help, but Miss Stewart will be looked after. Don't you worry. Everything will be all right.' But how could it be? she thought.

'Now, Nurse Cassidy will stay with you until arrangements are made,' Dr Clark said, who was sitting at the side of her bed. He took her hand and spoke, she knew, comforting words, like 'It'll get better, she'll support you,' but she felt a great grudge against him rising in her and she wanted to say, 'You should have taken him seriously,' but she knew it was no one's fault.

Book 2

Chapter 1

1939

The day of the funeral, everyone, it seemed including Grace McFarlane and Jack Drummond came from Waterside. Aunt Meg remained at the flat to make a ham tea for the returning mourners. The whole thing was like walking through a mist to Mirren, with frequent pats on the shoulder which seemed to direct her through the maze. What she did remember was that before they left, Jack Drummond said to her, 'I'll be there on the date of your flitting, Mirren. Josh asked me to help you. He's busy with the tail end of the harvest.'

She stared at him, not in disbelief, but surprise at his offer. He was a farmer too, and surely couldn't spare the time.

'There's no need, Jack. The removal men will see to everything.'

'Another pair of hands would be a help,' he said, and along with the others, he kissed her when they all left. She had persuaded Aunt Meg not to stay on. She wanted to be alone. Besides, her aunt was patently suffering. There were lines on her face. 'Arthritis, Mirren. It's caught up with me at last. A family complaint.'

So here she was, she thought, alone for the first time, in her new flat, 12 Limes Avenue, 'a dead end' as Miss Currie called it, actually a cul de sac off Albert Road running parallel with the railway. Jack had been very helpful at the removal, and taken her for lunch to the Ca'd'oro Café in Union Street, then got his train from the Central Station opposite, to Waterside, giving in to Mirren's request that he should go back home, although he had offered to stay on for another day. But that had worried her. Where would he sleep? He had said he would 'doss down' in the Kelvingrove flat, but there were only bare floors there, and she had persuaded him against that.
  She was in the bedroom which had been intended for her father, sorting out his books, when the finality struck her. She felt like a swimmer who had at last come up for air. The only thing which had saved her from the desolation of her loss was having to teach each day. She had got through her first week.

The staff had been sympathetic and suppor-
tive, indicating that although they hadn't
known the 'old gentleman', Annie Calder's
phrase, a girl about her own age, they
appreciated what a blow it must have been
for his daughter. Annie Calder had replaced
Jessie Fyfe, who had left to be married.
Mirren almost preferred the self-centred
behaviour of her class to the hush which fell
upon the common room when she went into
it.

I could have stayed on in the Kelvingrove
flat now that Dad's gone, she thought,
choosing a shelf for 'History'. What a lot of
books on that subject he had collected,
typical of his undirected reading. If you had
said to him, 'What's your period?' he would
have looked startled, she knew, and probably
said, 'Any, I think.' His chief source of books
was the public libraries, which occasionally
put on sale their discarded tomes, the bigger
the better from his point of view, particularly
if they were well-illustrated.

Then, his dictionaries, French, Italian,
Scandinavian, and here was a Japanese one.
Lately he had been interested in the origin of
words, and had demonstrated examples to
her with delight. 'There's a Latin root buried
in most of them, they're called the Romance
languages,' he had told her. She had thought
sometimes that he was like a thirsty man
drinking at a well which had been denied

him from birth. Perhaps I got my craving for learning from him, she thought. Once she had said to him, she remembered, as she arranged the books (in all of which he had written his name), 'You're an old bibliophile,' and had to explain what the word meant. His look of awe had been, she knew, at her knowledge, not at the meaning of the word.

He had been 'a bit of a scholar', he had told her, in his school in Lanarkshire, amongst the farmers' sons who had attended it, and they had pulled his leg, but they had all become men at fourteen and had left school then. There had been no great expectations from his father and mother. They were glad he would conform to the mould. Once she had said to him when they were talking about his schooldays, 'Anyhow, Dad, you made your own career in the city,' and he had said, 'Yes, thanks to Jane, but blood is thicker than water. I missed the farm life all the time here, but she didn't. She said she had always felt out of place in Waterside.'

She was finding she could think of other things. His terrible death was not now appearing in her dreams. Dr Clark had been aware of her suffering, and had given her sleeping pills to help her. 'I can trust you, Mirren. I wouldn't hand them out to everyone.'

There was Jack Drummond. There had been no further meetings with him. He probably felt, as she did, that it was not the time nor place for them. But he had said, before he left her to go to the station, 'You just have to let me know, Mirren, and I'll be there.' She had thanked him, thinking she was not likely to do that but she felt grateful to him. When she thought of him, his country speech, his lack of city polish, she knew they were not important; but they had nothing in common except a mutual attraction which would have melted away with time.

She had settled into school life fairly well. They made a nice little threesome, Mr Young (Alastair), Annie Calder, who taught the juniors, and herself. Although it was a primary school, the numbers were growing rapidly, and Alastair (he liked Annie and Mirren to call him that) was appealing to the board of governors for another teacher to be added to their quota. 'My role is to be a figurehead,' he had joked with them. 'Not to teach.'

He had met Mirren in the corridor one day, and said to her, looking serious and lowering his voice, 'I can't say this in front of Annie, but I'm impressed by you, Mirren. When I was taking your class yesterday for maths, I got nothing but enthusiasm from them for their teacher. Your history results are particularly good.' 'That's my chief interest,' she had told him. 'I'm afraid I can't say the same about Annie,' he had said. 'She doesn't manage to control her class. Have you any suggestions?' She hadn't liked this conversation. 'Give her time,' she had said, 'she's nervous. The children feel it. And there's Jimmy Grant in her class. He's the trouble-maker of the school.'

'Yes, I know,' she remembered him saying, 'she actually called at my flat the other night to complain about him.' She remembered this, because she'd thought at the time that it was an odd thing for Annie to do. He'd said he'd had a long talk with Annie, and explained the principles about not being in favour of strapping, but perhaps he'd have to resort to it. She remembered being glad when the bell rang, as she might have given him her views about corporal punishment, but she'd been able to say, 'Excuse me, but I must go and help Annie to bring them in.' 'Mum's the word,' he had said. When she had been helping Annie to marshall the pupils into lines to march them back to class, she had looked at her, and thought of what Alastair had told her. It was difficult to fit this in with Annie's baby-like face and unruly hair.

Astronomy. The trouble had been that her father's enthusiasm had quickly vanished, hence the preponderance of books on every subject. Then it would get too difficult for him. 'This old brain of mine,' he would say disconsolately. He it was who should have gone to university, she thought, but the times were against him.

When she had finished her task she felt tired, and went into the kitchen to make a cup of tea. She was lonely. I must ask someone in, she thought. Annie, for instance. Get to know her background. She was filling the kettle at the sink, when she caught sight of a man emptying rubbish into one of the dustbins in the back green. She thought she recognised him. He was wearing a dark overcoat and a bowler, and she could imagine his wife saying to him, 'On your way out, would you empty the rubbish for me?' He turned and walked across the grass in the direction of the ground-floor flat. She saw the face underneath the bowler, white, lugubrious, and she shut her eyes and thought. Who did she, or maybe her father, know who looked like that? She remembered the person she was thinking of had had a slight limp, like the man she was watching. Think, Mirren! And, slowly the picture eased into her mind. The man on the bench at the park when she and her father had sat down. He had looked embarrassed, and had stuffed the sandwich he had been eating into his briefcase. And hadn't he said, that on fine days, he couldn't bear going into restaurants. He liked the fresh air. Dad had agreed with him, and said he missed the countryside too and that was why they were in the park ... which had led to a conversation, typical of Dad, until the man got up and limped away. Yes, she remembered the limp. But, wait, hadn't she seen him on another day in the Mitchell when she was studying? He hadn't been wearing his bowler, and she had seen his face clearly, and when their eyes met he had smiled tentatively, in recognition.

How strange, she thought. Someone from the past. I must call and introduce myself. The woman in the bottom flat, his wife, whom she had met shopping, had seemed quite friendly, although haughty. She'd had a closed, no-nonsense type of face. You keep yourself to yourself and I'll do the same...

Never mind, she thought, if I don't call I might meet him outside and I could say, 'Excuse me, but I feel I know you. Do you remember me?'

She turned to get the teapot, feeling excited. It made her move here feel suddenly worthwhile, to have a point ... What point? she thought. And felt a wave of misery sweep over her. Loneliness ... was it worse here than it might have been in Kelvingrove? Worse there, she decided. Everything in the park and in the flat would have reminded her of him. She decided to make a cup of tea into a meal, made some sandwiches, and sat in her front room with them, as her father had done in the other flat. But there was no view of the park, just a railway. A train went rushing past. Where did they go to, passing through here? She must find out about the stations, but she wouldn't have any use for the train as she could walk to school. She wished she was there at this moment. It was the only place where she could count on sympathy. A bath, she thought, and got up purposefully.

But in the bath, she was suddenly overcome by such a storm of weeping that she kept her face buried in the sponge for a long time.

Where is he? she thought. Such a hole in her life, anyone's life when they lost someone they had loved dearly. They could have been discussing anything at this moment. Hitler's rejection of King Carol and King Leopold's offer of mediation, for instance. His healthy dislike, hatred of Hitler, had done away with her wish for peace. He was right, of course. 'I'm with Churchill,' he said often. And she remembered him laughing at the report he had read somewhere that there had been an attempt to paint New Forest ponies with stripes like zebras for camouflage. 'They're a daft lot, the English.' Like many men of his age he had never crossed the border.

Chapter 2

The next day when she woke up, she felt better – she had had a good sleep, thanks to Dr Clark's pills. She would plan her day, she thought. She would straighten up the flat in the morning, and take the tram to Pollok Estate in the afternoon. That way she would get through the weekend, and after that there was school on Monday morning. She wondered if she would hear from Jack Drummond, but hoped not. I'm not ready for emotional involvement, she thought. I've been drained of emotion since Dad died. She didn't allow herself to sit down and weep, but went to the kitchen to make her breakfast. While she was filling the kettle at the window, she looked out at the dismal prospect – the wash-house with its rows of dustbins in front, one for each tenant. That was where she had seen Mr Campbell, or the man she and her father had met in the park. If only Dad were here to confirm my suspicions, she thought.

When she had finished her breakfast, she purposefully went about the job of tidying up the flat. What is so traumatic about moving? she asked herself. The surroundings? Not as good as Kelvingrove with its view of the park and its proximity to the city. Wait a minute! The big thing is Dad. You're here alone. At Kelvingrove there had once been Dad and Mum, now here she was with neither of them, and she was singularly alone, and single. But hadn't she wished at times she could have a flat of her own? Here she was, then. And she had to adapt to living in a place where she could not help but imagine the previous occupant living, Miss Currie. Her presence was palpable, Miss Currie, now in her 'wee bungalow' with a view of the Clyde. 'I think you'll find my flat very suitable, it's handy for the trams, secluded, and near the shops.'

I'll have to blot you out, Miss Currie, with the wallpaper, roses in columns in the bedroom, the old grate in the kitchen, which could be replaced with the gas cooker from the other flat, the dark hall where there had been an attempt to jazz it up with a bold striped wallpaper. That could be banished with plain walls and lamps for good illumination substituted.

But in the bathroom. What could she do with the bathroom? The polished mahogany seat on the toilet bowl, the round mirror, freckled with rust, the bath which had been painted very obviously with pale beige paint, as had the linen cupboard. The washing basin was cracked. And the idea of sitting on the mahogany seat of the toilet bowl where Miss Currie's round bottom had rested, appalled her. And only in emergencies, like last night, having a bath in that dingy bath where Miss Currie had once floated, and where she had cut her nails: 'I always attend to my feet when I'm in my bath.' Why did one remember the throwaway remarks?

I have to imprint my personality, blot out Miss Currie, her old-maidishness, introduce my own, she thought. But have I a personality? Has it been crushed by looking after Mum when she was ill, and then coping with Dad's distress and illness after she died? Does that show on me?

Alastair had said she was doing well with the children at school, but how about grown-ups? Annie certainly came to her for advice. And Alastair confided in her about Annie. She got the impression that they were seeing each other apart from the school. Have I a look of responsibility, too old for my years? she wondered.

She went into the bedroom, which she had converted into a study with her father's books, but it would be hers now, she thought, sitting down on her father's old leather chair, at the table, and looking out on the green backyard with the row of dustbins in front of the wash-house. It had been the

107

first one, counting from the left, that the bowler-hatted man had used yesterday. If only Dad had been here, he could have spied on him and confirmed her belief that it had been the same man as they had seen in the park. 'Yours is the fourth dustbin in the row,' Miss Currie had told her, 'and I don't know if you'll want to use the wash-house. I never did. I took my bed linen to the laundry, and washed my smalls' – your 'bigs' Mirren had thought, listening to her – 'in the bathroom.' She remembered Miss Currie's coy smile in the fat face.

Had the mystery man really been Mr Campbell who lived downstairs, whom Miss Currie had talked about? 'Very genteel', with a son at the university? The husband of the woman whom she had spoken to while shopping?

'But then, Miss Stewart,' the voice echoed in her mind, 'you'll be like me, not wishing to hobnob with the neighbours, your interests will be outside.' Well, she didn't want to be like Miss Currie with her closed mind, and she didn't have many interests outside. Not yet. She thought of the school, a composite word, covering her attachment to her pupils, and her feeling of solidarity with Annie and Alastair.

Miss Currie had been glad to leave the school, and what would have been her interests? Washing her 'smalls' in the bathroom, having a few of 'the girls' in for supper, correcting her pupils' homework, and going to church on Sunday. I shan't be like that, she thought, I must get out and meet people here, join some societies, a choir, perhaps, mother had always said she had a 'sweet' voice, make something of her life. And there were men. When she felt like it, she'd write to Jack Drummond, and thank him for his help. But not yet, with her head full of Dad. Once, sitting at the window in the last flat, he'd said suddenly, 'I've been a drag on you, Mirren, and you've been a wee angel to me. I know you haven't had the kind of life that young girls are entitled to, and that you missed your mother when you were growing up.' Strangely enough, she hadn't, not like this feeling of emptiness, of being a wraith, a shadow, and not part of this planet at all.

She went into the kitchen to make something for her lunch, and while she was eating, with the intention of going to Pollok Park, the doorbell rang. I'm not ready, she thought, rising. Who could this be? Jack Drummond? She went slowly through the dark hall to the front door.

When she opened it, Annie was standing on the mat, her black curly hair awry as usual. Perhaps this time it was the wind. She had a bunch of flowers in her hand. They were chrysanthemums, and there was a torn piece of paper round the stems. 'Well, hello,

109

Annie,' she said, 'this is a surprise! Come in.' She held the door open and Annie stepped into the hall.

'I was helping Dad in his allotment this morning, and he said I could pick those, and give them to you. I've told him about you.' She held out the flowers. 'I knew this was your address, so maybe they'll help you to settle in.'

'Oh, that's kind of you! What a nice idea! People have Open House days, don't they, for all their friends when they move.'

'Do they? I didn't know that, but I just had the idea.'

'Well, thank you. Come into the kitchen while I put them in water. Would you like some tea?'

'That would be nice. How have you settled down?' Annie asked as she sat down in a chair Mirren had indicated. 'Does it make you miss your father more?'

Mirren, filling the kettle at the sink, nodded her head without speaking. Her throat filled. 'It was nice of your father to suggest you bring the flowers. Tell me about him.'

'Dad and I are pals. He knows how difficult it is for me at home. He says he feels guilty.'

'Why guilty?'

'Well, Chrissie is Dad's second wife, and they have twins, Douglas and Elizabeth (but they're called Dougie and Lizzie) and she likes to go out at night with her friends. So I'm left with them. Dad works late a lot. He's an engineer. He gets overtime – he says his firm's getting a lot of work because of the war coming, and Chrissie likes him to take it. She says the twins cost a lot.'

'I'm sure they do. How did you manage to study for your degree?'

'Chrissie is Dad's second wife. My real mother is a teacher, and she decided early on that I must go to the university. I was there when she left us.'

'For someone else?'

'In a way. She applied to teach in Canada, and went off there with a teacher friend. So Dad and I were left. It was a terrible time. And then he met Chrissie, and he says he married her partly because he didn't like me being left alone when he was at work. I think he was worried that I was getting into bad company.'

'And were you?'

'What do you think? You know what it's like at the university. I seemed to get to know the bad apples.' She laughed, running her hand through her hair.

'You've got lovely hair, Annie,' Mirren said.

'So the bad apples told me.' Her black eyes flashed. 'I was upset at mother leaving us.'

'Do you hear from your mother?'

'Yes. She's written to Dad and me. She

says she's started a new life there with her friend.'

'Oh!' It sounded strange to Mirren. 'Did they get a divorce?'

'I suppose they did. He couldn't have married Chrissie, could he?'

'No, that's right. It must have been bad for you when your mother left?' What a story, she thought. And as if Annie knew what she was thinking, she said, 'Mother's friend, Maymie, was always at our house, and I think that was why my father and mother split up. They were always quarrelling about Maymie being there. Anyhow, that's another story.' She gave Mirren a knowing look. 'I came to see how you're getting on. Chrissie has taken the twins in their pram to visit her mother.'

'Don't apologise. I was going for a walk in Pollok Park. Would you like to come with me?'

'Yes, I'd like that. Anything to get out of the house. Now that I've got a job I'd like to get a flat, if I could afford it, or a man!' She laughed. 'You've got the flat, at least.'

'Yes, there's that.'

Mirren brewed the tea, and sat down opposite Annie at the table. Her story had certainly given her plenty to think about. She remembered Alastair saying she'd called to see him. She's an enigma this girl, she thought. 'Don't you have any friends of your own age?' As she spoke she realised Annie must be about her own age, but she felt much older.

'I did have a boyfriend, Neil. But I'm trying to give him up.' Her black eyes flashed again.

'Why?'

'Dad objected to him. But he was fun...' She smiled, looking across the room. 'A girl's got to have someone.'

Mirren listened while Annie told her about Neil, who didn't want to teach, and was looking around for something which he would like to do, and she found herself thinking, I don't really need this girl as a friend. She had thought while Annie was speaking, that she would say to her, 'Drop in here, any time, Annie.' But it would be nice to have a boyfriend, someone she could talk to about world affairs, as she had done with her father, someone who would give her comfort and love. Someone like Jack Drummond, perhaps...

Chapter 3

The following morning, when Mirren wakened, she felt optimistic, as if she had adjusted to the flat, and her new life, without her father. Perhaps Annie's visit had helped, although she had been surprised to hear that she had called on Alastair with a trumped-up excuse. Was there something going on between them? But it didn't concern her, and she turned her mind to reflecting that this morning she didn't have to travel from Kelvingrove on the tram. While she was washing in the bathroom (and regretting the painted bath) she decided to do something positive about it. There was a plumber in Albert Road who she would ask to call and give her a quotation to renovate the bathroom.

It was a pleasant morning, although with the feeling of coming winter in the air, and when she turned the corner of Limes Avenue into Albert Road, she saw a black-coated figure of a man standing at the tram stop. Something about his stance alerted her. Was it Mr Campbell? He was wearing a bowler hat and a black overcoat, and leaning on a rolled umbrella. In his other hand he carried a briefcase.

He looked up as she drew near him and their eyes met. She thought she saw a flicker of puzzled recognition in his, and she stopped. 'Are you Mr Campbell?' she asked him.

He transferred his rolled umbrella to hang on his left arm to allow him to raise his bowler. 'Yes, I'm Mr Campbell.' He looked surprised at her question.

'I'm in Miss Currie's flat above you. She told me your name.'

He smiled, a relieved smile. 'Oh, that's it! I thought I recognised you. My wife told me she had met you in the shops. Have you settled down?'

'Yes, thank you, Mr—'

'I'm sorry,' he said interrupting her. 'Here's my tram.' It was drawing up at the stop with a thundering of brakes. He lifted his bowler again, 'I hope we meet again, Miss...?'

'Stewart.' She watched him get on to the tram, and go forward towards the inside. Well, he wasn't a young man. It was probably preferable to climbing upstairs. What a pity I didn't get a chance to ask him if he remembered me, she thought. She walked on, and began to scan the shops as she went. She stopped at one with sanitary fittings in the window. 'John Craig, Plumber,' was painted on the window. Ten minutes later, she had arranged with Mr Craig to call that evening. She looked at her watch as she left the shop, and saw she hadn't much time to get to the school by nine o'clock, and she began to hurry. She reached it, a grey stone building surrounded by an asphalt playground. Ahead of her she saw Alastair Young, holding open the gate for her. She hurried towards him, and they steered their way through the children, running in all directions. When they reached the steps going up to the entrance, he said, 'Impossible to have a conversation going through that melee. We're first, I think. Annie seems to have difficulty arriving here on time.'

'She called to see me yesterday. I think she has responsibilities at home. Her father married again, she told me.'

'Yes, and there's a young family. You and I are lucky, perhaps, with only ourselves to think about.' He held open the swing door for her.

'Thank you. I had my father up to a short time ago,' she reminded him.

'I'm sorry,' he said. His eyes were apologetic. 'Of course you had.'

Annie arrived when Mirren was in the common room. She was looking dishevelled, as usual, and her black hair was in need of brushing. It stuck out at odd angles. Her jacket was creased. Perhaps her appearance had nothing to do with the twins, she thought. It might be that she liked her bed too much and found it difficult to get up, and some people were naturally untidy. But she was as cheerful as ever.

'I told Father and Chrissie about our visit to Pollok Park. They both said I should invite you to come home with me.'

'That was kind. I must rush on, Annie. But thanks.'

When she came back from lunch at the flat, Alastair called her into his room. 'You'll be pleased to hear,' he said, 'that I've been allotted another teacher. It will relieve me of teaching except in emergencies, and let me get on with my desk work.'

'That's good,' she said. 'The classes are rather big to manage.' She had no difficulty, but Annie had trouble in controlling her pupils. She told her at break-time in the afternoon. 'Good news! Alastair tells me we're going to have another teacher added to the staff.'

'I bet she'll be glamorous, and he'll fall for her.' She looked displeased.

'You don't mind, do you? Have you fallen for Alastair?'

She shrugged. 'Well, he's difficult to resist, isn't he?'

'Handsome, but lacking in ... what it takes.' Mirren laughed. 'He doesn't appeal to me.'

'You don't know him.' Annie smiled a

knowing smile.

She was busy with the plumber in the evening, and agreed to his suggestion that she should have a completely new bathroom suite. 'I've found,' he said, 'that bathrooms take on, more than any other room, the character of the person who's lived there. This is a good block of flats, but if you've bought outright, you'll have to see to any renovations yourself. It's only now that tenants have been given permission to sell.'

'We bought it,' she said. 'My father believed in ownership,' and remembering the profit he had made, decided there and then to have the alterations done.

'I could start next week,' he told her, 'and have the essentials done if you can be away for a day.' She understood what he meant.

'Yes,' she told him, 'I can be at school all day.' All it would mean was that she'd take sandwiches with her.

She didn't tell Annie in case she would repeat her invitation to go to her house. She had no wish to become embroiled with Chrissie, or the twins, or indeed, Annie.

She enjoyed the peace and quiet in the common room, safe in the knowledge that Mr Craig was getting on with the installation and tiling. She could well afford to pay whatever he asked, she knew, and the thought of a pristine bathroom at the end of the week was cheering.

On the second day when she returned to the flat at half past four, he told her that a Mr Jack Drummond had called. 'We had quite a talk,' he said. 'He's a farmer. Well, you would know, wouldn't you, the way he talks, country-like.'

Yes, she thought, anyone would know. 'Did he leave a message?' she asked.

'Yes, he said he would phone you.'

'But I haven't had one installed yet!'

'Yes, I know. I told him that. And he said, just to say that he had called. He'd be in touch.' There had been a deal of rapport, she thought. 'I have to have a telephone myself, for the business. More and more of my clients are having them installed. They're a good invention if they're used wisely. Mr Drummond agreed with me there. Trouble is,' he went on, 'it's the moneyed people who are getting them, and they get attention first on the list. To tell you the truth, they bully you!'

'You'll just have to stand up against that,' she said. 'I promise not to bully you once mine is installed, nor am I in the moneyed class.' She laughed to soften her words.

She showed him out, relieved, and set about making herself a meal while she listened to the news on the wireless.

But a talkative plumber couldn't prevent her from feeling good today, she thought, unless she consciously thought of her father.

Her life seemed to be moving forward: teaching wasn't the anxiety she had feared and Jack Drummond wanted to see her again.

She sat down and wrote a letter to him there and then, deciding to go out and post it later. At the back of her mind there was still the puzzle. Were Mr Campbell and the man on the bench one and the same? Perhaps she would call on them, to introduce herself properly. It was like solving a mystery, something she could do for her father.

Limes Avenue was deserted and as she walked, a train went hurtling past on its tracks, lit up, with the occasional face at the window. They all have lives like me, she thought, all with their problems, big or small, turning over in their minds. Some will have husbands or boyfriends, some lonely like me. Some might even be worrying about the coming war, and what difference it would make to their lives, whether they would be called up or not. She thought of the men she knew who could be affected. Jack Drummond, for instance, Josh, but wouldn't they be exempted? Alastair Young, but he wouldn't be in the first batch, and there was Mr Craig, the plumber, who she had noticed was young and handsome, with all his talk about taps, basins, grouting and tiling, plumber's jargon, she thought. She had reached the end of the avenue, and when she put a hand out to touch the railings which enclosed a grove of lime trees, she found it was sticky. It must come from the leaves, she thought. Dad could have told me.

Chapter 4

A few days later when she entered the common room before morning classes, she saw that Alastair and Annie were there with another young woman. Alastair looked up.

'Here's Mirren. This is our new addition to the staff, Mirren...' he hesitated, 'Miss Black.' And immediately, turning to the stranger, said, 'I should have said that we like to use first names here.' He smiled at the girl, who was blonde and sparkling, these were the only words Mirren could think of to describe her.

'Good idea!' she said. 'I'm Muriel. And you're Mirren.' She held out her hand, smiling. Her smile was large, lots of white teeth, contained by a red-painted mouth. 'And hello, Annie.' Muriel Black looked around. 'I think I've got it now, Alastair, Annie, Mirren. Is that right?' She turned to

Annie, who was watching her, Mirren thought, rather than looking at her. 'It's terrible on your first day, isn't it? Mr Young ... oh, sorry ...' she giggled, 'I should say, Alastair, I think us girls should gang up together. I'm new here, but we would have more respect for you if we called you Mr Young.'

'No,' Alastair said, 'I don't agree. I'm running this school on modern lines. We're a team. And we can only have the feeling of a team by using first names. At least that's my theory.'

'Well, I've got used to "Alastair",' Mirren said. 'I don't know if it will work if we keep adding to our staff, but I'm quite happy with the present arrangement.'

'Right,' Muriel Black said, 'I'll go with the majority, although seniority is often the deciding factor, I mean in age.'

'I'm thirty,' Alastair said, 'if you're fishing, and I happen to know that is a few years older than any of you three. Isn't it, Annie?' A bell rang. 'Starting time! Come along with me, Muriel, and I'll introduce you to your class.' They went out together.

Annie said, 'What do you think of her, Mirren, facing up to him like that?'

'I admire her. She's very pretty, don't you think?'

'Yes, and bossy. Arrives here and tries to change the rules Alastair has laid down. She imagines her charm can win over every man she meets.'

'Well, we're here to teach, not to criticise. Come along, Annie, we'd better get to our classes.'

At the end of the week she saw how Alastair was giving in to Muriel's suggestions. Indeed he seemed to be conquered by her. Annie, on the other hand, was critical, saying to Mirren that Muriel had laid a spell on him. Thank goodness it doesn't concern me, she thought.

Mirren's new bathroom was now finished, and she celebrated by having a bath and a shower. Miss Currie's presence had been swamped completely and, lying in the bath, Mirren felt happy. She could make her own imprint here, because Dad had never lived here with her. The thought still brought tears, but she had to admit to herself that it had been a good move. She loved teaching the children, with whom, she flattered herself, she had established a good relationship, and she liked strolling along Albert Road with its good shops and friendly shopowners. Limes Avenue was pleasant with its grove of lime trees, with the interest of the railway running along beside it. She had decided that she must find out where the nearest station was for Glasgow Central. She was orientating herself very well, she thought, and there was the feeling that she was a person here, in her own right, and that if she had remained in the flat at Kelvingrove, she would still have been Mr Stewart's daughter.

Still feeling that she was her own person, she decided after she'd had her lunch on Saturday to call on the Campbells and invite them for tea on Sunday. Why not now? When she knocked on their door, a young man with a long university scarf round his neck, and wearing a coat, opened it. She had been expecting it would be Mr or Mrs Campbell, and she was taken aback.

'Yes?' he said. He had black glossy hair which flopped down on his brow, bright, lively eyes, spilling over with laughter. To her eyes he looked young, at least younger than Alastair, using him as her yardstick. University young, she thought, rather than employed somewhere, an air of freedom.

She stammered. 'I'm sorry. I was expecting...'

'Is it my parents you want to see?' he asked.

'Yes. I live in the top flat, in what was Miss Currie's flat, and I thought I'd introduce myself to them.'

'Well, you must come in.' His smile was youthful, like a schoolboy's. 'They're both inside.' He held open the door wide, and ushered her in.

Mr and Mrs Campbell were sitting in seats

124

by the window, he was reading a newspaper, and she was sewing something in an embroidery ring.

'Here's a visitor for you,' the young man said. 'Miss...?' he looked enquiringly at Mirren.

'Stewart,' she said, smiling because of the instant rapport she felt with him. 'I live in Miss Currie's flat. I think I've met you both.' Why am I doing this? she thought. I've only met them casually. It was really their place to get in touch with me.

'Please sit down, Miss Stewart,' Mrs Campbell said. 'Yes, we've met, haven't we, doing our shopping. And my husband tells me you spoke to him the other day.' Mirren felt her face flushing. She had pushed her way into this house, she realised. Mr Campbell was placing a chair for her.

'I'll get off, then,' the young man said.

'This is Jamie, our son,' Mr Campbell said. 'Have you a meeting, son?'

'Yes, worse luck. Maybe we'll bump into each other again, Miss Stewart, now that we know each other.'

'I hope so,' she returned his smile. 'My name is Mirren.'

'Well, goodbye, Mirren,' he said. 'Back about nine, I think, Mum. I'll have a bite there.'

'All right. Off you go.'

His mother took up her embroidery ring

which she had laid down. 'Always on the go,' she said, looking up at Mirren.

'It's not so long since I was at the university myself,' Mirren said. 'But I've finished with it now, and I'm teaching at the primary school in Albert Road.'

'Jamie graduated in 1937. He's serving his apprenticeship in a C.A.'s office. Another five years, I'm afraid. I think he still goes up to the university.'

He must be about two years younger than me, Mirren thought. There was a pause, then Mrs Campbell said, 'Well it's nice of you to call.' Her smile seemed to Mirren to dismiss her, and she more and more wondered what had driven her to make the decision to visit the Campbells. It was totally out of character. She heard herself voicing her thoughts. 'I have a distinct memory of meeting Mr Campbell in Kelvingrove Park.' She smiled at him. 'We lived near it, my father and I. He died recently.' She heard her voice thicken, and she abruptly stopped speaking.

'Oh, I'm sorry,' Mrs Campbell said. 'Have you no brothers or sisters?'

Mirren shook her head. 'No, and my mother died just when I started university.' The more she spoke the more she felt as if she was begging for sympathy, and the more she thought it was totally unlike her.

'This distinct memory you have about meeting my husband,' Mrs Campbell said.

'How long ago was that?'

'The year my mother died, nineteen thirty-five.'

'Nineteen thirty-five?' Mrs Campbell looked at her husband, 'But you were with John Nesbitt, weren't you?'

'Yes, I was.' Mirren thought the man looked pale and perturbed. 'Of course I was ... no time for gallivanting about Kelvingrove Park. It was that year that John shot—' He stopped suddenly. 'No, no time for gallivanting.'

The conversation trailed into generalities, and Mirren still had the feeling that she had made a mistake in calling. They didn't offer her tea, and her plan to ask them to come to her flat tomorrow melted like 'snow off a dyke', she remembered her father saying.

'Well, if you'll excuse me – ' she got up, making up her mind – 'I'll get on now. I've still got quite a lot to do upstairs. You know what it's like, moving...'

'Oh, we know what it's like,' Mrs Campbell looked at her husband, 'don't we, David? We had a large house in Manchester, Miss Stewart, and it was a difficult move, getting rid of quite a lot. We're not used to living in a flat.'

'Yes, I can understand,' Mirren said. 'Well, we'll know each other if we meet at the shops, Mrs Campbell.' She looked at the woman, who had her eyes on her husband.

'My husband will show you out, Miss Stewart. Goodbye.' She bent her head to her sewing.

Mirren, feeling dismissed, followed Mr Campbell through the dark hall. The whole flat was badly lit, and everything had an air of being well-worn and shabby. In the tall vases on either side of the fireplace, she had noticed some bedraggled grasses and thought, a bunch of flowers might have been acceptable.

But, going upstairs to her flat, she knew that her visit had been a mistake. She wasn't really a 'pushing' sort of girl, and her visit must have seemed to the Campbells to be peculiar, to say the least. When she got back to her flat, she made herself a cup of tea, and to cheer herself up, ate one of the pastries, a 'pastry horn' she had bought in the City Bakeries for the Campbells' tea tomorrow. The rest she put on her kitchen window ledge, and watched a small storm of sparrows feasting on the unexpected goodies. And then, dispelling the gloom, she remembered the son, Jamie, and his brilliance in the sombre darkness of his parents' flat, the shining hair, teeth and eyes, and felt that the meeting had been important, why she didn't know.

She continued to turn over in her mind her visit to the Campbells' flat. What a fool she had made of herself, practically accusing Mr

Campbell of being the man she had met in the park. You're becoming obsessed, she told herself, you have only yourself to think about, everything you relate to you. The world doesn't revolve round you. There are more men in Glasgow who dress like him, are middle-aged, and walk with a limp. Wasn't it a favourite subject for writers, illustrating the difference in class, the man in the bowler or the man in a cloth cap? She remembered her father telling her that at Cranston's Coffee Room which he frequented, the men sat round the tables wearing their bowlers. Was it that they all welcomed the respite from raising them to ladies whom they met? Margaret, the waitress, hadn't counted as a lady.

And as fast as she thought of the Campbells and felt depressed about her visit, the memory would come to her mind of the son, Jamie, and his youthful charm. How did he compare with Jack Drummond? she wondered. Jack's charm was adult, a man who knew women, even if they were only country girls. Jamie's charm radiated to all and sundry. Don't feel you were singled out, she told herself, he probably bestows it on tram conductresses too.

But there's more to consider than charm, she told herself, there were interests. Jack would be unsatisfying there, just as she would be to him. His wife would have to know how to be a farmer's wife, she would have to have country skills, work hard, and still not be too tired to please him in bed.

But Jamie. She couldn't contemplate being married to him. He had to grow up, be capable of adult love. Why can't people who are attracted to one another not be able to live together, until one or the other grows up?

And why are you thinking along these lines? she asked herself. You're not longing for marriage or children, it's only love you're longing for, so why is it so tied up with marriage? Are these questions girls of her age have always had to face, and was she only waking up to realities?

Chapter 5

There was no doubt about it: Muriel Black had affected the happy atmosphere in the common room. She came in with new ideas every morning, and Alastair seemed to be captured by them and her. But Annie was not. She complained to Mirren, saying that Muriel was 'always getting at her' and that Alastair did everything Muriel told him. Not feeling herself involved, Mirren took a back

130

seat, but watched what was going on. 'Oh, Alastair, by the way,' was Muriel's opening gambit, and he seemed to be captivated by her ideas.

Once when Mirren went to the ladies' toilet, she found Muriel and Annie there. Muriel was applying lipstick to her already red lips. She looked up when Mirren came in. 'This girl's accusing me of "sticking my nose in",' she said, 'her elegant expression for my helpful remarks to Alastair.'

Mirren didn't reply. She said, 'Excuse me,' and went into a cubicle. When she came out the two girls were still there, both flushed. Annie was saying, 'I know it's no good complaining to Alastair, but I can write to the Committee...'

'They won't listen to you,' Muriel said. 'Alastair hasn't given you a good recommendation.'

'You lying bitch!' Annie said. 'Isn't she, Mirren? There's been nothing but trouble since she came here.'

'You have to watch your language,' Muriel said. 'I could report you.'

'I think you should make your complaints to Alastair, Annie,' Mirren said.

'He won't listen to me. I've tried. Would you speak for me, Mirren? She's skimmed off my best pupils and taken them into her class, and left me with the dummies.'

'Don't listen to her,' Muriel said, smiling,

and peering at herself in the mirror.

'What I will say,' Mirren said, 'is that any changes you want to make, Muriel, should be put up to the staff, with Alastair there.'

'I agree with that,' Muriel said surprisingly. She combed her hair, patted it and, putting the comb into her handbag, snapped it shut and went towards the door.

'Did you ever...?' Annie said, looking at Mirren when Muriel had gone, her eyes full of angry tears.

'If I were you, Annie, I would watch my tongue when you're speaking to her. You're on shaky ground.'

'But I try! And I'm tired when I come to school. Chrissie's lazy and she leaves the twins to me to look after. I've complained to Dad, but he says he has to support her. I really do it for him. But you can see what I've to put up with.' Here we go, Mirren thought. Is she telling the truth about her home circumstances or is she making it up?

'Try and leave your worries behind you, Annie. And how about the boyfriend you mentioned to me? Neil? Couldn't you see him at night and make yourself less available at home?'

'No, I told you Dad didn't like him. But he's gone to some kind of training camp. "Join the Army and see the world," he says. It will suit him down to the ground. Besides I like Alastair better, and I know he was

132

quite keen on me before that one came!'

'That may be so, but I think you'll have to face up to it, he's keen on Muriel now. You and I should be in the playground supervising. Coming?'

'Right.' She ran her comb under the tap and applied it to her hair, but even with all her combing it still remained in its dishevelled state. She doesn't stand a chance with Muriel, Mirren thought.

That evening after she had had a meal, she decided to write a letter to Jack Drummond. She sat at the kitchen table, pen in hand, finding it difficult, but eventually wrote:

30.09.39
Dear Jack

The plumber told me you had called. I've been busy at the school, and have meant to write to you before this. I hope you're well, and all at Waterside. I'm afraid I shan't get there for some time as my weekends are full up with cleaning and shopping, but I really like the flat now. It doesn't have the view we had at Kelvingrove, but that memory includes my mother and father, and I think I'm better here, starting a new life. I always wanted to live on my own in a flat near them, but now I've got that and not them, which I have to get used to.

I hope we'll meet soon. You'll see I've got notepaper with my telephone number on it. It's quite a thrill, and I really feel like a bachelor girl now. What do you think of this phoney war, and how long do you think it will last? I miss my discussions with my father. Will you be exempted in the calling-up? I read that all who were working on the land were, since we are dependent on you for food. If I were a man I think I'd become a Conscientious Objector. I hate how the whole world believes that fighting is the only way to settle disputes. What do you think?

Looking forward to seeing you soon.

She puzzled over the ending, then wrote, 'Love, Mirren.'

Was that true? she thought, remembering how when she was with him, she had felt thrills coursing up and down her body. But was that love?

She posted the letter on her way to school. When she went through the hall, she saw a typed noticeboard, headed:

Staff Committee Meeting
Please meet in Room 2
22nd October 1939 at 4.30 p.m.
Alastair.

So Muriel had taken her advice, she thought.

On Saturday she walked along Limes Avenue and halfway down saw a train go speeding past her. Who were these people she saw at the windows? Were they speeding away from Glasgow? She felt cheerful. Partly because she was on her way to the station to go there. She turned into Albert Road, then caught a tram to take her to Pollokshields Station. When she climbed the steps and reached the platform, she saw there were quite a few people waiting and she walked towards them, intending to join the crowd. She realised as she came nearer, that one of them was the Campbells' son – she recognised him by the long striped scarf he was wearing and, unlike the other men, he was bare-headed. He appeared to recognise her also and came towards her, smiling. 'Hello, Mirren,' he said.

'Hello,' she said, not wanting to call him 'Jamie' but feeling Mr Campbell was inappropriate, 'I didn't expect to see you here today.'

'Oh, yes, I'm a working man. I'm in a chartered accountant's office. They fixed me up there from the university.'

'Yes, your mother told me. Do you like it?' she asked.

His smiling eyes met hers. 'No.'

'Why did you accept it, then?'

135

He shrugged. 'Money's useful. The job was offered to me because Maths was my best subject, but I don't think I'll be there long.'

'Why?' The sound of the oncoming train drowned out his reply, and he took her arm and opening the door of the coach which had stopped beside them, helped her in.

'Now we can continue our conversation,' he said. His smile was captivating, she thought, but then so was Jack Drummond's. The difference lay in the sexual attraction of Jack Drummond's, whereas this young man's seemed ... she looked for a word, found it, 'joyous'.

'Why,' she repeated, 'won't you be in your job long? I didn't hear your reply.'

'I'm going to join up. I want to go into the RAF. I was in the university air corps. I love flying.'

'Do you?' she said. 'If anyone I knew was involved, I think I'd be terribly worried.'

'Them's fighting words.' He laughed. 'You have no pride in your country?'

'That's a difficult one,' she said. 'I haven't given it much thought. I seem to have too much on my mind.'

'I can see you and I will have to have some discussions so that I can change your mind.'

'You could try,' she said. She looked around the coach, and saw there were only three men in it, all with their faces buried in their papers.

'I can't bear to read the papers,' she said.

'Tell you what,' he said, 'are you going to be in town for long?'

'Possibly all morning.'

'I finish at twelve. Would you like to meet me then? Say in the café at Central Station? We could have a coffee and go home together.'

'Won't your parents expect you when you finish work?'

'No, they're used to me coming in at any old time. I try not to have my mother cook for me.' She wanted to ask why but instead raised an eyebrow enquiringly.

'For quite a time she wasn't well. I think I know why but I decided not to give her any more cause for anxiety.'

'That sounds reasonable.'

'You strike me as a reasonable sort of girl.'

She smiled and said, 'I think I could be described as that. I've always felt older than my years. I'm twenty-five.'

'Are you? I'm about two years younger than you. It's nice to think I've got you handy if I need a guide, confessor or friend.'

'What do I get out of it?'

'Being my confessor and I'm a good listener.'

'Great! I need that. I'll be in the café at twelve o'clock, then.'

'Just a coffee, eh? I don't have set meals during the day. They expect me to have dinner with them at night.'

They walked through the Central Station, and at the steps leading into Union Street she said, 'I go down here. I'm going to Argyle Street, to Fraser's. Which way do you go?'

'Down here and along Gordon Street. The office is there.'

At the foot of the steps he looked at his watch, and said, 'Good God, I'll have to run. The more junior you are the earlier you have to be in.' She stood and watched him running along the street, his scarf flying, nearly two years younger than me, she thought, and dying to get into the RAF. She compared him in her mind with Jack Drummond. She had far more in common with Jamie. They seemed to think alike. With Jack she would have to adapt herself, learn a whole new language, farm language, a whole new way of thinking also. Both of them had charm. One would go away to fight, one would stay at home.

She crossed at the lights beside Boots. What was she going to buy at Fraser's? Possibly a black cocktail dress? (She felt better in black.) With it she would wear mother's gold chain and the bracelet with the inset diamonds. When would she wear it, and with whom?

Chapter 6

She had trailed through all the big stores with the picture in mind of the black dress she wanted. It had to be original, not low in the neck, short, striking. And just as she was giving up in her search and was walking through Fraser's, she saw one on a rail which seemed right to her. The salesgirl joined her. 'I don't know why this one didn't go. I think it's because it's too original. Girls all want to dress the same nowadays. It's distinctive, and you're just the person to wear it. Try it on.'

Mirren took it over her arm and retired to a cubicle. It was original, certainly. It was black marocain, buttoning from neck to hem, and when she tried it on, it fitted her perfectly, following her shape, small breasts, slender waist. She tried leaving two or three buttons undone to show off her knees. When she had gone to the swimming baths occasionally with Jessie Baxter, she had compared her own knees with her friend's, but hadn't drawn any attention to the difference – it was Jessie who had. 'Look at your knees and mine, Mirren. Yours are so rounded and smooth. You should wear a bathing costume all the time.' Mirren had laughed, but looking at them now, encased in silk stockings, she thought, yes, three buttons undone at the foot will show them off. The *pièce de résistance* of the dress was that there was a ribbed silk over-skirt, composed of two panels, a foot shorter than the dress, gathered on to a band which tied round the waist, with a cuffed pocket on either panel.

The salesgirl came into the cubicle. 'It's been waiting for you! Not many people have the figure or style to wear it. And the beauty is that you don't have to wear the extra skirt. You have two dresses then, one for a special occasion, the other for an office dress.'

'I'm a teacher,' Mirren said.

'Oh, it's too good for that! Children would not appreciate it. Wear it when you meet a boyfriend for coffee, and then when he asks you out on another special date, wear it with the extra skirt!'

Mirren was thrilled by the dress. It could not be worn at Waterside, where the girls wore flowered dresses, obviously run up by the local dressmaker, but it could be worn today to meet Jamie! 'I'll take it.' She had looked at the price and knew she could afford it. 'I'll wear it now without the extra skirt. Could you wrap it up with this jersey and kilt I'm wearing?'

'Certainly,' the salesgirl said. 'You've got a bargain there! It's a model dress, reduced. I'll put this into a bag – ' she lifted the silk over-skirt, and Mirren's kilt and jersey – 'and you can get it at the counter when you're paying.' She gave Mirren an approving glance. 'It's not often you find your dress, and you have the sense to recognise it.'

She was seated with her parcel in the café at ten to twelve, and she ordered and paid for a cup of coffee, slipping off her camel coat and hanging it over the back of her chair. In about a quarter of an hour Jamie came rushing in, scarf flying as usual, saw her and waved, then came and sat down opposite her. 'Sorry I'm late.'

'But you aren't,' she said. 'I'm early. I bought myself a coffee.'

'You shouldn't have paid for it. I say, your eyes are shining! Has something happened since I left you?'

'Just that I've bought this dress I'm wearing. You wouldn't know the satisfaction of finding something that seems to have been made for you.'

'The fact that it's made your eyes shine is good enough for me. I think I know the feeling, but with me it was for my Meccano set which I had bought with money from a rich uncle. The glow kept me warm all day!' He smiled at her. 'You look like a Parisian lady, although, truth to tell, I've

141

never met one.'

'That's what I feel like.' She remembered how, in the mirror at Fraser's, she had noticed how the black set off her fairness, and seemed to make her skin glow.

'I think you haven't given yourself many treats in the past,' Jamie said.

'You're possibly right. In the last few years I've lost both my mother and father.'

'That's sad,' Jamie said. His eyes held hers. 'I'm going to tell you something about my parents. I realise that dress has done something for you, it's made you more beautiful, and more ... receptive, and it's certainly done something for me. It's made me realise that I didn't look at you properly before.'

'I feel different.' Was it only the dress? she wondered.

They drank their coffee. Every time Mirren took a sip and looked up at Jamie, he seemed to be looking at her. 'I didn't realise your hair was so fair,' he said, on one occasion.

'It's the dress,' she said, smiling at him, and then as their eyes met and clung, embarrassed, she said the first thing which came into her head. 'Are you an only child?'

'Yes.'

'So am I. It takes one to know one. I always felt my mother wouldn't have liked a large family. She was fond of Glasgow, the city, and buying clothes – I could never under-

142

stand it...' She stopped. 'I've just realised that I experienced the same pleasure today! Like catching a fish! Maybe I'm two persons after all.'

'Would you like to know how you seemed to me when you called at our house yesterday?'

'Yes,' she said, apprehensive, and shaking back her hair. He had commented on its fairness.

'Someone who seemed quite sure of herself. I wasn't surprised that you were a teacher. I never could contemplate being one, taking charge of a class, and guiding children's lives, since I couldn't guide my own.'

'I may have looked confident when I called, but I wasn't. As a matter of fact, I was curious. When I saw your father one day from my window, I remembered that I had seen him, or thought I had seen him in Kelvingrove Park. I was with my father. I can see the bench where we sat. But he and your mother said yesterday it couldn't have been, so there must be two people going about who resemble each other, your father and this man we saw.'

Jamie surprisingly put a hand out and covered hers. He wasn't smiling, and he looked troubled. 'You and I will have to have a talk,' he said.

'What's wrong, Jamie?' she said. Her heart

143

was aching, why she didn't know. 'Is there something troubling you?'

'There has been. Are you in a hurry to go home?'

'I have nothing to go home for.' Her eyes filled with tears, but it wasn't pity for herself, it was this something else which had to be talked about with Jamie.

'What about you and I going to Kelvingrove Park, and you can show me where you met my father, or his doppelgänger? Would that distress you, going back to where you lived?'

'Possibly. But I won't let it bother me. Yes, I'm willing to go back there. Will your parents not worry about where you are?'

'I'm not in the habit of going straight home from the office. Saturday afternoon is more enjoyable for me wandering about, or going up to the university. No, they've got used to me drifting in and out. If I could afford it, I would have a room of my own somewhere.'

They finished their coffee, and left the café, Mirren carrying the large carrier bag with 'W. Fraser & Co.' emblazoned across it. When they got off the tram at the park gates, she made herself look across the street to where the flat was, where my life was, she thought. To her surprise Jamie put his arm round her. 'Does it hurt?' he said.

'Yes, but not so much as if I'd been alone.' She forced herself to say it. 'My father fell down the stairs there, and died.'

'How terrible for you! I'm so sorry, Mirren.' She met his eyes and saw they were full of sympathy.

'Don't be. I've got a new life now. I try not to think of it. In a way it was a blessed release for him. He never got over my mother dying of cancer. She was a shadow of herself when she died.'

His arm tightened, and he said, 'Come on!' They went towards the open gates. 'You lead me to where this meeting took place,' he said.

'Right.' As it was Saturday, there were children playing around the Stewart fountain, and filling the paths with their games. They had to be careful to avoid them; some had hoops, others had scooters, and still others were pushing small children in go-chairs. Mirren thought of Annie, and felt guilty for a moment. She should be doing something for the girl. She didn't quite know what.

'Have you ever been in this park before?' she asked Jamie as they climbed up towards the top of the hill and Lord Kelvin's statue.

'Yes, with various girlfriends in the university. It was handy.'

'Had you many?' she said, turning to smile at him to subdue a stab of jealousy. He's only a boy, she thought. Why should I mind?

'Yes,' he said. 'That may sound as if I were

boasting, but they were merely friends. They seemed to confide in me. They were generally the girlfriends of men friends. They said I was a good listener.'

'Well, that's a good reputation to have.' She felt the jealousy melting away.

'Are you teasing me, Mirren?'

'No. But you seemed to be praising yourself.'

'Sorry.' He shrugged. 'Are we near the place where you think you met my father?'

'We've reached it. This is the bench.' They stopped. 'I remember it because it was behind this oval bed of, what are they?' She peered. 'Winter pansies. Aren't they glorious colours? Father was good at flowers. It was May when we met your father, if it was him, so the flowers would be much the same. Shall we sit down?'

'Yes.' They sat down together on the empty bench. 'I'll begin,' Jamie said, 'and then you can tell me what you remember.' He put his arm behind her shoulders along the back of the bench. She looked down and saw that the camel coat had parted, revealing her knees which were showing where the buttons were undone on the dress.

'OK.' Her mind was full of her father.

'I shouldn't say this, I know,' Jamie said, meeting her eyes and smiling, 'and I'm trying not to flirt with you ... I like you too much for that...'

146

'Go on,' she said.

'You've got lovely knees.'

'Really?' She laughed, closing her coat. 'Funny you should say that.'

'Why? Has someone else told you?'

'Yes, a girl called Jessie Baxter.' She laughed at the expression on his face.

His arm slipped off the back of the bench to her waist, and pulled her against him. 'You're my kind of girl,' he said.

'Well, begin with what you remember. You're not the only good listener.'

'OK.' He turned to her. 'This is serious.'

'I know,' she said. 'It's serious for me too.'

'I'll have to give you the history of my family,' he said. 'I hope you don't mind. Well, father was in cotton. That's how it was always said. "You know David Campbell? He's in cotton." He seemed to be good at his job, and he was offered a similar one in a Manchester firm. I was born in 1915. We were living in Newlands at the time. I can remember the house. And the drive, trees down either side. I remember walking along that drive on my way to school, at five, mother holding my hand. Then, it seemed that I had just started, when my mother began packing, I remember helping her, being given a box to put my toys in. She told me we were going to live in Manchester, that Daddy had been offered a better job. I wasn't sorry, because I didn't like the school

147

in Newlands at all. We got custard and prunes often at lunch, and I didn't know what to do with the stones, so I swallowed them! I kept it as a secret.'

Mirren laughed. 'Did you get your lunch at school?'

'Yes, it was a private school. Miss Dempster ran it. She had a gold pince-nez.'

'That was posh. Mine was an ordinary school. We got milk to drink at playtime, with a straw, but I walked home for lunch. I was given money for the tram, but I cheated sometimes and used the money to buy sweets. Do you remember sugarally straps?'

'Yes, I do, but my mother said they were unhygienic. Boys strapped each other's hands with them. My passion was jelly babies. They made me feel like a cannibal, especially the black ones.' She laughed at him.

'I could eat you,' he said, and took a pretend bite at her cheek.

'Stop that! So you went to Manchester?' she said, still laughing.

'Yes, I got the feeling it was an exciting thing to do. Both parents seemed happy at the change. I remember them poring over maps spread out on the table. We went to Manchester in the train, it was the first time I had ever been in one, and then we got a taxi at Piccadilly Station, I remember the name, which took us to a large house, at least it seemed larger than our last one, and it had a garden with a ginko tree in it. Father said the owners had put a hundred pounds on to the price of the house because of it. And a swing on an apple tree, I remember swinging high amongst the apple blossom. They seemed very happy with the move, and I was taken to what my mother called "A Dame's School", which I didn't like because the children spoke differently from me and made fun of me, and called me a Glasgow keelie. I used to go home crying.'

'Poor Jamie,' she said, 'you were bullied.'

'Don't mother me!' He shrugged off her remark. 'I suppose I was, but my mother took me to school one morning and complained to the headmistress. Mother could be quite awe-inspiring. I'd seen her telling off the grocer's boy, and in shops, where they said, "Yes, madam," or, "It won't happen again, madam," the shop assistants.'

'She would be pleased with the step up to Manchester?'

'I suppose so. She could be quite haughty. I always seemed to be in shops with her and she would be buying furniture and material for curtains. I was fascinated by the salesman in the curtain department, how he measured the material against a brass measure nailed to the counter, and how he tore it with scissors rather than cut it. Anyhow things must have turned out all right,

149

because I can remember my sixth birthday, and a lot of children playing with me in the garden and we had balloons, and I got a lot of presents.'

'Nice memory.'

'Yes, well, that seemed to be the end of the good times because I then went to what I called the big school, Manchester Grammar. I didn't do very well there, I still felt like an incomer, and I know I had difficulty with the lessons. My reports were all of the "Could do better if he tried" variety, but the reason was that things at home were not so good. I always seemed to be interrupting their quarrels when I went into the room where you could see the ginko tree, and being told to go and play. Sometimes Dad's partner came, and they closeted themselves in the study, a room I was debarred from, and was told to go upstairs to my room.'

'It sounds to me that they might have been in dire straits. The Chinese started exporting cotton, didn't they?'

'Yes. Do you have any memories of the Depression?'

'Only what was in the papers, and hearing my father talking about it. We didn't have much to keep up, like your mother, and although my mother liked shopping, she was also a good sewer, I think most women were, and she would tell me that she was making her own clothes now. She didn't expect me to do the same, because Dad always insisted on me doing my homework. I know now that he wanted me to succeed because he hadn't been encouraged to study himself. We seemed to have enough money because his father had left the farm between the two sons. Roger and Cameron, and Roger bought my father out. It's funny how you see things more clearly once you grow up. He adored my mother, and I'm pretty sure he came to Glasgow to please her. But he obviously had a good brain, Maths was his best subject at school, he told me, just like you, but he had to earn money right away and he became an apprentice in the drawing office of a shipyard. When things were getting bad he used to say he had chosen wisely, because shipbuilding would save Glasgow. He was interested in the news, my mother wasn't, and he used to talk to me about it, looking up from the *Herald* and saying to me, "Listen to this, Mirren." He said that the reason for the Depression was that so many of the bright young men who could have built Glasgow up again were lost in the Great War, and those who were left weren't clever, or lucky enough, to substitute new industries. Glasgow was ashamed of itself, he said, and we were a proud nation and didn't like to admit defeat.

"That's interesting,' Jamie said. 'I wish I had known your father. I might have worked better than I've done. Look how he spurred you on. They kept from me how bad things were, and wanted me to have what they had planned for me, schools, good schools, university and so on. They had to apply to Carnegie to get a scholarship for me at the university, when we came back. They tried to make things easier for me, I was never given the impression that I had to work.'

'Well, you have a job now,' Mirren said, 'you can work at that. So when did you come back to Glasgow?'

'When I was twelve. In time for the Gorbals gangs. Do you remember their names?'

'No, I don't remember what I don't have to remember.'

'I'm different. Things stick in my memory which don't have any relevance to me. There were the Gorbals gangs, the Billy Boys, and the Bridgeton gangs, the Norman Conquerors, they called themselves. Why I remember that was that I travelled home on the subway from school and when I got off at Lower Pollokshields, I would hide my school cap, because boys hung around the entrance, and they'd go for me because of the cap if I hadn't hidden it quickly enough. "Here's the toff coming!" they'd shout. I knew they were from the local school, but wondered if they might be from one of the gangs!'

'Poor Jamie. Your childhood doesn't seem to have been very happy.'

'Oh, it was all right. I had lots of interests of my own. I made model aeroplanes with plywood, because I was interested in the various types, and there were lots of societies at school. I joined the ATC when I was old enough, to learn about real aeroplanes. I was desperate to fly. One of my favourite books was *Le Petit Prince* by Antoine de Sainte-Exupéry (it had been a French set book) – he loved the sensation of being in the air, the author. I read about him and how he became entranced with flying, and eventually he crashed and died ... it got to me.'

'I haven't read it, although I did French too. *Madame Bovary* was more in my line. So, you're back in Glasgow. Did your father get a job?'

'Not at first. "Cotton" was a dirty word, but after a few years when sometimes he was working, other times not, he had a stroke of luck. He met a man whom he had known and they set up in business together. Cotton again. This man, Mr Nesbitt, had the idea that he could supply specialist firms. It must have seemed to him as it had been in Manchester, because before that he had taken various jobs. I knew they were all over the place because he was often in late at night, always neat in his bowler hat and over-coat and rolled umbrella. Sometimes my mother would say, "Go round to the tram stop and see if you can meet your father." I would do this, and that's a happy memory. After a long time and many tramcars, standing in the dark, one would stop, and I would see him getting off gingerly – he had developed a limp, which he said was the result of playing football when he was young, and he would say, "Hello, son. Have you been waiting long?" I always said, "No," and we would walk home and he would say, "It's nice to have an escort." He looked weary and I could have wept. I remember saying to my mother that I could get a job delivering papers in the morning, I had asked the newsagent, and she was so angry! "What would the neighbours think?" she said. "Don't mention such a thing again."'

'Didn't you ask your father if you could?'

'No. She said I wasn't to mention it to my father. That he had enough to worry him.'

What an upbringing, Mirren thought. 'I'm thinking,' she said, 'that I probably would have been the same as you, if I had been in your position. I never asked my parents if they could afford to pay for me at the university, I took it for granted, and I was never expected to take a job to help.'

'I didn't ever feel guilty at the time, possibly because they were careful that I didn't. My mother always seemed to be sewing when we came back to Glasgow, and there were women who called and went away with handkerchiefs and pleated jabots for

154

bishops, she told me, which I saw her starching and ironing and wrapping carefully in tissue paper, ready for these women. Sometimes if she was busy she would tell me to open the door to them.

'Pin money it was called. Women like my mother didn't go out to work. Then my father had this stroke of luck meeting Mr Nesbitt. It must have seemed like manna from heaven because he was obviously taking any job he could, up till then. I expect he sunk what money he had into this partnership. This was a terrible time for us, with him nearly broke. I remember him going off to his new office: he had polished his shoes till they shone, and when he put on his coat, my mother brushed it all over, saying that she would have to get a new piece of velvet for the collar. Then she and I went to the window to wave to him passing. She said to me, "I hope they arrange to have a company car to pick him up, like in Manchester." I remember thinking, she wants to show off to the neighbours. But the good times didn't last for long. The new business failed, it must have been a risk because of the slump, and there were weeks when he came home, looking terrible. He would shake his head when Mother asked him how things had gone that day. I gathered by their conversation that the money he had put into the business was lost, bit by bit, and then there was the terrible evening when he came home, sat down and put his head in his hands. His partner, Mr Nesbitt, had shot himself, he said, committed suicide. I can still see the expression on their faces, and Mother looking at me and saying, "This won't make any difference to you, Jamie."

' "I won't go to university," I said. "I'll get a job."

' "It's not as bad as that, son," my father said. "They'll need someone to keep the firm going, or wind it up. I'm the only partner, now that John has ..." and he shook his head.

' "I'll have to go and see poor Mary," my mother said. I felt terrible for them, and protested that I wouldn't go to university but look for a job instead.

' "There aren't any jobs to be had because of the Depression," I remember my mother saying. Then I'll never forget her next remark and my father's face.'

'What did she say?' Mirren asked.

' "We don't want another failure in the family." ' He met Mirren's gaze. 'I looked at my father's face. It was as if he had been struck by her. I met his eyes and he gave me a wan smile.'

'That was cruel,' Mirren said.

'Cruel, yes. I realised the state of affairs between them at that moment. But she was right about there not being any jobs to be had. I trailed about the city, trying everywhere, and answered anything I saw in the papers, but with no luck. It was a bad time. You could feel the dejection. I went to see my proposed tutor at the university, and he advised me to take up my place. Then, Father seemed to be carrying on in the firm, and he and Mother assured me that it was still going, and he would be all right, that I didn't have to look for a job, and to tell you the truth, Mirren, I had been so disheartened by being turned down and realising what it was like to look for work in a Depression, and meeting other young men in the same position, that I agreed to go to the university. We seemed to be all right at home, there didn't seem to be any difference, Mother always had a good meal ready for Father coming home, and I tried not to be a burden to them by eating at the university.

'Can you remember when that was?' Mirren said.

'Yes, 1933. I had just left school and was beginning at the university. I would be eighteen. I had seen the Depression coming when we were in Manchester. More beggars in the street, friends at school disappearing – I suppose their parents couldn't afford to keep them there, or were moving away. My father had begun to walk to the office. At first a company car had picked him up, then I noticed our food was becoming plainer, no chicken or beef, they quarrelled all the time, and I guessed she was getting into debt with everybody – she liked the best – and the grocer and milkman and fishmonger who used to deliver stopped coming. She was the one who ruled our household; he was, is, a gentle soul. Then the day came when we were packing up, and there was an ignominious return to Glasgow, and finding this flat. That would be in nineteen hundred and twenty-six, I would be eleven, I think. But I was sent to the best school as I told you, though how they afforded it God only knows, and I often wished I was at an ordinary one. At least I shouldn't have been persecuted by the gangs of boys I told you about. After standing up to them and getting a bloodied nose and worse still, the badge torn off my cap, and having to tell my mother about that, all I could do was to run faster than them. Sometimes people getting off the train came to my aid, I would walk beside a man, preferably a big man, so that he would see what was going on and protect me, and that dodge worked very well. I never mentioned it at home except when I had to confess to having lost my badge...' He made a gesture of dismissal. 'Oh, I'm sorry to go on about this, I'm not begging for sympathy...'

'You'd be glad to leave,' Mirren said, picturing him jumping off the train with fear in his heart. She had the wish to put her arms round him.

'Well, it got better, as I grew older, and they got tired, but, yes, university was bliss, except ... well, I had enough qualifications to get there, but I had to apply to Carnegie, who paid my fees, though I remember feeling the indignity of collecting vouchers which had to be handed to my tutors. But it was the best time of my life, and possibly I could have worked harder, but to have friends who thought like me and didn't make me feel as if I was "different" was wonderful... if it hadn't been the worry about my father, who came home at night looking terrible. The stress in the house was palpable.'

'Money was never a problem in our house,' Mirren said. 'I can't remember during these years having any worries. I, like you, went to the university, but I felt obliged to work hard because I knew that was what Dad wanted. All his ambition was transferred to me. If I did well, he was delighted. Mother looked on, pleased if he was pleased, or if I had a boyfriend whom she liked.'

'Didn't you have one?'

'Oh, there were boys I was friendly with, but our troubles began when my mother began to feel ill. She got worse and worse and then cancer was diagnosed. She died when I was at Jordanhill Training College and as I had to study and sit exams around

159

that time, Aunt Meg, Mother's sister, took over the running of the house. Then Dad became ill and he got worse and worse, his memory went, and his temper, and I sat my Finals with the sorrow of him on my shoulders. I don't know who was worse off, you or me, it's a moot point. He began to wish he was back in Waterside, where he came from, and it was when he slipped out of the house one day intending to go back there, that he fell down the stairs. He died.' She felt his arm round her waist. 'I have good memories –' she tried to steady her voice – 'which you don't appear to have, Jamie, as far as your home is concerned. Dad and I used to walk in the park. He liked that because it was what he and Mother had done, and he loved the trees and flowers, and birds, and the Kelvin. The river at Waterside was called the Calder, and it reminded him of it.'

'So it was here that you met my father?'

'Yes, this very bench. It was when my Aunt Meg was looking after the house. I remember her glancing over Dad's bent head – he was sitting at the table, looking sad – and saying, "Take your father for a walk in the park." We set off, and I got out of breath walking, and he was teasing me, so we sat down on this bench beside your father.'

'If it was him. 1934, you said? What time of the year would it be?'

'It must have been the spring. May, I think. Yes, that would be right, I can work it out from when my exams were, at Jordanhill.'

'1934? My father was still in the office, clearing up after Mr Nesbitt had committed suicide. He went on running the business, he said it had picked up a bit. He went out and in as usual each day.' Jamie was beginning to look agitated. 'Tell me what you remember, Mirren.' She looked at him. His face was white.

'He, your father, if it was him, said that he hated to be indoors in good weather, and he made a habit of doing this, walking to the park and having a sandwich, rather than going to a restaurant.' She decided not to tell Jamie the impression she'd got of his father, what she had thought at the time of his 'hunted' appearance, and the down-at-heel shoes. 'And funnily enough, later, one wet day, I was studying in the Mitchell when I saw him again, but it wasn't lunchtime...' She saw Jamie was looking at her intently. 'Have I said anything wrong?'

'No, except that...' he stopped. 'What year did you think that would be?'

'I told you that. 1934. May. Yes, it was when Aunt Meg was with us. Is it important?'

'Just that...' he looked at her, 'that was the time when he was supposed to be going out to his office and keeping the business going.

161

But now I see what I didn't understand before. The balloon had burst. Mother had discovered that he wasn't going to any office during the day. He was leaving the house, as usual, pretending he was going to the office, and wandering about Glasgow, eating in parks, living on money he still had. I imagine she discovered at the bank that their savings had dwindled even further and when she challenged him he had to confess. She treated him badly: "Sweep the kitchen floor, David", "Make the tea". She still had friends in for tea, and that I hated because she would sort of "parade" me in front of them, and I would have to be polite to these women, and listen to her singing my praises, while Father was in the kitchen, making the tea ... I tumbled to this quite soon, but most of the time I stayed away, trailing round the town as he had done, or passing time at the university, until I felt it safe to go home. I tried to be friendly with him, but all he would say was, "Don't you worry about things which don't concern you." I once said to him in the kitchen when we were washing the dishes, "Dad, can't I help? I'm part of the family. Tell me—" But he interrupted me: "Your mother cares very much how we look to other people. If we can keep a front up, that's all that matters." Talk about being piggy in the middle!' He looked at Mirren with a wry face. 'So that's the state of affairs just now. He's got some kind of job. I think he's a clerk in a shipbuilder's, but he hasn't told me. You're right. I have to keep the job I have, it was my tutor who recommended me, and work hard ... or join up when the war gets going. At the moment I'm able to contribute something to the household expenses.'

'I shouldn't rush into the war. Wait till you're called up.'

'But don't you see that's the only way I'm going to be able to help them? My salary is very low just now, because I'm being trained. I'm a pupil. I'm lucky that they give me anything at all.'

In the tram going back to Pollokshields, they didn't talk much. Mirren looked through the window at all the shops she knew as they rolled along Sauchiehall Street: C. & A. Modes, Pettigrew & Stephens, Copland & Lye. She could differentiate, as most city folk could, which supplied one's needs, Pettigrew's slightly better than Copland & Lye, and for extra style and cost, Daly's, which had a fashion nous which the others didn't have. And there was the McLellan Galleries, where she admired the painting of the Glasgow Boys & Girls, but not the numerous Highland scenes with Highland cattle grazing in front of a towering mass of mountains, with perhaps a waterfall coursing down them. Glowering, she called them, but she loved the colouring and design of the Glasgow artists.

She said to Jamie, silent beside her, 'Are you interested in art?'

He shook his head, 'I'd like to be. I was put off by being taken to the art galleries at Kelvingrove. I remember my father taking me to see the skeletons of huge dinosaurs, and wished I could draw like the students sitting around them on stools.'

'Me too,' she said, 'we lived very near, of course. You really have to go to the art school if you're interested. Now I am. I'd like to find time to study art, maybe go abroad.'

'We'll go together,' he said, meeting her eyes. 'What do you say? Go in for educating ourselves, now that we've finished with being educated.'

'I'd like that,' she said, and as their eyes met, she thought I've never known anyone with whom I had such an immediate rapport ... the attraction she felt for Jack Drummond faded out of her mind.

'What do you say if we start next Saturday?' Jamie said. 'We'll go to the McLellan Galleries and see what's on there, and if there are any lectures we can go to. And then have a meal in town.'

'Great idea,' she said. 'But I insist on paying my own way.'

'We'll decide that at the time. Shall we meet in the afternoon, at three, in case it closes early on Saturday? I'll come up for you then. Will that suit?'

'OK.' She remembered Annie saying how it would be good to have a flat of one's own, and also a boyfriend. 'I'll be ready.'

In the entry, before she started climbing the stairs, he took her hands, drew her to him and kissed her. 'You don't mind, do you, Mirren, I wanted to do that so much.'

She thought again of Jack Drummond and how he hadn't asked if she minded him kissing her. 'No,' she said, 'I feel as if I have known you for a long time, Jamie. I wonder if it is because of your father?'

'I feel a bond too, as if we had to meet. I've never felt that before, about anyone. Do you think we're falling in love?'

'I don't know ... yet. There's certainly something different. Maybe it's because I'm older than many of the girls you know?' She smiled at him.

'I don't think that's important. What's a couple of years? It just means you'll be able to take care of me, instead of the other way round.' He drew her closer to him. 'Will you promise to think about me until Saturday, and tell me how you feel, when I call for you?'

He said this so naturally, that she thought to herself: What does it matter about general opinion, that a girl should have the backing of her father and mother if a suitor called, so that they could look him over? I have no family, he's independent, although he lives with his parents, and it has never occurred to him that he shouldn't call on me although I live alone. Besides, she was free now, with her own flat; she could do anything she liked.

In bed, her mind was full of him, the different expressions which seemed to pass over his face like a summer wind, which blew cloud and shadow, lightening or darkening his eyes, the general loveliness of his face as if he was attending closely to what she was saying. This wasn't like Jack Drummond, who had let her see what it was like to be aroused sexually. There's no point in comparisons, she told herself, you are a free agent.

Chapter 7

Next Saturday morning, Mirren washed her hair and dried it carefully. She decided to wear a grey suit and not *le tout ensemble* of the black dress with over-skirt. She had chosen the suit because it matched her eyes, and to freshen it up, she added a chiffon scarf of palest pink, which seemed to make her complexion look more delicately pink, and set off her fairness. She was ready long before Jamie was due to call for her.

The next problem reared up. Should she look as if she was ready to go out immediately? She compromised by not wearing the jacket, and leaving it over a chair beside her bed, with her handbag and gloves. She was contemplating if she shouldn't have left them in the hall when the bell rang and she went to answer it with her problem unsolved.

But when she opened the door and saw Jamie's bright eyes and smile, she was flooded with pleasure, and said, 'Come in, Jamie! You're earlier than I expected. I'm almost ready.'

He stepped in, and in the dark hall, he said, 'You seem to be barring my way. Am I allowed to kiss you?'

'I was hoping you would,' she said, and held up her face, and as he drew her to him, her arms went round his neck, involuntarily.

'I've been looking forward to this since last Saturday,' he said.

'You mean, to seeing my flat?' She laughed. 'Come in properly, then.'

'You know I didn't mean that.' He kissed her. 'Lead on.' He released her.

She took his hand and led him into the kitchen.

'This is nice,' he said, looking around.

'Ours is dark with a horrible cooker that's badly in need of cleaning. I tried to do it once, but my mother took it as an insult, so I gave up.

'She's not a housekeeper, she thinks it is beneath her, and we don't have a cleaner. One thing I do do because it offends me, is clean out a large cupboard which stands in the kitchen. It is large and freestanding, I think we had it in the larder in the Manchester house, and she seems to labour under a delusion that it's ice-cold. She puts dry goods in it and left-overs, even jugs of milk. The smell is terrible when you open the door, so, unnoticed by her, I clean it out and throw away anything that's gone bad. She came into the kitchen one day and saw me at it, and said, "That's not a job for you, Jamie. I've meant to do it for ages." What she likes is entertaining, and sewing, and I think the truth is that she's lost her spirit. She's had a blow, I think, and can't surmount it.' He crossed to the window. 'It was from here you saw my father?'

'Yes,' she said. 'I think now that I made a mistake in calling on them. It was quite unlike me. It must have been curiosity.'

'I'd had a theory about him for some time, and you telling me how you met him in the park confirmed it. The whole thing was a pretence on his part, leaving to go to the office after Mr Nesbitt, his partner, had committed suicide, wandering about the town until it was time to go home. I know now there was no office to go to. He would be drawing money from his bank account, and giving Mother a weekly sum. I don't know how long it took her to tumble to this, but whatever she is, she's a good business-woman and she must have had it out with him. I know there was a time when the atmosphere in the house was unbearable, but I deliberately divorced myself from it. I knew my mother was a spender and couldn't control it, and I suspect he reached the stage when he felt so guilty that he had to confess to her. I was never there when they were rowing, but I was certainly aware of the atmosphere.'

'It's a sad story,' she said.

'Yes, but I'm not here to talk about my father, Mirren.' He got up. 'You have to show me the rest of your flat.'

'OK.' She led him to her bedroom, and seeing her jacket on the back of the chair, she began to put it on. He took it from her and helped her into it. His nearness made her breathe quickly.

'Does this mean we're going now?' he said, laughing at her. 'I like it here. White and virginal. And very restful.' She thought he looked very pointedly at the bed.

'There's the rest of the flat.' She didn't meet his eyes. She led him to the room she

169

had prepared for her father, where he admired the shelves of books, and then to the bathroom, which he exclaimed about, and its modernity.

'I've just had this done, to erase Miss Currie. Do you remember her?'

'Unfortunately. She's certainly been erased.' She had the feeling that he was laughing at her.

'That's it,' she said. He followed her to the bedroom. There, she picked up her hat, and crossed to the mirror on her dressing table to adjust it.

'Yes, you look lovely.' He was behind her. 'You're acting as if you were rushing me out,' he said. 'Are you afraid I would have my way with you on that lovely bed?'

'Don't be silly, Jamie.' She met his eyes in the mirror.

He turned her around so that she stood in his arms. 'I'm just as nervous as you, Mirren. Being alone with you here...' He laughed down at her. 'Don't worry. If you want to know, I've never been in a lady's bedroom before.' He bent and kissed her. 'I know now I've fallen in love with you.'

'But we hardly know each other,' she said.

'There must be two types of love. One, where it's overwhelming, and the other where love grows slowly, don't you think?'

'I think the first one must be where you allow yourself to be overwhelmed, the other, the safer way.'

'What a psychologist you are! But it takes two to be impulsive. I've a feeling we wouldn't be discussing this, so obviously we're not.'

'We're both cautious,' she said. 'Let's see how we get on with each other first.' She wanted to tell him that she was afraid, afraid of the consequences, having a baby, afraid of her feelings.

'The chance to throw your cap over the windmill, as it's called, may happen sooner than you think.'

'You mean, because of the war?'

'Yes. Up until meeting you, that was the only thing I wanted. Now, I don't think I could bear not seeing you.'

She pondered in his arms. 'The stage we're at is very nice. Meantime, shall we go to the McLellan Galleries and be educated?' She crossed the room to lift her handbag and gloves. She looked at her bed, white and virginal, almost with regret. She knew she was not capable of taking time by the forelock. Her meeting with Jack Drummond had taught her that. There were girls like Annie, and perhaps Muriel, who were different from her and Jessie Baxter, who had got married in a tearing hurry, who didn't give it any thought at all. She wished for a moment that she was like that. She turned to him. 'I'm ready.'

'You're so correct, Mirren, in everything you do, precise.' He laughed, 'I don't possess a hat. Sorry. Perhaps in a year or so I'll wear a bowler like my father. But I don't feel like a budding C.A. either. Perhaps the war will rescue me.'

'Don't talk about it. Let's go, then. I think my key's in the door.' She was quite pleased with how she had managed a tricky situation.

On their way to the McLellan Galleries, she thought of how her heart had seemed to beat faster when Jamie was near her. She could tell that he was inexperienced with women, unlike Jack Drummond, who had given quite a different impression. But Jamie had been brought up, she felt sure, by a mother who had strict rules about the courtesy women expected from the opposite sex. She thought of those words because they could have been Mrs Campbell's. But now was a different generation, and she hadn't kept up with it. She still felt that a man shouldn't be in a flat alone with a young woman. It might lead to 'consequences'. You're hardly different from Mrs Campbell, she told herself, you should be able to behave as you want. You should have been mixing with young people of your own age, to get the feel of it, instead of being wrapped up in your studies, and the health of your parents.

'Jamie,' she said on the tramcar as it swung round into Sauchiehall Street, 'do you think you come to the state when you disabuse yourself of your upbringing and act as you feel?'

He looked round at her. 'Parents do influence us, but it depends on your character. You should be able to slough it off when the occasion demands it. Hi! This is where we get off! Conversation to be continued. Come on!' They rattled down the stairs, Jamie jumped off first, and held out his hand to help her off. I'm perfectly capable of getting off myself, she thought, but this courtesy presupposes women are frail creatures, who have to be guarded. They walked along the street, Jamie placing himself on the side nearest the pavement edge, and she thought, here we go again, that's to protect me from brigands, that's the word, or mud splashes from carriages.

'You're still doing it,' she said, as he pushed open the door of the galleries, holding it to let her in.

'Doing what?' he asked.

'Behaving like a gentleman.'

'Don't you like it? I'm trying hard.'

'We're both trying too hard.'

They agreed to accept that they knew nothing about art, and approached the pictures on view, prepared to look and criticise They sat down in a corner to study the

173

brochure. Jamie scored. He at least had heard of the artists.

'I'm ashamed of myself,' she said. 'There are huge gaps in my education.'

'Me too. Maybe we should have stayed in your flat?'

'Jamie! It's manners to wait until you're asked!' She laughed at him.

'Are you regretting you didn't ask me?'

'Of course not. And stop teasing. What would you have said if your mother had popped her head out when we were passing your door.'

'I would say ... I don't know what I would say. But I would decide there and then that I would have to move out of their house, get a room somewhere, and invite you to come and see me. I should be more hospitable than you.'

They left the Galleries, taking the brochures with them, reassuring each other that they had enjoyed going there, and Mirren feeling that she had to find out more about painting. She would get some books from the library before they went back again and study them.

'Meantime,' Jamie said, 'would you like to go to the cinema, or have a meal, or something?'

'I think we should go and eat, I'm ravenous. But remember, I'm paying my share.'

They walked down Sauchiehall Street to

Renfield Street, where they knew there was a good and cheap restaurant. It was cold and wet, and Jamie said, 'Take my arm. I'll lose you in this wind.' The street was busy with young couples, talking and laughing together, some were sharing umbrellas, and Mirren regretted that, in planning her outfit, she hadn't thought of taking one, or at least a raincoat.

They ran the last few yards, and stood in the vestibule while they got their breath back. 'We ought to have been prepared for Glasgow weather,' Jamie said, and Mirren, brushing her wet hair from her forehead, agreed.

In the restaurant, facing each other, they pretended to study the brochures, but every time Mirren looked up she met Jamie's eyes. 'You're not listening to me,' she said.

'You're right. I'm absorbing you. You're so shy, Mirren. I've told you I've fallen in love with you. Could you possibly feel the same?'

'I don't know.' His eyes were lovely, she thought, deep blue, almost black. He was very handsome. She would have liked to tell him. 'Give me time.'

'There isn't much time.'

'Because of that old war?'

'Yes, and we'll only be young like this for a very short time.'

'I don't know my own mind.'

'Will you promise to get to know it and tell

175

me on our next meeting?'

'I'll think about you in bed.'

'Well, that at least is progression.'

They both made short work of the cheapest thing on the menu, pie and chips, washing it down with copious amounts of tea. The restaurant wasn't licensed, and they were both typical Glaswegians, unused to drinking wine, so they didn't miss it. They finished with apple tart, and a cup of coffee each, smiling at each other when they had finished. 'Great grub,' Jamie pronounced, and she agreed.

When they got back to Limes Avenue, he said to her in the entry of number 12, 'I'll see you to your door.'

'All right,' she said. 'It would be embarrassing if we were standing here and your father or mother popped their head out.'

'That makes me feel about ten,' he said.

Outside her door, she said, 'Thanks for a lovely evening.'

'I enjoyed it too. Why are we suddenly being so polite?'

'I suppose because we're embarrassed.'

'Not me. How about next Saturday? We'll have lunch together, and decide what we're going to do.'

'OK. You have to work in the morning. I'll come on a later train, and meet you in the station café. Would that suit?'

'Fine. Well, I'd better get downstairs.'

'It's a funny situation.'

'You mean living so close to each other?'

'Yes. We might have a walk somewhere in the afternoon, and we can discuss art.' She smiled at him.

'You're a tease.' He put his arms round her, and she thought, this is where he asks if he can come in. When he didn't, she was sorry, not because she wanted him to, she assured herself, but that he didn't give her the chance to refuse him. He bent to kiss her. 'Little girl, aren't you? Try not to think of me as a pouncer, but most girls have an air of stand-offishness, or come-hitherishness. I never know with you.'

'What air do I have?'

'One of freshness, untouchability, and I do so want to touch you.' His face changed, his eyes became black.

'Don't look like that, Jamie.'

'What is "that" then?'

'You'll be annoyed if I tell you.'

He had his arm round her waist, and he tickled her ribs. 'Come on, tell me.'

'All right. Lecherousness.'

He reeled back, pretending to be shocked. 'Yes, that's exactly right, but as well, I like your mind, in fact everything about you. I'd better get downstairs. What a ridiculous situation! So near and yet so far.' He leant back on the banister. 'Shall I slide down?'

'I used to do that, in the other flat. Go on.

177

I won't look.' She turned and inserted her key in the lock. She felt him nuzzling her neck.

'Saturday. Central Station. See you, say, two thirty? Think of me till then.'

'Saturday. Central Station. OK, I promise to think of you.'

She closed the door, very very slowly. And it was as if she was shutting him out of her life.

Her bedroom still looked white and virginal.

Chapter 8

The telephone rang in Mirren's hall when she was having her breakfast. It was such a rare occasion since it was installed that she hadn't got used to it, and she automatically patted her hair and wiped her mouth with her napkin before she rose to answer it. Not many people, except those in business as Mr Craig had pointed out, and perhaps those whom he called 'toffs', felt it necessary, and Alastair had told her yesterday that he had had a phone call from Annie to say that she had a bad cold and couldn't take her class. 'Yet she was able to go along to the corner telephone kiosk and phone from there,' he had said aggrievedly.

Mirren lifted the receiver off the hook and said, 'Hello.' She knew it was Jack Drummond before he started to speak.

'Mirren, is that you?'

'Yes,' she said apprehensively. 'What a—'

He interrupted her. 'You'll be wondering why you haven't heard from me recently, but my mother was ill, and I was too busy with her to do anything else.'

'I'm sorry to hear that, Jack. Aunt Meg mentioned it in her last letter. Has she got worse?'

'She died two days ago, and I've been that busy fixing up arrangements and so on ... the funeral's on Thursday afternoon. Could you come?'

'Thursday...' She played for time. 'It's very difficult for me, Jack. It's the last week of term before we close down for the Christmas holidays, and I was planning to visit Waterside during that time' – this was a sudden idea – 'but that wouldn't be until next week. As well as that, one of the teachers is off. She may be back today. I don't know.'

'I just thought ... well, I had to let you know in case you were wondering ... but I've had a terrible time. She was down to skin and bone, but she refused to go into the cottage hospital. The day before she died, me and the district nurse tried to persuade her, but it was no good, and the next day ... well, she died. Maybe it was as well. She couldn't have borne sitting about all day twiddling her thumbs, at least that's what everybody's saying...'

'I'm so sorry for you, Jack. I know how you must be feeling. But I'll see if it's possible to get off, and let you know.'

'Thanks. I phoned you on an impulse ... I just thought ... well, never mind. I'll see you when you come to Waterside.'

'Give me your telephone number, Jack.' She opened her new book for addresses, and wrote it down as he dictated. 'I've got that. I'll not raise your hopes about me coming, but I'll do my best.' She felt awkward, and said, 'Must rush now to get to school.'

'Aye, that's right. I'll maybe see you, then?'

'Yes, Jack. Goodbye.' She hung up the receiver on its hook and sat down at the table, her head in her hands. She couldn't feel sorry for his news since she had never known his mother, but had imagined her as a small wiry woman with a tight grip on the affairs of the farm, and her son.

She met Alastair when she went into the common room. 'Annie isn't in?'

'No, nor likely to be. I know that girl.' I bet you do, Mirren thought. 'Thank goodness I can count on you and Muriel. Here she is.' He turned. 'Hello, Muriel.' Mirren thought they exchanged intimate glances. I never used to have a suspicious mind, she thought.

'Good morning, Muriel,' she said. 'Had you a difficult time on the train today?'

'No, it was easy.' She came from further up the Circle Line, Mirren knew. 'Sometimes you have to stand all the way.'

'Poor you.'

'It's the Christmas rush,' Alastair said, 'and we now have to get through this week without Annie.'

'What did I tell you, Alastair? That girl's most unreliable,' Muriel said.

Mirren decided not to mention the funeral. It would be the last straw. The janitor rang the starting bell, and she lifted her register. 'Off to the treadmill again.' She would tell Jack tonight that it was simply impossible, and order some flowers to be sent. She believed they delivered as far away as Waterside, or they telephoned a nearby florist.

When she got home that night, there was a long letter from her Aunt Meg, telling her about Mrs Drummond's death. 'Jack is very upset, and we've all been trying to help him as much as possible. A big strong man like that, but that's the kind who are most struck down, I've found.' There was no mention of her coming to the funeral. Obviously she wouldn't expect Mirren to attend since she hadn't known his mother. 'Well, Mirren, I know you'll be sad at Christmas missing your father, so I want you to pack up and come to me and stay as long as you like, or until you've to go back to the teaching. I could never put up you and Cameron, as I have only one spare bedroom, as you know, but there's that little room off the front room with a bed in it, and it suits you. It's better than staying on your own.'

She had never given much thought to Christmas, and now that Jamie was in her life, perhaps he would have some plans. Now there was Jack Drummond and Aunt Meg to be fitted in. She decided she would accept her aunt's invitation, and see Jack at the same time. She would phone him tonight and tell him that it was impossible to get time off for the funeral. She would decide when she would go to Waterside, after she had seen Jamie and found out what he was doing. They had been so absorbed in each other, that Christmas plans had been far from their minds.

Surprisingly, she had another telephone call that evening while she was writing to her aunt.

She ran to lift the receiver, pleasantly excited. What a difference it made to have a telephone in the house, she thought. She remembered Jack saying to her, 'The telephone is a godsend to farmers. It saves me driving to Hamilton to get what I need.' She heard Jamie's familiar voice, bright, young.

'Mirren, it's me, Jamie! I'm phoning you

from Glasgow. I remembered you had a telephone now, so I've nipped into a kiosk at the station. What are you doing for Christmas?'

'Christmas?' she echoed.

'You know, Father Christmas, jingle bells and all that. We didn't discuss it.'

'Can't it wait until Saturday when we meet?'

'Well, you might get booked up, or something.'

'I'm just writing at this minute to accept an invitation to go to Waterside for Christmas. I'll certainly go there during the holidays. I have other people to visit there.'

'I see.' He sounded disappointed. 'There's a dance at the university on Saturday, that's also why I'm phoning you. Would you like to come with me?'

'Yes, I'd like that. We could discuss Christmas then.'

'OK. The only thing I know I'm doing is going with my mother and father to my aunt and uncle in Jordanhill. He's a bank manager there. My Aunt Phoebe always gets drunk on these occasions and keeps having another nip in the kitchen. Everyone pretends not to notice, but it's laughable. I can't think what they do on their own. Wild orgies, maybe.'

'I don't have any colourful relations like that, I have to tell you. Everything at Waterside is jolly and uncomplicated with loads of food and drink and they all become very merry, and a good time is had by all. Then I'll probably visit my friend, Jessie, now married with a baby. In Partick. I promised her I would, and then my father died...'

'Well, I can see your time is going to be fully occupied. I don't get holidays like yours, of course. Christmas Day and New Year's Day.'

'What time on Saturday, Jamie? Is this dance a dress-up affair?'

'Far from it. Lounge suits for the men and no long skirts or white gloves for the ladies. Shall we meet at two thirty as we arranged, Station Café? We can easily put off time until we go up to the university.'

'That's fine, as long as you don't suggest a ten-mile walk. I'll be tired after my week at school. We're putting on a nativity play, and it's going to be nerve-wracking.'

'Oh, damn!' she heard him say. 'I have to put more pennies in the slot...' She heard his voice intermittently: 'Do they accept shillings? Oh, good! Now I can speak for as long as I like. Mirren, Mirren, are you there?'

'Yes, where else would I be?'

'I thought I'd lost you. Now I've to spend a shilling talking.'

'Don't be mean. But honestly I smell something burning. I was boiling potatoes, and the pan may have burnt dry.'

'That'll cost more than a shilling. I suppose you'd better go. Remember, I love you. Think of that as being repeated twenty times, which will use up my shilling.'

'OK. See you Saturday.'

Only one potato was ruined, fortunately. Life was hotting up, she thought: the school, Jack Drummond and Aunt Meg coming on the scene. And Jamie. Would she have to choose between Jack and Jamie?

When she got to school the following day Annie was back, red-nosed and sniffing, but otherwise all right. It was her turn to be aggrieved, apparently, when Mirren said to her that she hoped she was feeling better ... 'Alastair didn't give me much sympathy when I phoned him, said I had to get back as soon as I could, because I was letting the whole side down.' Muriel appeared in the common room and seemingly overheard Annie's last remark.

'Quite right too,' she said, going to her locker, 'if we all went off because of a simple cold, and on Christmas week, where would we all be?'

'Who's asking for your opinion?' Annie said. 'Or have you become Alastair's deputy?'

'I resent that,' Muriel said.

'Resent all you like, but I only take comments from the headmaster, and not from anyone else.'

'You're dead jealous, and spiteful into the

bargain,' Muriel said.

Alastair came into the room. 'Ah,' he said. 'A full complement today. I'm glad you decided to come back, Annie. I was just wondering how we were going to get through this week.'

'Oh, I shouldn't have thought you would miss me, with your deputy here!'

'What are you talking about, Annie?' His voice was cold.

'Don't play the innocent. You know who I mean.'

'This is intolerable,' Muriel said. 'Tell her, Alastair.'

'Yes, go on. Do what she says,' Annie said. The starting bell rang.

'We'll treat this scene with the contempt it deserves,' Alastair said. 'But I may tell you, your career is hanging in the balance, Annie. Unless you apologise to Muriel, I shall have to dismiss you on the grounds of insubordination.'

'Insubordination!' Annie's face was scarlet with indignation. 'Do I hear Muriel's voice? I would advise you to think very carefully before you do that, Alastair. If you don't I might have to tell the governors one or two things.' Mirren saw Alastair flinch. Muriel answered for him. 'You shouldn't use threats, Annie, not one in your position. From what Alastair tells me, you might blacken your own character.'

186

'And since when did you become one of the board of governors?' Annie said. Mirren had always thought Muriel was handsome. Now she saw that the girl's eyes had narrowed and become malevolent.

'Now, now,' Alastair said. 'We mustn't forget we are teachers first and foremost. Your classes are waiting.'

Mirren took up her register, books and handbag. 'We'd all better do as Alastair says. Come on, Muriel and Annie, your classes will be waiting, and don't forget there's a rehearsal for the play at three o'clock, in the main hall, isn't it, Alastair?'

'Yes, you're right, Mirren. Thank you for reminding me.'

Muriel lifted her register, and walked out of the door followed by Mirren and Annie. None of them spoke.

At three o'clock Mirren turned up in the hall, and helped to shepherd in the children. Alastair and Muriel were already there. The children were excited and talkative, and she admired the way Alastair subdued them. What was going to happen? Would he report Annie? Or have a private talk with her? Annie was subdued and sulky. Mirren decided to keep well out of the situation, and concentrated on placing the children for the play. She thought Jimmie Grant with his impertinent face and black fringe was a poor choice for Jesus, and wondered whose idea that was. Alastair and Muriel helped her. Whatever the situation, she saw that they were both first-rate, dedicated teachers.

She marched her class back to their room at four o'clock to be dismissed, and when she went to the common room, she found Alastair waiting there. Muriel was seated, and in a few minutes Annie came in. Alastair asked her to take a seat. He placed it for her, and seemed to smile placatingly at her, Mirren thought. Was Annie going to be asked to apologise? she wondered.

Alastair spoke: 'I'm afraid there hasn't been the Christmas spirit between us. Have we been working too hard, I wonder? I know, Annie, you were busy in the costume department, and I do appreciate that. We've all been tired out, but I've experienced this before. Everyone gets rather put off their stride, well, you know what I mean, words said, then regretted. I thought we had a good team here, but if we haven't then I take full blame. However . . .' he paused, and looking at the girl directly, 'Muriel has generously offered to apologise for her behaviour. She realises she's to blame.' Clever, Mirren thought. And arranged in a few minutes, behind Annie's back. Alastair was still speaking. 'She feels her appointment has thrown a spanner in the works, and she's ready to apologise to you, Annie, and I fully withdraw anything I may have said here in the common room before the classes began. Will you accept my apology?'

Annie had coloured, and looked non-plussed.

'And mine too,' Muriel said. 'I've always got on well in the school where I was teaching before I came here, and if I've been the source of annoyance to you, Annie, I'm sorry.'

'I don't know what to say,' Annie said, 'and I admit I have a short temper, but there are some people whom I find it hard to get on with. I retract any threats I may have made, Alastair, if that's what you want me to do.'

'In a way. Just please, don't make any assertions which have no bearing on fact.'

'I'll make a cup of tea before we all go home,' Mirren said. 'After all, it's Christmas!' Mirren fulfilled her role. She also felt she was the only one in the room free from guilt, and she made up her mind to make the nativity play a success if she could, as the only contribution she could make was as an onlooker in this little back-room drama, although surprisingly, Alastair had gracefully given in, probably acting on Muriel's advice. Would that close the matter? Time would tell.

Chapter 9

Buying this dress has been fortuitous, Mirren thought, as she tied the over-skirt on, and fastened her mother's pearls round her neck. A dress for every occasion.

And in its tube-like state, without this over-skirt, it would have been perfect for Mrs Drummond's funeral, with the addition of her camel coat, black hat and gloves. She thought of how it would have stood out amongst the tweed suits of the farmer's wives and the men in their stiff Sunday blacks, and chastised herself for such thoughts.

Was this her mother's temperament showing through at last? Planning outfits, and the pleasure when you knew you were dressed for the occasion? It would have given Mother such pleasure if she had known I had come round to thinking like that, she thought now, and that I might have enjoyed going with her on one of those endless trails through the city shops for just the item required, essential to the success of the expedition. It's all a question of attention to detail, she thought now, which had been manifest in my studies.

She sat down to put on the new pumps of black patent leather – never spoil the ship for a ha'penny worth of tar. Now the raincoat and an umbrella to protect her hair.

In the train she allowed herself to think of Jamie. If she followed her mother's mode of thought, he wasn't nearly such a good 'catch' as Jack Drummond, who could offer her a home, and freedom from worry about the war, probably ways of avoiding the rationing ... but that was not her way of thinking.

There were signs that the phoney war was at last coming to an end, and in one way, everyone would be glad to get on with it. What would she do to help? She didn't like the idea of carrying on teaching, perhaps she would join one of the women's services, or even work in one of the many munitions factories which were springing up.

When she walked through Central Station towards the café, she imagined everyone looked purposeful and quietly excited. She would like to be part of this, not shut up in the quiet of a schoolroom.

She was still surprised at the rush of pleasure it gave her to see Jamie coming towards her, his open smiling face, the scarf no longer flying but wrapped several times round his neck. He sat down, blowing on his hands. 'They say this is going to be a bad

191

winter,' he said. 'Don't you feel the cold?'

'Not much. But standing on the platform at Pollokshields, yes, it got to me.'

'It's lovely to see you. Have you got your pretty dress on under that coat?'

'Yes, but I'm keeping my coat on until I get to the university. I want to bowl you over!'

'You've done that already.' He took her hands across the table. 'Now I'm going to bowl you over,' he paused. 'I've joined up!'

'Joined up? You mean now?' She couldn't keep the dismay from her voice.

'I'm waiting for orders. I'm in the ATC, as you know, and that entitles me to opt for the RAF. I thought it would be better now than waiting for the rush.'

'But I thought you said—'

'That I couldn't bear to leave you? Well, neither can I. But I had a talk with myself and decided that I had no right to plan our future unless I won the war first ... that's the good part of me. I'll be able to send some money home, and the other advantage is that I don't want to sit in that office and wait till they haul me out of it.'

'But you'll lose your job!'

'No, I had a talk with them. The boss is an old Air Force man, and he said it would be there for me when I came back, and the years in the Air Force would be counted as part of my contract with them.'

'Well, you've made up your mind.' She was

bereft at the thought of losing him.

'I'm not away yet. It may take ages. Don't think I won't miss you, Mirren, but I wouldn't feel right with myself if I didn't do this.' She could see that he was excited at the prospect. His eyes were shining.

'Have you told your parents?'

'Not yet. But I don't think Dad will mind. Nor Mother. He was in the first one and she'll be proud. Besides I won't be a drag on them any longer.'

'There's that. Perhaps I won't stay in teaching. I was just thinking about it on the train coming here. I felt rather like you, I might want a slice of the action too. There are all the women's services.'

'You're beginning to think as I've been doing. I don't want to be like the last generation, who let it all happen. But we've had the Spanish Civil War to warn us, and we've behaved in the same way. Seen the signs and ignored them, watched Hitler goose-step all over Europe, and done nothing about it.'

'But we expect our Government to do this, don't we?'

'Yes, but we could have protested when we saw they weren't doing anything. I didn't bother joining any societies in the university? Did you?'

'No. I was engrossed in getting through the work and helping at home. We're all very good at closing our eyes.'

'Well, let's be different. Let's do what we can and push our happiness to one side until we have a peaceful world again.'

'It sounds noble, but very difficult to live up to.'

'We will be able to see each other, or at least to keep in touch.' She saw that his eyes were shining with excitement. The knight in armour, she thought. He's found a role for himself.

'Meantime,' she said, feeling she was the careful one, 'life goes on. I've arranged to go to Waterside for Christmas. You were asking me what my plans were.'

'Oh, Mirren!' His eyes were sad. 'It won't be for a long time, will it?'

'Certainly Christmas Day. I'll be having Christmas dinner with all my relatives, and probably spend a few days there, then you and I could meet in Glasgow. We'll arrange it later.'

'Well, I can bear that. I feel sad, but happy. I'm looking forward to joining up and the training, but not beyond that. It will be terrible going away and leaving you, but I've made up my mind. I shan't change that.'

'You must do what you think best.' In her mind she was thinking: Why jump the gun? But it was his decision, in keeping with his character. He was a romantic. She was the practical one. 'Well, we won't talk about it any more. Are we going to eat here, or do we get it at the university?'

'There, I think. Let's have a coffee here.'

In the tram, they passed her flat, and on the other side the bleak stretch of the park in darkness. In her mind's eye she saw herself walking with her father on the path leading from the fountain, and sitting down on the bench where they had met Jamie's father. Which had led to her meeting Jamie. His life had been led mainly away from home, whereas in her case, her home had shaped hers. Had it made any difference? She thought of Jack Drummond, whose life had been ordained for him, that of a farmer within a community.

'How often I've sat on the white tram going up to the university!' Jamie was saying. 'And here we are, going back in different circumstances. What a different person I was then. But I hadn't met you.'

'This is our stop,' she said. 'Come on.' The noise of their feet on the iron staircase linked up in her mind with her father falling downstairs to his death and before that, memories of rushing up the stairs two at a time to tell her parents that she had got her degree, and before that again, the learning stage in climbing them with her mother, 'One, two, three...' How innocent we all were to begin with, and how it begins to be complicated...

Jamie was helping her off at the university gates. How imposing she had thought they

were on her first day there. 'Happy memories?' he said as they walked quickly through
them because of the rain.

'I wasted my time here,' she said.

'Why?'

'I worked too hard.'

'I was the opposite. I didn't work hard
enough.'

'Well, here we both are. The products. And
it didn't solve a single thing for us.'

'It's not supposed to. It's to teach you how
to think.'

They were in the great hall, joining in the
dancing. They didn't talk much, but she put
her arms round his neck and he held her
closely. Her mood was one of poignancy and
Jamie evidently felt the same. It was as if
they felt the weight of the unknown future
on their shoulders but couldn't talk about it.
Once, Jamie, looking down at her, said,
'We'll have to wait and see what's in store for
us. It's as if we were being swept along by a
huge tidal wave to an unknown shore.'

'That's quite poetic.'

'Is it? I feel sad.'

'So do I.'

'We'll not stay long.'

'No, we'll not stay long.'

They left at midnight, and caught a tram
into town, where they changed to one for
Pollokshields.

'I should have said that I liked your dress.'

196

'I call it my lucky one.'

It was snowing when they rounded the corner of Limes Avenue. The branches of the limes at the corner were lashing themselves into a frenzy. 'These trees don't like the weather,' Jamie said. 'Like me. I have a poor circulation.'

'Well, you must come up with me and I'll give you a hot cup of tea.' (Is that me talking? she thought.) She could see the surprise in his face and knew he was trying to hide it.

'Have you anything to put in it?'

'Some whisky which I keep for hot toddies. My father thought it was the remedy for colds, with lemon and sugar.'

'Well, let's have that.'

'OK.' They both burst out laughing and he bent and kissed her.

They looked at the closed door of his parents' flat as they passed it but didn't say anything. Once in her flat she led him into the kitchen, where it was warm because of the stove. She busied herself with putting on the kettle, and taking the whisky out of the cupboard. When she reached for the tea caddy, Jamie said, 'Let's go the whole way and have hot toddies without tea. That's the proper way to drink it.'

'I know that, but I think it was a solace to my father to put whisky in tea, then he wasn't getting his daughter drunk.'

'You mean calling it tea instead of hot toddy?'

'Yes. Get two glasses down, Jamie, and the sugar, while I get the lemons from my larder.' When she came back, he had poured whisky into the glasses, and added hot water.

'Now, squeeze your lemons into it to salve your conscience,' he said, laughing. She did and they took their glasses into the sitting room. They sat down on the sofa together, and raised their glasses to each other.

'I shall tell everyone you got me drunk,' Jamie said.

'I shall tell everyone that it was your suggestion.'

'No it wasn't. You put the idea into my head by telling me about your father giving you a hot toddy.' She laughed at him, and he took the glass from her hand and put it down on the table where he had put his own. 'You have to be punished for lying.' He pressed her back in the sofa and kissed her on the mouth.

She felt the whisky flushing her cheeks, and, stretching her arm, she took up her glass again. 'But you're not going to deprive me of my drink. You have yours.'

'I tell you what. We'll both have a drink and see what effect it has on us.'

'All right.' She was laughing. 'You're crazy, Jamie.'

'I must be, crazy with love.'

They both drank and kissed, and she felt the whisky stinging her lips.

'We'll try that again,' Jamie said. They both drank, laughing at each other as they did so.

'You're crazy,' she said. 'You're pulling me down to your level of craziness.'

'It's nice, isn't it? Finish your toddy. It's good for colds.'

'I haven't got one.'

'It's good for the one that you'll get. If this weather continues, we'll go into the country and skate. What do you say?'

'Yes, I'd like that.'

This time the kiss was a lingering one. Mirren felt the taste of whisky on her lips, or from his lips, and she imagined the spirit was coursing through her body, setting it on fire. 'Your cheeks are on fire,' Jamie said, caressing her face with his hand.

'I'm not a toper like you. We didn't keep it in the house.'

'Didn't you ever drink in the university bar?'

'No.'

'What a deprived life you've led.'

She didn't know if Jamie had suggested it, or she had stood up, saying she was hot, but she found herself lying with him on the cool counterpane of her bed with Jamie beside her.

'Better?' he said.

'Yes, this is nice. You're not going to …

199

Jamie?'

'That's what you want, isn't it?'

'Yes.' She was quite clear in her mind. 'This room's too white and virginal.'

The bit she had often played through in her mind, how you got your clothes off, how you started, seemed to be dismissed with no trouble. They were both naked and shivering, and Jamie pulled the rose-patterned quilt over them. She thought how thoughtful he is, how caring, and then, but it's for his own benefit, he's the cold one. Certainly his body was shaking.

'You're shaking, Jamie,' she said.

'It's not the cold. I'm on fire. Aren't you?'

'Yes, and worried stiff.'

'Don't. I'll take care of that.'

Then there was a hiatus in her thinking. It was all pure feeling. She discovered herself, knew why she had felt incomplete. This is it, she thought, this is what I wanted. She was on fire too, and knew desire, lost herself in desire. 'You're a greedy girl,' he said.

They lay for a long time afterwards, and she thought they dozed off. In any case, she opened her eyes and saw Jamie dressing.

'Where are you going?' she said.

'Home.'

'But you can't go home in the middle of the night.'

'My God!' He lifted his watch. 'You're quite right. It is the middle of the night. Half

200

past three! Don't worry. They're used to me slipping in during the night.'

'I don't believe it. I can't have you frightening them. Come back to bed.'

'What a demanding woman you are!' He had divested himself of his trousers, and had leaped in beside her.

'You can't deprive me of my play-back.'

'You mean, "How was it for you?" kind of thing.'

'That kind of thing.'

The next part was almost more enjoyable, she said to him, almost. At six o'clock he got up and made tea, and brought it into the bedroom. 'This is what husbands do, I believe. And light up. But I don't smoke, do you?'

'Never.'

He left at seven, saying that was best. She didn't know where he would go, possibly sit in a café until it was time to begin work at his office. She got up too, and had a bath and leisurely dressed. She was on holiday now. She would get ready to go to Waterside. She looked at herself in the mirror. Shall I look different to everyone? she wondered. Her body felt alive, stimulated, as it ought to be, the feeling was of someone who had sloughed off a skin, or rather discarded, and revealed herself to herself. And to others?

On her way to Waterside the next morning, she still felt different. Would Aunt Meg see any difference in her? She felt the other passengers in the carriage were taking quick glances at her, which they turned away when they met her eyes. Suddenly, the whole enormity of what she had done, hit her. She looked out of the window and saw they were in the country now, and the sheep grazing in the fields didn't appear too disturbed. What if, in spite of Jamie's care, she did have a baby? Would he marry her? Or would she keep it from him? Scenarios came and went in her mind, having to give up teaching, having to tell Jamie. But he was too young to be a father! That was what was wrong with him. He thought it was some kind of adult game. He was excited just now. He was going to fly, the thing he loved, he would be engrossed in that, wouldn't want any encumbrances. Stop it! When he came home on leave, it wouldn't be to Mirren whom he knew in her black dress, but a misshapen woman whom he didn't recognise. Stop it! She chided herself again. You're going to meet your relatives soon, you must look your best. You're bound to meet Jack Drummond soon. How will you deal with that?

She made herself stop thinking, by force of will, and when she stepped down at Waterside Station, she saw Josh on the platform. He waved, and she saw him running along the platform to help her out of her carriage. She lifted down her luggage, and opened the door. Josh helped her out.

'Great to see you, Mirren. Aunt Meg asked me to pick you up. You look marvellous!'

Chapter 10

In the car Josh and Mirren chattered away, thoroughly at ease with one another. Is it because we're cousins? she wondered.

'Has Jack got over his grief at losing his mother?' she asked him.

'He's taken it very badly, and is missing her in more ways than one. A woman is needed in a farmhouse, and she was a devil for work, Mrs Drummond. I think Grace has been helping him.'

'That's good of her,' Mirren said, thinking, doesn't he mind? But, of course, he and Jack are good friends. Why should he?

'Remember the last time you were here and I took you to the dance and the barn went on fire?' he said, turning to her with a smile.

'Could I ever forget it? Did everything turn out all right?'

'Well, of course, there was an inquest. The girl died. The girl whom the firemen got out. She'd been overcome by the smoke before they found her at the back of the barn. The situation became very nasty. Four of them had come from Cambuslang together. The girl's parents have sued the owner of the barn, and it happens to be Jack. This, coming along with losing his mother has been very hard on him. He had to pay a sum of money to the parents in compensation, although witnesses say these four were smoking. The whole thing caused quite a commotion in the village, and Jack was considered to be well out of it.'

'So perhaps the girl was a victim of her own carelessness?'

'You never know. Young girls fall in love with what their friends are doing. And she was only seventeen. Jack has changed recently. I think he feels badly done to. He used to be great fun in company, now he seems suspicious, and...'

'Truculent.'

'That's the word. It takes a school teacher to know.'

'I don't think I'll be one indefinitely. I'll probably go into one of the women's services.' He looked at her in surprise. 'I'm beginning to get a conscience.'

'I bet you know someone whose joined up. Is that what's influencing you?'

'No, not really.'

'I would have thought teaching was helping just the same.' He was sharp, she thought, Josh understands me. 'I'll take you on as a Land Girl any time.' He laughed.

'No, thanks. I'm not cut out for that.'

'I must admit I get qualms about the war too. Nothing will be the same afterwards. The whole world as we know it.'

'You'll be exempt, won't you?'

'For the time being. But Father is still able-bodied, and I wouldn't feel right if they didn't call me up.'

'I never thought of you in the Army, Josh. I imagined you and Jack would be exempted.'

'He will, because he's now running the farm alone. Ours is a different case.'

He dropped her off at her Aunt Meg's, saying he would see her tomorrow for Christmas dinner at their house.

Her aunt greeted her with arms wide. 'Look at you, so smart and trim in that suit! And the white blouse and black bow at the neck just right! What is it about Glasgow clothes that gives them that air? Jane discovered the secret early!'

'It's strange, Aunt,' she said, when they were having a cup of tea, 'I'm finding myself getting quite interested in clothes now.'

'Ah! Is there a young man on the horizon? Girls usually dress for men.'

She felt herself blushing. 'Well, I'll tell you, Aunt Meg. I have met someone. I'll tell you about him later.'

'He must be quite special. You and I will

have a quiet meal tonight and a chin-wag. Did Josh tell you we've been invited to the farm for Christmas dinner?'

'Yes. Is it just a family party?'

'I think I heard Margaret say she had invited Jack Drummond. Everybody's sorry for him, and no doubt Grace McFarlane will be there. Margaret and Grace keep hoping that Josh will toe the line there.'

Later, when they sat round the fire for Aunt Meg's 'chin-wag', she said, 'Now tell me about your young man.'

'Well, it's strange how I met him. Coincidence, really. Remember you were staying at our flat when Mother died, and you sent Dad and I out for a walk in the park?'

'Yes, I was worried about him. The time when you came back and told me you had met a man ... you sat on the same bench?'

'Well, it's a long story, but he's turned out to be Jamie's father!'

'I thought you said he had looked a bit down-at-heel?'

'Yes, I did, but I'll tell you why.' She ran briefly through the story of how she had met him again at Pollokshields.

'Well, fate seems to have brought you and this Jamie together.'

'We've fallen in love, but he told me last night that he's joining up. He's desperate to fly.'

'Ah, that's hard. But that's how it was in

the last one. So many wives and sweethearts left behind. Some of us buckled to: I was helping at the Cottage Hospital, others had to stay at home because they had babies. I'll tell you a secret, Mirren,' she leant forward, and the firelight lit up her strong face, the dark eyes, still beautiful. 'I fancied Roger, but Margaret was there first, and she's made a far better wife for him than I would have done, so everybody's happy.' Mirren looking at the shadowed eyes, wondered if this was true.

'Josh was saying he's eligible.'

'Strictly speaking, that's true, but Roger has a great influence in these parts. I don't think he'll want to see his son going away to fight. Jack Drummond is all right. He owns his farm, he'll be exempt. But you were telling me about your Jamie. What does he look like?'

'He's tall and dark, boyish. I'm older than he is but he has a grown-up way of speaking. He has a great sense of fun, but I think his home life hasn't been too happy. His mother strikes me as having been a demanding woman, who couldn't put up with setbacks, and didn't support her husband when she should have done.'

'So, he's looking for a mother?'

'No, Aunt Meg. He doesn't need that. He's a most independent young man. If he has a passion, it's for flying.'

'More than his passion for you?'

'Oh, no! It's difficult to convey his charm to you, Aunt. He's the kind of person who is bound to be popular wherever he goes.'

'Ah, well, that's good. As long as he doesn't seek that popularity away from you.'

'Oh, no, Aunt. He's a contented person, except for this wish to get into flying. It makes me want to volunteer too.'

'Don't do that. Wait and see how things go and you get an idea of where you might be needed or want to go. I was desperate to nurse. The war gave me the opportunity. I presented myself one day at the Cottage Hospital and asked to see the Matron. She said to me, "Are you fond of babies?" and I said I was. She needed someone for the maternity ward, and I started there and then. I wasn't allowed to go near the women until she had trained me, and then I was in clover! Suddenly everyone was having babies, and if I wasn't busy in the ward, I was busy outside it. I took my exams and became a matron. And here's a strange thing, Mirren. I was so content helping the women, that I never wanted one for myself!'

Mirren's cheeks had begun to burn with all this talk about babies. She didn't want any more of it. She put her hand to her face.

'What a fire that is, Aunt Meg! You wouldn't think there was a war on.'

'Oh, there's no shortage of coal here. This

208

is mining country, and somehow a sackful gets put behind my house in the yard, every week, as sure as the moon waxes and wanes. There's a lot of men in Waterside who are gey good at setting off with their makeshift barrows and gathering the black diamonds that lie about the bings. I often think some of them are my babies! I don't look a gift horse in the mouth, oh, no!'

Mirren laughed. 'I'm surprised at you, and you a pillar in the community!'

'Fair dues! Do you think we should redd up and get to bed now? We must be at our best for the party tomorrow.'

'Maybe we should. And I've got my presents to wrap up. I was busy last night, and didn't get time.' That's true enough, she thought.

She went to her little room off the kitchen. There she looked round with satisfaction. Just the same as when she had stayed here as a little girl: the rose-patterned quilt, the low window sill where she could stand and see the garden and the lights of other houses in the village twinkling along the road, the white fluffy rug at the bedside, and yes, she investigated, the rose-patterned bed-pan beneath the bed. Aunt Meg had insisted on her using it during the night if she were caught short and didn't want to go through the parlour and then the kitchen to the toilet at the foot of the stairs. She remembered how her aunt had disposed of the contents, lifted the window, leant out and emptied the bed-pan into the flower bed. 'Make the pansies grow,' she used to say.

When she was snuggled up under the rose-patterned quilt, she imagined Jamie was with her. He had pulled her quilt over them, and she had known the delight of a man's naked body against hers. No regrets, she thought. It was natural; it was wonderful. She dismissed the tiny morsel of worry which still hung about in her mind. Many women must have been in the same state in the last war as would be in this one. You're not alone...

Chapter 11

Mirren and her aunt set off on Christmas morning to walk to the farm. They were both carrying baskets of Christmas gifts, but they had insisted to Josh last night that they were perfectly able to come 'under their own steam', as Meg had said. The pavement was icy, and she kept on telling Mirren to watch her step. 'I don't suppose the roads freeze up in the city,' she said.

'Not much,' Mirren said, 'but we get terrible fog. Sometimes I've had to feel my way from the flat at Kelvingrove by the railings of the houses!'

'Oh, my! Well, you and I will walk on the road here. There's never much traffic through the village and we'll be safer.'

They were greeted on their way by villagers calling out to her aunt, 'Merry Christmas, Miss Calder.' 'Mind your step,' and such like, and 'I see you've got your niece with you,' and 'Good morning, Miss Stewart.' It necessitated a few stops to introduce Mirren to some of her friends, but fortunately, the farm was quite near, and they arrived without mishap. 'You can see how they keep an eye on me at Waterside,' she said to Mirren. 'There's no chance of me having a fancy man without the whole village knowing. It's not like that in Glasgow, eh?'

'No,' Mirren agreed, thinking of the night she and Jamie had spent together, and how easy it had been. Any worries they had had certainly not been because they might have been observed.

They were greeted by Margaret, beaming, arms wide, and each enveloped in a welcoming hug. 'Well, you got here safely. And look at those baskets you're both carrying! You should have let Josh pick you up. Come along now, we're all in the parlour, you're about the last to come.'

'Stars always arrive late,' Aunt Meg said. 'Lead on, Margaret.'

They were ushered into the room and greeted by Roger. 'Here you are, then. Merry Christmas! Now I think you know everyone here.' The room seemed to be full of faces raised to them. 'But I don't know if you'll remember Martha and Jake Allan, who help us about the farm, and the old gentleman smiling at you, Mirren, is their grandad. He used to work here, and he has a place with us at Christmas.' Mirren saw a sprightly old gentleman like Father Christmas himself, waving his stick at her.

'Come and sit beside me,' Martha Allan said to Mirren. 'I remember you when you were a little girl coming with your mother and father.'

'Do you?' Martha Allan had a permanent smile which she kept while she was speaking, and a pulled-in chin, giving the impression of an onlooker, well-pleased with what was going on around her. 'Now, just ask me if there's anyone you don't recognise, and I'll tell you who they are.'

'I think I know everyone, Mrs Allan.' She waved to Grace McFarlane who gave a half-hearted wave in return.

Uncle Roger was at her elbow. 'A toddy, Mirren. I've given you plenty of water in it. They're all whisky drinkers here.' Mirren noticed that Martha Allan was clutching a glass of whisky which looked undiluted. She looked round, and her eyes fell on Jack

Drummond, who raised his glass to her. He was standing beside Grace.

Josh came into the room, resplendent in Highland dress. He caught sight of Mirren. 'Hello!' he called. 'I'm the star turn here!'

'Come on, then, Josh!' Jack Drummond shouted. 'Gie us the Highland Fling!'

'Later, Jack,' Josh said. 'Mother wants you all to drink up. She's taking the turkey out of the oven.'

'Josh decorated the room,' Martha Allan said to Mirren. 'Isn't it lovely?'

'Yes. I noticed it when I came in.' There were garlands of coloured paper strung from the four corners of the room, and hanging from the centre, a large silver ball, which reflected the light from the oil lamps placed round the room. The windows were decorated with tufts of cotton-wool, presumably to resemble snowflakes. The effect with red candles on the window sills was Christmassy, Mirren thought, hoping that the tufts were on the outside in case of fire.

'Roger had electricity put in the house, but he likes lamps at Christmas. It's quite a job filling them and trimming the wicks, but it's only once a year, and Jessie, the maid, doesn't mind. We all help.'

'It's a lovely soft light,' Mirren said.

'Yes, romantic.' Mrs Allan's chin was pulled in, if possible a little further, to emphasise that she approved.

Aunt Margaret's flushed face appeared in the doorway. 'Come on, everybody, before the turkey flies away!' Obediently, they all made for the door. Mirren saw Aunt Meg helping the old man, and she let them pass before she moved. Jack Drummond was at her side.

'I hoped I would see you tonight, Mirren. Thanks for your letter.'

'It was nothing. Josh was telling me you've had more worries – about the barn.'

'Aye...' He was looking straight ahead. 'Whit aboot you and me having a walk tomorrow afternoon?'

'Yes, that would be nice. I think Aunt Meg will want to rest.'

'Good. I'll call for you.'

They moved on to the entrance of the big kitchen. Her Uncle Roger was directing them, flushed and smiling. 'Mirren. You sit on Josh's right. Facing your aunt. That's it. All the family together. And here's Maggie and Tom. You sit beside Mirren. Good. Now, the bairns. My, how they've grown! Old enough to come to a Christmas party, eh?'

Mirren greeted her cousin and her husband, Tom, a speechless young man. 'You must be proud of them, Tom.' He seemed more speechless than ever, and she bent to speak to the little girl. 'Rita, isn't it? What a big girl you've become!'

'They're very shy in company, Mirren,'

Maggie said. 'You won't get a word out of them. Josh is the only one who gets them to speak.'

'What does he do?'

'Tumbles on the floor with them. But today he's too busy. He's a marvel, Josh. Anyone who gets him for a husband will be lucky.'

'I thought Grace was the chosen one,' Mirren said softly, looking around.

'Not by Josh.'

They were interrupted by the serving of the food. Mirren noticed Martha Allan was helping her aunt, and her uncle was busy carving the turkey. 'This is an old custom here, Mirren!' he shouted above the din. 'Christmas turkey is our speciality, and then a good old-fashioned dumpling. Your aunt is a dab hand at that. Done in a cloth.'

'Aye,' Jake Allan said, 'and there's no one can beat Roger at the carving. And yet when it comes to slaughtering any of his beasts on the farm, he turns white!' There was general laughter.

Everyone declared the turkey to be done to a turn and Margaret was duly compliment-ed, and again when it came to the dumpling, which was rich, studded with every variety of fruit and, as if that were not enough, drench-ed with sugar and cream. There was wine for the lily-livered, whisky for the real men, and sherry for the ladies, and when they all got up from the table, everyone seemed merrier than before.

The hall had been cleared of furniture for dancing. Strip the Willow, waltzes and polkas, were soon following fast on each other. More people came in during the evening, when tea and mince pies were served, and they overflowed into the farmyard. In the cold clear night Mirren saw a crescent moon in the blackness of the sky, and heard voices ringing clear in the darkness concealing everything except where the grey stone walls of the farmhouse shone in the moonlight.

'A memorable night for me,' she said to her aunt and uncle when she and Aunt Meg were thanking them and taking their leave.

Jack Drummond offered to take them both home, and in his car they laughed and exchanged anecdotes about the party. Aunt Meg thought Josh's Highland Fling the *tour de force* of the party, but he was clearly a favourite of hers, and she said she would need to take a long rest tomorrow afternoon, as the clootie dumpling had floored her.

'We're quite merry, you see, in Waterside, Mirren,' she said, 'and the next thing to look forward to is the school play and then the social evening in the village hall on Ne'erday.'

'You'll be staying on for that, Mirren,' Jack said.

'I'm afraid not.' She had made up her mind as they spoke.

'I'm taking her for a walk tomorrow afternoon,' he said to Meg, 'while you're resting from the clootie dumpling.'

'Did I say that? Have you asked Mirren?'

'Yes, he has, Aunt. I've decided that the best medicine after the clootie dumpling for me is a good walk.'

'You see, Miss Calder, it's all fixed up behind your back.'

'You're a tearaway, Jack Drummond, but you take good care of my niece, and bring her back safely.'

'I'll do that.'

In the house later, Meg said, 'He's a schemer, that Jack Drummond. But I'm glad to see him cheered up a bit. He's had a lot of trouble recently. Did you want to go with him tomorrow?'

'Well, he asked me at the farm, and I said, yes.'

'Are you going to tell him about Jamie?'

'Yes, I think I will.'

'It's none o' my business, Mirren. You're a young woman now, quite able to run your own affairs. Now I think we should both get off to bed. I'm whacked. What about you?'

'Well, you've just said I'm able to run my own affairs, but I agree with you. So I'll get off to bed too.'

'Oh, I'm getting to be a bossy old woman.

You do what you want, Mirren.'

She craved her bed. She wanted to think of Jamie and not the Christmas party, clear her mind. She felt too far from him here. She'd get back to Glasgow before the social evening at the village hall in case she was swept into that too, she decided.

Jack duly called for her when she was sitting in the parlour waiting for him. Aunt Meg had declared herself worn out and retired to bed. 'It's cold outside,' he said, 'and there's been a sprinkling of snow. Wrap yourself up.'

They set off down the Calder Road, the 'Pech Brae', as Jack called it.

'Do you know what "pech" means?' he asked her as they walked down the slope. He had taken her arm in case she slipped, he'd said.

'Don't worry,' she said, 'my parents came from Waterside. They brought the dialect with them, "pant", isn't it?'

'Right first time, but no' the way down. You'll find out on the road back.'

The river was flowing sluggishly between boulders. They stood on the grassy bank, watching it ripple over the stones and boulders in its path. 'I loved it when I was little,' she said. 'I was allowed to play down here with the older girls who took me, and we waded in, looking for pieces of red stone, which lay about in its bed. We coloured the boulders with this red chalk, each choosing one, and worked away like diligent house-wives. I've often thought of these sunny days, and when I got back to Glasgow with my parents, I thought I had been in a different world. My grandfather's garden was another delight. He used to pick me some roses to take home, they grew over his door, a red one and a white one, and the scent comes back to me still, and for sustenance on the way home, he would give me a piece of rhubarb which he would strip, and a little bag of sugar to dip it in. That conjured up Waterside for me. I always felt I had another life tucked away, a secret life that no one else had.'

They walked along the river bank, Jack saying that they might get to the Falls of Clyde if they hurried on.

For a long time they didn't speak. Mirren thought of Jamie, and the life here in the country which was so different from Glasgow. Would he like it, she wondered, or was he a city man? He had always lived in towns, Manchester and Glasgow, and he had never shown any enthusiasm for the countryside. But she knew so little of him, and so much, she thought. She was walking in a daze of pleasant recollection, when Jack said, 'You're away in the clouds. I hope you're thinking about me?'

'I'm not, Jack,' she said. 'I must be frank.'

'About somebody else?'

'I have to say, yes.'

'Well, I hope it's not important, because I have something to say to you. Would this be too cold for you?' He pointed to a fallen log.

'We could try it and see.'

When they were seated, he put an arm round her and squeezed her to his side. 'Do you remember the barn dance?'

'How could I ever forget it?'

'Don't joke, Mirren, this is serious. I always felt I had got off on the wrong foot with you because of that dance, and yet you were quite friendly when Josh and I came to see you and you and I went to the pictures. To tell you the truth, I can't make you out. You're not like the girls around here, ready for a tare, an' that.'

'Jack...' She thought, Surely I must tell him now, but he silenced her.

'Let me speak. You know I lost ma mither. Well, that was a blow, but since then I've had trouble with that fire. I don't want to go into it, but it's cost me a tidy penny. Anyhow, when I've been sitting alone these last months, I've thought to myself that I need a wife here, I need Mirren. Now, that may surprise you, but to tell you the truth I find you tantalising—'

'That's the last thing I am,' she interrupted.

'Well, to me at any rate. Ma feeling of

220

being not right in myself has made me miserable for a long time until I realised what it was...' He turned to her, and took her hands. 'I want you, Mirren. This is a proposal. Would you consider marrying me?'

'Oh, Jack,' she said, 'this has gone much further than I wanted it to. I wanted to tell you about Jamie, but wondered if I was being presumptuous in thinking that you ... were interested. But I've fallen in love, since I met you. I couldn't think of being married to you, but I would like you for a friend with Josh.'

'You're telling me you're not interested in me.'

'Yes. I'm not used to these situations, Jack, so I don't know if I've behaved badly or not. But I'm in love with someone else, and I think we're going to be happy together, if this old war doesn't get in the way.'

'I wouldn't be called up. And I've got a nice home to offer you, now that Mother's gone.'

'I'm sure someone else would be flattered with your proposal, in fact there must be many girls you know.'

'Aye, plenty. But none that I would want.' He looked at her with tragic eyes, then seizing her by the shoulders, he kissed her roughly. 'There,' he said, breathing hard. 'Does that not make a difference?'

She was shaking. 'No, Jack. I'm sorry. It's

too late. I'm in love.'

He got up from the log and strode about the grass. She sat, feeling miserable and wondering how she, Mirren, had managed to get into such a mess. Had she led Jack on? She didn't think so, and then she remembered being at the cinema with him, and anxious to feel desire again, and encouraging him. I was innocent, she thought. Now I'm not – I'm Jamie's – but I can't tell Jack that.

He came back, and sat down beside her. 'Just subduing masel'. For two pins, I'd have made you change your mind about this Jamie. I suppose he's one of those sophisticated office types you get in Glasgow, bowler hat and rolled umbrella?' He sneered, and she no longer felt sorry for him.

'He's not at all like what you imagine, he's young and enthusiastic, and dying to fly...'

'Well, here's hoping he escapes the Germans when he's up there.'

It was like a sword driving through her heart. It was all right for her to have fears, but she didn't want him voicing her thoughts. Besides there was no comparison between them. Jamie was young, pure, this man was older in everything you could think of except tact. 'I don't like that sort of talk,' she said.

He put an arm round her. 'I didn't mean to hurt you, Mirren. But I'm hurt too, I thought you would be glad to accept my

222

offer. I know many a girl who would jump at it.'

'Do you?' She wanted to say, 'To be your wife, and live in a farmhouse, and work as hard as your mother did?' What a nerve, she thought. Now you're thinking like him, she told herself, but if he were the last man on earth, I wouldn't marry him. 'Well,' she said, 'why don't you ask one of them?'

He turned and looked at her. 'Do you know what you are? A bitch.' His face was ugly.

She was afraid. She got up, and said in her best teacherly tones – she knew it would annoy him, 'I'm not used to that kind of language, Jack Drummond. The matter is closed. I'm going back to Aunt Meg's.'

He rose too. 'I'm disappointed in you. Maybe I've got too big an opinion of myself, but I thought you'd be flattered by my proposal.'

'But I've been honest with you. I told you I was in love with someone else.'

'Aye,' he glared down at her. 'Well, it's a hard one to swallow. I guess I've got my fingers burned. But, to be honest, Mirren, I had never met anyone like you before, you were so cool and yet so fiery. I thought you'd make a good mate for me, but I see I was wrong.'

'I'm sorry, Jack, but it seems we've both made mistakes. I don't think we should continue with this conversation. It's not getting us anywhere. Can we go back now?'

The walk back was distressing to her. Anything she said to him, he answered in monosyllables, and she gave up, hurrying her footsteps. She didn't like this place now. It was too smothered with trees, too lonely, and she was afraid of him. She kept reminding herself that he was a village lad and a friend of her family, but he was obviously upset, and not able to accept her refusal. 'Cheer up, Jack,' she said, when they were at the foot of Calder Hill, the 'pech brae'.

'You don't understand, how dreaming of you got me through. It's a great disappointment to me that you haven't been doing the same.'

'That's it. I've let you down. I'm sorry,' she said, feeling safer as they climbed the hill to the village. It was dusk now, and she put an arm through his. 'Can't we remain friends, Jack?'

'I'm not used to being friends with girls. I don't think of them like that.' He shrugged her away like a child.

'I'm sorry. And I hope you get over your disappointment soon. I'll be going away tomorrow. So you won't have to meet me again.'

He left her at her aunt's gate with a brief 'goodnight', and when she went into the house, she found her aunt in the parlour. She looked up with a bright smile, 'Well, did you enjoy your walk, Mirren? I thought you'd bring Jack in for a cup of tea.'

'No, he's annoyed with me.' She sat down and burst into tears.

'What is it, ma dear, tell your aunty.' Meg got up and put an arm round her. 'He's got a bad reputation, that Jack Drummond. Did he insult you?'

'Far from it!' She looked up, mopping her face. 'Sorry about that. I don't usually cry. Just, I'm glad to be back. I'd never make a country girl, Aunt Meg. Unfortunately.'

'What do you mean, "unfortunately"? We're all very proud of you, just as your mother and father were.'

'He didn't insult me, Aunt. He asked me to marry him. He was disappointed when I refused.'

'Well, you had to, hadn't you? There's...'

'Yes, there's Jamie.'

Chapter 12

It was a peculiar thing, Mirren thought, on the way home, how disassociated she felt when she was in Waterside. Now Glasgow looked almost strange to her as she stood in the Central Station, waiting for her train to Pollokshields. So many people everywhere, so much noise, compared with the quietness of Waterside, with its few roads and stretching pastoral scenery. Was it her roots pulling her when she was there? she wondered. But she had made Glasgow her place, and now there was Jamie to hold her there, or until he was called up.

When she arrived at the entry to the flats, she passed the door of his parents' flat, before she started climbing the stairs. Was he in there, she wondered, and wouldn't it have been nice if she had been able to knock and announce to whoever answered it, 'I'm back!'

Her own flat seemed empty and cold when she got inside, and strangely alien, and she quickly became absorbed in lighting two fires, one in the kitchen and one in the front

226

room, and putting away her clothes when she had unpacked. With the curtains drawn against the cold darkness, she began to feel more secure, and having further settled herself by making a tour of the flat, and plugging in a radiator in the cold bedroom, she felt she could sit down and drink a cup of tea. With the radio turned on for the six o'clock news, she was able to say to herself, 'This is nice, a place of my own. Well, here you are again, Mirren,' she addressed herself in her thoughts, 'a woman on your own with a career. But there's Jamie. When you see him again, everything will fall into place.' She longed to see him. Would he look different since that night, how would she seem to him, perhaps he would get in touch with her soon? She had still a week before she went back to teaching, and he knew that. There was no doubt a small community like Waterside was comforting, but here she had to stand on her own, and the phrase came into her mind, 'Be your own woman.' Remember, she told herself, your father and mother left Waterside because it was too constricting. In the midst of her meandering thoughts, a process of settling, she was beginning to realise, the telephone rang and she fell over a chair in her haste to answer it.

She heard his young, enthusiastic voice when she lifted the receiver. 'Oh, Jamie,' she said, 'I was just thinking about you. I'm so glad you phoned me. It makes you real again.'

'I'm real all right. I've tried each evening in the hope you had just stayed for Christmas and come back. I've never stopped thinking about you – ' his voice lowered – 'since that night.'

'I'm just back. I ran away. I'd had enough of Waterside. I thought of you all the time too.'

'Weren't you enjoying yourself?'

'Oh, yes, I was made very welcome. What about you?'

'It was as I told you. I went with my parents to visit the drunken aunt and her husband again. It's becoming an annual family treat, something that's forced upon you and you haven't the courage to break away from. Mother says, "Poor Phoebe," and father says, "I don't know why John doesn't put a stop to it." I'm afraid my Uncle takes the easy way out. He has a good snifter before we come, to get him through the evening, and she fortifies herself in the kitchen after each course, and a good time is had by all. The pretence that goes on is stifling, and yet, if I didn't go it would cause more trouble than it's worth.'

'Well, never mind, you can call it your good deed for Christmas.'

'Yes, well, that's enough about my affairs. When can I see you?'

'Well, I'm on holiday for another week, so I have all the time in the world.'

'Right. I tell you what. Remember we talked about skating? It's cold enough, and I've been told about a pond near East Kilbride, which is frozen over, and good for skating.'

'East Kilbride?'

'Yes, I know it's far away, but we could take a tram to Burnside, and get a bus or walk from there, or if you don't like that, we could get a train all the way. How about Monday, at five thirty? I'll be working.'

'Right. I'll meet you at Central Station and we'll take the train the whole way. We don't want to wear ourselves out before we start skating. Besides it will be dark. That'll be fun. I'll bring sandwiches.'

'I've got something to tell you. It will be best in the dark.'

'Tell me now.'

'No, I can't.' So his talk about his aunt and uncle had been because he couldn't bear to tell her whatever it was.

She spent Sunday cleaning her flat, and in the afternoon she took the tram to Pollok Park and walked for an hour amongst the trees. It was a damp, cold evening, but no snow, and the pond at East Kilbride would no doubt still be frozen.

When she woke on Monday morning, her room seemed whiter than usual. There was a peculiar light which made her bed look less white than usual, and she pulled the rose-patterned quilt over the counterpane to bring a touch of colour into the room. When she drew aside the curtains she saw that Limes Avenue had been transformed. The pavement and road were covered with snow, and the trees were drooping with its heavy weight. Jamie will already be in his office, she thought, and he'll have his skates with him. I'll have to meet him, and we'll have to make up our minds in the station whether we'll set off or not.

She got ready after she'd had some lunch, dressing in a white Arran jumper, thick enough to keep out the cold, a waterproof jacket, and a white knitted cap with bobbles on top. She wore a short red skirt, and red stockings to match. Carrying her skates, she felt as if she were in an advertisement for Klosters. She had read somewhere it was one of the smart places to go for winter sports.

She saw him from afar off, wearing a zipped jacket, and like her, a knitted cap, and trousers tucked into boots. The inevitable scarf was wound round his neck and tied under his chin. She waved when she drew near, and he hurried towards her. When they met he put his arms round her and kissed her. 'Jamie,' she said, 'it's not the place...'

'It'll do till later.' He took her hand, saying,

'Platform twelve! Come along!' They ran, their skates bumping against their legs, and boarded the train. There were several people in the carriage, and they looked up when they both came in. A lady like Miss Marple, Mirren thought, kept her eyes on them, as they settled down. 'Going skating?' an elderly man addressed them, as if to welcome them into some fraternity.

'Yes,' Jamie said. 'East Kilbride.'

'Quite good.' He nodded judiciously. 'Used to be all right when I was a lad.'

'There can be some terrible accidents on those ponds,' Miss Marple said. 'Be sure and don't skate in the middle. My father used to say that to us.'

Mirren and Jamie said they would be careful, exchanging glances, and she thought, how young Jamie makes me feel compared with Jack Drummond.

She whispered to him, 'I've got something to tell you too.'

He nodded. 'Good.' He sat back, and didn't speak again, until they reached the station. 'East Kilbride!' they heard the porter shout, and as they got up and jumped out, they heard the man who had spoken to them call, 'Good skating!'

'Thank you!' they both shouted. They noticed quite a few people got out after them.

'All locals,' Jamie commented, as they

presented their tickets at the exit. 'How boring to live outside Glasgow and travel into it each day on the same train. I should hate that sort of life.'

That, she thought later, should have given her some sort of warning.

They walked briskly through the village, and found the pond by the directions Jamie had. They saw by the light of the moon that there were a few people skating, and some young people stood round a van which was parked at the side. They joined them, hoping to buy a hot drink. Everyone was in high spirits. The skating was excellent, they were told, and they found a bench at the side of the pond where they took their cups of coffee. Mirren opened her packet of sandwiches, and they sat close together because of the cold. People went skating past them, and they watched and ate, enjoying the scene, the darkness lit only by the moonlight, and diffused by the thick belt of trees round the pond. 'It's like a dream,' she said.

When they were skating together, slowly, as she wasn't as expert as he was, the cold and the movement made her feel excited, and soon glowing with warmth. 'This is marvellous, Jamie,' she said, 'isn't it? I didn't know you were so good.'

'I've been practising, but I love it.'

They stayed on the ice for about half an hour, by which time they were skating round the pond at a fair speed, hands clasped and pleased with themselves, until Mirren took a tumble, and they had to skate back to their bench. Her knee was bleeding through her stocking, and the pleasure of skating had gone for her. She felt shaken and cold. 'Pride goes before a fall,' she said as they sat down. She tied his proffered handkerchief round her knee, and pulled up her stocking again. She felt slightly sick and he put his arm round her. 'Poor you!' he said. 'Shall we call it a day, or a night?'

'Yes, I've had it.' She got up, felt dizzy, and then all right.

On their way back to the village, she said to him, 'Well, what had you to tell me?' He didn't answer. 'Jamie?' she queried.

He turned to her. 'You won't like this, I know. Remember I told you I had volunteered?'

'Yes.' Now her heart felt cold.

'Well, it was a long time ago, when I was at university. I was getting training in the ATC, and I fell in love with the whole idea, of flying, I mean. I filled in a form for a Short Service Commission with the RAF, and sent it off. My father had to sign it too, which he did. I don't think he realised what it meant. Well, it looks as if they are getting desperate for men, because I've had instructions from them to hold myself ready to being called up.'

233

'So, what will that mean?'

'Just that I've been elected to go to a training school in England.' When she looked at him she saw the excitement in his face. His eyes were shining.

'You're pleased?'

'Yes, it's what I've always wanted. I told you. Of course I'll be sorry to leave you. In fact, I daren't think about it. Just when we've met. But there will be leaves, and there's a little time before I go.'

'They won't waste time, I'm sure. Oh, Jamie.' In the dark road she turned to him, and he took her in his arms.

'Try not to worry.'

'It's easy for you to say that. When will you be leaving?'

'In a week's time.'

'Oh, no!'

His cold cheek was against hers. 'It's better this way. The time will soon pass, and you'll be busy teaching. Remember, I love you. And I didn't know you when I volunteered.'

'It doesn't alter your decision. Oh, I realise that! And that there's a war on.'

'That's right. It's "Your Country Needs You" and all that sort of thing. And there will be leaves, and we can write to each other. Who knows? The war might be over by the time I finish my training, so there's no point in worrying too much.'

'I understand, Jamie,' she said. 'Don't say

any more. Your commitment comes before me, us. We aren't the only couple in such a situation. Those who have known each other for a long time, got married, for instance...'

'You're not regretting that night?'

'No. But we didn't wait.' She heard the wail in her voice.

'I don't know many people who do. Aren't you a little old-fashioned?'

'Maybe.' Of course she was, or out of touch with how other young couples were behaving. There were probably thousands of girls willing to take risks, but there was still the stigma ... Yes, she thought, I am old-fashioned. It's how I've been brought up, chance remarks of her parents, attitudes ... old-fashioned was the word. She had been out of touch with how opinions were changing, barriers being broken, because of the war. Of course there had always been girls like Annie, what her parents had thought of as 'bad girls'.

'To tell you the truth, I never thought of getting married,' Jamie said.

She laughed at him, genuinely amused. 'You're too young. It doesn't matter about my age, but you would have to be a lot older for the idea to occur to you.'

'But I love you. If I begin to think when I'm away that we should get married, or if you do, we'll decide. What do you say?'

'All right. It obviously needs more thought.

I'm beginning to believe in that song, "love and marriage, love and marriage", you know?'

'"Go together like a horse and carriage" – yes.' In the darkness on the deserted road, they stood together, looking at each other. I shall remember this night, she thought, the bleakness, a lonely road on the outskirts of Glasgow. Had there been no blackout, the city would have been shimmering in the distance, lying cupped in its hills. From here, we could have seen it easily since we're high. Therein lies my future, or is it in Waterside?

'Well, we've both got each other,' Jamie said. They stood close in the darkness, but didn't kiss.

'But I don't regret it,' she said. He seemed to know what she meant.

'Nor do I. But I'm glad. If I don't come back, I've got that night to look back on.'

'Don't talk like that.' She raised her face to his, and he kissed her.

'You're crying.'

'I know. It's this old war. We haven't been given much time.'

'I'll write you wonderful letters. I feel I get the best of it. It's going to be very exciting for me, whereas you have just to carry on teaching.'

'Perhaps I won't. I might volunteer too.'

When they were walking again, she remembered that she had said she had

236

something to tell him, but there didn't seem much point now in telling him about Jack Drummond. They had enough to think about.

She was back at school again. Of course Jamie had come up to her flat with her, after East Kilbride, and of course they had made love again, this time in desperation at the thought of being parted.

'Shall you tell your parents about me?' she'd asked him.

'Possibly. They know there's someone in my life. But they have never taken me into their confidence, so I don't feel the necessity to take them into mine. I shall send them some money out of my allowance in the RAF.'

'I think that would be good.' Had we got married, she'd thought, I shouldn't have wanted anything from him; then she'd reminded herself that married women weren't allowed to remain in teaching.

She had cried into her pillow in the warm bed which he had left. They had agreed that they would meet in town on the following day to have a talk before he left Glasgow, and they had met in the café in Central Station, 'our café' it was in danger of becoming, she had said.

And now she was back at school, and had been met by the momentous but not

237

surprising news that Alastair and Muriel had become engaged over the Christmas holidays. Muriel had met Alastair's parents, and everyone had been most satisfied with the news. Since, so far, they were in exempted professions, their intention was to get married and look for a dual post in a country school where they would live out their dream, apparently. Annie had been scathing, to Mirren only, and had said to her, 'Typical of men,' which reinforced her belief that she and Alastair had had a short affair.

'We've both given in our notice,' Alastair told them, 'so there will be some changes in the staff.' He looked so happy that Mirren felt sure he was in love with Muriel and she with him.

Tonight the four of them were going to the Rogano to have a meal in celebration, and before that, Annie and Mirren were meeting to buy a present for the happy pair, a present from colleagues, not a wedding present, they had decided.

'Things are certainly moving,' Annie said to Mirren, 'and I've made a decision too. 'I'm going to get a room near Neil. He's been posted to the Territorials at Maryhill. If he gets married quarters there – well, we'll get married.' Everything which was happening reinforced Mirren's belief that people were obviously good at making up their minds when it came to relationships. She

238

was glad to think that she was in the swim, and no longer the innocent daughter of her parents. Where have you been all your life, Mirren? she asked herself several times in the following week.

She and Jamie had met once again. He had rung her yesterday morning at school. 'Mirren, it's come!' She was in no doubt what he meant.

She saw him off at Central Station the following morning. He had persuaded his parents not to come in. The train which went from Platform One seemed busy. It was going to London, and there was a febrile air, she thought, amongst the porters and travellers. She saw a few men in uniform and a girl in ATS dress, surrounded by friends.

She and Jamie clung together, speechless, until he said, 'Better be off. I'll write.'

'It's come too soon. Take care of yourself.'

'Same goes for you.' His look was loving, but his eyes were full of excitement. He went striding up the platform, away from her, not looking like anyone but Jamie yet. Soon he would be kitted out, and he would know he was in the RAF. It was what he wanted.

She was behind the barrier. A woman was standing beside her. 'Is yours away too?' she asked.

'Yes,' Mirren said.

'To hell with this war! A'm gawn fur a drink noo. Wid ye like tae come?'

'No, thanks,' Mirren said. 'I've to get back to school.' She had telephoned Alastair with the excuse of a headache, so that she could see Jamie off, and he had said, brusquely, 'Get back as soon as you can. Take an aspirin.'

'Tae school?' The woman looked at her curiously. 'D'ye mean, like yin o' these typin' colleges, you know, that yin?' She screwed up her face. 'A canna mind the name.'

'Skerry's?'

'Aye, that's it. Aye. Where you become a typist. I'd like that fur ma youngest. She's bright, give her her due.'

Book 3

Chapter 1

1940

Suddenly Mirren was aware of the war. 'There's a war on' was no longer an empty phrase. Up till 1940, she appeared to have been living life from her own point of view, with one-way spectacles.

There had been her time at the university in the old flat, her parents' death, and her meeting with Jack Drummond at Waterside, moving to Pollokshields, teaching, then Jamie. I've been completely self-absorbed, she thought, now that he had gone.

Other people surely were able to stand on the outside and comprehend what was happening around them. Not so she. For the first time in her life someone else was there, unlike her parents, to worry about, not a filial concern as it had been for them, but someone whose eyes she could see through,

Jamie's eyes, and having to read the news and understand where she stood in relation to the world, and him.

His letters were not numerous, but then she could understand that. His perspective had changed, he was in a new milieu which changed as he was posted from one place to the other. Sometimes his letters came from Croydon, other times, South Wales.

I've never known tiredness like this. We're at it from morning to night, assimilating lectures, learning to fly, which incidentally is the best way of getting to know oneself. Remember I told you about Antoine de Sainte-Exupéry. I'm experiencing all the feelings he described so well, the loneliness up there, sometimes the elation, the terror ... but the best thing is comparing notes with the men like me engaged in the same discovery. We have such a bond, we hardly have to express it, but it becomes a love, a caring for each other.

So far I've distinguished myself in the air, but not on the ground. I'm bad at navigation, and I've given myself a few frights which I shan't forget, but that is outweighed by this other element I've discovered for myself, a natural one, denied to most of us, but now mine. And when you do something right, the elation can only be compared to the times you and I were together and I seemed to have been granted the gift of knowing what life was all about ... I have to stop myself when I go on like this.

I think a lot about you, Mirren, darling, and I'm sorry now I didn't tell my parents about you. I find it difficult to write to them, they kept from me things I should have known, my path had to be cleared for me, even Father signing my form of entry for a short commission was done without query, because I wanted it. I realise they were activated by the kindest of motives, but it only succeeded in isolating me from them.

If you ever feel you would like to speak to them, take your courage in both hands and call and see them, and say we write to each other, that there is a bond between us ... anything to make them realise what we mean to each other. Perhaps you would find it easier than I did.

Perhaps it's not fair to tell you how much I'm enjoying myself, and about the comradeship of the other men. Most of them have somebody they write to and we exchange photographs. I haven't one of you, nor you, me. For a lark we all went to Croydon one day and had our photographs taken in uniform, we must have seemed like a gaggle of laughing schoolboys. I enclose the result. Could you get one done and send it to me? We all keep them in our breast pockets as a lucky charm.

I love you, love you. I don't see much prospect of leave at the moment. I'm on three-monthly courses, and although we get rest periods in between, it hasn't been possible to make the journey to Glasgow. It's nice here amongst the hills of Wales, peaceful...

Please write to me and tell me all you're doing. I sometimes wish we'd had more background together, but we never had a chance to do any of the normal things which most people do. I remember that night when we skated, the moonlight and the noise of laughter coming to us from the other skaters as we sat close together on our bench, and how pathetic you looked when you hurt your knee and wanted to be comforted.

Things are hotting up on the war front. Our boys have been in Bremen, and we're told we'll be in it soon if we work hard and don't make any stupid mistakes. We relax sometimes in chairs by a log fire here, or in the pub with a pint, and talk about it, long to be in it. As yet there's no feeling of fear about the prospect. Better stop now.

I send you my dearest love,
Jamie

Things were different at school now. Muriel and Alastair had departed for a country school in Ayrshire, and Annie had left. Neil had been in the Middle East and had been injured at Sidi Barrani, and when he returned home, they had got married, and were living in married quarters at Maryhill. They had had a little girl, and Mirren visited them there. They seemed to be supremely happy. Neil, whom she hadn't met before, was a rangy young man on crutches (he had broken his leg the first week he was in the Army) and looked as if events had happened too quickly in his life for him to comprehend. He seemed devoted to Annie and his little daughter. Annie appeared to run his life for him and took care of the baby, as if they were both her children. 'They both need me,' she said to Mirren. 'We're happy. I don't know if Neil will go back, but he'll get a good pension, and I'll get a job in one of the factories. He can look after Bessie.' She had made her peace with the war, Mirren thought.

She was racked with worry about Jamie. He now had his wings, and had been moved to the south coast, and was flying in sorties from there. His letters became fewer and fewer. Life for him was a routine of sleeping, eating, flying, but he seemed to be still enjoying it, and still talked about the elation he had first felt.

Just before the school closed down for Easter, she got a shock. Aunt Meg wrote to tell her that Grace McFarlane and Jack Drummond were getting married.

She was always in his house helping him, and she didn't seem to care that the village talked about her. People made snide remarks about Josh, saying that Jack had pipped him at the post, and worse, and the village has been in a turmoil of gossip all through the winter. You wouldn't think there was a war on.

Have you had an invitation to the wedding? If you're going to accept, there's your wee room here waiting for you, I know you've been busy with the school and your extra war work. You could do with a rest.

It was true. She was more than busy at school. She had two pupil teachers and a qualified teacher, Mrs Thompson, a widow, and Mirren had been appointed in Alastair's place. She found the work tiring, the pupil teachers needed a lot of training, and she was always rushing into Glasgow to the canteen at night. She would be glad of the break at Waterside during the spring holiday.

The invitation to the wedding duly arrived. She hadn't thought she would be included, but she guessed it might be Jack's way of telling her about his marriage to Grace. Also she would like to see Josh.

She duly wrote and accepted; she was having a week off, which would cover the date of the wedding, April 12th, and also told her aunt she would like to come and stay with her over that date. It was fitting in nicely, she thought. As well as the canteen, she had taken on weekend work at a children's hospital where she was an auxiliary nurse, filling in for the full-time ones who had volunteered for the Army. Altogether, she did her best to quieten her conscience that she was not doing enough for the war. Annie was working in an aircraft factory full-time, and Mirren's old friend, Jessie, whose husband had been called up, had volunteered for the WAAF (her grandmother was taking care of their two children). Everybody was anxious to do their bit, and she tried to instil this outlook into her pupils, giving them weekly talks on the progress of the war, and how they could help.

In spite of what Jamie had said about his parents, she had never called on them, nor had she seen them, and passing their door daily she had occasional qualms. When she came back from Waterside she would do it, she promised herself. She wanted to be honest with them.

She enjoyed shaking off the worries of living in Glasgow, which had been with her throughout the winter. Her mind, also, had been full of anxiety about Jamie's safety, the running of the school, the dashing across the city to the canteen at Hope Street, then at weekends going out to Carmyle, where the children's hospital was situated. Food was scarce. Since she had only one ration book, her supplies were strictly limited, and her Aunt Meg had assured her she would 'feed her up' when she came to stay. She had to admit that the appeal of a soft-boiled fresh egg with toast, was strong. And she would probably indulge her passion for cream, which she remembered her Uncle Roger giving her in a full gill can, 'for your porridge, Mirren', when she had stayed with them as a child.

She got a taxi to Aunt Meg's house. The usual warm welcome awaited her, with apologies. 'I don't see much of Jack nowadays, so I couldn't ask him to pick you up. The same goes for Josh. Margaret tells me he's become very quiet, but she doesn't think he's missing Grace. I don't think he was keen on her,' her aunt commented. 'They were seemingly good friends, and Grace was the one who was keen on getting married.'

They sat down that night after they had eaten, to have a 'good crack'. 'Tell me, then, what's Glasgow like these days?' her aunt asked.

'Much the same as usual. There's a feeling of waiting for something to happen, and we all try to do our best to help. I have training sessions in the school, about wearing gas masks and cookery and so on, but luckily the children treat it as a game. I've been very lucky, but we all feel we should do our best. If the men are too old to volunteer for the Army, they volunteer for jobs at home, the Home Guard and so on. I look at the huge balloons in the sky to deflect enemy aeroplanes, and wonder when Hitler is going to strike. "Be Prepared" is the battle cry.'

'Aye. We don't know anything about it here. We're living in cloud cuckoo land. I lost a very good friend in the last one. I sometimes wonder if we would have got round to getting married. How about your Jamie?'

'He's in the Air Force.'

'No' flying one o' these Spitfires?'

'Yes, and he loves it. He always wanted to fly.'

'Where is he now?'

'On the south coast.'

'Probably waiting for the invasion. I didn't believe what the papers said, then one by one, I saw the signposts being taken down at every crossroads, and I realised that they meant business.'

'Oh, they mean business all right, and Churchill recognises that.'

'You said Jamie's parents lived very near you. Do you go in and have a cup of tea with them sometimes and give them all the news?'

'No.' She hung her head.

'What is it, lass?' Aunt Meg's hand was on her shoulder.

'It's a strange situation. His parents know nothing about me, and although Jamie loves me, I don't think he ever tied it up with getting married. He suggested in his last letter that I should call and see them. They live in a flat beneath me.'

'In the same close?'

'Yes, strange, isn't it? I called to see them when I first moved in, but that was before Jamie and I fell in love ... it's a funny situation, Aunt. He lives on another planet from most people. I think he only feels at home when he's flying.'

'Is he young for his age?'

'About ordinary things, yes. He's had a strange upbringing. You know how involved I was with my parents, well, he seems to be quite different from that.'

'He sounds as if he has to grow up. Being in the Air Force will do that for him.'

'Yes. He's asked for a photograph of me.' She laughed, and the tears rushed into her eyes. 'That's the first normal thing I've noticed.' And there's another thing, she thought, remembering the feel of his naked body.

'Everybody's different. What age is he, Mirren?'

'Two years younger than me.'

'Oh, well, he seems quite normal. I'm glad you've told me about him. Now, if you get worried, you need someone to talk to. I'm getting the phone in too, so we can speak that way. We'll keep in touch.'

They discussed the wedding of Jack and Grace, and her aunt said it was the talk of the village. 'Grace wanted a white wedding, even though there was a war on. They're both alike these two, fighters, heads up, they don't mind being talked about, and they'll show the village ... I think that's the general idea.'

'Will Josh go?'

'Yes, I'm sure he will. His father and mother will be there. One of the jokes that go round the village is that Josh will be the best man.'

'Oh, no! I can't see Josh agreeing to that. He hasn't the same temperament as them.'

'You're right. Oh, well, the whole thing is a nine-day wonder. It even eclipses the war!'

'It would be difficult to do that.' Villages, Mirren thought, so self-centred. She'd hate that. She was glad she lived in a city.

Chapter 2

Mirren had decided that her black dress was too funereal for a wedding. Besides, it was too closely associated with Jamie – it was his dress, she thought. Instead she bought a patterned chiffon dress, with a large-brimmed hat picking out the dominant colour, cerise. The hat suited her, as large brims suit all small-featured women. I'm like a mouse peeping out of its hole, she thought, not realising that it gave her a slightly pathetic yet winsome look.

'You'll outdo the bridesmaids,' Aunt Meg said. 'I bet you bought that outfit in Daly's. You couldn't find that style anywhere else.'

Josh picked them up in an old farm Ford. His father and mother had gone on before. He looked admiringly at her. 'The town comes to the country,' he said. 'Is it you under that brim, Mirren?'

She took it off and rested it on her knees. 'I'm hiding,' she said.

'I think that's what people expected me to do.'

She was sitting beside him at the front. She

didn't know if Aunt Meg would hear their conversation. 'Are you hurt by Grace and Jack deciding to get married?'

'What can I say? In one way, yes, but if I look at it the other way, I think Jack's done me a favour.' He lowered his voice as he spoke, and she decided to leave the subject. Was he implying that it took the pressure off him?

When Jack and Grace walked down the aisle together, Mirren thought they both had the same expression on their faces, chins up, smiling, confident: 'You can talk all you like, and feel sorry for Josh, but it doesn't affect us.'

The reception was held in a hotel in Hamilton, and again, she was sitting beside Josh. Aunt Meg had been picked up at the church by Margaret and Roger. Josh was quiet, and Mirren decided she wouldn't talk about the wedding pair. 'You won't be called up, then, Josh? I have a friend in the RAF and he says things are hotting up.'

'They certainly are. If there's anybody I admire, it's the boys in the RAF. They're going to bear the brunt of it soon.'

'Don't say that,' she said involuntarily.

'I'm sorry. I expect you're worried about your friend.'

'Yes, I am. But he seems to be like the rest of them, enjoying the challenge. He says it's a wonderful sensation to be in the air, alone.

It's what he'd always dreamt of.'

'I envy them. I worry about not taking part in the war. Jack always said we should consider ourselves lucky, but it would be impossible for me to volunteer. I suggested it to father, and he looked quite shocked. He says he's dependent on me to help him. I suggested perhaps three land girls might take my place, but he didn't take the hint. As a matter of fact, he doesn't look too well these days. Kind of tired.'

'I know how you feel. I have a job where I'm depended upon, and I do some war work, but I still feel it's not enough. I feel that, like Jamie, I should be doing more.'

'Is that your friend's name, Jamie?'

'Yes.'

When they got to the hotel, her place was marked between Josh and his father. He wasn't the Uncle Roger she remembered. His zest for life had seemingly diminished, he looked decidedly older, all his liveliness gone. He seemed to be on a different plane from her, and although he listened to her with attention he had changed. The war touches the older generation too, she thought.

'How does the war affect you in Glasgow, Mirren?' he asked, as if he knew what she was thinking.

'It seems to be hitting us now. Just a general awareness. Do you read the papers,

254

Uncle?'

'Oh, aye. Things don't look good. London will get it first. They tell me it's all sand-bagged. But I have faith in Churchill. He'll see us through, and the RAF. That Douglas Bader in his Hurricane! What do you think of that for courage, and him losing both legs?'

'He calls them his tin legs. He must be a splendid example to them all.'

'Aye, we're all depending on the RAF to keep Hitler back. But this is gloomy talk at a wedding. Here's Jack's Uncle John on his feet.'

It must be an ordeal for Uncle Roger, this wedding, Mirren thought, but compared with the war, there was nothing to grieve about. Jack and Grace certainly looked as if they were enjoying themselves. She looked over at the table where they sat in its centre, and her eyes met Jack's. He raised his glass to her.

The speeches went on and on, becoming more farm-like in their innuendo, the laughter more raucous. Two of Jack's friends spoke, hinting that there would be a few girls disappointed in Waterside today, which was greeted by applause, and 'Good old Jack'. Mirren, watching him, didn't see any embar-rassment, and when he got up to speak, he raised his glass to Grace, saying he had won the hand of the best-looking girl in the

255

village, and 'I should know,' this being greeted with applause and knowing looks. He looks like a man who's won a prize at the County Show, she thought, and nodded when Aunt Meg, on her other side, said, 'Quite pleased with himself, Jack.'

The floor was cleared for dancing, and Mirren seemed to be popular with the young men. Most of them knew her as the Stewarts' niece, and they were much friendlier than the girls. She was able to have a word with Grace, who asked her, chin in the air, if she was 'surprised'.

'Surprised? Why should I be surprised?'

'Well, the last time you were here, I was Josh's girlfriend, but some folk are too slow in coming forward.'

You can't say that about Jack, Mirren thought, remembering him at the barn dance, and afterwards, when he had come up to Glasgow with Josh.

'One thing,' Grace said, 'Jack won't be called up. He owns the farm. With Josh, there's a possibility that he might be, since his father could get land girls in Josh's place.'

'Well, Jack being exempt must be a relief for you, Grace.'

'Aye. We'll settle doon in his folks' house, and rear a fine wee family.'

'You seem to have a good future ahead for you. I wish you all the best.'

She and Aunt Meg discussed the wedding

day over a last cup of tea. They hadn't the appetite for anything more. 'For war time, the food at the wedding had been generous,' Mirren said.

'That reminds me,' her aunt said. 'Your Uncle Roger left a fine gill of cream for you, and some fresh eggs.'

'Well, that sounds great! You and I will share them before I go away.'

'No, there's no need for that. Folks around here don't forget me.'

'By the way, Aunt, what do you think of Uncle Roger's appearance these days? I saw a decided difference in him this time.'

'Margaret hasn't said anything to me. But you confirm what I've been thinking too. He's no' himsel'. But Roger has always kept his feelings to himself. He'll be depending on Josh to help him with the farm.'

'Yes. I suppose. Well, everyone has their own worries these days, but I didn't see any sign of that with Jack and Grace.'

'No. They deserve each other. I just wonder how that marriage will go?'

'Time will tell.'

'There's a few wagging tongues already. I keep thinking of you, Mirren, and your worries about Jamie. You've got no parents to support you. When I get my telephone it will help people to get in touch with me quicker. If I'm needed. I think we'll see a rise in the birth rate amongst lassies who've had their boyfriends called up.' She added, 'I mean in Waterside.'

She thinks she's sailing close to the wind with that comment, Mirren thought, but her worries about being pregnant had long since disappeared.

'Nothing to what there will be in Glasgow,' she said.

'I haven't been too careful in what I've said.' Her aunt laughed. 'No, you're not the kind, Mirren.' Was that a compliment, or not? she wondered. 'I just mean that if you get worried, or sad, or get bad news, don't forget your old aunty's here. Just ring me up and we'll have a nice crack on the phone.'

'I'll do that, Aunt. I've only got you.' Should she tell her about Jamie's parents?

She felt in the train that she had been living in a different land. But Glasgow Central with all the bustle brought her down to earth. As she scoured the noticeboard for her train to Pollokshields, she felt glad to be back, with the prospect of plenty to do. There was a rhythm about Glasgow life, or was it the routine which she had missed in Waterside? You haven't travelled enough, she thought, to see what it's like in other places. Did she need a structure to her life? A husband – which took her back to thinking about Jamie. He had said that if the idea occurred to either one of them, they were to say. She made up her mind as she wrote, that she was ready now. She was beginning to feel that there was something missing from her life, companionship. She had never made many friends; she had learned to like living alone. It wouldn't matter where you lived, she told herself, you take your personality with you.

When she got home, she sat down and wrote the letter to Jamie.

I've just been to a wedding at Waterside, two friends there. I must admit, Jamie, that I wished I was married too. I would feel I could then go ahead, loving you, having you to write to, and feeling we belonged. I'm surprised to hear myself saying that, because I've always been an independent girl. The war is affecting most people's lives. I want it to be known that if affects mine, not some hole and corner affair that only you and I know of.

No, I haven't been to see your parents, but I thought if you asked me to marry you when you get some leave, we could come out in the open. I want the whole world to know, I want to be recognised.

When I read this through, it's like me proposing to you, but the war has changed everyone's thinking, stripping away any subterfuge.

I think of you constantly, and I want to do that, knowing you are my husband, not someone I slept with twice.

I sat down to write you an account of the wedding I went to at Waterside, and to tell you that the photographer took a picture of me. He promised to send it to me, and when I get it, I'll send it on to you.

Well, I've never proposed to anyone before. I hope you don't get too much of a shock, and that you understand how I feel.

Yours, Mirren (that's how I feel)

Chapter 3

In the days following writing her letter to Jamie, Mirren bitterly reproached herself. His mind would be fully occupied with flying. She shouldn't have troubled him. She knew what had made her write. There had been the wedding, then the weddings of Annie and Jessie, and other people she had heard about. Everyone seemed to be jumping into marriage if they had boyfriends. Another thing disturbed her. When she went to the children's hospital at the weekend, she often had to nurse the babies, and when she and another nurse were changing beds, she would lift the child in her arms. The emotion she felt was keen enough to surprise her. The children in the hospital were frail, generally tubercular, and the feeling of protectiveness overwhelmed her. This was a far cry from teaching, something fundamental, and natural, and she would think, I could have had a baby with Jamie, something of his to take care of. She was surprised at the depth of her feeling. One of the nurses had said to her, 'You cuddle these children as if they were your own. I've got two. You soon lose that feeling when you've got to get up in the middle of the night when they're bawling their heads off.'

And her conversation with Uncle Roger about things 'hotting up' seemed to be coming true.

Her photograph came from Waterside, showing a slim girl holding on a large hat with her face in shadow. The wind was blowing her skirt round her legs, and she thought it would do, although her face was hidden but her legs weren't. She wrote a short note to Jamie, enclosing it, telling him that she was thinking of him all the time, and wondering if he had got her last letter.

There hadn't been anything in the papers about Spitfires, but she supposed they escorted the bombers who were bombing the towns on the Ruhr. 'Take care, Jamie,' she wrote. 'I'm looking forward to our life together when you come back.'

Yes, she thought, 'hotting up' was the right expression. President Roosevelt, she read, had said that the United States was not liable to attack, because of the German successes. How can we escape? she thought. Someone at the canteen said there was a rumour that American troops were being shipped to the Gareloch for disembarkation to Glasgow.

With renewed zeal she drilled the children at school in evacuation, and at night the picture stayed in her mind of them all assembled in the playground, their gas-masks over their shoulders, their faces excited at the unknown prospect. Their numbers had depleted, as some parents had taken the offer to evacuate their children to the country, but many of them had straggled back, preferring home comforts and busy streets to the peace and quiet of the countryside. She instigated a weekly meeting at the school for women whose men were in the forces, so that they could talk with one another. The difference in the attitudes of the women was surprising to her. The ones who worked on night shifts talked about the extra money they earned, and how they went up to town for a 'tare', others looked worried and worn out. She realised it was an attitude of mind, and hoped she was setting the women a good example, although they wouldn't know how her heart ached for Jamie.

The time wore on, and there was no letter from him. Sometimes when she passed his parents' door she longed to ring the bell, in the hope that they would invite her in and they would have a good talk with each other, comparing letters, remembering him, perhaps they would have photographs of him at various ages, the young Jamie, but only the blank door faced her. Funnily enough, she never saw Mrs Campbell in the shops, nor her husband, perhaps standing at the car stop – it was as if they had been spirited away.

At the end of May there was the great evacuation from Dunkirk. Mirren knew Jamie would be involved in fighting the Germans in the air, and daily expected news, but none came. The newspapers were gloomy, but as Aunt Meg said on the phone, 'Trust Churchill to turn defeat into victory,' quoting his stirring messages to the country, but Mirren heard many stories of the scenes on the beaches. The graphic descriptions came from soldiers in the canteen, who had been put on the train to Glasgow. They seemed dazed, like men who had been permanently wounded, although most of them showed no apparent damage. 'I saw

British shoot British in a frenzy,' one man told her, 'men who were hanging on to the laden boat I was in, being shot. Watching their bodies floating in the water as we sailed away, was a picture I'll never forget. One had his fist raised, and was cursing our skipper ... a terrible sight. But the greeting we got when we landed at Dover was amazing. There were scores of people there helping us, giving us cups of tea, blankets, and then we were put on the train ... "Take me back to dear old Blighty",' he said. 'We haven't any songs like that, have we?'

The morning came when a letter dropped through her letter-box from Jamie. She had looked at it for a long time before she dared open it.

Dear Mirren,
    Too tired to write much. We're at it day and night. Got your picture, and it's safely in my breast-pocket. It's lovely. A windswept maiden! We all think we'll get leave after this. So many of us shot down. The sadness in my heart for them is indescribable. Now I'm fighting in revenge for their deaths, not my country. See you very soon, I hope. Prepare the fatted calf.
    Your loving Jamie

She was overjoyed, and telephoned her aunt immediately to give her the good news.

'He seems to be a survivor, Mirren. You must go on thinking that,' she said. 'Now, what's the news here? Aye, sadly Roger's been diagnosed with cancer, and Josh is virtually running the farm. And Grace is expecting a baby any day now. Otherwise we go on here very much as we always did, quite jecoe, and much better than those in towns, I fancy. Have you shared your good news with Jamie's parents?'

She hadn't. She argued that if he was getting leave he must have told them and thought she would wait until he was here, and then he would take her to see his parents, and say, 'Mother, Father, this is Mirren, the girl I'm going to marry.' She had seen the scene so often in her mind, that she had begun to half-believe in it. This feeling was so strong that one morning when she met Mrs Campbell in the grocer's, and they exchanged comments about Dunkirk, she found herself saying, 'Your son is away, Mrs Campbell, isn't he?'

'Yes,' she replied, looking enquiringly at Mirren.

'I hope you get good news of him,' Mirren said, faltering, and only now anxious to get away. It had been a mistake. The woman looked frail, her eyes sunk in her head, and Mirren suddenly ashamed of herself, moved away, saying, 'Must get on. Nice to meet you.'

The following morning, as she was preparing to leave the flat for school, she heard her doorbell ringing. When she dashed to the door, thinking it was the paper boy, she found Mr and Mrs Campbell standing there.

'Oh, hello,' she said. She was shocked at their appearance. Jamie, she thought, and then, saying his name, 'Jamie...' She stood looking at them, and felt a rush of dread, like a wave, flooding over her. She put out a hand to the wall to steady herself.

'May we come in?' Mr Campbell said.

'Yes, please...' She led the way to the front room.

When she had seated them on the sofa, she said, 'It's Jamie, isn't it?'

She didn't know where this calmness came from. She still felt dizzy, and sat down on a chair opposite them.

'I've lost my boy,' Mrs Campbell said.

Mr Campbell produced a letter from somewhere. 'The news came in this morning's post.' He handed it to her.

She only read the first few words, 'We regret to inform you...'

'How did you know about Jamie and me?' She raised her head to them. Mrs Campbell's face was buried in her handkerchief. She shook her head.

Mr Campbell put his arm round his wife's

shoulders, and looked at Mirren. 'I just don't understand—'

'Our time together was so short. We only knew each other for a few weeks before he went away. I think he must have felt it too difficult to tell you.'

'I don't understand...' Mrs Campbell repeated. 'We've sacrificed everything for him, and now he's gone...'

Mirren sat, transfixed. The school, she was thinking, and we'll have to have a talk. 'Will you both sit there and I'll go and phone my deputy, Mrs Thompson, to start the school without me. And I'll make a cup of tea ... just, don't go away...'

She telephoned the school, and said she would be there as soon as she could, that she'd had bad news, then went into the kitchen, and ran water into the kettle, watching her own movements, thinking, how can I do anything as mundane as this when Jamie's gone? She would like to throw herself on her bed, and weep, but there were his parents, she would have to help them somehow, the tragedy was theirs, their son, their only son ... she waited for the kettle to boil, then jolted herself into thinking, cups and saucers, and biscuits, had she bought any yesterday, yes, there were some in the tin fortunately, but who would want to eat biscuits when Jamie was dead, dead ... she repeated the word several times, trying to make the fact sink in, but all she felt was a sense of nausea and dizziness. Is this grief, she asked herself, as she assembled teapot and cups and saucers, milk, sugar, very little left, she hoped they didn't take it, but these are sweet biscuits, that should make up. She pushed open the door, and went in, putting the tray on a table beside her chair. One glance had let her see them, sitting straight, waiting.

'We've been talking, Miss Stewart...' Mrs Campbell said.

'Mirren.'

'Mirren. We realise that the news is as much of a shock to you as it is to us. We have to share our grief.' Her voice suddenly wailed, and she put her handkerchief to her eyes. 'But I don't understand Jamie...'

'There's nothing to understand, Mrs Campbell, we met when I called at your house, we fell in love, time rushed past for us, I knew he had volunteered, the time was precious, maybe that's why he didn't tell you about me...'

'I can see that,' Mr Campbell said. 'But now we've lost our son, and you've lost him too, although it's difficult for us to...' He hesitated.

'To understand,' Mrs Campbell said.

Mirren felt a flash of anger. If she says that again, I'll go mad, what is there to understand, Jamie and I fell in love, I've lost him.

'I know it's bad for you,' she said. 'But it's bad for me too. I don't know how I'm going to be able to...' Keep your tears, Mirren, they'll go soon, then you can throw yourself on that bed, where you and he ... Say something, they're waiting for you to say something ... 'How did you know Jamie and I were...?'

It was Mr Campbell who answered. 'We were sent his effects, your photograph was amongst them. There were other things, his watch which we gave him when he graduated—'

'It's funny how you recognise people by their gait...' she said. 'That's how I knew you, or thought I knew you as the man Dad and I had met in the park, your gait, it's the most important thing about anybody...' What's that got to do with it? she asked herself.

'The way you were looking up from under your hat, and your stance...' he said.

'I know what you mean,' she said to help him. 'Oh, I haven't poured out your tea.' She filled the cups and passed one to Mrs Campbell first, who took it with a trembling hand. Her eyes were brimming over with tears.

'Sugar?' she asked. The woman shook her head. 'A biscuit? They're sweet.' She shook her head again.

'We've just left our breakfast,' Mr Campbell said. 'We had to come and see you right away.'

'Just tea for you, then. Sugar?' How did she manage to go through this rigmarole?

'A little if you can spare it. I'm afraid I've a sweet tooth.'

'He generally takes two teaspoonfuls,' Mrs Campbell said, in a hostessy voice.

'I can spare it. I don't take any.' She handed Mr Campbell his tea, then sat down again, opposite them.

'We'll go when we finish this,' Mrs Campbell said. 'Then you can get back to school. Do you teach near here?'

'Yes, the Primary. But I shan't go in today. I couldn't face them all ... I'll maybe go out, wander...' like a lost soul amongst the crowds, saying, 'Jamie, Jamie, Jamie...' over and over ... put on my black dress, his dress, very appropriate ... She realised another silence had developed and it was up to her to break it.

'Have you relatives to tell?' she asked.

'Only a brother and his wife,' Mr Campbell said. 'They live on the other side. We only visited them at Christmas. Jamie came with us. There aren't any other nephews or nieces, "not very prolific," John used to say. He and Phoebe have no family, nor had my elder brother. My wife had only one sister and she's unmarried. So there's no one to tell.'

270

'Except friends,' Mrs Campbell said. Her husband nodded.

'Yes, there are friends.' And me, Mirren thought, me.

They finished their tea and got up to go. They were very awkward with each other. Mrs Campbell had stopped crying.

At the door Mrs Campbell said, 'Come down and see us in the afternoon and we'll talk.'

'Yes, do that,' Mr Campbell said, looking relieved. 'That might help all of us.'

'Mind the stairs,' Mirren said to them when they turned away. Jamie had slid down on the banister, hadn't he? One of the nights. Or was that a dream?

When she had shut the door behind them, she ran to her bedroom and threw herself down on the bed, burying her head in the pillow. You'll never feel Jamie again near you, his nakedness. All their future gone ... the tears came, like, like, the Falls of Clyde, she thought, searching for a metaphor. Who had told her about the Falls of Clyde? Jack Drummond. Waterside. She'd have to telephone Aunt Meg and tell her that Jamie no longer existed for her, for anyone. How had it happened? Had he been shot down into the sea? She saw his head above the water, his arms raised. Or had he hurtled through the air in his Spitfire? Would he be able to say to himself, 'This is how I wanted it,' like

Antoine Sainte-Exupéry, his hero? Would he have time to think of her, regret that they would never meet again? 'Oh, ye'll tak' the high road, and I'll tak' the low road,' she remembered the song. 'But me an' my true love will never meet again.' They said if you were drowning all your life went whirling past your eyes ... but what was it like if you went hurtling through the air, strapped into a box with wings? She hadn't had any information from his parents about how he ... They would tell her when she went downstairs to see them ... the tears were drowning her ... and then she turned over in the bed and pressed the pillow to her, the one his head had rested on, and began a monologue, repeating his name over and over again, 'Oh, Jamie, Jamie, Jamie, where are you?' That was the question you always asked when you lost someone dear to you, perhaps if she had been a believer she would have known the answer...

The outdoor bell sounded in her ears. Was it the Campbells? They had something to tell her they had forgotten. She lay listening to what sounded like imperious ringing, got up slowly, examined her face in the three-sided mirror on her dressing-table, and wiped it with her handkerchief ... The bell sounded again. She went to the door, stood inside it for a second, and then opened it. It wasn't the Campbells.

'Oh, Mrs Thompson, I'm sorry. I've had bad news, come in, please...'

'I thought I'd come round to your house, it's lunchtime, but we were all worried.'

'Yes, come in, please...' She led the woman into the front room. The tray was still there with the cups and saucers, milk and sugar, and biscuits. 'Sit down, Mrs Thompson. I'll make you...' She sat on the same chair she had sat on facing the Campbells. 'The thing is...' She buried her face in her hands. 'Oh, I don't know what I'm going to do.' The tears suddenly came.

'You make yourself comfortable on this sofa.' Mrs Thompson had stood up and put her arm round Mirren's shoulders. She helped her to lie back, placing a cushion in the corner for her head. 'Oh, poor dear, that's more comfortable, isn't it? Would you like me to make a cup of tea for you...?'

'No, thanks. I've had some. Oh, that's very rude, what about you?'

'I had a cup before I left the school. Have you any aspirin?'

'Yes, in the bathroom cupboard.'

'I'll get them. Let it go, let it go.' She produced a handkerchief from her handbag and handed it to Mirren. 'There you are, cry your heart out, and you'll feel better.'

She was glad Mrs Thompson took a long time to find the pills. It gave her a precious space. She wept and wept, and found she was repeating Jamie's name over and over again, as she had done in her bedroom. The sound of it in her ears, seemed to contain all her sorrow, 'Jamie, Jamie, Jamie.' When she looked up after an unconscionable time, she saw Mrs Thompson was in the chair opposite her, holding a glass of water and the pills...

'You've had bad news. Was it your boy-friend?'

She nodded her head. 'My lover,' she wanted to say. 'I don't feel I can come to school...'

'Of course, you can't. I've talked it over with the two girls, and we've let the children go home after lunch. I hope I did right?'

'That was wise. But I'll be in tomorrow morning. I'll get over this...'

'Have you got anyone who'll be with you?'

'Oh, yes – ' she didn't know where the words came from – 'his parents are quite near.'

'That's good, then. I'll go now and give you a ring in the evening. I know what you're going through, I lost my husband, not in the war, but a death's a death, it takes a lot of getting used to. Have you a minister?'

'No, I'm not a member of any church here. I haven't been in this flat long.'

'I could phone the nearest one...?' The woman was being kind, but she was an intrusion, she wanted to get on ... Get on with

274

what? She wanted peace, to be alone with her grief.

When she had shown Mrs Thompson out, she attempted to tidy up, but left the dishes at the side of the sink. She couldn't see for the tears. She went to the telephone and dialled Aunt Meg's number. 'Aunt Meg,' she said, when she heard her voice, 'he's gone ... Jamie's gone...'

'Have you had word?'

'No, his parents have. Killed! Can you imagine it? And I thought he was going to be lucky...'

'I'll come right away, Mirren.'

'No, Aunt.' She had become fearful of interruption, she wanted space ... 'His parents are quite near. And I'm seeing them later today. They might even persuade me to stay...'

'Well, that certainly would be better.' She knew her aunt was suffering with her arthritis, and moving about was painful to her. It would be unfair to bring her here. Besides, she wouldn't find it easy to walk up the stairs leading to the flat.

'I'll phone you again tonight, Aunt Meg. I may have some more news for you...'

'Mirren, I'm worried about you. You were always such a self-contained girl. I know how much you loved Jamie, and although I never met him, I know he must have been quite special. Will you promise to ring me again?

'I'll be here, waiting...'

For the first time she felt impatient with her dearly beloved aunt. Everybody wanted to crowd her. She had to have time, time to lie in bed and imagine Jamie, alive and loving ... but that was wrong. She had to come to terms with Jamie's death. She would tidy up and then go downstairs and see the Campbells again. They would be disappointed if she didn't turn up.

Mr Campbell opened the door to her. 'Come in, Mirren,' he said. He led her into that large room with the withered grasses in the tall vases, and the grimy windows. She had noticed it the last time she was here. There was a window-cleaner who came round each month. Perhaps she could tell him to call on them...

When she was seated, he said, 'I'm afraid my wife is in bed, Miss ... I mean Mirren. She was so overwrought when we got back from your flat, that I gave her two aspirins with a cup of tea and she's still asleep. How are you coping?'

She shook her head, unable to speak for a moment. 'I feel more at ease with you, Mr Campbell. I think it's because of having seen you that time when I was with my father, that time in the park.'

His face froze. 'Yes, we discussed that. But it's in the past now...'

He wasn't going to make a confidante of

her, she thought. Shutting her out, as they had done with Jamie. 'Would it be possible for you to let me see Jamie's effects?' she asked him. 'It would make it real to me.'

'Yes, they're on a table over here.' He led her to a table by the window. She saw a kit bag, a cap, uniform, a watch, and her photograph. She lifted it, turned it over. On the back he had written, 'Mirren.'

'Could I have this?' she asked.

'Yes, I don't see why you shouldn't. After all, it's yours.'

Getting up to walk to the window had made her feel dizzy. She didn't know whether to resume her seat at the fire or not. Mr Campbell made no movement. 'I'm sorry your wife had to retire to bed,' she said. 'I don't think I'll stay...' She felt herself sway and he put out a hand to steady her.

'You must admit,' he said, 'it's terribly difficult for us to realise ... realise ... that Jamie...'

'Had me?'

'Yes.'

'I do see that.' Her head had cleared. 'I think this visit was too soon for all of us. I'll give you a ring at the end of the week.'

'I'm sorry. We haven't got a telephone. I always meant to get round to it...'

'Yes, I understand. Well, thanks for my photograph, anyhow. I'll get away upstairs. We'll keep in touch.'

As he was showing her out, she heard Mrs Campbell's voice coming from another room: 'David ... has she gone?'

He looked at Mirren, embarrassed. 'Yes,' he called. 'I'm coming...'

He opened the door for Mirren, and said, 'It's a terrible time for everybody. We're getting our share of it. Thanks for calling. I'm sorry...' Mirren nodded. She felt like an unwelcome visitor.

She lay all afternoon in her bed, torturing herself with memories – Jamie, scarf flying, on the station platform, his smile of recognition, meeting her in the station café, brimming over with life, now lying, where? At the bottom of the sea, on some field with the tangled wreckage of the Spitfire, or flying with his hero Antoine, in an unknown sky, eyes shining, flying, on and on...

The telephone rang around six o'clock, and it was her aunt, worried ... 'Mirren, what are you doing about your school?'

'It's closed down this afternoon, but I shall have to go in tomorrow.'

'This is Thursday. Are you going to be able to go in tomorrow?'

She hadn't thought about it. Her mind suddenly clicked into action. 'Yes. I'll have to, but I'll have the weekend then, Saturday and Sunday.'

'Why not come to Waterside? You're better planning, it makes you look ahead.'

278

Why not? she thought. Nothing mattered now.

'All right.' She thought suddenly that she would be able to tell Mrs Thompson that she was going away for the weekend, which would relieve her of the necessity of agreeing to any suggestions the woman might make.

Mrs Thompson, a woman of her word, duly presented herself at the flat that evening. 'How are you feeling now?' she asked.

'Better, thank you, Mrs Thompson. Come in.'

Mirren saw by her face that the woman had her mind made up. Immediately she sat down, she launched forth. 'I've been talking to my daughter. She's seventeen, and wise for her age. That's what it's like when you're left. You have to fend for yourself, and your family. Ethel thinks you should come to our house this weekend, and we'll attempt to cheer you up. She's a very jolly girl, Ethel.'

'That's kind of you, Mrs Thompson, and your daughter. But I'm going to my aunt's. She lives at Waterside, and she's suggested that, and I've agreed.'

'Oh, well, as long as you're not alone. Ethel will be disappointed. It was partly her idea.'

'That's kind. Now about the school, Mrs Thompson. The children are coming back tomorrow morning?'

'Yes.'

'I'll be able to come in tomorrow. I'll

manage.'

'Oh, are you sure?'

'Quite sure.'

'Well, I'll get back, but Ethel will probably have the bed made up.'

'Oh, I'm so sorry. You've been very kind. But I'll see you tomorrow at school. That's best.'

Mrs Thompson got up. 'Now, I want you to promise me that if you're lonely tonight, you'll just walk round to us, we're in Nithsdale Road, number twenty-nine.'

She would have promised anything if she would just go. She was able to usher Mrs Thompson out with renewed and grateful thanks, and stagger to her bedroom. She wakened at three o'clock in the morning, and touched the bottom of a black pit of grief. Jamie, Jamie, Jamie, smiling at her, his blue-black eyes shining, his grown-up way of talking which had secretly amused her, helping to pull up her stocking over her bruised knee, his eyes meeting hers, full of love... Jamie, Jamie ... But she was able to go to the school in the morning, secure in the knowledge that she had no tears left.

Chapter 4

Stepping off the train at Waterside Station, Mirren thought, this is my other life where my alter ego lives, my bolt-hole. Does it represent the two sides of my character, the peace I find here at Waterside, the busyness of Glasgow? Which suited her better? Had her father known the same dichotomy? Not her mother, she had craved for the city, hating the enclosed atmosphere of a village, longing for the scope of Glasgow, and had he been so much in love with her that he had given in to her wishes? Now she could understand the need for two houses, the restlessness of a city, compared with the haven of a place like Waterside.

She went through the station hall and out to the front where one taxi stood waiting. The driver reached back and released the door. 'Frae Glesca?' he said. 'You'll be Miss Calder's niece? Hop in.'

Mirren duly hopped. 'Did Miss Calder send you?' she asked.

'Aye. Does your cousin usually pick you up?'

'Yes.' One's affairs were public property here.

'Mr Stewart isn't so well these days. A good thing he's got Josh to look after things, eh?'

'Yes.'

'And how d'you like living in Glasgow?'

'Very much.'

'A teacher, uren't ye?'

'Yes.' You know it all. She wasn't surprised at the next remark.

'A fine turn-up for the troops, Jack Drummond and Grace McFarlane marrying, eh?'

'Very nice, I thought.' Would that shut him up?

'A stirring lass, Grace. She'll keep him on his toes.'

'Yes.' It was back to the affirmative.

'Josh was ... oh, here we are at Miss Calder's. Suffers from rheumatism now. Still she must be a good age.'

'How much?' At last a variation.

'Five bob'll dae me. On ye go. I'll carry your case.'

She walked up the path with the pinks on either side, catching their cinnamon smell, and rang the bell. 'Just leave it here,' but the door was opened at that moment by her aunt. 'Mirren! And Geordie picked you up. Good!'

'Always willing and able, Miss Calder. And how's the rheumatism the day?'

282

'It's arthritis, Geordie. I'm fine. Ready for my niece. Come away in, Mirren. How much was that, Geordie?'

'Your niece squared with me.'

'But I told you ... well, never mind.' Mirren was standing beside her now in the doorway. 'Good-day to you, Geordie,' her aunt said, 'put the case there.' He deposited Mirren's case in the hall and, touching his cap to both of them, went out, standing expectantly on the doorstep.

'Thank you, Geordie,' Aunt Meg said, and closed the door. 'That man!' she said to Mirren. 'He was told not to charge you. I'll square up with you later, Mirren. Come into the parlour, I've got a cup of tea ready for you. You look pale, lass. You haven't had much sleep, I suppose, you poor soul.'

'No. But I'm getting used to Jamie not being here any more.' She managed the sentence without tears rushing into her eyes. 'Funnily enough I managed at school very well. Children live for the moment. I think Mrs Thompson must have told them not to misbehave, that I had had bad news, because when I went into the classroom there was a sudden hush, then Jean Scobie stood up and said, "We're very sorry, Miss Stewart." That nearly finished me,' she said, looking at her aunt, 'their eyes were on me as if I had changed.'

'They're funny, children. Now, I made

your favourite pancakes, and there's straw-berry jam there, this year's picking. And here's a cup of tea, good and hot.'

Her aunt's fussing made it unnecessary to speak after her first outburst, and the bright little fire, even the embroidered table napkins and the fine egg-shell china gave Mirren a feeling of being cosseted, which helped to assuage her grief.

She was able to tell her aunt later about Jamie's parents, and how she felt that she would never be accepted by them. 'I'm an interloper,' she said. 'They've been so busy planning Jamie's life, that they never took into account that he might meet a girl. Theirs was a smothering kind of love, all done for the best, but they weren't a close family as a result.'

'Nevertheless, Mirren – ' her aunt laid a hand on hers – 'I think when you feel able to do it, you should call on them. Even if you only talked about Jamie, you would get to know them, maybe help them in some way.'

'Yes, I'll try to do that sometime in the future. I do feel a bond with Jamie's father. You know he's never admitted meeting in the park. But it was because of that meeting that I called on them and met Jamie.'

Her aunt was a good listener. Mirren was able to tell her how much she and Jamie had loved each other, and gradually she began to see that it had been a good thing and how it

284

had made her grow up. 'I'm sure we would have got married when he came home, if he had come home, and glad—' She couldn't shock this celibate aunt with the disclosure that they had slept together, but she was fiercely glad that it had happened. She was a woman now, and what did it matter that they hadn't been married? She had memories of him which she might not have had.

The following morning, her cheeks were wet, and she knew she had wept in the night, but when she joined her aunt at the breakfast table, she said, 'Would it upset you to go and visit your uncle, Mirren? You know he's got cancer. Margaret said she would be glad if you would call and see him.'

She said she would like to go, and her aunt said she would phone and say they would look in that afternoon.

She offered to shop for her in the morning, and she set off with shopping basket down the village street, enjoying the fresh air, compared with Glasgow, and the gardens of the houses lining it. The traffic which passed her was mostly composed of farm tractors, combined with a few cars, and when she came to the shops she dawdled at their windows, comparing their displays with those in Glasgow. They had an individuality which reflected the owners, the hardware had farm implements and tools, and the drapers sensible dresses and under-which spoke of comfort rather than display. No wonder Mother longed for city smartness, she thought, looking at lisle stockings in a sensible grey shade, and thinking that she herself hadn't known of their existence in a world of silk stockings and lace-trimmed underwear.

In the grocer's, she met Grace McFarlane, who was pushing a pram, and she stopped to speak to her.

'I didn't know you were in Waterside,' Grace said.

'It's just a short visit,' she said. 'I'm going back on Sunday.' And, bending down to the pram, she took the little hand of the baby lying there and, looking up at Grace, she said, 'She's absolutely lovely, Grace. I heard from Aunt Meg you'd had a little girl. What is she called?'

'Ella. It's a favourite name of Jack's.'

'Is it? How is he?'

'All right. Very busy with the farm. I'm not able to help him because of Ella. I think he would have liked me to be outside with him helping the way his mother did, but there's so much to do with the house and the baby.'

'Yes, I'm sure there is.' She looked down at the child. Jack's eyes, she thought. They seemed wiser than they should be for such a small baby, and she had Grace's hair, fair and curling. 'A little beauty,' she said, her filling with tears. She kept her face down, waiting until she felt able to look up, and find her handkerchief. 'I've got a cold,' she said. 'I hope I haven't passed it on to Ella.'

'Oh, she's as tough as old rope. Squeals the place down if she doesn't get what she wants. Look in and see us if you have time.'

'That's kind of you, Grace. But I doubt if I'll have time. I'm going to see my aunt and uncle this afternoon. And tomorrow I expect I'll have to go to church with my aunt.'

'Aye, she's a holy one, Miss Calder.' The baby was whimpering. 'Well, I'd better push on. Nice to have met you.'

'I'm glad too, and to have seen your lovely baby.' Mirren walked away in the opposite direction, keeping her head up because of the tears.

She found her uncle to have changed for the worse when she and her aunt called that afternoon. He had lost weight, and his old forthrightness had gone. He appealed constantly to Josh, who seemed chastened, as if he had a weight on his shoulders. Before it had always been a jolly table, but even her Aunt Margaret was quieter, still with her rosy cheeks but her hair had gone grey at the temples, and her smile was not so frequent. Evidently her uncle's illness was affecting the whole family. Josh's sister was there too with her children, but she noticed her uncle didn't chide them as he had done before, tease them. He gave the impression of a man who had lost his will to live.

'And how's Glasgow?' Josh asked. 'Do you feel the effects of the war more there?'

'I suppose so,' Mirren said. 'Darkened streets and houses and people with families complain about the lack of food, but it doesn't affect me.'

'At least you haven't a man away in the Army,' Maggie said. 'It affects me all right.'

There was a pause. Mirren caught her Aunt Meg's eye. She answered for her.

'We don't know who Mirren may be missing, Maggie. There aren't many people unaffected in some way.'

'I'm sorry if I've said the wrong thing.' The girl, looking embarrassed, spoke sharply to the child next to her. 'If I've told you once, I've told you a thousand times. Look at your sister! You've got to behave when you come here. You're upsetting your grandpa!'

'The weans are all right, Maggie,' Roger said. 'They're no' bothering me.'

'And how is your teaching getting on, Mirren?' Aunt Margaret was the peacemaker.

'Fine, aunt. Quite a number went to live in the country, of course.'

'Aye, we have some here in the village.'

The talk turned to the evacuees, in the middle of which Maggie said she must get 'ome and get the children to bed, and shortly after their departure, Aunt Meg said she and Mirren must go.

'You should have waited for Josh to come back,' Aunt Margaret said. He had offered to run his sister home with her children.

Mirren had said to Aunt Meg that she would prefer to make it a short visit, but she saw her aunt and uncle were upset about the sudden end to their entertaining. 'That would be kind, Aunt,' she said, 'if it suits Josh. Aunt Meg will be glad of the lift, I know, with her arthritis.'

'Aye, now that you mention it,' her aunt said, 'I wouldn't say no.'

'Another cup of tea, then?'

They both accepted, Mirren saying she would like to have a talk with her uncle about Dunkirk. 'And I'm sorry if Maggie was upset,' she said, 'I didn't know her husband had been called up.'

'He was in the Territorials. He had to go. I think there were a few lads here who liked parading about in the uniform in peacetime, but hadn't realised what it meant.'

Mirren was talking to her uncle, and Aunt Meg was 'having a crack', as she put it, with her sister-in-law, when Josh came back.

'Poor Maggie,' he said, 'she misses Tom.'

'Was she crying again?' his father asked.

'A bit, Dad, but you know Maggie. She has always made a heavy load of her worries.'

'I can't think of a bigger load than she's got

now,' Mirren said.

She said an affectionate farewell to her aunt and uncle, and she and her aunt followed Josh into the yard.

'You're better in the back, Aunt Meg,' he said, helping her in. 'You in the front, Mirren.'

'Right.' When he was driving towards the village, she said, 'Your father is feeling his illness now, Josh.'

'Yes. He has his own cross to bear.'

'It's difficult running the farm on your own?'

'Not so bad. But I've applied for a land girl to help me out.'

'I've had the feeling for ages that I should be doing more,' Mirren said.

'I would have thought teaching the young ones quite a contribution.'

'In a way, yes. But...'

'Have you lost someone?' His voice was concerned.

'Yes, as a matter of fact, I have. A very dear friend.'

'I guessed as much.' He lowered his voice. 'I want you to know, Mirren, that if there is any way I can be of help, don't hesitate to get in touch with me.'

'That's kind of you, Josh. But this is something I've to get over on my own. Nobody can help me.'

'Don't say that. A cousin is quite good at

helping. Blood is thicker than water. You know I've always ... well, you know.' He turned and met her eyes.

'He died...' She felt his hand on hers.

'It hurts?' His eyes were full of sympathy. 'Well, don't forget,' he said.

When they reached Aunt Meg's house, he helped her out, and escorted her to her door, Mirren following.

'Well, isn't it nice to have a kind nephew to help me,' their aunt said. 'Here's the keys, Mirren. You open the door.' When she had done this, her aunt invited him in.

'No, thanks,' he said. 'Not that I wouldn't like to. But I generally help Dad to get into bed.'

'I understand.'

'Well, I'll say goodbye for the present.' Mirren held out her hand, but Josh drew her to him, and kissed her cheek. 'We're cousins, after all.'

'And what about your old aunt?' Aunt Meg said.

'A hug for her.' He threw his arms round her.

When she had closed the door, she said to Mirren, 'That lad has a heavy cross to bear, and unlike Jack Drummond, Margaret said he was dying to go and fight, but he knew his place was at home.

Chapter 5

1941

Mirren soon found that there was no time for grieving. Everyone seemed to be settled into the pattern of the war, which meant getting on with things, as they saw it, commiserating with those who were grieving. In the case of women, it often meant replacing the men who had been called up. Factories had been set up all over Clydeside for the manufacture of Merlin engines, and such like. Lots of the mothers of the children at school were working in those factories, and Mirren tried to alter the curriculum at school to suit, so that the children didn't suffer. She instituted school lunches, and extra care after classes were over, until the exhausted mothers were able to collect their offspring. On the whole people 'kept mum' about where they were working, as instructed, and Mirren noticed the women didn't talk about what they were engaged with in the factories.

She also noticed how busy the centre of the town was, and how Sauchiehall Street became a promenade for the American soldiers who had been disembarked at the Gareloch. As a result the canteens, especially the one for the Allied soldiers, were bursting at the seams, and most of her evenings were spent in one or the other. She made many friends amongst the women helping, and occasionally went out with them to the cinema, but she didn't join them in the nightly parades in the busy streets. Sauchiehall Street was the favourite place for the Americans.

She had learned to conceal her grief for Jamie, but after one or two visits to his parents she stopped going to their flat. They were a dispiriting couple. It was evident that life had been ruined for them by the death of their son, and while Mrs Campbell seemed to have become a recluse, Mr Campbell was in a happier position as there were many jobs to be had, and when she saw them, she learned that he was a cashier at one of the shipbuilding firms on the Clyde. 'A very responsible job,' Mrs Campbell said to Mirren. 'Only someone with David's experience could do it. But life will never be the same for us.'

She still visited Waterside on any holidays she got from the school. Her uncle had died, and Josh had handed the running of the farm to a manager, and volunteered. His mother always said she was proud of him, and his father would have felt the same. She had retired to a cottage near Aunt Meg's and was one of the team of ladies who met in the village hall to knit socks for the soldiers. Aunt Meg was now an invalid, and had various people popping in to look after her. She didn't want to leave her house, she said, and occasional visits to the Cottage Hospital were all that was necessary when she had a bad bout of arthritis. Mirren took over her care when she went to Waterside.

She had visited Grace and Jack occasionally, and found them happy enough, although she suspected they quarrelled when they were on their own. She noticed that Grace seemed to take a delight in contradicting him, eyes flashing, and that Jack looked apologetically across the table at her, a look she didn't return. She suspected he still flirted around, and gave Grace cause for worry. Her aunt confirmed this. He adored his little daughter, and spoiled her outrageously, Mirren thought, glad that she wasn't involved with them.

She carried the responsibility of the school on her shoulders, and because of that, felt her job was essential, although at times she would have liked to volunteer for one of the women's services. Mr Churchill had widened the calling-up to include most of the fit, within the age limit, but when she discussed it with one of the inspectors who visited the school occasionally, he advised her to stay put, that she was highly appreciated, and that she was doing a very necessary job. 'And I don't think you're the type to be attracted by the uniform,' he commented.

There had been a small raid on Glasgow in July the previous year, but now in the spring of 1941 it was shaken by three massive air raids on the Clyde. Mirren's desire to be in the Forces disappeared, since canteens had to be established in the city to feed the Clydesiders who had to flee from the desecration of their houses. Anyone who could help was welcome, and she found herself busy most nights in Glasgow with those canteens, as well as the ones for the Forces. By dashing into Glasgow every night after teaching she had hardly any time for herself, and consequently she was able to forget Jamie for longer and longer periods.

Everyone was aware that Glasgow was a significant port since Liverpool had been bombed, with a new harbour at the Gareloch. A lot of her information came from the soldiers and bombed-out people in the canteens, and she felt that she was at least one small cog in the war effort. She was driven by the thought of Jamie's sacrifice, and the need to emulate it herself, and sometimes when she got home late at night at Limes Avenue and lay soaking in her bath, she would feel a fierce sense of satisfaction.

At the Allied Forces canteen one night she was serving tea to an American – not unusual since Glasgow was awash with Americans who charmed the local girls with offers of silk stockings and candy bars. And also their physiques, no doubt since the average American soldier or airman towered over the average Glaswegian youths, who were often referred to by the girls as 'wee smouts' in comparison. There was a vacant seat near this man, and he said to Mirren in his American drawl, as she handed him his tea, 'Why don't you sit down and give me the pleasure of your company?'

'All right,' she said, smiling. 'I must admit this job is hard on the feet.'

'Do you work during the day?' he asked her.

'Yes, I'm a school head,' she said, 'and that's tiring enough, I must say.'

'You strike me as being driven,' he said, 'you know, intense. I've been watching you dashing about all over the place.' His white smile in his tanned face was attractive.

'Intense?' Mirren said. 'Yes, I suppose I am. It's good to be so busy that you haven't time to think.' And in case she would find herself telling him about Jamie, she said, 'Where are you from?'

'New York. It has the same kind of buzz as

Glasgow.'

'Buzz?' she said. 'I never thought of Glasgow as having a buzz. What's your job in New York?'

'I'm a broker,' he said.

The word didn't mean anything to her, and she asked again, 'What's that? Here we just have pawnbrokers. That's where you take any jewellery or valuables to pawn. You get money for them at the time. And you can buy them back within a certain period.'

'Are you in the habit of using them?' he said, smiling at her. 'You seem to know all about them.'

'Local knowledge.' She had got used to being teased here. 'But I know people who depend on them. You recognise the shops by three golden balls hung outside. The shops are generally at the corner of a street.'

'And tended by a man looking like Shylock?' His smile was charming, she thought.

'Almost.'

'You see I don't fit into that category.' He ran his hand round his smooth chin. 'A broker is rather like being in your stock exchange here. We deal in money, not jewellery.'

'I see. Do you get a chance to make money for yourself?'

'Occasionally. My wife likes jewellery. It means I can satisfy her craving.'

'Well, that's nice for her,' Mirren said. 'Are

you near shops in New York? I've heard of places like Madison Avenue.'

'Quite right. No, we live in Upstate, Westchester, about forty miles from New York. We have the Hudson lapping at the foot of our garden.'

'Have you any children?' She was aware of seeming curious.

'Yes, a boy and a girl, Greg and Tansy, eight and six. Are you married?'

'No.' She must try and say it. 'My boyfriend was killed flying a Spitfire.' She managed it without the tears flooding her eyes, but her annoyance at having to say 'boyfriend' instead of 'lover' which Jamie had been, and not being able to say, 'my fiancé' or 'my husband,' saved her from the tears.

'I'm sorry.'

'Oh, it happens all the time. Tell me.' She tried to concentrate on what he had told her. 'Can your children swim in the Hudson?'

She knew he was answering her silly question to take her mind off Jamie. 'No, it's not advisable. But we have a holiday home in Cape Cod, two miles from the sea, and it's on a little lake. We all swim there, or we pack the car with towels and picnic stuff and drive to the coast.'

She would have liked to ask more questions, but now the tears were perilously close. 'It sounds an idyllic place to live. Of course we're lucky in Glasgow. A half-hour takes you to the coast.'

'I loved the place where our ship docked. The Gareloch. Or should I be saying that?'

'It's all right. Everyone in Glasgow knows how busy it is. Mr Churchill sails from there. And the King and Queen.'

'Oh, well, I'm honoured to have been in such select company.' He smiled again at her, and she noticed a spasm of pain cross his face. She had seen his crutches resting against a chair. She also noticed he was wearing naval uniform. 'You've been wounded,' she said. 'Where did it happen?'

He put a finger to his lips. 'Careless talk costs lives. Isn't that what they say? But you'll probably know that US Navy destroyers have been deployed on escort duties.'

'Yes, I knew that. Food supplies, isn't it?'

'Right on. Well, accidents can happen. But this old leg is giving everyone a lot of trouble. I've been deployed here waiting for a posting. There's a scheme about exchanging wounded. It's taking a hell of a time.'

'Poor you. Does your leg hurt?'

'Sometimes,' he shrugged. That's enough about me.

'I'm afraid I'll have to go,' she said. She had seen one of the helpers giving her a quizzical look.

'Can I see you again? Shall you be here tomorrow night?'

'I expect so. I'm here most evenings.'

'Come and sit beside me, then. I'll order your whole menu to keep you here.' Again the charming smile.

'I'll try,' she said. She knew she would.

'My name is Don Bartlett, by the way,' he said.

'Mine is Mirren Stewart.'

He held out his hand and she put hers in his. 'Howdy, Mirren Stewart. I'm sure glad to make your acquaintance,' he said. She laughed. 'After sundown then, at the Old Canteen.'

She felt laughter bubbling inside her, a new feeling. 'Sure thing,' she said.

She went home that night, with this new feeling still inside her. But it's nothing to do with Jamie, she assured herself, it's just on the surface, an amusing happening. Everyone was entitled to a bit of amusement those days.

It seemed like no time at all before she found herself sitting beside Don Bartlett again, and after that, exchanging confidences, and in time she was able to tell him about Jamie, while he told her about Betsy, his wife, and Greg and Tansy, until one night he said to her, 'Do you think our friendship has progressed far enough for me to ask you to accompany me to the cinema tomorrow night?'

She made up her mind. He had been honest about his wife and children, and she had told him about Jamie. 'Why not?' she said.

She turned it over in her mind, going home. She liked him, she felt sorry for him, but had it been her longing for male company that had made her accept his invitation? She could add it to her war effort, she thought. If she had been his Betsy, would she have minded? She had never felt jealous when Jamie was away. She had been so sure of his love.

In the morning, which was fortunately a Saturday, and she had no school duties, she had a letter from Josh. It was on thin Army paper. She read it slowly.

Mother would tell you that I had volunteered. She approved of me going, and of getting a manager for the farm. She wanted away from it, and I could understand that. The man who is running it for me is willing to buy it if I don't come back to it, so it leaves me free. I might learn another trade in the Army.

I'm sure you must know that I care deeply about you. I wanted to propose to you but you told me about the loss of your boyfriend and I knew it wouldn't be the right time. I've loved you for years, ever since you came to the farm as a little girl. I used to lead you by the hand, and you were someone very special to me, my cousin from Glasgow, different from the Waterside girls, different from Grace. I never loved her, and was pleased when she and Jack got married. I think they're well suited. She's a firebrand, and Jack will give as good as he gets. She felt I should have lost my temper with her, but truthfully, I never cared enough.

Would you consider being my girl while I'm away, Mirren? I'm in this training camp at present, but we'll be going on duty soon. Please write and tell me if I can write to you, and if you could begin to think of me as I do of you?

The rest was composed of news about Waterside and the people there and questions about her life in Glasgow, which she skimmed over. She was not surprised at his proposal. She had always felt a bond with him, but presumed it was because he was her cousin, but she doubted if she could think of him as anything else.

However, she would make it part of her war contribution, she joked with herself. She would tell him that she was willing to correspond with him, but not as his 'girl'. 'I don't want to be tied down, Josh,' she would say, 'or consider myself as anyone's girl. I'm not ready for that, but I'm fond of you in a cousinly way, and if that would do meantime, keep writing, and I'll be willing to become your pen pal, as we used to call it.'

She wrote immediately, and posted it when she was doing her shopping in Albert Road.

She went to the Allied Canteen that evening, wondering if Don would be there. When she went into the room, she saw him immediately, and she waved to him. It was after eight before she could find time to sit down at his table, and he welcomed her with his sweet smile. 'Bingo!' he said. 'You managed it.'

'Just. We're especially busy tonight.'

'I knew you were a girl of your word, but I wondered if you might regret it.'

She shook her head. 'One thing I've learned is to stick to what I've said. My staff and the children wouldn't like it if I didn't.'

'Well, I'm glad. We can still go to the cinema, then?'

'Of course. They have two showings. I'm sorry I couldn't get to your table earlier.'

'That's all right. You're here.'

'I've told them I'm knocking off early tonight. There's a good film on at the Odeon, Judy Garland.'

'Good girl. You and Judy Garland. Suppose you meet me outside in fifteen minutes? That will give you time to make your excuses and get your coat, and time for me to get myself out of here.'

'Wouldn't you like me to help you?'

'No. No nannying, please. I'm very good at

being independent. That's what I've learned.'

'And I'm very good at making up my
mind. So we're both boasting.'

'Which proves we're trying to reassure ourselves.' He made to get up. 'See you outside.'

'Right.' She got up and left him, not
looking back, but having to restrain herself.

He was leaning against the wall outside
and she went forward to him again. 'So you
made it?'

'Sure. Hello again.' She had a sudden
desire to bend forward and kiss him, because
he looked so frail, but she thought it might
surprise him.

'The cinema is in the next street. Can you
make it?'

'Sure. Exercise is good for me.'

They started walking at a slow pace, to suit
him, and looking at him, she saw him wince
once or twice. She restrained herself from
asking if he was managing all right, but kept
her hand on his arm, trying to act as a
bulwark from the crowds in the street. Most
people were careful of him, giving them a
wide berth, but she was glad when they
reached the cinema. Here they were well
used to helping the wounded. A wheelchair
was quickly got for him, and he was wheeled
to the lift, and from there to the theatre.
They were put in two back seats of the stalls,
which was more accessible, and when they

settled down, she remembered that long ago she had sat in a similar seat with Jack Drummond at the Regal cinema. But this was different. There was no romance, just friendliness.

He seemed to be happy with the American film they saw, and hummed along with the lyrics, and when Judy Garland was singing soulfully, he reached for her hand and held it. They didn't speak for the duration of the film.

The attendant helped him to the lift again, providing a wheelchair, and Don asked him if he could get him a taxi at the entrance. The man was kind enough to do that, helped by what Mirren saw was a substantial tip. She remembered that it was said that Americans were taken advantage of in Glasgow. This thought she kept to herself.

When they were in the taxi, Don said to her, 'What's your address, Mirren, I'll drop you off first.'

'Oh, there's no need for that,' she said. 'I was going to go back with you to your barracks, and see that you were delivered safely.'

'No, no, that's not necessary,' he said. 'Give the man your address, it's much better to see you home first.'

'Well, that's kind,' she said, saying, 'Twelve, Limes Avenue, Pollokshields,' to the driver, but feeling as if she was in the same category as the cinema attendant whom she had suspected.

It didn't take long, to drive down Renfield Street, then Union Street, and into Argyle Street, and then to turn right at the Trongate and across the bridge over the Clyde, and on to Pollokshields, with Don asking questions all the way about the route. 'I'm trying to get a picture of Glasgow in my head,' he said. 'It looks to me that you'd be better with our grid system.'

When the driver stopped at her address, Don looked suitably impressed. 'These tenements,' he said – he had picked up the name from her conversation, 'are rather like our brownstones in New York. Is it a cold-water flat that you have?'

'Certainly not,' she said laughing. 'I've got a lovely bathroom, and the flat is quite modern. You must come up and see it, sometime...' She stopped speaking. She hung her head, thinking of Jamie coming upstairs with her.

'What's wrong, Mirren?' Don said. 'Have you said something you regret?'

'I forgot for a second you couldn't come up in any case, and then I was reminded of Jamie.'

'You haven't got over him yet?'

'I don't think I'll ever.' The tears were running down her face. He handed her a handkerchief and put an arm round her

306

shoulders.

She took the handkerchief, thanking him, mopped her face and returned it. She was acutely aware of the taxi driver, sitting motionless in the front. 'Sorry. I'll have to go upstairs, Don. I have fits of crying still.'

'On you go. Thank you for coming with me tonight and helping me to the cinema. It was a great treat.'

'Thank you for taking me and being so understanding.' She got out, aware of the driver's curious look.

She stood at the pavement's edge, and waved to Don as he was driven away. Then she went running up the stairs to her flat, still weeping. She had trouble opening her door, but when she was in, she ran to her bedroom, and flung herself on the bed.

She didn't see Don Bartlett for some time at the canteen. She was unable to go for a week, because of a bout of 'flu, and when she did, she saw no sign of him, nor for the following week. She even asked some of the helpers if they had seen him, but no one had. She was worried, then said to herself, 'ships that pass in the night,' and tried to put him out of her mind. He had regretted making a date with her, she decided, and was keeping out of the way.

Time passed. People were getting weary of the war, she thought, and yet it had becom a way of life, and everyone went doggedly on, spurred on by Mr Churchill's encouragement. He had become an icon, she thought.

Josh was in the desert, but so far lucky, and their correspondence continued, with Mirren dutifully answering his letters, and realising as time went on it was no longer a duty. His sweetness of temper came through in his letters, and she began to feel concerned about his safety. She followed, as far as she could, the progress of the war in the Middle East. She knew he was in Tobruk, but he was unfailingly cheerful, saying that the worst enemy was the sand. 'It gets into everything, eyes, ears, mouth, tanks, guns ... we spend most of our time scratching ourselves, in unmentionable places...' She heaved a sigh of relief when she read about the fall of Tobruk.

One evening when she went to do her usual stint at the canteen, she saw Don at his usual table, and when he caught her eye, he waved and beckoned to her. She went over and sat down opposite him.

'Long time no see,' she said.

'Did you think I had disappeared?'

'Yes, but men come and go here, and we never know what's the reason. Would you like some tea?'

'I'd love it. But let's exchange our news first.'

'Mine is simple. I've been carrying on as usual. And I had 'flu, and then when I was

308

back here, you had disappeared. But!' She suddenly noticed. 'You haven't your crutches! I was hoping you weren't having trouble with your leg.'

'Not trouble. I've been in one of your hospitals. My exchange didn't come through, and they got fed up with me hanging around, and arranged for me to be transferred to the Royal Infirmary. There was a surgeon there who could deal with my type of injury – my kneecap had been shattered. Well, he did, and after the operation and a fortnight's rest, I was sent back to my barracks, so here I am. And now, today, I've had a letter to say that I've to hold myself ready for embarkation soon. I wouldn't be surprised if there was something else boiling up.'

'Well, you'll probably get leave first, and a discharge.'

'Who knows?'

'So you might be back with your family before long?'

'I might. You've been very sympathetic, Mirren, and I've appreciated it. Especially as you've had your own worries.'

'Who hasn't? You've helped me too. It takes a long time to get over a bereavement, but I'm feeling more resigned now.' She wondered if she should tell him about Josh, but decided to keep it for later. 'Well, I'll get you your tea.'

When she returned with it, he said, 'We must have a proper goodbye. I see *Citizen Kane* is on at that cinema you took me to. Would you like to see it with me?'

'Yes, I would.'

'What about tomorrow?'

'Yes, I can be here.' There didn't seem any point in being coy.

'Seven o'clock?'

'Suits me.'

She left him, feeling happy for him. He would soon see his wife and family, and that would be the end of their friendship, she presumed. I'll miss him out of my life, she thought.

Chapter 6

They were informed that they would have to wait for the commencement of the film.

'Let's have a coffee while we're waiting,' Don said. This time he didn't need a wheelchair, and they made their way to the coffee room. She noticed he had to lean heavily on his stick, and she offered him her arm. He smiled at her and put his hand through it.

When they were seated, she said, 'Tell me about your life in Westchester, wasn't it? Or what your day's like.' She was going to lose this quickly-made friend, and she wanted to have a picture in her mind.

'Well, I get up in the morning, I have to be up early to beat the traffic into New York. Betsy takes the children to school. When I arrive at Wall Street, the fun begins.'

'Fun?' she said.

'Yes, the balloon goes up. Everyone starts bidding, I get stuck in right away, and often there's no time for lunch. Suddenly I find it's four p.m. and it's time to knock off.'

'Do you feel tired after "brokering",' she hesitated over the word.

'Sometimes tired, sometimes disappointed, sometimes elated. I often join some of the other brokers for a drink before we set off for home.'

'Are there women too?'

'Good gracious no! Although with the smart cookies working in offices, I don't think it'll take long.'

'Perhaps it's just as well. Betsy might get jealous.'

'American wives are suspicious, by nature. But she's busy too: she swims, plays tennis, lunches with friends, picks the children up from school, and we have a drink when I get home. Then, while I romp with Greg and Tansy, perhaps take them riding – Tansy is particularly good – Betsy cooks their supper. When they've eaten we settle down to our meal, or we might be going out to dinner at friends' houses, or having some of them to our house. So I make time for a shower, and get the drinks ready if we're having guests, and then before I know it, I'm getting up at six a.m. and the whole circus begins again.'

'I never knew what sort of married life I would have with Jamie.'

'What did you imagine?'

'Well, he was training to be a chartered accountant, and we might have started off in my flat, to save money. I, of course, would have had to leave the school, as married women aren't allowed to stay on. It may be different in America. But I should have quite liked being a housewife, and perhaps going in the train to Glasgow at night to the theatre with him, but, of course, if we had children, that would not have been possible.

'Did you intend to have children?'

'We never discussed that. When you're not married, the aim is not to have children. That's frowned upon here. But we had so little time together, that we were concerned only with our love for each other and Jamie being called up...' She felt she was giving too much away.

'You hadn't known each other for a long time?'

'No. But we fell instantly in love when we met, and being together was what was uppermost in our minds.'

'You're a victim of your upbringing and your background, I think,' he said. 'In New York we played about a bit before marriage. But I notice the ones that last are where friendship comes before marriage, and then when the love dies, you have something to keep the marriage going.'

'Is that what it was like with you?' she asked.

'No. Betsy was a much sought-after girl in our circle, and I fell in love with her. I suppose you could say I was one of the competitors, but she chose me.'

'But your marriage is a success?'

'We keep it looking like that, because of the children. I adore them, but Betsy isn't a natural mother. She likes the good life. So when Tansy was born, she grew tired of me, and...' He looked away. 'Well, she went looking for excitement, and had an affair with a friend of mine. It wasn't unusual.'

'Did you do the same?'

'No, I think my love went to the children, and, I guess I'm not naturally promiscuous ... which probably comes from my New England background. I knew my friend, a ladies' man, and she wanted to come back when he soon grew tired of her. And then I was busy in Wall Street, building up my career, and our life went ticking along.'

'That's sad. Are you implying that it' wrong to marry when you fall in love, should you wait till you have a friendship, and build on that?'

'I'm not saying that, exactly, but it's what I've found. I had to have Betsy, and then when I had her, I found we had very little in common.'

'Well, I'll never know if it would have been the same with us. One thing I do know is that Jamie was a restless creature. I don't think he was interested in having children. His parents doted on him, and that didn't do him any good.'

'I suppose, if you could come to see it that way, it's better to imagine a life you might have had with your Jamie. I'm only giving you my opinion.'

'It gives me a lot to think about.'

'Have you had many men in your life, Mirren?'

'When I was young I knew men at the university, but I think I must have been a late maturer, and also my parents were both ill, and I was taking care of them.'

'That wouldn't have made any difference. I'm pretty sure you're a girl of strong emotions, and therefore when you were attracted to Jamie and he to you, you were completely bowled over.'

'You speak as if you had written the book.' She laughed. 'What age are you, Don?'

'Thirty-two. No, you asked for my opinion ▪d I'm giving it to you. I was in the Naval

Reserve, that's how I happen to be here. I volunteered, because I thought it would give Betsy time to make up her mind about what she wanted. I think it's going to be all right when I go back. It's been good for me, and in any case I was quite glad to get out of my rut. It's a bit of a rat race in Wall Street.'

'So your marriage may have benefited with your enforced absence?'

'I'm hoping so.'

They were both suddenly devoid of words. He put out his hand and touched hers. 'Now, you, Mirren, are a girl whom I could form a firm friendship with any time, and later, well, one shouldn't speculate...' She wanted to say, 'Don't smile at me like that.' Instead she said, 'I think your marriage is going to be all right. And you've got your family to go back to. I'd love to keep in touch and know how your life turns out, and let you know about mine.'

'Let's do that.'

Her thoughts were on Josh. She didn't have to tell Don about him. She had worked it all out for herself. She knew she had cared for him for a long time, without realising it. So it shouldn't be difficult to think of marrying him with that as a background.

She saw Jack Drummond now as an episode in her life, curiosity on her part, not love, her first experience of attraction, a sexual awakening. And what a mistake it would have been if she had married him! Grace and he were suited to each other. They lived on confrontation. Babies would always be an afterthought.

'I can tell you, Don Bartlett,' she said again, 'you've given me a lot to think about.'

'Good. But you're bright. You would have found your way through the maze.'

'Perhaps.'

'Gosh,' she said, 'isn't life difficult? Do we ever get it right?'

'Only if we're very clever. How about our film now?' he said.

'I had quite forgotten it. Yes, let's go and see *Citizen Kane*.'

Once again, they were in the back row of the stalls, 'where the courting couples go,' she whispered to him, laughing. She was impressed by the actor, Orson Welles, but while she appreciated his performance, her mind kept going back to her conversation with Don. She had never known a man with whom she could have such a rapport, like the brother I never had, she thought. She felt his arm round the back of her seat, and knew he was feeling the same. She would never forget this film, she thought, nor Don, who had opened her eyes to relationships. She saw how her life had been affected by her parents, and how she had never really been young when she should have felt young. I was naive – the thought that Jamie and I could have grown up together. Or could we? Would he always have been a kind of Peter Pan due to his background, where, instead of being allowed to take responsibility for himself, he had been deprived of that.

Jack Drummond, without knowing it, had helped to educate her, could have taught her how to enjoy life, and the life he was now having with Grace suited him, because they were essentially of the same temperament. They had recognised this and drifted together. Their frequent quarrels would lead to frequent making-up. She had never known quarrels with Jamie. She had never known how they would suit each other had they been married. Maybe, she decided, their love affair ended before they had become deeply disappointed in each other.

When the lights went up in the cinema hall, she and Don looked at each other.

'Good,' she said.

'Makes you think. There are lots of good things to look forward to when the war is over,' she said.

'Right.'

He joked and laughed with her as the taxi drove towards her flat, but when they were nearing it, he stopped talking.

'What's wrong, Don?' she said.

'I'm sad.'

'If you like,' she said, 'you can come up to my flat.'

He looked at her. 'Would you like me to?'

'Truthfully,' she said, 'no. Let's leave it as it is. I prefer to remember you as a friend.' And that's the most mature thing you've ever done, she thought.

'You think it might change things?'

She had thought of Jamie, and Don's wife, Betsy, the glamorous woman, and the two children whom he adored. 'Have you read our poet, Robert Burns?' she asked him.

'I've heard of him.'

'He wrote poems which seem to fit every situation. I'm reminded of one of his, "Ae fond kiss, before we sever".'

'Which being translated means?'

'One fond kiss before we part...'

'Why not?' He took her in his arms, and his kiss seemed to be an amalgam of Jack Drummond's practised art and Jamie's passion. And Josh's? After the barn fire he had kissed her before they went into his house, and she had wondered why. 'Will you send me a copy of that poem some day to remind me?' Don said. 'No, on second thoughts, I shan't need it. I'll never forget you, Mirren.'

Again, she noticed the curiosity of the Glasgow taxi-driver. The tilt of this one's head showed that he was listening, and his mirror was angled so that he could see the back seat.

'I'll get out, Don,' she said, 'but you'll have

to write first, so that I have your address, that is, provided your wife won't mind and you want to.'

'We don't read each other's mail. But, yes, I'll write first. Because I'll want to.' They looked at each other for a long time.

'I better get out,' she said.

'Why not another?'

'Another what?' she said.

'Ae fond kiss.'

'Why not?' she said. 'Provided the driver doesn't mind.'

'You'd noticed too?' he said, laughing.

She held up her face. This is comforting, she thought, no greediness, just a warm friendship which nourished but didn't ask for more. I've had that, she thought. This is what it ought to be when one is married. This is what I have to aim for.

When she got out of the taxi, she stood at the edge of the pavement and waved to Don as he was driven away. This is right, she thought, but I hope he feels as deprived as I do. She turned and ran towards the stairs, passing the Campbells' door on the way. That's the end of one chapter of my life, she thought. The shut door with its blank look seemed to echo her thoughts.

Archives and the Computer

To my Colleagues of the Third World,
with respect

Archives
and the
Computer

Michael Cook

Archivist, University of Liverpool

Butterworths
London   Boston
Sydney   Wellington   Durban   Toronto

United Kingdom	Butterworth & Co (Publishers) Ltd
London	88 Kingsway WC2B 6AB
Australia	Butterworths Pty Ltd
Sydney	586 Pacific Highway, Chatswood, NSW 2067
	Also at Melbourne, Brisbane, Adelaide and Perth
Canada	Butterworth & Co (Canada) Ltd
Toronto	2265 Midland Avenue, Scarborough, Ontario
	M1P 4S1
New Zealand	Butterworths of New Zealand Ltd
Wellington	T & W Young Building, 77–85 Customhouse Quay, 1,
	CPO Box 472
South Africa	Butterworth & Co (South Africa) (Pty) Ltd
Durban	152–154 Gale Street
USA	Butterworths (Publishers) Inc
Boston	10 Tower Office Park, Woburn, Mass. 01801

First published 1980

© Michael Cook 1980

ISBN 0 408 10734 0

British Library Cataloguing in Publication Data

Cook, Michael b. 1931
  Archives and the computer.
  1. Archives – Data processing
  I. Title
  025. 17'1   CD971   80–41286
ISBN 0 408 10734 0

FG (Coo)

283

Printed and bound in Great Britain
by W & J Mackay Limited, Chatham

Contents

Figures

Preface

It is time that there was a manual of archival applications for the computer. Archivists have been investigating the subject and seeking practical computer development since early in the 1960s. Dr Califano's paper to the International Congress on Archives at Brussels in 1964 marks the first co-ordinated effort by the profession to agree on the principles of automatic data processing as applied to archival materials. Since then the subject has been developed rather patchily by archivists. Beginning at about the same time, librarians and documentalists have made better progress, and, using the advantages of their greater numbers, their greater need for current awareness and real time working, and their generally better access to organizations which run large computer systems, have devised several practical and elegant systems for cataloguing, indexing, information retrieval and general management of their offices. None of these amounts at present to a widely recognized national or international network, and all display individual characteristics which mean that each system has specific advantages and drawbacks. (Perhaps all human systems will ultimately prove to have this disadvantage.) Nevertheless these systems are now available as models and packages, and archivists may hope to learn from the experience of their near colleagues.

This may suggest that there has been no advance in the development of purely archival automatic systems. This is not so: the leading national archives services of the developed world have established or promoted sensible practical systems which, in some cases, are already being offered as the basis of co-operative projects or as embryonic networks within their own countries. There have also been a few independent innovations as the result of the work of smaller archives services and one or two from the Third World.

It is well known that computers and everything associated with them are changing and developing so rapidly that writers cannot

keep up with them. There are also fashions in thinking about them.
At present we seem to have moved from a period of excessive
optimism to a period in which the limitations and drawbacks of
automated systems are much to the front of users' minds; no
doubt we should aim at a point somewhere between these
extremes. In spite of the drawbacks and of the risk of systems
failure, computers do offer the most important new development in
archives work since the opening up of archive-based research in
public education in the second half of the nineteenth century. This
is a good time therefore to attempt an assessment of what has
been done so far, and to offer a simply worded explanation to
those who have hitherto not taken much notice of these
developments. The time has now passed when the archives
profession as a whole can ignore the subject.

The present study is addressed primarily to two groups of
people. It is hoped that archivists who have had no experience with
computers, and with little mathematical or scientific background in
their education, will find it a useful guide to this rather complex
new world. At the very least, it may help them to master its new
vocabulary; and with the new vocabulary the new battery of
concepts which has had such a vitalizing influence on information
work generally. The second group is that of students who are about
to enter upon careers in archives administration which will stretch
well into the next century. The need to reach the minds and
interests of students at the universities of both Liverpool and
Ghana is the immediate inspiration of this book, and I would like to
offer public thanks to all the students with whom I have discussed
computer applications over the last five years or so. They have, as
they may recognize, provided many of the ideas.

It is important to state clearly what is included in the present
study and what is left out of it. It is clear that the theory and
practice of archives administration as it exists nowadays must be
the co-operative work of many people. No one individual or
published work should try to cover too wide a spread of subjects.
This book therefore concentrates upon giving a general
introduction to the computer and its possibilities for operating as a
tool in archival management. After a general discussion on the
nature of automated systems, and their relation to manual ones, a
select group of important systems is described in as much detail
as may be needed for a reasonably secure understanding of their
operation, and with enough information to guide further study.
Records management systems are included, for this is an area in
which there is good opening for versatile and practical systems,
which if properly planned go far to solve problems never really
tackled heretofore. Finally, a brief discussion of the problems
involved in the treatment of machine-readable archives offers a

field of action which is open to many archivists working in large organizations, and highlights a problem which has good pioneering studies and a body of practice, but which is as yet little known to the profession at large.

What is not attempted here is any treatment of computer systems which aim to use the contents of archives. This book is about records management, archives administration, the conduct of archives and services, the building up of finding aids to archives (including indexes to these). It is not about the exploitation of archives in research; that interesting and worthwhile subject has a literature of its own, but still lacks a practical manual. This book also avoids any very detailed and thoughtful study of indexing and its associated world of thesauri, syntactical and semantic structures and contextual data retrieval; there is a very considerable literature already upon this, and it would indeed be desirable if more archivists interested themselves in the technicalities of indexing. But for the moment the possibilities inherent in systems for the general description and listing of materials is taken as the central point of interest of this book.

I would like to offer my most sincere thanks to many who have helped to produce this study. I have taken their advice, used their facilities or claimed their support. The book is much the better for it, but for its errors and omissions I am solely responsible. I would particularly like to thank the following: Lionel Bell at the British Library; S. C. Newton, at that time at the British Steel Corporation; Annette Kennett and her staff at Chester City Record Office; Guy Cangah and his staff at the Archives Nationales of the Côte d'Ivoire (with kind recollections of my visit in 1977); Maureen Patch and Glyn Evans at the Dyfed Record Office; Margaret Whittick and (at the relevant time) Ron Chesterman at the East Sussex Record Office; H. S. Cobb at the House of Lords Record Office; F. Burke, C. M. Dollar, and S. E. Hannestad at the National Archives and Records Service of the U.S.A.; M. E. Carroll, H. Naugler, and (at the time) Hugh A. Taylor at the Public Archives of Canada; Michael Roper at the Public Record Office; A. L. Bain at the Smithsonian Institution, Washington; David Butler, Bruce Jackson and Alan Seaman at the Tyne and Wear Archives Department; Sam Kotei at the University of Ghana; Maynard Brichford at the University of Illinois; and at the University of Liverpool a whole army of colleagues, including Adrian Allan, Peter Baker, Stephen Foga, Andrea Rudd, Zafar Siddiqui in the University Archives, and John Martin of the University Computer Laboratory. I am also grateful to acknowledge the kindness of the following institutions who have allowed publication of material from their own systems: Chester City Record Office, Dyfed Record Office, East Sussex Record Office, the House of Lords Record Office, the National Archives of the Côte

d'Ivoire, the National Archives and Records Service of the U.S.A.,
the Public Archives of Canada, the Public Record Office, the
Smithsonian Institution, Tyne and Wear County Record Office, and
the University of Liverpool Computer Laboratories.

The University of Liverpool   Michael Cook
                                                       October 1979

1 Computer Systems

A computer is 'a mechanical or electrical device for processing information'. This recent definition makes it quite clear that a computer is something relevant to the work of those who deal with information. It is not an instrument only, or primarily, of use to mathematicians or natural scientists, or to accountants, whose main concern is computing figures. The term 'computer' (which, we are told, arose accidentally) does not describe the most characteristic action of the computer in its outward relationships, though it may describe the internal methods which it uses. The French term *ordinateur* – implying a machine which arranges collections of disparate items into a significant order – is more suitable to the computer in its everyday use as a processor of information.

Archives offices, or archives units in libraries and museums, are, for the purposes of the present argument, examples of specialized data banks. On the analogy of a monetary bank, they are places where large amounts of a certain kind of information are stored in safe keeping and can be utilized, because it is felt that the information in them is of significance to society. Generally, the difficulty experienced by the archivist is that it is a slow and technically demanding job to extract usable information from the documents, or to construct finding aids that are complete enough to allow others to do so. Work on archives is usually funded from public money, or from money set aside for a cultural rather than a utilitarian purpose. This is rightly so, for, as the Grigg Report laid down in 1954, it is the duty of a civilized state to make provision for its archives.[1] But it means that there are normally not enough people or resources to do the job under ideal conditions, and that it is important to provide results within quite a short time. This predicament is even more acute in countries of the Third World, where there are too few resources to devote to the problems of archives, but where the information contained in them is a particularly valuable part of the general stock of information, and is needed to support development work. It is also compounded by the great bulk and rapid accretion of most archive accumulations, which means that, if they are not controlled rapidly and effectively when received, the problem of doing so later will be insoluble.

Archivists therefore are under pressure to provide results rapidly, and not to get swamped by unlisted mountains of paper. The computer has provided an instrument which for the first time offers the possibility of improving radically both the rate of output of finding aids and the depth of access they give to the raw material. With their aid, the same type of manually constructed material already produced by archivists could be used to give a vastly more productive output. The all-important factor is the design of the system.

In this situation the computer does nothing to impair or replace the personal and professional skills of the archivist. It is there simply as a tool, rather as microform systems are. Like them, the computer is part of a complex system, in which a number of operations is combined. The archivist is needed to plan and define this system, and it will not work without him, or without the use of his skills and judgement.

The Scope of Automated Systems in Archives

A rapid survey of existing archival applications shows that there are several areas in which automated processes could be or have been introduced.

1 In records management, computer systems can be used to control the inflow of records into custody, the identification of documents required by users, the control of documents issued to users and their return (circulation control), and the identification of records due for disposal at a particular time.
2 In archival management, the control of archives passing through processes (sorting, fumigation, repair, description, storage, etc.); description and listing of archival material; production of systems of finding aids; retrieval of documents and/or information from the stock; and indexing.
3 Special archival projects, such as the construction of large-scale indexes, the control of microforms, publishing, or the exploitation of archival sources in research.
4 The management of archives offices and records centres. Applications here include compilation of user statistics, ordering-up procedures for moving documents to and from

users, controlling the allocation of storage space, and control of stocks of consumables. Probably this group of applications will be most apt for larger institutions.

5 A separate group of activities concerns the management of machine-readable archives and records. Computers are clearly necessary in order to make use of, or even to store on a long-term basis, valuable archives which have been generated by computer-based projects. This is a problem which is beginning to impinge upon the work of many archivists, but which is still regarded as a rather specialized area.

These are processes which have been developed or suggested as suitable for computerization. If an archives office is interested in doing this for any of them, it will have to carry out an enquiry into its own methods, objectives and needs, so that it can determine to what extent an automated system could be found to suit it. It will be necessary to carry out an analysis of its current systems. On the one hand this may clarify the logical steps in existing processes and the objectives they are aimed at; on the other hand it will take account of possibilities offered by a computerized version.

These possibilities are quite various. A choice may be made, for instance, between specialized piecemeal operations and general ones. In the former case, the computer carries out a particular series of tasks (such as indexing personal names) in a general context of manual systems. The latter situation attempts to automate whole processes and to combine a number of different operations. The more complex the computerized system, the more difficult it is to fit all the bits together, the greater the disruption of the established method, and the greater the possibility of failure. But also the possibility of radical improvement in access to archival information is the greater, and this must be a main aim in introducing computers. It is one which, if successful, justifies the cost and trouble involved.

Archivists are not accustomed to regard their services as similar in kind to those offered by, for example, manufacturing industries. Yet, from a systems point of view, an archives office has many of the same characteristics as the business control of such an industry. Consequently archives offices may hope to benefit from technological innovations which were conceived as aids to efficient business administration. The development of data-base management systems is a good example of this. Like any administration, an archives service works by carrying out a series of different operations upon a data base which holds all the information it needs. In a business administration, this data base includes lists of creditors and debtors, together with details of their financial operations, and stock lists; in a university administration, the data base consists basically of lists of students and of staff, with relevant information. Once the necessary system has been installed, these data bases can be manipulated so that they will automatically provide the most useful pieces of data when and where they are needed. In the case of an archives service, the data base consists of lists of archival holdings, together with all the detailed information which goes with each item. The system is required to arrange these data in a variety of particular orders, and to produce sections at every necessary point. For example, the repository staff will need shelf or location lists; the conservation staff will need lists of items in need of repair or which should be inspected; the searchroom staff need to produce guide entries, inventories, handbooks and indexes; the publications section wishes to publish selected descriptive entries; and all sections, as well as the users, wish to have access to particular archival documents held in the store. It will be seen, then, that an archives office can organize itself around a central data base just as a business organization can. Computer control of that data base will involve much careful planning, but is inherently likely to provide a much more effective control than any form of manual operation. It is also likely, incidentally, to alter the working conditions of the archives office staff for the better. Many of the tasks which have to be done in manual systems of archival management are dull and repetitive. In a computerized system much of the repetitiveness is eliminated, and instead there are problems which are intellectually taxing and interesting. A well-designed computer system is a tonic to the staff.

If computerization of a general system is possible at all, it carries possibilities for the radical alteration of the product. So far, it has been assumed that computers are an alternative way of executing what has been effected in the past by manual methods: the establishment of administrative control over archival processes, and the production of traditionally defined finding aids like guide entries or inventories. But in fact the computer has the potential to produce quite new products. Out of a single data base (basic descriptive lists of archival holdings) it can, for example, produce an infinite number of specially selected finding aids in specific orders; this possibility has been referred to by K. Darwin.[2] Finding aids therefore could be tailored to any specific user's needs. Beyond this, any computerized data base can be used for two kinds of purpose. It can print out various descriptions in various orders; these descriptions may be sorted and selected by the system in order to achieve a particular objective and may include updated information. It can also (if the system is so designed) allow a searching procedure, in which the user interrogates the system until he identifies exactly those documents held within it which answer his enquiry. Both these possibilities carry important implications for archives administration, and both arise from the computer's basic feature: its ability to carry out logical operations on data fed into it, at very great speed.

Finally, the data base of one office may, if it is suitably structured, be linked with the data base of one or more other offices, so as to form a network. National or regional networks for the storage, retrieval and publication of archival data are a real possibility.[3]

Systems Analysis

It has already been mentioned that archives services interested in automation must undertake a study of their aims, processes and needs. Such a study is known as 'systems analysis'.

The basic concepts of systems analysis are quite simple. The work of the office as a whole is regarded as a system (containing sub-systems) in which every process or operation can be analysed, broken down into a logical sequence of steps, and displayed in a series of analytical charts or descriptions. In a professional setting, there should be a clear statement of aims and objectives, methods for evaluating the progress of the organization towards achieving these, and the demands made on the service by its users. This part of the analysis cannot of course be reduced to any mechanical or computerized programme, but must remain in the hands of intelligent human agents trained to exercise their judgement. If any part of their work contains processes which cannot be explained by a series of logical steps, one following from another, then those processes will hardly be suitable for computer assistance, and will continue to depend on human intervention and manual operations. Analysis of needs (in particular) also demands an imaginative approach, for examining an existing system is not always the best way of discovering what the true demands upon it are.

Fig. 1 illustrates in summary form some of the steps involved in the construction of an archival inventory. This omits several detailed steps; these can be plotted in a subchart if necessary.

The symbols employed in the construction of flow-charts are laid down by British Standard 4058 of 1973.

Charts such as these are often more useful than textual explanation because they avoid the need for much solid reading matter and display the essential relationships of parts of the process at a single glance. It may be of interest to note the looping elements in the chart. These loops show one of the ways in which computer programs can be said to be in part self-directing. Wherever there is a repetitive series of actions, which must be undertaken in order until the job is completed (a very common condition for all human tasks), this can be set out in a program by means of loops; these are instructions that when a single cycle of

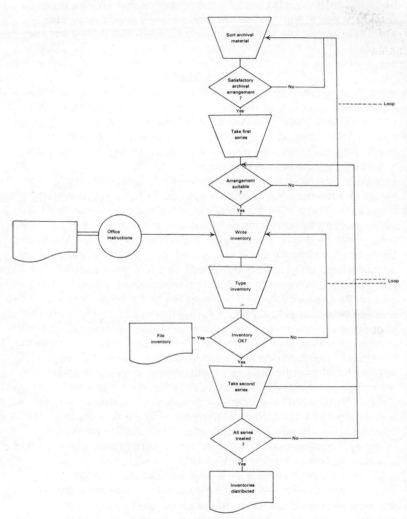

Fig. 1   Steps in the production of an archival inventory

processes has been completed, the operator should return to the starting point and complete an additional cycle; and so on until all completed. It is also worth noting that no value judgements are made on such matters as the layout, accuracy, explicitness, or level of the inventory which is being produced. The probable existence of prior instructions on these points is hinted at by the symbol (shown as a magnetic tape, but actually more likely to be a typed document) for 'office instructions'. It is assumed that the policy behind the construction of finding aids has been worked out by the office and embodied in such instructions. The computer, of course, can have no opinion where a comparison of value-judgements is concerned.

To determine whether or not computerized systems would be of value in the particular circumstances of the office involves a new enquiry in which each sub-system is examined and the computer's capabilities set against those of the existing manual methods. There are several steps in planning and carrying out the enquiry.

Initial Planning and Assignment Brief
Who is to be the analyst? There is a strong theoretical case for appointing a specialist systems analyst. He will be able to judge the processes involved with an unprejudiced eye, and no doubt will be able to suggest improvements on established practices; he will also be able to draw on previous experience of computer operation. However, apart from cost, there are also other drawbacks involved in importing outside people. They will always know much less about the tasks than internal staff, and perhaps be less sympathetic to their aims. On completion of the job they will depart and if there is no knowledgeable and enthusiastic permanent member of staff, it will be difficult to maintain the system, if it is introduced. An external analyst may fail to appreciate staff prejudices which in the long run may be of vital importance. Generally in archives work the best way is for a member of the permanent staff to take up the tasks of systems analysis and computer appreciation, and for him to see through both the enquiry and the subsequent implementation of a new system if one is decided upon. The analyst must in any case be given all necessary authority to spend time, enter relevant offices to make enquiries, and to have access to external advice at senior level. A timetable for completing the analysis should perhaps be added at the outset. Having studied the situation and isolated problem areas the analyst is in a position to report suggesting a plan or alternative plans.

Computer installations are separated from the staff of user organizations by three intermediate groups: operators, programmers,

and systems analysts. This is a useful arrangement, since it allows
for the blurring of boundaries between these groups. Programmers
often extend their interests into systems analysis, and users tend to
drift in the same direction. Systems analysis is therefore a sort of
common ground between user staffs and technical staffs, a ground
where the nature of tasks and goals may be thought out and
discussed, and where achievements can be evaluated and
appreciated. On the other hand, the user is not required to
understand all the technicalities of computer operation and
maintenance, nor to speak the jargon if he does not wish to.

Feasibility Study

At this stage the investigation should confine itself to broad issues,
not with program details. The possibility that computers will *not*
prove to be the best means of achieving the organization's ends
must be taken seriously. Computer systems are not always a good
answer: sometimes they introduce inflexibilities, unnecessarily
complex methods, or antagonise the staff so much that the end is
worse than the beginning. Costs will be a significant feature, and a
comparison of costs as between automated and manual methods
will be included in the final report. If a computer system does
survive the tests applied at the feasibility stage, the report which
terminates the study will give tentative answers to the following
questions:
  What are the problem areas?
  What sort of computer facilities would be needed, including
    software packages, special programs, memory store, etc.?
  What will the likely cost be, including staff time, testing and the
    need for specialized staff?
A particular problem for archivists is the treatment of backlog
accumulations either of incompatible finding aids or of
unprocessed archives.

Full System Investigation

If the feasibility study report has recommended a computer system,
and this has been accepted and budgeted for, the next step is for
the analyst to construct a detailed plan, and to include in this plan a
full and specific system design. At this stage decisions will be made
which will be irrevocable in practical terms, and may cause much
trouble later. Full discussion of the alternatives, with specialist
advice, should be arranged. Decisions will include whether to use a
particular proprietary system (hardware or software), or to what
extent a tailor-made system should be developed. A specific
programming language will have to be chosen, the structure of the

data base, format of input and output documents, method of data
storage and retrieval, and the requirements of developing a second
or later generation of the system. A successful project may attract
other users and there is always the possibility of joint or communal
use of a system, or the setting up of a user network. The
acceptance of unnecessarily restrictive programmes has brought at
least one well-known computerized system in archives to nothing,
and there are of course many examples of the same thing in the
wider world of government or business.

Implementation and testing
The period of change-over to a new system is always difficult. An
ideal way is for the new system to be run in parallel with the old
(manual) one for a trial period, during which the drawbacks and
'bugs' of the new one are identified and dealt with. Test runs
should include as many of the foreseen problem situations as
possible; unforeseen problems will appear of their own accord. Full
consultation with all staff who will be at all affected, at every level,
is most important: hostility of members of staff, however
unreasonable it may seem, can be a most important factor in the
failure of a new system. Computer systems should help people to
work more effectively in a more interesting environment; if they fail
in this, or appear to fail, there is something wrong, and it would
perhaps be better not to introduce the change.

   Though several exist, computer systems involving archives are
not yet common. Any new venture in this field has potential
repercussions in the archives world generally. It would be highly
desirable if those who are considering the introduction of computer
systems in any way would publicize the facts among colleagues,
and allow inspection soon after implementation, and perhaps
discussion at planning stage.

Input
All information systems have three stages: input, processing and
output. These may be analysed in turn.

The Structure of Archival Description
An important feature of archival services is their variety and
individuality. Archivists are conscious that each archival
accumulation presents unique problems in its ordering and control,
even though basic principles of action have been long established.

The kaleidoscopic variety of systems of archival endeavor . . . developed not
because each archivist deliberately set out to create an esoteric system.

Rather it represents the application of the basic rules of archival enterprise to the situation of the time and place. No two operations enjoy the same complement of personnel, budgetary resources, administrative independence, collecting goals, and so on.[4]

The first problem in designing an automated system for archives, therefore, is to achieve such a degree of flexibility that it can be adapted to the circumstances of a wide variety of pre-existing systems. Alternatively it may be necessary for archivists to adapt their procedures and outlook to accommodate the needs of an automated system. The determining factor is the practicality of the proposed system: the main thing is to achieve the objectives of the archives service.

One of the main problems is that of the level of description. There is a certain amount of agreement among archivists that there are five levels, though not all are agreed upon the name that should be applied to each.

	1 Group level	The major divisions of archival holdings based upon common provenance.
MACRO-DESCRIPTIONS	2 Sub-group level	Organic subdivisions of the group.
	3 Series (class) level	The basic division of archives into cohesive describable units, usually large in size but capable of control as single items.
MICRO-DESCRIPTIONS	4 Sub-series level	Divisions of series based upon some common feature.
	5 Unit level	The basic physical unit, individual documents, or files.

Each level of archival control tends to require a different type of finding aid.

Despite the idiosyncracies of particular archives offices, there has evolved a family likeness between the different sorts of archival description. There is, for example, a general assumption that there should be at least a two-level system in any given office. In this the primary component consists of a set of summary descriptions at a fairly major level ('macro-description'); this will often be at series level. The secondary component ('micro-description') may embrace levels 4 or 5. A particular user may go first to the guide (descriptions at levels 1–3), and this will direct him to the more detailed lists covering the series he is likely to be interested in. This is the system, for example, in a local archives office. It is only where the holdings are very small and simply constructed, as perhaps in the local history collection of a library, that a single level of description, usually a micro-description, will allow sufficient control. In a similar way, a calendar (a set of very detailed descriptions of individual documents) is a micro-description within a set of macro-descriptions consisting of collection lists.

It is assumed in the foregoing that there are two main purposes behind the design of an archival finding aid. One is the establishment of intellectual control, whereby users can be helped to undertake searches for the information they seek. The other is the establishment of administrative control, whereby the office staff can ensure that the archives are properly accessioned, processed, stored and retrieved. Finding aids which are designed for one purpose must contain information different from that in the finding aids designed for the other. Administrative control, for instance, requires data of physical characteristics (size, condition) and location (shelf-number). Intellectual control demands access, if possible, to the subject matter contained in the archives; this leads to the need for a third level of finding aid, in the form of indexes, which are a second means of access to the micro-descriptions.

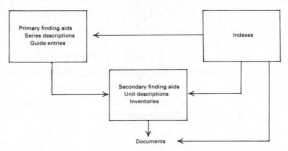

An automated system may aim at providing for either macro or micro level of description, or both. It may be used to make up guides or inventories, or a complex in which the user is directed from one to the other. It may also provide for either administrative or intellectual control, and so include the specialized data required for each, as well as the specialized forms of output. In particular, a complex system will probably need an index or set of indexes.

A. Arad and L. Bell (1978)[5] have attempted to construct a universal terminology for archival descriptions falling into any of the categories that have been discussed. They propose general concepts with these labels:

Archival entity. Any archival material which is being described as a unit, whatever its level.
Archival description set. Any set of similar archival descriptions which are kept together and can be ordered in different ways. Thus a guide consists of a set of descriptions of series or a detailed inventory consists of a set of individual piece descriptions; either can be ordered in different ways to produce, for instance, a location register or a subject guide.
Archival record (using 'record' in the computer sense). Any description of an archival entity, whatever the level of

operation. Archival records, like all components of data bases, must be structured, and in that structure elements will be *fields*. In any archival description set, each record will have an entry in each of the fields provided by the system. *Notations* are devices such as reference codes attached to an entity which serve to identify, classify, arrange or locate it *Tags* are specialized notations attached to an archival description set, to an entity record, to a field or sub-field, to allow the computer to manipulate data items.

Within suitable contexts, these terms are employed in the following chapters.

A source of possible confusion has been that it is possible to construct a computer system to operate at any of the levels of archival description, or even at several of them. From the computer's viewpoint there is no difference between one archival description set and another, even though from the human user's viewpoint there is a great deal of difference: a summary guide, which is an archival description set of summary entries at series level, looks very different from a detailed inventory of documents, which is a structured list of file titles. It is, of course, of vital importance that levels of description should not be confused with each other, and that where several levels are in use there should be notations which will clearly make the distinction between them. Users, whether staff or members of the public, should be in no doubt as to what level of description they are dealing with.[6]

Before leaving this subject, it is important to point out that archival descriptions often require two quite different sections of text:

(i) An introductory section containing a record of the archival entity's provenance. This might include, at its fullest, a history of the originating organization, the development of the administrative functions which caused the creation and use of the archives, a summary of their content, a note of their physical forms, and the history of their provenance and transfer to the archives.

(ii) A second section would then consist of the operative archival description, record by record, including entries in each of the fields provided by the system structure.

This dual nature of many archival finding aids is a complication which sharply distinguishes them from those used by libraries, and it is a great cause of difficulty to systems designers. It is interesting to see how archivists have overcome the problem in different ways in different contexts. The problem is at a minimum where the description level is at macro, for then there is a minimum difference in format between the first and second sections.

The question has already been raised whether one should try to adapt computer systems and operations to existing forms of archival description, or use the opportunity offered by the computer to devise something new, more suited to its capabilities. At this point a more technical comment can be quoted:

We may opt to use more complicated, expensive and flexible systems to accommodate data of the sort we are most used to; or we can change our methods of description and our output requirements to use fields of more uniform, limited, and definable lengths and benefit from more efficient automated systems. Such systems could completely replace the layers of intellectual control we now maintain, from inventories and descriptions of individual collections to repository level descriptions and national catalogs; but they would not be used primarily to print guides such as those we have prepared manually for years, but rather would comprise a data bank, linked in a national network, searched interactively, and available to archivists and the end user. In the long run I suspect that the decision to retain traditional formats rather than adapt ourselves to the possibilities of large scale information systems may prove unwise.[7]

The possibility of being judged by posterity to have been unwise is always with us. At the present time, in a prevailing atmosphere of retrenchment and mild pessimism about the success of complex systems, the wiser part may be to keep to the familiar, and to start the construction of computer systems with the production of finding aids which may look rather like the kind we already produce, only in a somewhat more developed and co-ordinated form derived from a single data base. But flexibility must be an important feature of any new system.

A parallel dilemma also exists between choosing predesigned package software offering the possibility of eventual networking, with appropriate adaptation of archival finding aids, and designing individual programs to produce more specific kinds of output. Very careful planning and experiment are doubly important.

Whatever its level, an archival description set must contain a field structure which embraces all relevant data. A full list of data items that could possibly be included in any system is an impressive one, but it is important to remember that in any particular application not all these items may be needed; on the other hand, if the structure of the data base does not allow for them to be included, the system may prove to be excessively limited in practice. Here is a list of possible fields within an archival entity description:

1 *Entry number/description key.* Unique notation identifying the record.
2 *Archival level identifier.* Notation indicating the level of description.
3 *Archival reference.* Unique code provided by the archives service, as in manual operations.
4 *Sub-status number.* A code may be necessary to record the relationship between a record and its series and group, in order to preserve a note of its archival context.

5 *Former reference.* Notation of the record in a former administrative state.
6 *External reference.* Facility for the general index to refer to relevant information not contained in the archival description (e.g. where the archive has been the subject of a published work).
7 *Provenance.* Description of the organization which created the archive or from whose administration it was transferred. Sub-fields may be necessary.
8 *Opening date*
9 *Closing date*
10 *Title.* Brief description of the record's main content or character.
11 *Narrative.* Free text description of the contents and nature of the record, in extension and support of the title.
12 *Numerical quantity*, to be expressed in terms of the most appropriate unit (e.g. boxes, volumes, pages).
13 *Physical form*
14 *Volume.* Space occupied by the entity.
15 *Volume unit.* The units of measure used (e.g. cubic or linear footage).
16 *Location.* Sub-fields may be needed where the entity is dispersed.
17 *Diplomatic form*, indicating units with a particular characteristic.
18 *Classification code.* The entity's place in a code operated by the archives service (e.g. in the code for Quarter Sessions archives).
19 *Index entries.* Set of fields which should be designed to produce index terms tailored to the precise conditions of the archives service. The narrative field may also produce index terms or become the basis of whole text retrieval systems.
20 *Access.* Data which determine the date of opening to public access, or any other restriction.
21 *Location of further descriptions.* Note of the existence and nature of other lists or indexes to the entity.
22 *Language.* Note of the language in which the original is written (e.g. Latin).

On scanning this list, the reader may feel that it is longer than would be necessary for his own purposes. This may well be so; for example, a 'closed' archive does not need fields to describe the conditions under which archives are transferred, and probably not those dealing with access restrictions or the effect of closed periods. However, the difficulty is that if a system is adopted which, after a period of experience, is found not to provide for a function which exists, or which comes to exist, then it ceases to be helpful and becomes a hindrance. This is true also where a particular field proves not to be capacious enough to hold all the information needed; for example, if the fields for index terms cannot allow complex phrases but only single terms, this might prove to be a serious drawback when after a period of use the indexes have become very bulky.

Many, though not all, of the fields listed above may be restricted either to save space or to provide for a degree of automatic verification. Thus locations may be indicated by a code rather than by textual description; and dates may be limited to year numbers or the like. Unfortunately it is not possible to place similar restrictions on the main fields, such as the title or the narrative;

with these it is often not possible to foresee any limit to the space that could be demanded for a long description. Archivists must therefore choose between accepting fixed length fields, variable length fields or a combination. Fixed length fields are the simplest to handle from the computer's viewpoint, and from the systems designer's viewpoint they are the easiest to lay out on the final page; but, where there are many vacant fields in a record, they may be wasteful; and their biggest drawback is that they do not give flexibility to the archivist. Where fields are of variable length, it is less easy (though not impossible) to arrange for their regular layout on the output page. In particular it may be difficult to arrange for arrays of data to occupy single lines on the page, for naturally there is a fixed limit to the amount of material that will go into one line. This limit is normally about 120 characters, but the use of special peripherals can extend this to about 160 characters, possibly at the expense of not being able to use the office's standard equipment.

It may be dangerous for an archivist to accept a system in which there are inflexible limitations on the length of fields: archives are likely to vary considerably, one from another, and therefore need different ways of description. The East Sussex Record Office's system, ARCAIC, is an example of one in which the field limitations were extremely restrictive; in the long run these became so irksome to the staff to be finally an important contributory cause of the abandonment of the system. At the same time, there may be important reasons why in a particular context a close limitation of field lengths may be accepted: in the case of a records management system, the advantages of being able to set out in one line all details of each listed record may well occasionally outweigh the need to abbreviate such fields as file titles. The ARMS system illustrates this well. The matter is one for the archivist to consider in the context of his immediate objectives.

Single-line displays may be extended by adding second or subsequent lines of material below the field in the top line; Fig. 3 shows this clearly. Arranging for this elaboration may cause complications in the programming of the input data, particularly if punched cards are used.

Restrictions on the length of fields in some systems may also be dictated by the form in which the data are stored electronically within the computer memory. Serial storage on magnetic tape is perhaps more suitable for variable-length fields than the main alternative – key-address storage. Which of these is used depends on such factors as the need for on-line access, the amount of total data stored, and the need for long sequential searches by the computer; of course, technical advice must be taken on this. The choice can be of some moment, since the modes of scanning for data retrieval, writing-in amendments and transcribing the file – all

```
0 FIN/69/07/03P12&3SELECTION TRUST LTD       1?247683/K 776? TRUST,SELECTION
1 SCY/06/02/04SEFTON PARK HOUSEHOLDS SURVEY:  1970 P    7313- SEFTON PARK
2           COMPLETED QUESTIONNAIRES & ANALYSIS1970      -7327 HOUSEHOLDS
3 SCY/06/02/02NORRIS GREEN HOUSEHOLDS SURVEY: 1969 P    7313- NORRIS GREEN
4           COMPLETED QUESTIONNAIRES,CODE KEY            -7327 HOUSEHOLDS
5           AND PART ANALYSIS                                  SOCIAL SURVEY
6 FIN/70/01/01RESEARCH GRANTS IN SCIENCE      1970688/1 8010 GRANTS
```

Fig. 2   An example of a proof report, showing data base arrangement during input (Source: CMF).

```
SCY/06/02/01   FORMBY & FRESHFIELD MIGRATION SUR-   1968   P   7313-   FORMBY
               VEY;COMPLETED QUESTIONNAIRES                   -7327   FRESHFIELD
                                                                      MIGRATION

SCY/06/02/02   NORRIS GREEN HOUSEHOLDS SURVEY;      1969   P   7313-   NORRIS GREEN
               COMPLETED QUESTIONNAIRES,CODE KEY              -7327   HOUSEHOLDS
               AND PART ANALYSIS                                      SOCIAL SURVEY

SCY/06/02/03   NORRIS GREEN HOUSEHOLDS SURVEY:      1969   P   7313-   NORRIS GREEN
               CODING SHEETS, COMMENTS FROM                   -7327   HOUSEHOLDS
               SCHEDULES                                              CODE KEY

SCY/06/02/04   SEFTON PARK HOUSEHOLDS SURVEY;       1970   P   7313-   SEFTON PARK
               COMPLETED QUESTIONNAIRES & ANALYSIS           -7327   HOUSEHOLDS
```

Fig. 3   An example of output. The data base material has been sorted and arranged on the page (Source: CMF).

of which are operations which will be needed – will have to be designed; in a system carrying much data, considerable expense may be involved.

The power of the computer lies in its ability to manipulate data, and in practice archival programs identify data by their field characteristics. A computerized inventory can be re-sorted and printed out in any predetermined order, taking the fields as the basis of the order. Thus one inventory could be produced which is an alphabetical ordering of document titles; and another inventory might be based upon alphabetical-numerical ordering of reference codes. Each list may include the corresponding information from the other fields in the record, or it may exclude some of them. Thus in records management a list of documents in order of disposal data may be printed out which includes the location references but excludes data not immediately relevant to disposal, such as index terms.

Output Formatting

The objective of any system is to arrange for the input information – the archival description – properly arranged into its records and fields, to be input into the computer's memory store. Once there, this information acts as a data base and is available for further processing. The data base need not itself be in any set order of entry, provided that the computer has a program which allows it to distinguish any field, and any record, from all others.

Figs. 2 and 3 illustrate this, and show that the actual layout of data or data fields on paper in the end product is important when designing the input document.

Possible forms of output from an inventory might include the following:

(i) Inventory in reference code (archival) order, for use in the guide, searchroom, handlists. Updated yearly.
(ii) Inventory in location (shelf) order for staff use. Updated yearly, or after a major re-arrangement.
(iii) Special inventories (handlists) on subject bases, for searchroom or publication. Updated yearly.
(iv) Inventories of material emerging from period of restricted access. Annual.
(v) Place, person, subject indexes. Updated quarterly.
(vi) Type-set inventories of select series, for printing.

In a records management context, the following will be needed:

(vii) Disposal lists in order of effective disposal date. Updated monthly.

(viii) Reports giving data on the degree and frequency with which records are used. Updated six-monthly.
(ix) Reports on space occupied by records of user department. Updated annually for report, or on particular occasions in order to support a case for extension of storage.
(x) Vacated locations report. Updated frequently.
(xi) Lists of records for review. New lists monthly.

Design of Input Stationery

Input data must be processed. It is usually desirable to enter them on an input form which is designed to allow key-punch operators, or any other clerical personnel, to prepare the data in the right order, add the proper procedural data, and observe the correct field lengths and other characteristics; examples of input data forms are given in later chapters. Where field length restrictions operate, it is usual to mark off spaces for individual characters, one letter, figure or symbol (including a space) to be written in each space. Otherwise these are not necessary, but some clear division must be given to each record and field, and the necessary identifiers must be written in.

If the data preparation is to be done exclusively by the archives staff, who are familiar with both the system requirements and the character of the rough listing they are working from, there will be no strict need to write out raw input data on special forms. Key-punching or input by whatever means could be done directly from the archivist's notes. However, this condition does not always apply, and in any case there is a good reason for systematizing data on a special input form bearing a note of all the input formalities. Computers are particularly sensitive to incorrect input data (this is the meaning of the famous saying, 'garbage in, garbage out'), and what is saved by short cuts in the preliminary arrangement of the data to be prepared may well be lost in error reports or in data incorrectly input.

Usually two input data forms will be needed: a complex one for inputting new archival descriptions, and a simpler one for inputting updating information (amendments and deletions).

Direct data entry coupled with strong automatic verification facilities may make input forms unnecessary. This is discussed below (page 43).

The design of input stationery is also affected by the method used for preparing the data for input. Two alternatives are possible. *Batch working* is the accumulation of data sent as a batch to the data preparation staff; this method is usually employed where the data preparation equipment and personnel are sited elsewhere, perhaps in a central computer unit; or where data preparation is being done by a bureau. The alternative is *on-line working*, where data can be input into the system immediately, through input devices kept in the archives office and operated by its own staff. With on-line working it is not necessary to let amounts of data pile up, but new input can be made from minute to minute. The choice between these may be determined mainly by the kind of hardware available and by the parent organization's general system of administration. Where on-line input is used, it is likely that there can be interactive searching and output facilities.

Software and Computer Languages

Any form of writing, including numerals, can be fed into a computer, but the computer itself is not able to carry out any operations on the data stored within it unless it has complete instructions, covering every single step to be taken. These instructions (programs) are written in computer languages, of which there are many varieties. Some, covering very basic technical operations, never need come into the ken of a non-technical computer user: these are machine languages or codes and assemblers. Normally, users will only come into contact with high-level languages, which allow the program instructions to be written out in something approaching normal language and still be capable of translation into terms which the computer will be able to handle. The user therefore requires some knowledge of the high-level languages, because it is important that his system should be designed to use one of them.

Like all man-designed systems, computer languages have specific aptitudes: they are good at some things and not so good at others; so that choice of language is important. However, it is not necessary to be a computer expert, a scientist or a mathematician to understand the composition, terms and powers of a computer language, or even to learn to write programs in one. Equally, it is not usually necessary for a user to learn a computer language in depth, or to write his own programs. The best condition is one having a close dialogue between the user and the programmer.

Some languages are specific to one particular make of hardware. The high-level languages are, in principle, compatible with all makes, but still need a technical interpretative system, the compiler, in order to make them work with any particular machine. Obviously, no system should be adopted which is not fully interfaced with the available equipment, and which local computer staff are not familiar with.

A high-level language often used in information work is COBOL (Common Business Oriented Language), which originated for use in business administration. Intended to be a language understood by the layman, it uses English-language terms and is aligned

towards non-mathematical uses. There are several useful textbooks
for beginners in this language, but an unfortunate feature of this
literature, from the archivist's point of view at any rate, is that the
examples are invariably taken from business administration:
payrolls, invoices and ledgers. However, in both areas the
analytical process of dividing up the initial data into manipulable
fields is a useful one. The real trouble is that, if an archivist always
has to use a language which is – perhaps not very finely – adapted
from the needs and usages of another discipline, sooner or later he
will find himself unable to exploit the full potential of the computer.
All adaptations eventually demonstrate some degree of misfit.

It is therefore a good idea to look at other high-level languages of
possible relevance to archival work. These include FORTRAN
(Formula Translator), which is often regarded as primarily intended
for numerical and mathematical applications. It would not on the
face of it seem the most suitable language for programs aimed at
handling textual data, but recently some computer experts have
recommended it for this, and it is apparently less cumbersome than
COBOL in expressing certain kinds of data manipulations. It has
certainly also been used to good effect in historical research
projects using archival material, and it is taught to student
archivists at the training school in Marburg.

Another internationally used high-level language is ALGOL, whose
literature is usually couched in strictly mathematical terms. More
interesting to archivists is PL/1 (Programming Language 1), which
was designed to combine features of commercial languages such
as COBOL and scientific languages like ALGOL and FORTRAN. The
strength of the commercial approach is its ability to deal efficiently
with large masses of data, and sophisticated input/output facilities
have therefore been developed. The scientific languages have
emphasized fast and accurate definitions and the analysis of
complex problems. To do this they have developed sophisticated
algorithmic languages, but have neglected the facility to carry
packages of data through the processes. PL/1 is a language which
attempts to put these capabilities together.

Where there is any possibility of interactive working (see p. 45), a
language should be chosen which the user will feel able to use
confidently. BASIC (Beginners All-purpose Symbolic Instruction
Code) is a very simple language which can be learnt by anyone in a
few hours. Through it a user may work with the computer, using
on-line devices such as the Visual Display Unit (VDU). In this way he
can develop the flexibility inherent in his programs, particularly in
the area of information retrieval, and will not have to work at one
or more removes from the computer all the time. The value of an
elementary language such as BASIC is enhanced by recent
developments in operating systems.

Operating Systems (os) are programs which control the running of other programs and supervise the use of peripheral equipment. They incorporate instructions for all the operations which computers are commonly asked to do, and arrange the regular processing of all the different tasks of the computer unit. In practice, nearly all the operations an archivist might require of his system are likely to be common ones. Archival programs are mainly concern to record data, sort them into different predetermined orders, select certain items of data, add or subtract particular items, and compute transactional data. These are all relatively straightforward steps, complicated only by the large amounts of data that are often involved. An advanced operating system would be able to carry out most of them, and would not necessarily require a specially written program, or at least not a very complicated one. Where this is so, specific programs compiled for archives would be based upon the powers and facilities of the operating system in use with the computer; they would assume its capacity to support the programs, and would take advantage of the facilities it offers. Where the operating system is as useful as this, there is little reason why archivists should not undertake interactive work with the computer, perhaps using the BASIC language mentioned above. It is likely that the development of software in the immediate future, especially software packages which can be used with mini-computers and micro-processors, will make it less necessary for archivists to develop their own special programs.

An example of working interactively, using operating systems and a simple set of programs, is the records management work at the University of Liverpool. The data base consists of a file containing a list of records transferred to the records centre, each record containing seven fields (reference code, document title, first date, last date, disposal date, location and keywords). Three programs cause the data base to be sorted into three orders: reference number order (alphabetical-numerical); disposal date order (numerical); and subject-index keyword order (alphabetical). When all this has been done, the system retains four files in store: the original data base, which is in random order, and the three sorted files. Using an interactive terminal, usually a VDU, and the normal facilities of the operating system, the archives office can then call up either a visual display or a hard-copy printout of any of the above files. They can also call up any specific part of the files; for example, the first ten records which follow a certain reference number can be retrieved. Any of the files can be edited and amended through the VDU. When the data base is so edited, the alterations incorporated in it (which might be new records added, obsolete records deleted, or corrections made) will be incorporated in the final print-outs whenever the programs are run again. The three special programs are needed to carry out the major sorting of the items in the data base, but all other operations can be done through the normal use of the operating system. The computer in this case is an ICL1906, and the operating system is GEORGE 4.

Software packages are also of possible interest to archivists. These are interrelated sets of programs which have been developed by computer manufacturers or by specialist institutes to provide a tool for carrying out commonly required types of job on the computer. There are packages in the data management field which may be of interest in particular cases, and there are certainly some in the area of data retrieval. Examples of these which have been used by archivists are FIND2, a package for information retrieval which has been developed by ICL; and KWIC, a package for constructing indexes, produced by IBM. Packages can be bought or leased from the copyright holder, but in many cases are provided free by the manufacturers as part of the bargain for buyers of their hardware. Consequently archival users will probably find that, if there is a package suitable and available, it will be because their computer department already has it. In practice, it is necessary not only to have the package available, but also to have computer staff who are experienced in using it, or are willing to learn. Libraries or bibliographical packages are widely disseminated, and are at first sight likely to be adaptable to some archival uses. Many commentators, though, have pointed out that there are severe constraints in the structure of bibliographical data. 'Our finding aids do not fit well into these procrustean beds.'[8]

Many software packages are linked to mini-computers or micro-processors. These are also likely to be of interest to archival users, particularly as they become more common and more versatile. Small hardware like this is not likely to contain enough memory store to be directly useful in an archival context, since archival systems usually need storage for a considerable quantity of data. But a mini-computer can be used as a means of access to a larger computer, allowing specialized uses, or a greater range of facilities for input and output.

A relatively recent development in packages and systems is the Data base Management Systems (DMS). Although they are at the moment not widely available and are complex, these systems must be of interest to archivists, as they are essentially concerned with the manipulation of a data base. The root concept of a single multi-purpose data base used as the core of a complex system for supplying information to an organization would seem to be appropriate. One of the most difficult problems in DMS is the structure of the data base and the standardization of means of data capture. This is because, in an organization like a business, data are recorded by different departments in diverse formats, and it is very difficult to standardize and to maintain the strict standards required by the computer. This is not such a difficulty in an archives office, since there is less departmentalization, and the recording of data in set forms is after all the main purpose of the organization. Ultimately the prospect of jointly accessible data bases, including material from different institutions, but with selective access, is attractive. At present, however, it is likely that DMS packages are likely to be too complex and expensive for archival use, except where they are being developed by the parent organization for its current administration.

It is clear from this discussion that an important part of the study by an intending computer user consists in evaluating existing systems for their applicability. This evaluation must be both rigorous and imaginative; the analysis behind it must correctly identify the real needs of the system, and at the same time ensure that it will be able to accommodate features which will become available in the future. In an important article, D. Bearman (1979) has set a major systems evaluation in an archival context, the automation of the Survey of Sources for the History of Biochemistry and Molecular Biology.

The automation of archival information may be considered in a number of broader contexts. It may be part of a strategy for expanding institutional services, co-operating with other archives, reducing the demands of routine tasks on staff time, or integrating the archives with other departments of the institution of which it is a part. Whatever the larger purposes are, automation will succeed only to the extent that it takes into account the specific needs and goals of the archives. When systems that meet these needs are successfully adopted they will almost certainly change traditional archival practices.

To the extent that they force us to standardize within and between institutions and to pay closer attention to the problems of establishing intellectual control through subject access, they will result in an improvement of our methods. If the systems we adopt are chosen with attention to our needs, we may discover how many of our practices have developed because of the constraints of manual processing, and we will be able to alter these and retain only those descriptive techniques which truly provide more accurate and rigorous control.[9]

Indexes and Searches

Intellectual control over archival holdings remains a fundamental aim for archivists. Here automated systems are likely to have a profound influence: computer systems have the ability to generate indexes, and can carry out searches at great speed; they can also compare and co-ordinate index terms, and provide for searches at a depth and precision that would be impossible, in ordinary human terms, by manual methods. Naturally, there is a cost, both in financial terms and in terms of labour and design, and in designing facilities for data retrieval, indexing and machine searching an archivist must take into account very complex considerations. In practice, most archival systems do not yet provide for machine searching, although they do provide for some sort of index. The design of indexing or searching facilities goes back to the early analysis of the aims of the system. Both are based upon the descriptive information which is contained in it. In archival terms, the main descriptive material is likely to be one of the following:

(i) *Title*: a brief label usually originating in the administrative organization which is the archive's provenance, which may or may not give an accurate and meaningful summary of the document or series' content.

(ii) *Narrative*: a free text summary which sets out to give keys to the actual contents of the document or series. Fullness and level are determined by policy decisions.

(iii) *Full text* (not common in archival contexts): full text transcription, or something approaching it: in traditional language, transcription or calendar.

Data retrieval devices, of whatever kind, must be based upon the words included in the above descriptions, and their success must be limited in the first place by the accuracy and fullness of the descriptions given in these fields.

In index construction there are choices possible between using humanly assigned index terms and machine extracted terms. Combinations are possible. Where the index terms are humanly assigned, there must be provision for them in the input material. An example of this is the project PROSPEC-SA, where a variable-length field is provided for the inclusion of index terms by the archivist who is completing the input form. These terms can be names of persons or places, or subject keywords. An example of machine-extracted index terms is any standard KWIC index.

KWIC indexes, being entirely automatic, are often useful where the title and attendant data of a document (reference numbers, location numbers, dates) are sufficient in themselves to allow for retrieval; this would apply, for instance, in records management, where the index is being applied to a simple list of files. The KWIC system produces a permuted list of file titles, in alphabetical order, giving in each case the relevant context: files with more than one keyword in the title will appear more than once in the list. The drawback to this system is that it is of limited use in a wider archival context. The title of an archival document is normally not a sufficient guide to its contents, particularly where the listing is at macro levels. Where the title is composed by the archivist drawing up the description, the existence of a KWIC facility may also influence his choice of language. Nevertheless KWIC does provide a ready possibility for many working lists. Fig. 4 gives an example from records management.

KWIC Indexing: an example of machine-generated indexing which preserves
contextual meaning; suitable only for brief file titles.

 e.g. File titles :   ref. no.

    Conference of northwestern registrars 1
    Maintenance of main-road bridges   2
    Regional planning in consultation with 3
     District Councils

```
                    MAIN-ROAD BRIDGES. MAINTENANCE OF                  2
                    REGISTRARS. CONFERENCE OF NORTHWESTERN             1
          REGIONAL PLANNING IN CONSULTATION WITH DISTRICT COUNCILS.    3
     CONSULTATION WITH DISTRICT COUNCILS. REGIONAL PLANNING IN         3
        IN CONSULTATION WITH DISTRICT COUNCILS. REGIONAL PLANNING      3
             MAINTENANCE OF MAIN-ROAD BRIDGES.                         2
                    BRIDGES. MAINTENANCE OF MAIN-ROAD                  2
          CONFERENCE OF NORTHWESTERN REGISTRARS.                       1
     DISTRICT COUNCILS. REGIONAL PLANNING IN CONSULTATION WITH         3
       WITH DISTRICT COUNCILS. REGIONAL PLANNING IN CONSULTATION       3
             NORTHWESTERN REGISTRARS. CONFERENCE OF                    1
```

KWOC indexes : also machine-generated, but extracts the keyword, followed
by the full title.

```
        BRIDGES:
          MAINTENANCE OF MAIN-ROAD BRIDGES        2
        CONFERENCE:
          CONFERENCE OF NORTHWESTERN REGISTRARS 1
        etc.
```

Fig. 4 KWIC and KWOC **machine-generated indexes of file titles**

The output formatting of the index or search facility must also be
borne in mind at the design stage. The choice, as before, is between
batch working and on-line working (see pages 30–1, 44). Using
batch mode, a good choice might be to produce printed indexes,
which can be distributed in several copies and easily updated;
electronic typesetting and the use of upper and lower case might
be an advantage for this. Printout results of document searches are
also useful. In these cases, the system can print out the entry for
any document or series (depending on the level at which the
system works) which contains either a selected keyword, or a
predetermined combination of selected keywords. The selection
may be expressed in terms of Boolean logic; for example:

Please print out documents containing the combinations
XXXXXXXX *and* YYYYYYYY *or* XXXXXXX *and* ZZZZZZZZ, *and
not* QQQQQQQ (where QQQQQQQ is a possible component of
one or more of the preceding terms).

The resulting print-out will be an example of Selected
Dissemination of Information (SDI), and may be sent to potential users.
 However, there are disadvantages in using batch mode,
especially where there is machine-searching. Users do not always
select the best index terms, and archivists do not always give either
the best terms or the best combinations while they are doing their

listing and preparation of the input material; better terms or combinations of terms may occur to the user when he sees the result of his first search attempt. If he has to wait until another batch is ready before refining his request, there will be loss of time and frustration. This would be avoided if the interrogation of the system could be carried out interactively. A second search, using alternative terms, could then be mounted as soon as the results of the first were displayed, and the most acceptable result could still be printed out for reference as hard copy later. A system for interactive searching should therefore contain sufficient command terms to allow the user to modify and pursue his enquiry until some sort of conclusion had been reached.

An example of such a command language is the one used by EURONET in connection with an information retrieval service for technological documentation in Europe. This allows the user to enter the following simple commands:

CONNECT = 'Logging on': introducing the user
BASE =   Identify the data base to be searched, XXX being its name
FIND =   Institute search
DISPLAY = Cause alphabetically linked terms to be displayed
RELATE = Cause locally related terms to be displayed
SHOW =   Cause document references containing chosen terms to be
                  displayed
PRINT =   Cause these document references to be printed out
MORE =   Cause the system to continue further references or to continue
                  displaying alphabetical terms
HELP =   To get on-line guidance on procedure from the operators
STOP =   'Logging off': end of interactive session.

There are further commands in this system.

The mechanical operations involved in operating indexes are not in themselves difficult for automated systems. The problems encountered are really the problems of indexing in itself. These are exacerbated by the computer's ability to compile large indexes very rapidly, thus emphasizing defects which were always inherent in the indexing plan. Similar defects in a manual index might not become burdensome until the index had grown large over time. It is clearly important to have a coherent policy for the construction of indexes, even manual ones, and this policy should take account of physical constraints, not only of time of staff involved, but also of space and format. An indexing plan linked to an automated system should consider the number of terms to be permitted, the depth of indexing (the degree of detail which can be recognized by the insertion of more and more specific terms) and the level at which the documents are to be indexed (series level, individual document level).

Following decisions on these points, a choice must be made between free language indexing and the use of a controlled indexing language. In the context of a smaller archives service, particularly where there is specialization in archives covering certain subject areas, there is much to be said for choosing free language indexing. Archivists who are at home in their subject field, and used to working with colleagues, already, in a sense, are using a controlled language: their use of terms is exact, they operate (perhaps unconsciously) a 'preferred term' policy, and they are aware of the main pitfalls involved in choosing synonyms. On the work-bench free language indexing has the inestimable benefit that the indexers do not have to refer to an authority list or permitted vocabulary. In more general situations some kind of authority list must be established. There are, broadly speaking, two kinds of these: classification schemes, such as the one promoted in the 1970s by the Society of Archivists,[10] and thesauri.

The advantage of the scheme is that it provides a universal subject classification tailored to the needs of (British) archives services, but which is comparable in subject coverage to the universal classification schemes known to the library world. It is controlled by an alphabetical-numerical notation, which has the effect of making it rather formal in structure, and also implies difficulty in adapting it to the machine generation of index terms. Its other defect is that its very comprehensiveness makes it less suitable for specialized archives services, which would still have to develop a specialized classification system for their own use within the general umbrella of the wider scheme; from a computer viewpoint this is a serious defect, for it is precisely the specialized archives services which are most likely to develop automated systems, or to join automated systems proper to their areas of specialization. The advantages of this scheme to generalized archives services, such as county archives offices, are less likely to be immediately appreciated. However, it exists, and it is an interesting model for the construction of a general classification scheme.

An alternative approach is through a thesaurus, which is a listing of terms which sets out the logical relationships between them. From a thesaurus, a user may obtain a more or less complete determination of the conceptual context of any term. These are usually set out under such headings as NT (narrower term); BT (broader term); RT (related term); SA (see also); UF (use for). An advantage of the thesaurus is that, through tracing the logical linkages which it contains, it gives useful ideas for the choice of terms (either to insert into an index or to use in conducting a search) and for controlling the concepts documented.

It is a complex and lengthy task to compile a thesaurus, and there is as yet no general version (perhaps there could not be one) which is available as an archival model. A simplified version of a thesaurus is a subject-heading list, which can be much more easily compiled as a by-product of any indexing work. This simply lists index terms, and indicates which linked term is preferred. PT (preferred term) and SA (see also) or UF (use for) need be the only linkages used.

Another policy choice for the construction of indexes must be the choice between pre- and post-coordinate indexing. In the latter, index terms refer to simple concepts, and are combined only in so far as the system provides for the combination of terms, as in the Boolean examples mentioned above. This approach may be very suitable for automated systems which can provide the necessary combinations. Pre-coordinate indexes use compound headings or strings which can give a great deal of specificity. Combination is difficult, but a number of index strings can be given for any one document. This approach is very suitable for some kinds of simple machine-generated indexing, such as KWIC.

Generally speaking, any indexing method can be implemented by computer systems, provided of course that the system will accommodate it. At this point, the systems designer must decide whether his system should depend on machine generation of terms or humanly assigned and input terms. In either case there may be benefits in storing a thesaurus of some kind in the system. In its simplest type, this may take the form of a stop-list, which would prevent certain words (such as 'the' or 'about') being chosen as index terms; the stop-list would contain some hundreds of words, and could be extended simply. At the other extreme a full thesaurus could be held in the machine by which index terms would be checked and the necessary relationships displayed. The most important determining factor will be the general objectives of the system and its chosen output formats but, as in all aspects of systems design, compatibility with wider systems or developments of present systems will be important for the future.

Totally free indexing is not recommended. It will result in the generation of long indexes in which different terms appear referring to similar subjects, and unqualified terms carrying large numbers of undifferentiated references. Cross-reference to double or related terms would be difficult.

This very brief and simplified discussion of indexing questions is not sufficient to deal with this most complex subject. It is intended merely to provide a framework for a discussion of the choices which lie before the designer of an automated system for archival management. There is a considerable literature on the related questions of indexing, classification of information or documents, and information retrieval, and this should be consulted.

Computer Processing

Computer installations (configurations) correspond to the
conceptual divisions apparent in all information work: data in, data
manipulation, information out. A computer is, after all, simply a
tool with which one may carry out certain tasks more easily. Many
of the problems in using computers, however, stem from the
limitations imposed on the work by the input and output
equipment rather than from the operations which go on inside the
computer itself. A survey of some of the input/output devices is
therefore useful.

Input Equipment

The purpose of all input devices is to change the format of the data
to be fed into the computer, in such a way as to allow the computer
to accept and use it. Data produced and used by archives offices
consist of descriptions, inventories and indexes, which are written
or typed out on sheets of paper or on cards; to allow the computer
to work on these, it is usually necessary to translate them into
different formats.

It is true that there is equipment which allows computers to
absorb data by directly scanning the source documents. These
include mark sensing, where predesigned cards can be marked off
by an ordinary pen or ballpoint; magnetic ink character recognition
(MICR), familiar to most people from the codes now printed at the
bottom of bank cheques; and optical character recognition (OCR),
where characters typed in a special fount and situated in
predetermined places on the document (as in the case of invoices)
can be read directly. All systems of course require special hardware
in the form of reading machines. While there is of course a great
potential in this field, and it is likely that there will be technical
development in future, the present situation is that the capabilities
of systems such as these are too limited to be useful in an archival
context; they may be useful where a large number of uniform
documents must be processed, but this is not usually the case with
archival lists.

An exceptional instance of the use of OCR is to control the
photographic collections in the State Archives of North Rhine
Westphalia, at Dusseldorf. Their experience shows that this may be
a practical approach for a small archive service, since the only
hardware required is a special typewriter with which material can
be processed in the office. However, this presupposes that the
computer service to be employed has compatible equipment and
expertise.

More normally, input data are prepared by translating them into
machine-readable forms. The most common of these are punched
cards, punched tape, and magnetic tape.

Punched cards. These are familiar to most people because they have been used for many years to carry uniform types of data. Payrolls, for instance, could be recorded and processed on punched cards even before the introduction of computers. They have been found to be a particularly apt and flexible means of feeding in information to computers, and card-punching machines and operators are present in most large organizations today. It is possible to hire machines or to send punching work out to an agency.

Basically a punched card is a rectangular card measuring 83 × 188 mm, and on it are printed (usually) 80 vertical columns. Each column represents one character (letter, number or symbol), and the card puncher pierces a combination of regular holes down the appropriate column to represent the character desired. Many card punchers also print the characters in the usual symbols along the top of the card when it has been punched. The cards that have been punched can then be fed through readers which transmit the data to the computer very rapidly.

From an archival point of view, the punched card has the drawback that it is of limited length and is a discrete object, like an index card. Archival descriptions of documents are usually of greater length than 80 characters, and this means that more than one card may be needed for each description; and archival inventories are usually designed to document the interconnexion between one document and the next. However, these are difficulties which can be overcome, and the punched card in most cases is a suitable mode of input for archival data, given certain safeguards. A particular virtue of the punched card is that it is not difficult to retype a card which contains an error. Stacks of punched cards can also be stored very easily, and, though they cannot easily be read by eye, they constitute a permanent record.

Fig. 5 A punched card, showing the punch combinations for letters and numerals

Punched tape (paper tape). At first sight this mode of input seems to be inherently more suitable for archival data, which is often lengthy but with variable components, and yet demands a connected treatment. Paper tape is supplied in long reels, and these are fed through a paper tape punching machine. The machine punches patterns of holes across the tape representing characters, and the tape is then read by special readers.

Unfortunately, paper tape has inherent defects which have tended to make it increasingly unpopular in the computer world, and it is no longer so common to have paper tape punching facilities. In particular, it is difficult to insert updated information or to correct errors in typing. To correct a spelling mistake, for example, it is necessary to retype the entire tape; and though this may be done automatically, by switching an instruction to copy the good parts of the original tape, this is expensive in time and resources. Paper tape remains a data input possibility, however, and at least one important current archival program uses it.

Magnetic tape. It is possible to type data directly on to magnetic tape and, with the advent of word processors and other advanced office equipment, it is likely that this will be an increasingly popular method of preparing input data. The particular advantage is that the typewriters which prepare the tape can also produce a hard (i.e. eye-readable paper) copy at the same time. Magnetic tape is easy to correct, and can be copied or read into the computer at high speed. Generally the speed of this system is greater than that of the others. Some equipment allows visual display of the characters typed, correction by backspacing, and some degree of verification of the data which is being input. Modern tape encoders often use cassettes, which of course makes the tape much easier to handle and to preserve as a record.

All input systems must provide for verification, that is, the checking of the material which has been prepared to see that it is accurate both in its content and in its format. Computers are intolerant of even trivial errors, and mistakes which would be insignificant in a manual system will cause major trouble in automated ones.

There must therefore be a way of ensuring that all input data is correct. A common way of arranging this is to type the input data twice, by different operators. The resulting input material (punched cards, tape, etc.) is then run through the reading equipment, which will reject any item that does not tally with its counterpart. These can then be examined manually and the necessary amendments made. Double keying is an efficient but expensive method, and obviously doubles the initial typing costs. A small archives office probably would prefer to rely on visual proof-reading by its own staff. In this approach, input data are keyed only once and read into the computer. The system will reject items which do not conform to the program format, but otherwise will read in possibly erroneous data. To check this, the system is asked to produce a direct print-out of the material it has stored, and this can then be proofread by a member of staff.

Most systems will also provide a set of checks on the correctness of the input data as part of their design. The structure of the fields in PROSPEC is a good example. Field limitations, including the number and type of characters used, and other simple logical restrictions can be enforced, and entries which do not conform with the restrictions are returned as errors. A list of the type of field restrictions which can be self-verified mechanically includes the following:

(i) Permitted characters: numerals, alphabetic characters or their combination.
(ii) Character length limit: fixed or variable, justified to right or left margins.
(iii) Range limits of numerals (e.g. the earlier date should not have a higher numerical value than a later date).
(iv) Compulsory co-presence: if one field is given a value, then other linked fields must also contain significant information; alternatively, if one field is left vacant, related fields must also be vacant. This kind of restriction may also be used in supplying selected information in output formats.[11]

Input devices can sometimes incorporate these program restrictions in their off-line data preparation. However, when all is said, the correctness of the input data, and the verification of the data which have been processed, must remain the responsibility of the supervising staff and must involve a cost element.

So far all the input devices mentioned have implied that the data are to be fed in in batch mode: that is, a quantity of data is to be prepared off-line, in the office or bureau, and then later fed into the computer system in one batch. At present this is the most usual way of feeding in large amounts of data, and it is likely that it will continue for a time to be the most usual method for archival programmes. However recent years have seen a very rapid development of on-line data input methods, and with the advent of micro-processors and mini-computers in large numbers it is possible than on-line data insertion will become much more feasible. Batch mode has the advantage that all the slow work of keying and verifying the material can be done away from the computer. Once prepared, material can be read in quickly, saving costs in computer time.

On-line Processing Equipment

Teletype. This resembles a telex machine. It can communicate
directly with the computer, and produces hard copy in the form of a
long sheet of paper on which the transaction is typed; it can also
produce punched paper tape. Teletypes are used in the Public
Record Office to produce the orders for documents (i.e. primarily as
output equipment). Their main disadvantage is that they are slow,
since one letter must be typed out after another, and the overall
speed is less than that of a good typist.

Visual Display Unit (VDU). This is now the normal method of on-line
data preparation. It consists of a cathode ray tube (CRT) similar to a
television screen, together with a typewriter keyboard. Characters
typed out appear on the screen, as does information supplied
by the computer. This method allows very rapid access to the
information held by the system, and is a very simple direct way of
inputting or of correcting and editing data held by it. It is not so
suitable for inputting large amounts of data, since this would
require the terminal to be connected to the computer on-line for a
great length of time; this can be expensive and wearisome, since it
may not allow flexible use of office time. There is no doubt, though,
that access to the computer's information via VDU is the most rapid
and convenient method of using it and there will undoubtedly be a
rapid growth in the numbers of VDUs and the sub-systems which
support them in the near future.

If VDUs are available, an interactive mode of data retrieval and
system interrogation is also possible. Interactive interrogation may
be contrasted with batch mode interrogation, where questions to
be asked are stored until there are a quantity, and answers received
by print-out at intervals. In interactive mode supplementary
questions may be asked, and of course the waiting time for results
is reduced to virtually nothing.

On-line input/output through VDUs requires the installation of
linking equipment, known as 'modem'. More than one VDU may be
used in the link, and these may be in different locations.

Processing

The main body of the computer, often referred to as the
'mainframe' (especially to distinguish it from micro-processors or
mini-computers), is officially known as the Central Processing Unit
(CPU). The details of the structure of the CPU are not of direct interest
to the user; they can be read in many manuals, and there is no
need to give any further information here, beyond stating that the
CPU has a control unit, an arithmetic or arithmetic/logic unit where

the actual manipulation of data occurs, and a memory store. This last is the most important part of it from the user's point of view, and it is important to understand some of its characteristics.

Data held in memory by the computer can be divided into that needed instantly at hand and a backing store where long-term information can be kept until it is wanted. The instantly available memory must include at least the basic parts of the programs which are being used by the system together with the operating system and other regulatory material which governs the computer in carrying out its work; data being processed at the moment must also, of course, be held in the immediate access memory. It follows that the capacity of this memory is most important for the success of any system. Archival systems in particular are likely to demand that a large amount of information be held.

Computers are often defined in terms of the size of their memories. They are said to hold so many K bits of data, where K indicates the number 1024 (or in casual use 1000); 'bits' are the basic units of data when translated into binary code. 40K describes a memory which will hold some 40,000 basic units, at any one time, which in practice may mean about the equivalent of about 5000 eye-legible characters. This refers only, of course, to the main memory of immediately available data. Additional data may be stored, either on a short or a long-term basis, in the backing store.

Data are usually transcribed into some form of magnetic medium, usually a drum or a disc; they can be read from these surfaces by means of a reading head which rather resembles a record-player pickup. Batteries of these discs, usually constructed in sets, are a feature of a computer laboratory. Current technological development includes new versions of these memory storage units which enable much larger amounts of data to be stored on smaller surfaces.

Data which are less currently in use can be 'dumped' on to magnetic tape. This tape, usually standard half-inch tape capable of accommodating many tracks, is normally kept on reels, each reel encased in a circular plastic box. Arrays of these tapes can be observed in any computer installation, and constitute its working archive. When data held on the tapes are called for, an operator has to fetch the reel and fit it to a tape drive. This operation can take some minutes, and adversely affect a large-scale archives program at least if it is being used on-line.

The magnetic or electronic impulses which actually form the basic units by which the data are represented are extremely tiny. Reading or recording them would therefore be affected by particles of dust or other atmospheric pollutants, and all computer installations are carefully protected from these hazards. Installations are air-conditioned and usually screened from public areas; there

will be restrictions on the number of people who can enter. This
feature of computer installations is not a drawback to the user in
practice since he does not require access to the CPU itself, but only to
input–output equipment. These are usually kept in quite different
places from the CPU. Input–output peripherals will normally be put
where they are most convenient to the user.

Output

The most common form of output equipment is the *line printer*,
which prints out line by line (hence the name) information which
has been processed by the system, on to long lengths of paper. This
paper is of different widths, but normally allows the printer to
produce a line of up to 120 characters; wider papers and printers
allow lines of up to about 160 characters. This line length is an
important restriction in archival programs (see the discussion of
output formatting (page 29). Line printers are of various speeds
and sizes, but they are all much faster than typewriters. They are all
noisy, and are not suitable for siting in a searchroom.

Other forms of output which are relevant for archival programs
include output magnetic or paper tape (which may be used to
produce hard-copy output in remote locations); but of increasing
interest is the possibility of *output to microforms* (COM). Computers
can produce microfilm, either as reel film or microfiche, at very
great speed and with a high degree of excellence in the definition
and clarity of the film. COM units are becoming increasingly
popular, and are likely to be of particular interest to archival users.
This equipment is particularly suitable where there are multiple
access points, where there is a publication element in the system,
or for long-term data storage.

Most on-line devices naturally are useful for output as well as for
input. Output data can be printed out on teletype or displayed on
VDUs. In the former case, the process of printing is likely to be slow,
since teletype prints one character at a time rather than one line at
a time; in the latter case, retrieval of the data is instantaneous, or
virtually so, but the visual impression leaves no lasting record.
Neither instrument is therefore likely to replace the line-printer, but
a combination of VDU and line-printer allows for very flexible
interaction between the user and the computer, and will provide
for instant access to data and for the production of updated hard
copy which can be used in the office or searchroom.

Normally output from computers is printed in capitals only, since
this allows a much simpler mechanism and does not detract much
from the usability of the result in ordinary applications; transfer
lists in records management clearly are as useful when printed in
capitals as they are when typed in upper and lower case. However,

many archival applications may require more sophisticated
presentation. Guides to repository holdings are normally intended
for publication, and it would not be suitable to produce material
like this in majuscules or minuscules only; large areas of text in one
or other would be tiresome in the extreme, and there would be a
good deal of resistance from both staff and users. The service itself
will wish to maintain its reputation for fine work by the quality of its
publications. Here systems will need to include upper and lower
case printing facilities.

To do this two things are necessary: access to the necessary
output equipment, and the necessary control instructions in the
system, which will instruct the printer to change between capitals
and lower case. These add considerably to the complication of the
system, and must be provided for in the initial design. The
mechanics of printing out are not quite so difficult. If a two-case
line printer is not available in-house, output onto magnetic tape
would allow the printing out to be done elsewhere, and would also
provide a record which could be re-run when required. Computer
type-setting is feasible, and archival systems should in general at
least consider the possibility of using it in their printing operations.
The major national archival systems, PROSPEC and SPINDEX included,
do in fact provide for printing out in a variety of types.

Access to Computer Facilities

Only the largest archives services will be able to consider buying
their own computer installation, presumably in the form of a
mini-computer with its associated hardware. Mini- and
micro-computers are likely to become a more feasible proposition
for smaller organizations in the future than they have been, though
their usefulness still greatly depends on the availability of suitable
software. A mini-computer on its own is not likely to have the
storage capacity to be able to handle a large archival system. Such
equipment can be used on the 'front-end' of mainframe computers
to control one or more input–output terminals and to regulate their
connexion to the main computer. Such an installation can be very
useful in tailoring the system to the exact needs of the user.

In most cases, the archival user will seek to use the computer
installation already possessed by his organization. Most large
employers have a computer unit which has considerable capacity –
governments, universities, local authorities, businesses, and
specialized institutions and services. The costing of computer time
to internal users is likely to be favourable, and the expertise of the
computer unit's staff will also be available on a non-commercial
basis. There is likely to be a pre-planned system of input–output

devices, which will allow for the insertion of another means of access, or it may be possible to use the facilities of a neighbouring large department. There is generally spare time available on peripherals.

An alternative is to use the services of a commercial computer bureau. The development of a new system by this means will have to be fully costed out and the money paid over, whereas by using internal systems these costs may often be absorbed by existing budgets. Once the difficulty of finance has been solved, though, there are many advantages in this approach. The resources required for the initial development of a new system are precisely what an internal unit often does not have. The bureau, if well chosen, will be expert in appropriate systems and will pay close attention to the customer's needs. On the other hand one is dependant on the outside agency, which may decide at some future period to change its speciality, raise its prices or switch to new hardware which will involve difficulties of compatibility.

A fourth possibility lies in shared or co-operative working. Shared hardware and technical services can be arranged with little technical difficulty between, say, local authorities, specialized institutes, or firms; indeed such link-ups are nowadays quite common. Even if this is not feasible, the shared use of existing software certainly is. There are many precedents. In the field of documentation and information retrieval, many of the existing systems were developed by particular organizations, and later made widely available. For example, the system known as CAIRS (Computer Assisted Information Retrieval System) was developed first by the Leatherhead Food Research Association, and subsequently has become widely used by many information services. There are at present several archival systems which are sufficiently developed to be used as the basis for wider employment and there are several which could be so developed. In Britain, one which is already available, on a experimental basis, for co-operative use is PROSPEC-SA. In the USA, SPINDEX is the core of a user network.

Costs

The question of cost is one of the most crucial in deciding whether or not to introduce automated systems. It is quite clear that extra costs will be involved; it is not at all clear whether these extra costs will be enormously higher than the cost of existing systems, or that they will not buy extra productivity and means of access which are not available at any other price. Archivists who have published views on this question are divided into the pessimists, who point to large-scale projects which have incurred (or might have incurred) astronomical costs in money and in staff time, and the optimists, who calculate that if manual processes were truly costed, then automated processes, costed on the same basis, are only marginally more expensive, and vastly more productive. It may be useful to draw together some of these observations.

Representing the optimistic school, S. C. Newton published an analysis of the costs of his program ARCAIC, introduced at the East Sussex Record Office.[12] Costing was based on two assumptions: (a) that there would be a period of two years during which intensive activity would allow conversion of backlog lists to automated form; (b) that on the basis of 7500 key depressions per hour, data preparation would require up to 14 man-hours per month during change-over, dropping to 1 man-hour per month for normal running.

	Annual costs (£)
Cost elements (1970 figures)	
1 Punching and verifying: £1 per hour	
change-over period: 400,000 key depressions per month	1280
normal running: 100,000 key depressions per year	27
2 Machine time: £26 per hour	
change-over period: $1\frac{1}{2}$–$2\frac{1}{2}$ hours per month	780
normal running: 30 minutes per month	60
Added special charges for periodical printing: about	120
3 Stationery costs: input forms	—
special output stationery	133
(perforated cards)	
Annual totals: Change-over period	£2313
Normal running	£340

At this period the total annual budget for this archives office was less than £13,000. In the foregoing analysis no indication was given of the true initial development cost, that is the cost of the time of record office staff, analysts, programmers, or of the software and hardware that were available during the experiment, trial and planning. No doubt this is because it was an in-house development, using the county council's computer and staff, and the record office's own personnel; the system itself was a local adaptation of an existing library package which was available free. Nevertheless it could well be argued that in circumstances like that, the absorption of these costs is quite legitimate and normal.

Newton confirmed his optimistic view four years later, in 1974, by supplying the following table of annual costs involved in a theoretical situation, in this case providing a figure for development.[13]

Capital cost of system development, using package or employing organization's own programmer, £11,000. Write off over 15 years, annual cost £733.

Automated system		Manual system	
System development	£733	Input preparation	
Input preparation		(typing)	£635
(punching time)	£1086		
Computer time (charged		Indexing	£1057
as internal user)	£400	Stationery, equipment,	
Print-out materials	£750	overheads	£750
Establishment	£2500	Establishment	£2500
	£5469		£4942

The net marginal cost of automation in this case was therefore £527, in a budget of about £5000. These figures would justify the statement that costs are comparable if an honest comparison between automated and manual systems is attempted. Such a comparison is of course very difficult: there are many imponderables, and the costing of typing and key-punching time, based on the number of key depressions achieved by the operator over a period of years, tends to be a very variable factor.

In 1971 M. E. Carroll of the Public Archives of Canada carried out a study of the cost of indexing by automatic data processing and by manual methods.[14] His findings were that for a project covering the indexing of 100,000 items of correspondence the total costs would be:

manual:	$35,100; 2200 man-days.	Unit cost	$0.351 per card.
ADP:	$24,300; 1000 man-days.	Unit cost	$0.243 per card.

Items taken into account in costing the ADP side of this equation included systems analysis by an archivist, key punching, hire of card puncher, verification, machine sorting of the cards (including hire of the machine), line printer, and use of pre-existing program. A note was added however, to the later discussion of this report, on the unreality of costing the time of employees by counting the number of card operations they can do in one minute, and then extrapolating this: in practice no-one can maintain norms established in this manner, and the figures so derived must be regarded as giving only a general or comparative indication of costs.

To give consideration to the advocates of pessimism, it must be admitted that an important element in the costing of programs is their cost in staff time: an over-ambitious program can fail because it makes impossible demands. This is shown by a recent article by A. Calmes surveying the experience at the National Archives of the U.S.A. on their computer-based finding aids.[15] This article reports on a project (NARS A–1) for compiling series-level inventories into one master file so that subject retrieval would eventually be possible. The project was a very large one, involving an initial input of 3 million characters, and a eventual total of 100 million. The system study (analysis), carried out largely by NARS staff and occupying 4½ man-years, cost $70,000, and the eventual investment was $1,168,000, with an annual budgeted cost of $74,000.

Two general points are worth making, though of course very few archival users will operate on this scale. One is that the NARS service had reached a point where its work problems were too large to solve by traditional, manual methods. The analysts found that the costs of creating an integrated finding aid which would allow access to the archives for subject-based searches were in fact comparable, whether the job was done manually or by automated methods. However,

This was a moot point, since creation of the file would represent about 60 per cent of the total cost, and the Archives administration could not hire a large enough number of clerk typists and provide them with enough office space for typing and maintaining an active file of complete inventories of all the record groups.

If the work was to be done at all, then, it would have to be by ADP. However, on the other hand,

the overall cost of the system is high. If a fully automated system with on-line retrieval by index terms had been implemented, the cost would have been excessively high, and the production rate so slow that it would have taken sixty years to catch up. The A–1 system is a fair warning, therefore, that automation of archival finding aids must be approached carefully.

These general assumptions about cost are confirmed by a study of more recent projects undertaken by local authorities in Britain, involving the development of computer systems for the control of records centres. The extraneous development costs here were in the order of 2 per cent of the total budget of the archives office, but it is likely that in both cases a significant proportion of both the system development costs and of the data preparation costs was borne by the central computer services unit of the employing authority, for reasons connected with central finance and the maximizing of the use of the computer system.

In return for the expenditure of the net marginal cost of adapting to an automatic system (and, perhaps one might add, for the mental effort of changing systems and all that goes with that) the archives office thus has a radically more flexible and multi-purpose finding system. The manual operation produces only a typed inventory and a card index. The computerized system produces a variety of products, including inventories based upon different orders, selectivity of information, plus an updatable index incorporating at least some degree of term linkage. New uses for the automated system possibly can be developed, making the data base more widely useful, and ultimately making networks a possibility.

More information is required on the costing of computer projects in the field of archives, both on the costing and staffing of initial analysis and study projects and on the implementation problems of new systems.

General Capabilities of Computer Systems

Computers handle their data extremely quickly and can carry out routine processes almost instantaneously. This means that they offer the possibility of a solution to the traditional difficulty of archivists: their inability to get the results of their work completed within a reasonable time.

Computers are also accurate. A computer can break down, but it cannot make a computational error. Where errors are made in computer systems, they arise from mistakes in the content, presentation or format of the input data, or from the misdesign of the controlling program. Together with accuracy may be added diligence. Computers do not, as human agents sometimes do, get tired and lay aside the task; they are systematic and logical, and to perform a task with computer aid demands that the whole job, its objectives, its material and its method should be carefully thought out and logically analysed and explained. Every job gains from this treatment, and everyone's work becomes more effective and successful when it undergoes such a thorough analysis. On the other hand it must be admitted that computers are stupidly intolerant of small errors which in ordinary life we can accommodate, and that it takes a long time and much care to set up a computer program or system.

Computers are versatile, but only within narrowly defined limits. To some extent these limits are mechanical and derive from the input–output equipment upon which the computer depends. More fundamentally, the range of possible activities is determined by the limitations of the software available. However a large computer can always do more than it has been asked to do; it is an exercise in imagination and in analytical power for a programmer to find ways to allow it to undertake new tasks, or to develop new ways of manipulating data. It is difficult to set up a computer system; but, once it has been set up and proved, a computer can exercise its power to arrange and organize data in ways which would have been impossible manually.

Computers are automatic; and in a sense one may say that their systems are self-directing. It remains true that human judgement and direction are essential, for computers can only follow strictly logical and literal instructions. These instructions, however, can include patterns which allow the computer to carry out some functions unsupervised and spontaneously. This makes it different in kind from any previous tool used for data management.

These four characteristics – speed, accuracy, diligence and versatility – make computers particularly suitable for information handling and data manipulation, especially where very large quantities of data are involved.

Word Processors

A recent development of the specialized microcomputer, designed for use in offices, is the word processor. This is intended to carry out the preparation, editing, storage and retrieval of texts, and as such is of great interest to the archivist. Ordinary office purposes for which it can be used include sending out form letters (to prospective depositors, etc.), distributing publicity material, and updating statistics and reports. Ultimately, when the in-office data storage capacity provided by the microchip and the floppy disc has increased, the possibility of holding archival lists on this type of machine is likely to be a very attractive one.

2 Systems for Records Management

There is no universally acceptable definition of the scope of records management as a discipline, or of the boundaries between the administration of archival documents and the management of current records. These questions have frequently been debated. However, a pragmatist will notice that there are operational systems for the management of records centres, so that these provide a practical starting point. There are two groups:

(i) Dyfed, Tyne and Wear County Record Offices and the University of Liverpool have programs for the control of the movement of records into and out of the records centre: intake, listing, location, retrieval and disposal of records.
(ii) Chester City Record Office and the University of Liverpool have programs for controlling the issue of records from records centre and their recall.

Dyfed Record Office (CAR)
This is a simple and practical system to service the records management programme. A complication is that the new county authority was formed in 1974 from three previous county authorities, and is still administered from three geographically distant centres. The system must allow for this.

CAR is based upon a series of COBOL programs using an ICL 1904S computer installation, which is the county's central computing service. The programs were developed internally by the county's own programming staff.

55

The essential principle of the system is the creation of a data base containing the following fields: document reference; document description; dates (first and last dates, 'relevant' date); location (room, bay, shelf, box number).

Document reference. The system uses the reference number of the document given to it by the originating department, to which is added a simple alphabetical code identifying place of origin. No other unique reference number is given to any record. Problems were encountered in ordering and listing documents with disparate systems of referencing (e.g. 77/LSB/8; ACCOMM/CARMS; OSS/2), but were overcome by a simple operating device. The field is limited to 20 characters.

Document Description. Free text description up to 80 characters. Where a number of documents are listed sequentially and have the same general description (e.g. Register of Electors–information returns; Register of Electors–instructions to canvassers; Register of Electors–appointment of canvassers) there is a facility for reducing the common element to the ditto sign.

Dates. The date fields must either be completed or omitted. Each date allows two numerical characters for month, followed by two numerals for year. The 'relevant date' is the date on which action must be taken by the records centre in respect of that document; it is followed by one of the following code letters which indicates what that action should be:

P=Transfer document to archives for permanent retention; public access after 30 years.
D=Destroy in accordance with agreed schedule.
R=Review document and take further action as a result.
T=Transferred to another site or to Archives.
I =Indefinite retention for legal or administrative reasons.

Location. Two numerals each are allowed for codes indicating storage room, shelving bay and shelf upon the bay. For the box number 5 numerals are allowed.

Input uses batch mode and is based upon the traditional control document in a records centre, known in Dyfed as a 'transmittal list'. This contains fields for all the above information, together with boxes for the insertion of batch control information in the header. There is an initial box on each record which allows the archivist to insert a machine instruction. This instruction may be N (insert new record) or A (amend existing record). The checked and completed transmittal lists are sent in batches of up to 55 records to a central office for key punching, and a report print-out is received by the archives office for proof-reading and verification. Error reports are submitted with the proof list. Punching in fact is on to paper tape, but in other applications a small word-processor, typing direct to magnetic tape cassettes might be used.

There is also a deletion form for removing from the data base any document which has been destroyed or otherwise removed from the system. This provides batch information header, departmental reference number of the document, departmental identifying codes and the box number. Deletions are batched and processed as with the transmittal lists.

Output. Apart from the error reports and proof list (housekeeping output), supplemented by statistical reports on the number of records input, amended or deleted, there are two main output print-outs:

(i) The site inventory list is ordered by site (the geographical location of the centre, one of three county council centres), department and sub-department, and then the document reference number. This is effectively a master list of all records held by the three records centres, together with descriptive, action and location data relevant to each. Copies are produced for each centre and for headquarters.
(ii) The action list re-sorts the data to provide a list in order of the type of action required (e.g. destroy, transfer to archives etc.), then by site, department, and sub-department. Within these headings the documents are listed in order of relevant date.

There is no index, which is perhaps a limitation, but for the purposes of the records management service in Dyfed this is not required. The site inventory lists can provide rapid access to any document requested by a participating department, under its own reference number. The system is not designed for subject-based searches which run across departmental boundaries. Documentation includes a user manual, *Modern Records Procedure* (1979).

CAR has been officially in operation since February 1977, and has proved itself a simple, practical and inexpensive system. It does not do anything which could not have been done manually, but it is clearly very convenient to have alternative listing from a single originating input document, the transmittal list, which would otherwise be done either by duplicating and sorting copies of the transmittal list or by creating new records such as an action/location index; thus there is appreciable saving in manual documentation and clerical procedures. Control over the documents is generally better than would be possible manually. Little staff discomfort or rejection has been experienced.

CAR was developed by a programmer of the county computer
unit, in association with the record office. Costs are allocated to
central establishment servicing charges.
   (See Fig. 6 for input data form CAR/1.)

Tyne and Wear Archives Department (ARMS)

Although the starting point of this system is similar to that of CAR,
it is a much more elaborate and ambitious approach using one of
the data-base management systems. The county record office
maintains a single unified records centre which serves the
departments of the metropolitan county council and its associated
bodies, of which there are about twenty. It is worth pointing out
that this is a less complex situation than that of Dyfed County
Council: the records are administered at one centre, by one staff
team, instead of three, as at Dyfed. By the vagaries of the Local
Government Act, 1972, the metropolitan counties in England are
new creations of that year, and hence do not have a massive
backlog problem for records management. They have quite
restricted ranges of powers and duties, and consequently there are
relatively few user departments. The general effect is that a
metropolitan county is a relatively well-resourced authority, with
few but important functions.
   This is a setting for automated management systems that would
not necessarily work so well in a more complex situation.
Nevertheless, the ARMS system introduces advances in the practice
of records management which deserve acknowledgement.
   There are three innovations for which ARMS is remarkable:

(i) From the beginning it is based, not upon the master list of
     documents held, which is the aggregate of transfer lists, but
     upon a records retention schedule constantly updated. This
     schedule is in turn based upon the records class (series), and
     not upon individual files or documents.
(ii) Each class of records generated in the county council is
     allocated its own class number, which is used to designate
     that class throughout all the records management
     operations. The class number provides such a powerful
     control that, in the opinion of the records management staff,
     it will be possible to drop free text class titles or descriptions
     altogether from future amendments to the systems design,
     though of course the records centre will continue to retain
     class descriptions manually.
(iii) A sequence of rapid reviews is given to records which cannot
     be allocated clearly either to archives or to destruction after a

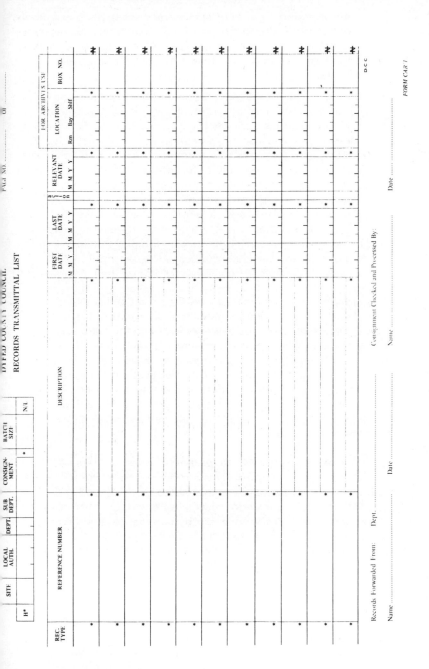

Fig. 6 Input data form (CAR/1)

definite period. The records management system as a whole
is based upon a tripartite division between records received:
for destruction after an agreed period of years; for review at
predetermined intervals; for permanent retention as
archives.

The automated system makes it feasible to bring up records for
review at much more frequent intervals than a manual system.
ARMS therefore includes a facility for review at 2, 5, 8 and 15 years
after a document has ceased to be current, as indicated in Fig. 7.

The system uses two data bases: the retention schedule file and
the master file. The former, naturally, contains the data from which
the records retention schedules are generated. Data are input to it
by means of an amendment to retention schedules form (Fig. 8),
also used for new records and deletions. The master file receives
data from a different input form, which is the traditional records
transfer list adapted for computer use by limiting the field lengths.
This results in a form basically similar to the CAR input form.

The retention schedule file contains facilities for the following fields:

Class number. This is allocated by the archives office when the
record is first received, and is used thereafter to designate the class
in every transaction; individual records within the class are
distinguished by their departmental record reference. However
there is also an unique record number, for which see below. Class
numbers consist of: two alphabetical characters denoting the
department of origin, four numerical characters allocated serially,
and one character chosen from the set: O (= record having a fixed
retention period), P (= record to be retained permanently), X (=
record to be reviewed).

Departmental Reference Mode (DRM). A numerical character chosen
from the set 1–4. Each numeral is a code for one of the common
methods by which reference numbers are made up and sorted:
date, alphabetical, alpha-numerical, numerical; this instructs the
computer to sort the reference numbers in that category by the
means indicated. This device avoids the problems involved in
sorting records bearing departmental reference symbols of very
disparate origins (cf. Dyfed, p. 56), and yet allows the records
centre to use the departmental reference as its own sorting and
identification code.

Action code of two numerical characters. This is supplied by the
archives staff, and its purpose is to indicate the type of action to be
undertaken in relation to that particular record. The following codes
are available:

01 = Destroy the whole class after retention period has expired.
02 = Normal review procedures to be followed.
10 = Review the record after a specified number of years (these will be
   further specified in the remarks column of the input form).
20 = Preserve the record permanently; transfer immediately to archives.
21 = Preserve permanently; retain it in the records centre for thirty years
   before transfer to archives.
22 = Preserve permanently; retain it in records centre indefinitely.
30 = Destroy the whole class after the expiry of the retention period, with
   the exception of random samples.
31 = Destroy the whole class after the retention period with the exception
   of specimen copies of documents.
32 = Destroy the whole class after the retention period with the exception
   of specific documents, specified in remarks column.
80 = Consult the archivist in charge of records management programme,
   who will give a ruling on suitable action.
90 = Departmental responsibility. The record is to be retained permanently.
91 = Departmental responsibility. To be destroyed after the retention
   period.

It is not certain that in practice all these codes are used. It would be
possible within the system to add further action codes if they
turned out to be useful. The archives staff of course rapidly become
familiar with the meaning of these code numbers.

Retention period. To be expressed in whole years (two numerical
characters).

Access code. This field is used to record any special conditions or
restrictions as to access that there may be. In practice most
records are entered with this field blank, indicating normality.
Otherwise a two-letter code can be entered.

Class title or description. A total of forty characters is allowed,
divided into two columns of twenty each, for the main title and any
subsidiary series. The class title provides the records centre with a
register of classes in use within the authority, matched against the
class numbers allocated to them, and of course their agreed
retention periods. The titles however are not entered into the main
file, since they are not needed for the actual administration of
records movement controls, but are registered at the records centre
as a means of overall control.
   Data for the main file are input by means of an adapted records
transfer form. This has six fields:

(i) Class number.
(ii) Departmental file references or numbers. Forty characters, divided into
       two columns of twenty each so as to allow for 'from . . . to' ranges.
       No class or file title is given, the class number and departmental
       reference being a complete and unique identification.

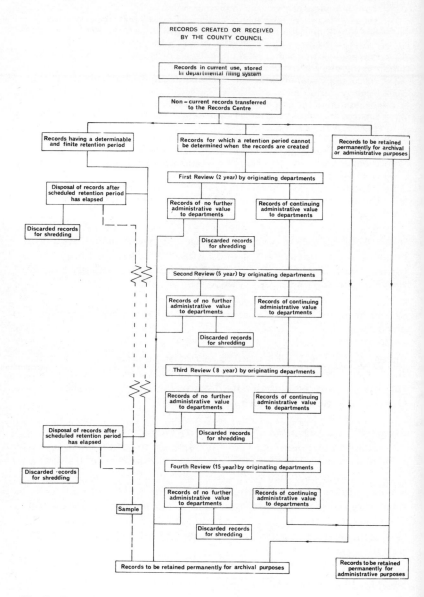

Fig. 7 Records management processes (ARMS).

TYNE AND WEAR COUNTY COUNCIL

ARCHIVES DEPARTMENT — RECORDS MANAGEMENT SYSTEM

Amendments to Retention Schedules

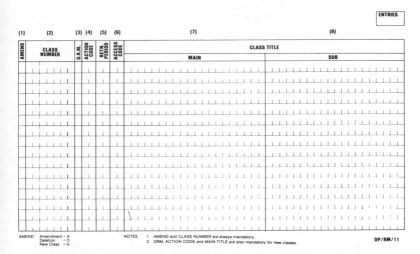

Fig. 8   Amendment to retention schedules input form (ARMS)

(iii) Covering dates (months and years).
(iv) Quantity. Three numerical characters can be used to indicate the size of
the record which is being described on this line. The system can be
used equally well as a class-level or as an individual document level
control. Most entries refer to a single document, such as a file, or to a
couple of linked documents, and so a low number appears. Where a
whole class is included, there will be a high number. However, since
the records centre is committed to the retrieval of individual
documents on demand, the input description is usually made to
relate to single documents.
(v) Special format. A simple code indicates whether the record is a volume,
a plan, or presents any other handling problem.
(vi) Storage location. Five characters allow a code for room, bay, shelf and
box numbers.

All input data are dealt with in batch mode, so that input forms
need batch data headers to be completed by the records centre
before processing. An important extra field on the transfer list
therefore provides space for the date of receipt of the records and
the receipt number.

There are also input forms to provide amendments and to record
requests for documents.

Once these data have been input into the system, the computer
itself will generate five additional data fields:

(i) Status code. The action code is scanned and a code of four alphabetical characters is taken from the set:

ARCH = transfer to archives
DEAD = not included in a retention schedule
DEST = destroyed
DISP = disposal
HOLD = holding
REVW = review

In practice most records come into DISP or REVW categories.

(ii) Event date ('relevant date' (CAR)). This is generated by matching the action code with the retention period.

(iii) Request indication. If at any time a document is requested by and issued to its originating department, the fact is recorded by the system by means of the record requests input. This information appears in several of the subsequent reports. Where there have been several requests, the date of the last one is given.

(iv) Requests per year of storage. A cumulative total of the number of times a component of each record class is referred to by departmental users is kept by the system, and the data are printed out annually.

(v) Internal Record Number (IRN). The system generates a unique reference number of six characters plus one check digit. Any further transactions in relation to any record need only be identified by the IRN, which is useful in several contexts.

In addition, the date of receipt and the receipt number are added automatically to the file. When all this has been done, the master list contains seventeen fields. Print-out can still be set with one line for each record.

Output

An elaborate input makes possible an elaborate output. The system provides for a total of 18 reports (RM01–12, with some subsets). Some of these produce documents which are directly usable by the records centre's clients; others are for housekeeping purposes:

For service use	*Housekeeping*	
	RM01	Report of validation and updating of amendments to records retention schedules
RM02 Records retention schedule. Issued to departments and frequently updated (see Fig. 9)	RM02	also gives a summary of records received which fall into each of the retention categories O,P,X
	RM03/1	Master file validation report: transfer lists
	RM03/2	Master file validation report: amendments
	RM03/3	Master file validation report: requests
	RM03/4	Master file validation report: review decisions
	RM03/5	Master file validation report: validation totals

RM04 List of records received by
the records centre. Issued to
departments with a date and
number and used as a receipt

RM05   Master file update report

RM06   Monthly exception report:
this lists issued records
overdue or other exceptional
states

RM07 Monthly review schedule
(see Fig. 10 and below)

RM08 Monthly disposal notification
(see Fig. 11)

RM09 Monthly master list, sorted
by departments, then by
departmental reference
numbers (see Fig. 12)

RM10   Monthly vacant locations
report

RM11   Yearly list of archived or
destroyed records

RM12   Yearly report of use of
records by class number
(see Fig. 13)

RM07 is a report to the originating department that records are up
for review. There is a space for the department to give a decision
on whether or not to destroy them at this stage; this is interpreted
into an action code on the right-hand column by the records centre
staff. Occasionally, in the light of an archival appraisal, they may
decide to keep something which the department needs no longer.
RM08 simply reports that records already condemned under the
retention schedules are due for destruction, and gives the
department an opportunity, if they wish, to amend the schedule in
this regard. RM12 is an interesting facility providing an annual
statement on which records have been requested for use during
the whole period of their storage (up to twenty years). This
information is not normally available in records centres and is a
powerful instrument for correcting the judgements made in the
retention schedules.

By the use of the ARMS system, the Tyne and Wear Archives
Department is able to run a large records centre, serving the whole
council and its associated bodies, under the day-to-day supervision
of two clerks. An archivist and a systems analyst from the Data
Processing unit were involved in developing the system, and the
former gives general supervision and maintenance. A reasonable
evaluation would seem to be that the system serves as at least one
additional clerk, and also carries out functions (such as recording
document movements and cumulating data on locations, space
cleared and occupied, etc.) which could not be achieved in practice
by a manual system.

DATE 17/10/79   TIME 12.30.57   REPORT RM02   PAGE 9

TYNE AND WEAR COUNTY COUNCIL

* * * ARCHIVES DEPARTMENT - RECORDS MANAGEMENT SYSTEM * * *

RECORDS RETENTION SCHEDULE

DEPARTMENT/SECTION: DATE:

THE SCHEDULE BELOW GIVES DETAILS OF THE CLASS NUMBERS ALLOCATED BY THE ARCHIVES DEPARTMENT TO THE CLASSES OF RECORDS PRODUCED BY YOUR DEPARTMENT OR SECTION.

**** THESE CLASS NUMBERS ARE IMPORTANT. ****

IT IS ESSENTIAL THAT, WHEN YOU TRANSFER RECORDS TO THE RECORDS CENTRE OR REQUEST THE PRODUCTION OF RECORDS HELD IN THE CENTRE, YOU GIVE THE CORRECT CLASS NUMBER.

YOU SHOULD DESTROY ALL EARLIER ISSUES OF THIS SCHEDULE.

CLASS NUMBER	DRM	ACTION CODE	RETN- (YRS)	ACCESS	MAIN TITLE	SUB TITLE
AJ0001P	2	21			DISTRICT COUNCIL AGENDAS	- GATESHEAD
AJ0002P	2	21			DISTRICT COUNCIL AGENDAS	- NEWCASTLE
AJ0003P	2	21			DISTRICT COUNCIL AGENDAS	- NTH TYNESIDE
AJ0004P	2	21			DISTRICT COUNCIL AGENDAS	- STH TYNESIDE
AJ0005P	2	21			DISTRICT COUNCIL AGENDAS	- SUNDERLAND
AJ00060	2	01	3		METROPOLITAN CTY AGENDAS	- GT MANCHESTER
AJ00070	2	01	3		METROPOLITAN CTY AGENDAS	- MERSEYSIDE
AJ00080	2	01	3		METROPOLITAN CTY AGENDAS	- STH YORKSHIRE
AJ00090	2	01	3		METROPOLITAN CTY AGENDAS	- WEST MIDLANDS
AJ001C0	2	01	3		METROPOLITAN CTY AGENDAS	- WST YORKSHIRE
AJ00110	2	01	5		COUNTY COUNCIL AGENDAS	- NORTHUMBERLAND
AJ00120	2	01	5		COUNTY COUNCIL AGENDAS	- DURHAM
AJ0013P	1	22			DAILY ABSTRACT NEWSPAPER CUTTINGS	

Fig. 9   Records retention schedule (ARMS RM02)

DATE 10/10/79 TIME 17.05.41 TYNE AND WEAR COUNTY COUNCIL REPORT RM07 PAGE 22
*** ARCHIVES DEPARTMENT - RECORDS MANAGEMENT SYSTEM ***
REVIEW SCHEDULE FOR THE MONTH ENDING 30/09/79

TO:
DEPARTMENT/SECTION:

THE FOLLOWING RECORDS WERE TRANSFERRED BY YOUR DEPARTMENT OR SECTION TO THE RECORDS CENTRE AND ARE NOW DUE
FOR REVIEW AS LAID DOWN IN THE COUNTY RECORDS RETENTION SCHEDULE. INFORMATION ON THE NUMBER OF REQUESTS MADE
FOR A RECORD AND THE DATE OF THE LAST REQUEST IS GIVEN BELOW.

WILL YOU INDICATE IN THE DECISION COLUMN (*) WHETHER THE RECORDS SHOULD BE DESTROYED OR RETAINED UNTIL THE
NEXT REVIEW. (REVIEWS TAKE PLACE 2,5,8 AND 15 YEARS AFTER THE RECORDS REACH THE RECORDS CENTRE.)

PLEASE SIGN AND DATE THIS FORM AND RETURN TO THE RECORDS CENTRE.

SIGNATURE: DATE:

<<<<<<<<<<<<<<<<<<<<
+ FOR THE USE OF THE
+ RECORDS CENTRE ONLY.
+ BATCH + SHEET
<<<<<<<<<<<<<<<<<<<<
+ DECISION CODES
+ 20=ARCHIVE (+CAT.NO.)
+ 21=HOLDING (+OPTIONAL EVENT DATE)
+ 98=DESTROY
<<<<<<<<<<<<<<<<<<<<
+ ENTRIES
<<<<<<<<<<<<<<<<<<<<
+   DECN. OPTIONAL
+ I.R.N. CODE   DATA

CLASS NUMBER	DEPARTMENTAL FILE NUMBERS/REFERENCES (FROM)	(TO)	COVERING DATES (FROM)	(TO)	QTY	FORMAT	REVIEW (YRS)	RECEIPT NUMBER	<<REQUESTS>> NO.	DATE	DECISION COLUMN *	I.R.N.
DZ0005X 5510				75	1		2	77/0440	0			0076738
DZ0005X 56452	56456				5		2	77/0500	0			0133773
DZ0005X 56457					1		2	77/0498	0			0133569
DZ0005X 56458					1		2	77/0498	0			013357X
DZ0005X 5700I			74	75	1		2	77/0440	0			0076530
DZ0005X 5700I			75	76	1		2	77/0440	0			0076341

*** END OF DEPARTMENT/SECTION ***

Fig. 10 Monthly review schedule (ARMS RM07)

```
DATE 28/11/79    TIME 21.25.52        * * * ARCHIVES DEPARTMENT - RECORDS MANAGEMENT SYSTEM * * *       REPORT RM08     PAGE 3
                                            TYNE AND WEAR COUNTY COUNCIL
                                      DISPOSAL NOTIFICATION FOR THE MONTH ENDING 31/10/79

TO:                                    DEPARTMENT/SECTION:

THE FOLLOWING RECORDS WERE TRANSFERRED BY YOUR DEPARTMENT OR SECTION TO THE RECORDS CENTRE AND ARE NOW DUE FOR DESTRUCTION FOLLOWING
THE EXPIRY OF THE PERIOD LAID DOWN IN THE COUNTY RECORDS RETENTION SCHEDULE.

THE RECORDS WILL BE DESTROYED ACCORDINGLY UNLESS THE RECORDS CENTRE IS NOTIFIED TO THE CONTRARY WITHIN ONE MONTH.
                                                                                                       ========
```

CLASS NUMBER	DEPARTMENTAL FILE NUMBERS/REFERENCES (FROM) (TO)	COVERING DATES (FROM) (TO)	QTY FORMAT	RETENTION (YEARS)	DATE OF RECEIPT	RECEIPT NUMBER	ACTION CODE
AN00060		09/75 07/76	2	3	21/10/76	76/0459	01
AN00070		10/75 03/76	1	3	21/10/76	76/0459	01
AN00080		10/75 07/76	2	3	21/10/76	76/0459	01
AN00090		10/75 07/76	2	3	21/10/76	76/0459	01
AN00100		10/75 07/76	2	3	21/10/76	76/0459	01
AN00110		09/75 07/76	2	3	21/10/76	76/0459	01
AN00140		04/75 03/76	1	3	21/10/76	76/0459	01
AN00150		02/75 07/75	1	3	21/10/76	76/0459	01
AN00150		08/75 03/76	1	3	21/10/76	76/0459	01
AN00150		04/76 07/76	1	3	21/10/76	76/0459	01

```
                                        *** END OF DEPARTMENT/SECTION ***
```

Fig. 11   Disposal notification (ARMS RM08)

DATE 28/11/79   TIME 21.36.20

* * * ARCHIVES TYNE AND WEAR COUNTY COUNCIL
RECORDS DEPARTMENT – RECORDS MANAGEMENT SYSTEM * * *
RECORDS MASTER LIST FOR THE MONTH ENDING 31/10/79

REPORT RM09   PAGE 487

DEPARTMENT AP

CLASS NUMBER	R D M	DEPARTMENTAL FILE NUMBERS/REFERENCES (FROM)	COVERING DATES (FROM)	(TO)	QTY	ACTION CODE	RETN.	ACCESS CODE	LOC.	RECEIPT DATE	NUMBER	I.R.N.	STATUS CODE	EVENT DATE
AP0111P	1	327			1	22		75	03247	15/02/78	78/0208	0196343	HOLD	
	1	446			2	22		75	03248	15/02/78	78/0209	0196514	HOLD	
	1	605			1	22		75	03250	15/02/78	78/0211	0196864	HOLD	
	1	722			1	22		75	03250	15/02/78	78/0211	0196853	HOLD	
	1	969			1	22		75	03251	15/02/78	78/0212	0197131	HOLD	
	1	1132			1	22		75	03252	15/02/78	78/0214	0197426	HOLD	
	1	1181			1	22		75	03253	15/02/78	78/0214	0197506	HOLD	
	1	1439			1	22		75	03253	15/02/78	78/0215	0197674	HOLD	
	1	1567			1	22		75	03255	15/02/78	78/0226	019819X	HOLD	
	1	1610			1	22		75	03257	15/02/78	78/0227	0198280	HOLD	
	1	1631			1	22		75	03257	15/02/78	78/0227	0198305	HOLD	
AP02000	1	YE/76/1	01/76	01/76	1	01	2		03665	27/06/78	78/0427	023875X	DISP	06/80
	1	YC/76/2	02/76	02/76	1	01	2		03666	27/06/78	78/0427	0238760	DISP	06/80
	1	YE/76/3	03/76	03/76	1	01	2		03674	27/06/78	78/0427	0238771	DISP	06/80
	1	YC/76/4	04/76	04/76	1	01	2		03675	27/06/78	78/0427	0238782	DISP	06/80
	1	YC/76/5	05/76	05/76	1	01	2		03677	27/06/78	78/0427	0238793	DISP	06/80
	1	YC/76/6	06/76	06/76	1	01	2		03677	27/06/78	78/0427	0238807	DISP	06/80
	1	YC/76/7	07/76	07/76	1	01	2		03678	27/06/78	78/0427	0238818	DISP	06/80
	1	YC/76/8	08/76	08/76	1	01	2		03679	27/06/78	78/0427	0238829	DISP	06/80
	1	YC/76/9	09/76	09/76	1	01	2		03680	27/06/78	78/0427	023883X	DISP	06/80
	1	YC/76/10	10/76	10/76	1	01	2		03681	27/06/78	78/0427	0238840	DISP	06/80
	1	YE/76/11	11/76	11/76	1	01	2		03682	27/06/78	78/0427	0238851	DISP	06/80
	1	YC/76/12	12/76	12/76	1	01	2		03683	27/06/78	78/0427	0238862	DISP	06/80
	1	YC/77/1	01/77	01/77	1	01	2		04233	20/11/78	78/0853	0322903	DISP	11/80
	1	YC/77/2	02/77	02/77	1	01	2		04233	20/11/78	78/0853	0322914	DISP	11/80
	1	YC/77/3	03/77	03/77	1	01	2		04233	20/11/78	78/0853	0322925	DISP	11/80
	1	YC/77/4	04/77	04/77	1	01	2		04234	20/11/78	78/0853	0322936	DISP	11/80
	1	YE/77/5	05/77	05/77	1	01	2		04234	20/11/78	78/0853	0322947	DISP	11/80
	1	YC/77/6	06/77	06/77	1	01	2		04234	20/11/78	78/0853	0322958	DISP	11/80
	1	YC/77/7	07/77	07/77	1	01	2		04235	20/11/78	78/0853	0322969	DISP	11/80
	1	YC/77/8	08/77	08/77	1	01	2		04235	20/11/78	78/0853	032297X	DISP	11/80
	1	YC/77/9	09/77	09/77	1	01	2		04235	20/11/78	78/0853	0322980	DISP	11/80
	1	YC/77/10	10/77	10/77	1	01	2		04236	20/11/78	78/0853	0322991	DISP	11/80
	1	YC/77/11	11/77	11/77	1	01	2		04236	20/11/78	78/0853	032300X	DISP	11/80
	1	YC/77/12	12/77	12/77	1	01	2		04236	20/11/78	78/0853	0323010	DISP	11/80
	1	YC/78/01	01/78	01/78	1	01	2		05059	23/07/79	79/1107	0497725	DISP	07/81
	1	YC/78/02	02/78	02/78	1	01	2		05085	23/07/79	79/1107	0497736	DISP	07/81
	1	YE/78/03	03/78	03/78	1	01	2		05090	23/07/79	79/1107	0497747	DISP	07/81
	1	YC/78/04	04/78	04/78	1	01	2		05083	23/07/79	79/1107	0497758	DISP	07/81

Fig. 12   Monthly master list (ARMS RM09)

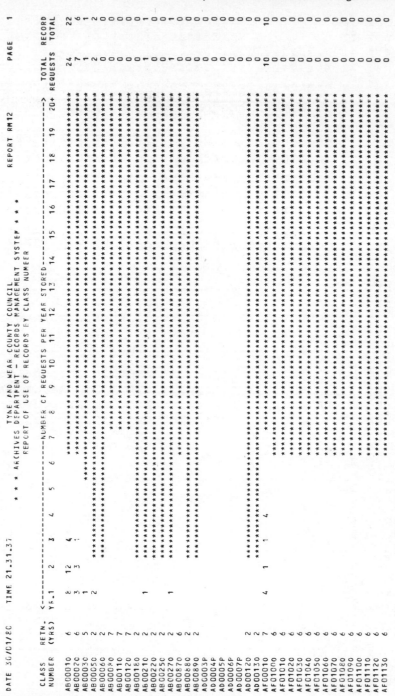

Fig. 13 Yearly report on record use (ARMS RM12)

Although the facility has not yet been much used, there is the possibility of linking archival information (the archival reference code, or 'catalogue mark') with record classes which have been or are due to be transferred to the archives. These data can be added to RM07 under the 'optional data' field.

No index is employed, since, as in the case of CAR, record retrieval is limited to issuing documents to their originating offices, who ask for them by their class number and reference number. Circulation control (using RM06) is achieved through these numbers also.

ARMS has been in operation since early 1978, and can be regarded as proved in practice. The system was developed by the staff of the county record office and the county's computer unit, and both development and maintenance costs are allocated to central establishment and servicing charges.

University of Liverpool (CMF)

This system is a very simple application of similar principles to the services available from the University's computer. It uses an ICL 1906S computer GEORGE 4 operating system, an elaborate infrastructure of access peripherals, and three simple COBOL programs. There are a number of data centres scattered strategically about the site of the University, which are available for the use of any member, with terminals in academic areas and in the libraries and central administration. This infrastructure has made possible a records management system based on interactive communication with the computer at multiple access points. System security is maintained by standard user-code and password procedures.

Input is keyed direct from the transfer lists, which are of the traditional type. It would be possible, of course, to overprint them with character spaces, as has been done by CAR, but in practice this is not necessary if the input is done by records centre staff. Data keyed on the VDU is visually displayed on the screen, and it is easy to alter the position of any character or column by using the screen editing facilities. If there is a considerable amount of data to be input at one time, punched cards could be used to save on-line time. In practice, the secretarial staff use the VDU at intervals during the day, so that it does not disrupt office routine unduly.

New data are added to the main data base in any sequence. Deletions may be made either by screen editing the data base or by a simple program in which the operator enters the document's reference code with a deletion instruction. Programs may be run when desired, and are activated by appropriate instructions at the VDU. These produce the following output:

(i) a master list of records held, arranged under departments by document
      reference codes:
(ii) a list arranged by disposal date;
(iii) an alphabetical list of subject index keywords.

A print-out of any of these can be obtained on demand. Updated
print-outs are usually ordered after there has been a considerable
influx of new material.

The VDU will also permit interrogation of the system, and will
display any record, or any consecutive group of records in any of
the files, up to a maximum of twenty lines of display at any one
time. Longer sets of records can be given in a print-out.

CMF is unusual in that it provides for a unified index of places,
persons and subjects. It was felt that a records centre serving a
relatively small and cohesive institution should be able to provide
information in response to requests, rather than confining itself to
producing specific records on demand. Index keywords are given in
free language, at the choice of the input operator (that is, records
centre staff). There is a special input field for index terms, which is
limited to sixteen characters; any number of terms can be entered
for any record. Updates of the index are produced whenever the
programs are run, and incorporate any deletions or amendments
made to the data base.

Development of the system was by archives staff, programmers
employed under temporary work-creation schemes, and the
University's computer laboratory. Apart from the programmer's
salary, which was borne by the Manpower Services Commission,
costs are carried by the computer service and by concurrent
large-scale administrative computer systems in the University. It
would be difficult to cost CMF specifically, since a number of other
systems, including some for the support of academic research,
were being developed together with it.

Other Records Management Systems

Automated systems for records management are in operation in
several countries. In Canada the Public Archives designed the
RECODEX system (Records Management Control and Indexing),
which was intended to provide a common format for the listing of
all records produced in government service. The Archives found
that it was difficult to persuade other departments to follow a
common form, a difficulty often experienced in common services
such as records management. They were also interested in a
system developed by one particular ministry, STARR (Systematic
Tracing and Retrieval of Records). Details of both systems are in
Bell and Roper.[16] It must be remembered that all complex
organizations are plagued with problems of information retrieval

and management, and are constantly devising systems for their solution. Bell and Roper refer to document-indexing systems based on standard KWIC and KWOC indexes at Imperial Chemical Industries and at BP Chemicals International Ltd. Probably something similar could be found in any large firm.

The French National Archives service operates an automated system for *pré-archivage*, the records management operation which transfers records, by way of the services of *archivistes en mission* to the *Cité Interministérielle des Archives*, the Paris records centre.[17] Input is based upon the equivalent of a transfer list but in rather an elaborate form. It includes fields for free-text description of the administrative function of the record services, and indexes. As in ARCAIC and PARC, 'author' fields are used to give details of the department of immediate and original provenance, and there is a classification code which is intended to record the structured organization of the archive group to which any record belongs. Output includes the usual listings; master lists of documents transferred; lists of documents allocated to the three retention categories; cumulations of data on the operation of the service (total numbers of records handled, and so on); selected and general thesauri generated from the indexes, and a KWIC index of keywords in the system.

Circulation Control Systems

Some records centres, including those of Chester City Record Office and the University of Liverpool, run systems for the control of circulation of records issued to departments. These are quite simple systems which do not seek to solve all the problems associated with circulation control, but which allow an improved degree of control over records removed from and not regularly returned to the records centre.

Input in both cases is by way of a form which allows basic identification of the document issued (reference number, title, dates, location) together with the name of the officer who has requested the document, his department, and the date removed. To confine this into one line of print-out requires fairly stringent field limitation. Chester uses a personal number in place of the officer's name, his payroll code provided by the salaries office; Liverpool uses initials, with an alphabetical code for the department. Documents duly returned can be removed from the list by a simple deletion entry.

At predetermined intervals a print-out may be required which will give a list of all documents issued by the records centre and still outstanding, together with a list of officers who have withdrawn documents, indicating the documents for which they are responsible after their names. It is simple to add to the program a print-out heading requesting these documents to be accounted for, and then to conduct an audit by sending copies of the print-out to the departments concerned.

A development at Liverpool is that the system will generate a separate list of documents which have been on issue for more than three months (or any other specific period which can be written into the program instructions).

The ARMS system is able to use its exception report (RM06) for a similar purpose. Basically this is a more interesting approach, in that it uses the principal data base to include this degree of circulation control rather than creating a new data base.

It might be thought that records centres could utilize the experience of public libraries and adapt a circulation control system from one in the library world. No records centre, as far as is known, has yet done so. This may be because library circulation does not resemble records centre circulation. Libraries have to issue books to a very wide readership, and their documents are controlled by bibliographic descriptions in strict format. Neither of these are particularly suitable for records control, but this is perhaps a field where there might be more intercourse between library and archive systems analysts.

Although circulation control seems a simple operation at first sight, it has a number of difficult procedural problems. One of these is the matter of input of data to the system. Manual systems of issue control usually require that a simple take-out slip should be completed; once this slip is written out, there is a formal record of the transaction. In a computerized system, however, there must be a delay between the transaction and the time when the computer returns some print-out record of it. During this time there must be some manual record that the document is out; perhaps this may be done by storing a copy of the input document. The only real solution to this difficulty seems to be the use of on-line access equipment. If the issue can be recorded immediately on an interactive terminal, the transaction is immediately filed in the system, can be referred to at any moment, and can be printed out at convenient intervals. However even where batch mode input has to be used – and therefore there must be a period when the transaction can only be recorded by some informal means – there may still be sufficient advantage in using the computer. If very large numbers of documents are withdrawn, and there is a complex departmental system of users, it is probable that the alternative to a machine-generated 'overdue' list is that no audit is held at all. The latter is indeed an option taken by many records centres, but if the computer can provide a means of carrying out at least simple primary checks on unreturned documents, it would seem to be a direct advantage.

Since it is not feasible to introduce machine-readable identification of users or of documents, there remain a number of tiresome technical problems connected with circulation control. Such a procedure is not recommended as an easy introduction to computer services in records management.

Linked Administrative Systems

There may be possibilities for co-operative projects with other areas of administration considering the introduction of automated systems. These will alter radically the nature of the records produced by the administration, and inevitably this will affect the services and design of the records management system. Problems involved in the handling of machine-readable records and archives are dealt with in chapter 4, but records managers will be interested in a number of other applications of automated systems.

Examples of interaction on administrative computer programs are: financial operations, particularly maintaining ledgers; personnel records; case records; registration of property (a specific example might be the computerization of the property terrier); registration of title deeds (this was the subject of the PARC (Pre-Archival Record Control) application of ARCAIC at the East Sussex Records Office, and there are other examples); equipment and stores maintenance; addresses and circulation lists; printing and publication; control of documents held in microform.

The question of computerizing registry systems in administrative departments is one which has been tackled by several central government archives services. The Canadian Public Archives has attempted to take a leading position in the design of record description produced by registries.[18] The British Public Record Office carries out periodic surveys, and has found some applications in registries.

3 Systems for Archival Description, Retrieval and Management

In this chapter a rather more detailed description is attempted of some of the leading systems which have proved themselves in operation or are being developed. It is not intended to be exhaustive or comprehensive. Other systems not mentioned here may be found in Appendix A.

There are three types of system that seem relevant:

(i) Systems for producing series (class) lists or descriptions for purposes of administrative control and general archival control, including publication.
(ii) Systems for information retrieval, that is, for the intellectual control of archive accumulations and access to or publication of the result.
(iii) Systems for the control of processes in the archives office or for the management of the service. These include systems for identifying archives and providing them for consultation for readers; and systems for controlling the enrollment and conduct of readers and for producing statistical information.

PROSPEC AND PROSPEC-SA

The computer system adopted by the Public Record Office in London, known as PROSPEC, is a set of programs for compiling

finding aids based upon the description and indexing of archives at
the class (series) level. In this it extends into automated form the
basic method of the office for establishing administrative control
over its holdings; in characteristically pragmatic fashion, this big
archives service has adapted its procedures to accommodate the
new disciplines involved in using the computer with a minimum of
innovation in format. PROSPEC is not a program for listing archives
piece by piece, nor for indexing them at depth; though of course it
does provide for an index at class description level, and there is the
potentiality for developing the program at least as far as including
descriptions of sub-classes. This has been done in the PROSPEC-SA
extension.

PROSPEC was developed from an existing package, INSPEC,
produced by the Institute of Electrical Engineers. INSPEC is a system
for handling abstracts of technical documents with facilities for
information retrieval and SDI, including print composition in upper-
and lower-case type. The system was introduced after a careful
study by a specialist team in the Public Record Office. Development
work and data input are handled by an agency but data preparation
is done in-house.

There is a single data base, compiled from data produced by
different departments and sections of the office as part of their
processing of archival material in the office. The system for data
capture is therefore an analysis of all those processes.

PROSPEC is aimed at producing a variety of finding aids, including
printed and published guides; in particular, to provide the basic
user's finding aid, the *Guide to the Contents of the Public Record
Office*. This is also used by the staff, but in addition the system
produces location lists for some parts of the service, and a
Summary for general use. Catalogues of searchroom lists and
indexes are held in the system but are not at present updated or
output; clearly this was regarded as an important facility. Originally
a microfilm catalogue was also proposed, but this has now been
abandoned. Since large numbers of lists and indexes exist, these
are rather complicated records, each covering a certain part of the
archives, and compiled at various dates and to varying depths of
description. Over many years microfilm has been built up covering
different parts of the archive.

Data capture
Input is by punched paper tape submitted in batches. The data
produced by particular sections are arranged in specific batches
which are identified by an initial consonant ('a' or 'n') and each
section is supplied with special stationery. A master flow-chart has
been designed to control these rather complex channels; a

simplified version of this appears in Fig. 14; since it was drawn up there have been further modifications, reducing the number of input channels.

Data either relate to fresh archives received for the first time in the office, or are amended on additional information relating to archives received in the past. In the latter case, the co-ordinating office writes the appropriate amendments on forms which are sent for keyboarding and verification. In the case of new material, information must be supplied by the Records Administration Division (basic data about the class); the Modern Records Department (class descriptions, administrative histories, index entries); the Repository Section (foot-run and location). Originally microfilm data were also required. These were obtained by completing sections of the main accessions form (the 'blue form'). In introducing the system for the first time, the transfer of backlog data was included as a special operation. Different forms are available for the recording of data other than that arriving with the documents. A complication is the brief administrative history which is an important part of the archival description of a class; this, with its index, has to be treated somewhat separately from the list itself, and is discussed below.

Input

Each class has a total of eleven items of information about itself. In the original project a sub-file covering a further six items was added to describe sections of the class which had been microfilmed. Each of these items is allocated to a field, and has a code number:

00 *Group and class code
02 *Last piece number
03 *First date
04 *Last date
05 Physical character of pieces in the class
06 Class title
07 Class description
08 *Index terms
09 *Cumulative foot-run of shelving occupied
10 *Location
11 *Means of reference in the searchroom

Those fields marked * above have a built-in verification. The system automatically rejects any input which does not come within the agreed field descriptions. Thus fields 03 and 04 in the main record are for dates. Only five variations are allowed: a year number (e.g. 1946); an approximate year number (e.g. c. 1946); an inferred year number (e.g. [1946]); a reign (e.g. Eliz 2 (a list of abbreviated royal names is provided – regnal years are not at present possible); 'no date' (n.d.). If a word which does not

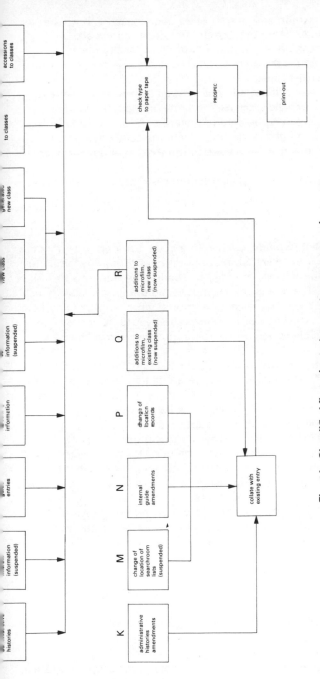

Fig. 14 Simplified flow chart: data capture processes in PROSPEC

correspond in form to any of these has been inserted, it will be rejected with an error report. Similar field restrictions are established for the other fields marked*. This facility does something to reduce the stress of the considerable proof-reading involved in a large project.

On the other hand, the fields not marked * above are free text fields. Here the archivists are free to write, in plain language, whatever they feel must be said to describe the class. Field 07 in particular allows a full description which normally covers at least a paragraph, and it is from this description that the index terms in field 08 are derived.

The precise rules covering all the field restrictions are set out in the manual.

Output

This arrangement of fields, each with a code number, is a way of listing archives vertically instead of horizontally, thereby avoiding the horizontal limitations imposed by the line printer. This flexibility is reinforced by the quality of the input medium, paper tape, which does not impose rigid physical limitations of the length of any field; though given this system of numbered fields, probably it would have been possible to use more rigid input systems such as punched cards.

To provide output, the system allows fields to be selected and arranged in different orders. Thus the guide employs fields 00 to 07, the location list uses 00, 02, 03, 04, 06, 09, 10. The result in each case is a specially arranged and printed list in which the appropriate details are given and kept up to date.

Outputs vary in their format. There is a straight line-by-line print-out of the input data which can be used for proof-reading and verification. Apart from this, PROSPEC uses a higher quality of print-out than normal. Internal lists use the ordinary upper-case line printer, but the updated guide appears in upper and lower case. There is a facility for using a computer typesetting system to produce high quality printed text, and another for outputting direct to COM which is likely to be of increasing significance in the future.

Administrative histories

Each class is preceded by a brief administrative history. These are necessary both for the support of research and for the use of records managers who have to recognize classes of records and fit them into their administrative context.

Compiling these histories is part of the professional work of describing archives. Regarded as input data for a computer project, however, the administrative histories have many defects. They are too variable in length and too diverse in content to yield easily to being handled as items of data. The PROSPEC solution is to keep the histories apart from the computer store and to handle them manually, but to include an index to them in the print-out. This is done by including an extra sub-file, the administrative history record, which includes three fields: 00 (departmental title) and 08 (index terms), derived from the main record, and a new field, 12, which gives a coded reference to the administrative history narratives held on paper files.

Costs

PROSPEC costs are based upon processing that is partly internal and partly external. Internally it has involved a certain amount of restructuring of processes and office systems, but this has perhaps been of general benefit. Keyboarding also has been carried out internally, using purchased and maintained machines, naturally employing an operator. The completed input material is despatched to INSPEC for processing, and this is charged for on the basis of on-line time plus services.

In 1974 it was stated at the International ADP symposium that the development cost of PROSPEC, including the pilot project, had been less than £5000. Some further figures were given for running costs: for data-base creation (including input listing and corrections) about £750, with an annual running for updating and checking of about £100 (1974 figures); £600 for upper and lower case line printer versions of the various outputs. The total given by this analysis would appear very low for the development of a major system for one of the world's busiest and most complex archives services, and the relative success of the project, both financially and operationally, is probably due to the P.R.O's ability to select a suitable and effective package which they could adapt. Perhaps one might add that if the P.R.O. had started to plan a new computer system in the late 1970s instead of five to ten years earlier, they would probably have been tempted to experiment with rather more sophisticated in-house equipment, and with at least some on-line access factors which would increase both the potential value of the computer working and the financial cost of it. From the standpoint at the time of writing PROSPEC looks rather conservative, and its lack of searching facilities may prove an important disadvantage.

Networking

The possibility of extending a system such as PROSPEC to organizations outside the P.R.O. was noticed from the beginning, and was made the subject of a specific proposal in 1974. Response was slow, since at that time the natural conservatism of the archives profession was not yet being seriously assailed by the practicalities of computer applications. However a pilot project known as PROSPEC-SA (SA standing for Society of Archivists) was assembled by 1977, in which ten smaller archives offices eventually participated, and the first print-out from this was available in the autumn of 1978. This project, although it doubtless delivered to its users a number of printed class descriptions, did little but demonstrate the possibilities of the system for the compilation and publication of nationally co-ordinated archival descriptions. A number of fairly minor adaptations of the system were developed by the guiding committee. The most important of these was the possibility (actually inherent in the ordinary PROSPEC scheme) of including descriptions of sub-classes. In PROSPEC-SA it is possible to produce lists which include both a general description of a whole class and particular descriptions of sub-classes within it.

Since there is no definition of the terms 'class' and 'sub-class' which would prevent them being used in practice for any division or subdivision of an archive accumulation, theoretically this would permit PROSPEC-SA, or a variant, to be used for the publication of virtually any type of archive unit with sub-units – though it would probably never be economic to use it for the description of individual pieces. This limitation may well be a feature of any networked system, which must have a national or widely conceived plan of action. The major objective of the PROSPEC system is the publication, at a high level of accuracy and readability, of brief guide-type descriptions of archival classes. Final judgement on it must await the appearance of published guides compiled mainly through the system.

A further adaptation of PROSPEC for the Society of Archivists includes a field for 'local codes' (the call number or title of the class or sub-class by which it is known in its own home); a field for recording the origin or provenance of the class (useful where deposited or non-official archives are being described); a rather crude index categorization which would allow selected parts of the final list to be printed out separately as part of a broad subject guide.

It is this last characteristic which is one of the most interesting of all. Rapidly updated selected print-outs of material from many different quarters but bearing on similar subjects would be a most important addition to the national apparatus for putting original source material to use. It would be the first serious step towards an effective dissemination of archival information at national level. There are of course many obstacles in the way. Apart from the difficulty of encouraging very large-scale participation, and the problems of finance that are likely to go with it, a considerable refinement both of the subject categorization will be necessary, following a major overhaul of the indexing standards in field 08 of the main PROSPEC scheme.

NARS A-1

The system A–1 in use at the National Archives of the U.S.A. must necessarily be included in the present series of descriptions, since it is one of the most important operational systems for archival ADP. However it is not proposed to give more than a most summary account of it, since it is a very large system suitable to an extremely complex archives service.

It was designed during the course of a major systems analysis at NARS, covering $4\frac{1}{2}$ man-years and costing $70,000. It must be assumed that any other large and complex archives service will need to put in a commensurate amount of resources into designing an appropriate system for itself; smaller and simpler archives services, however, may be able to adapt a pre-existing system or enter into cooperative systems.

The NARS system study carried out between 1972 and 1974 is interesting, in that it identified the professional problems of the service and formulated the aims of the service for a generation to come. At policy level the most important decision was to abandon large-scale attempts to establish intellectual control over the holdings in favour of solid administrative control. Plans for deep-level indexing were abandoned, and a system of series-level brief descriptions, with administrative details added, was chosen. The background to this decision was a situation where there was an enormous amount of archival material, both backlog and new accruals; staff were failing to keep up the necessary rate of production; and there was much lack of uniformity in the manual listing which had been done.[19]

In the resulting system, input is done in-house. Data capture is initially by the completion of form GSA 6710A (Change of Status Record (corresponding to a transfer list)), which is completed by archivists when the series comes into custody. Processing is done by four key operators direct to magnetic tape, and data are keyed twice for verification. It is reckoned that this method achieves quick and accurate data entry, and is sufficiently fast to prevent backlog accumulating. Data input, batch mode, is supervised by an in-house mini-computer which allows a certain amount of on-line working. Although the main data base is held at a central computer unit, the mini-computer holds statistical information on series held and their location, and allows interactive control of output printing.

Input data are given a control number broadly resembling the

NEW ACCESSIONS REPORT

12/30/1972

RG NO	SUB-RG A	LEVEL B	NUMBERS C	D	E	SERIES NO	UNIT OF ARCHIVAL CONTROL	UNIT OF PHYSICAL CUSTODY	TITLE
029	05	01					NNFS	NNG	Records of the Census of 1970
									The Records of the Census of 1970 include administrative records relating to the census, statistical summaries, and machine readable data files with detailed statistics for individual census tracts.
029	05	01	001				NNFS	NNG	Statistical Records
029	05	01	001	000	000	00001	NNFS	NNG	Statistical Summaries Compiled From the Returns of the Nineteenth Census of the United States. 250 linear feet 1/2/1970 to 9/15/1972
									These records consist of published compendiums; maps anotated by population density, type of industry, and trends in population growth; and, manuscript statistical reports. The published compendiums are arranged by Bureau of the Census publication number. The maps are arranged by state, thereunder by type of anotation. The manuscript reports are arranged by subject.
									6 Maps 126 Bound Volumes

Fig. 15 NARS A–1 report (Source: NARS (1974), p. 35)

SPINDEX control number, allowing twelve hierarchical levels from record (archive) group to sub-subseries.

Speed and accuracy are extremely important when working on this scale. It is reckoned that the whole operation of transferring the master file of series descriptions to the computer will take some twenty years. It includes about 200,000 series descriptions, and will require more than 100 million characters to be stored. A data base of this size is too costly to maintain as a unit, and will therefore have to be sub-divided, each segment covering one or more archive groups.

Output is by batch print-out and by machine-readable magnetic tape. This tape can be processed to provide various forms of page print-out by the in-house mini-computer. Output is also to COM in the form of microfiche.

Output includes a location register by record (archive) group and by Unit of Physical Control (subsections of NARS which include many units based in areas remote from the headquarters building); a new accessions report, which supports current awareness among the staff and users (see Fig. 15); an accessioned microfilm report, arranged by record group and by microfilm publications number; and a list of finding aids arranged by record group.

SPINDEX

This is a particularly interesting example of a purpose-designed system for archival description and indexing at high level. It originated in the Library of Congress Manuscripts Division and in the National Archives during the late 1960s (aided by a grant from the Council on Library Resources), but the project is now concentrated in the National Archives and its offshoot the National Historical Publications and Records Commission (N.H.P.R.C.); there is also a network of participating archival repositories. Three versions of the system are now available (SPINDEX I, II, and III). There are indications that, under the stimulus of the N.H.P.R.C.'s programmes for the collection and publication of national guides to both repositories and collections of archives, participation in SPINDEX will grow, and that there will be some further development of its capabilities as a central resource.

Because of its flexibility, the co-operative advantages of its use of the electronic photocomposition features of the latest version of the software (SPINDEX III), SPINDEX is becoming a leading contender for the all-purpose archival information system.[20]

The outstanding characteristic of SPINDEX (Selective Permutation Index) is its flexibility. It is designed to be of use for the control (description and indexing) of archives at any level, from the macro (group) to the micro (item), by any number of small or large institutions, and at reasonable cost. This is a formidable requirement, and, in one respect, there is a major limitation. Owing to difficulties in programming a system which would contain such variables, the N.H.P.R.C. were obliged to program in IBM assembler languages. These were DOS/ALC, for use on IBM 360/30, and OS/ALC, for use on IBM 360/40 or 370/145 and upward. This gives it a reasonably wide circulation in the U.S.A., but may well prove an important limitation if there is a question of extending it elsewhere. Here is a clear example of the problems posed by the need for very large-scale systems with long-term applicability. However in other respects SPINDEX conforms well to ideal requirements. All its versions are mutually compatible; it is capable of being developed yet further; and it is generally transferable to any bureau or institution where IBM hardware is available. On the other hand, it has no on-line search capability.

The flexibility of SPINDEX is achieved by three devices: the control number; the variably usable fields into which the record is divided; and the variably operated permuted index. The system aims at the description and printing-out of archive accumulations, and at indexing them fully; it is worth making this point since most descriptions refer to it as an indexing system, rather than as one for description or cataloguing – possibly a relic of its early origins within a library.

The control number

This enables the system to be used for any level of archival accumulation. The first field in any input must consist of a control number, which in the standard version of SPINDEX consists of a 3-character repository code, an 18-character identifying sub-field number – which will permit any record to be retrieved for updating or for printout – and a single-position record-action code.

This action code will perform one of two alternative functions:

(i) It can be used to identify the level at which the description is being done, on a scale from 1 to 8.

On this scale level 1 indicates the largest possible grouping of material: description at repository level; 2 is the next major division, the archives group; 3 the sub-group or series; and so on down through subseries, box or folder, and finally the individual item or piece. Distinctions of level may also be indicated within the 18-character sub-field number. The extreme flexibility of this level indication may be illustrated by examples below.

(ii) The action code may be used to instruct the computer to carry out appropriate actions with respect to the input entry it is attached to: i.e. add, correct or delete. SPINDEX can therefore update and vary any type of archival list carried by it.

To illustrate the flexibility given by this control number field and its components, two examples may be given. Although the principal use of SPINDEX within the National Archives was the description of two groups, the papers of the Continental Congress and the captured German records, where the archival levels were those normal to arrangement and listing exercises at group and series levels, the next important use of the system was by the N.H.P.R.C. to construct a guide to archival repositories.[21] In this guide, the work for which was done during 1977 and 1978, the level indicator was used to provide a classification of repositories and their contents. Thus a chain would be formed as follows:[22]

(State) (2 characters);	(Arizona) 04 . . .
(city) (3 characters)	(Phoenix) 04550 . . .
(institution within the city) (3 characters)	(Phoenix Historical Society) 04550630/1

This is taken as level 1 of the archival description.

(collection or group) (4 characters)	(John Butler papers) 045506300005/2

Level 2 of archival description.

(series in a collection) (1 character)	0455063000054/3
box (1 character)	04550630000546/4
folders in a box	045506300005462/5
items in a folder	04550630000546256/6

Standard SPINDEX II control number sub-field allocations. For normal archival descriptions the standard subdivisions can be used:[23]

level	characters	description
1	1–4	Collection/archive group identification. 4 numerical characters (0001–9999) allocated as a group identification by the archival institution concerned.
2	5–8	Series number. As above, but at the series (class) level.
3	9–12	Box (or volume) number.
4	13–15	Folder number. Chapters in volumes may appear here.
5	16–18	Item number. Pages in volumes may appear here.

From this formulation, it is possible for selections of the control data to be made which would allow selective print-outs, for example, of all repositories within a State, or of collections/groups, and so on. Not all levels of description need to be used in any particular case (in the case of the guide to repositories there will be little description below level 2), and if blanks are left in the input data, the system will supply the necessary number of zeros. On the other hand, there is a very wide choice of arrangements and levels which may be used if required. The control number method therefore allows SPINDEX to be used for the description of archive accumulations of virtually any size or complexity, within a repository or cooperatively between repositories.

Fields

As with PROSPEC, the data provided with any descriptive entry are divided into fields, each of which is identified by a tag consisting of three numerical characters. In the standard form of SPINDEX II these are as follows:

Tag
000 Control field: the control number (see above).
100 General heading (for very general and unspecific titles).
110 Subject title. Titles given here will be permuted; the permutation will include all words appearing in the title, except single characters and words in the stop-list. Compound terms should be hyphenated.
120 Personal-name title. This field is for the special case of material identified by a personal name, as with a collection of personal papers. The surname should be entered first, and the whole field will be indexed as one word.
150 Index cross-reference. This field provides an entry in the index listing, but does not appear in the register listing (inventory listing): it therefore allows cross-references to appear without redundant terms reproduced from the main list.
200 Supplied subject entries. This field allows the archivist to insert appropriate index terms which are implied in the archival subject but do not appear in it. Terms should be separated from each other by a single space, compound terms being hyphenated.
210 Alternative personal-name entries: allows names appearing as 'author', or originator of an archive, to be separated from names appearing as subject.
250 Span dates (first and last dates). Dates can be entered in any form, though years must be 4-character numerals and there is an overall limitation to 21 characters. Year dates can be used to create chronological listings, but in this case dates must be entered year-month-day, since the computer sorts the left-hand characters first.
300 Quantity of material. The symbol for identifying the unit of measurement appears first, e.g. I (items), F (folders), B (boxes), V (volumes), M (microfilm units), C (cubic feet), L (linear feet). This is followed by the amount measured. Standard abbreviations of large numbers include K for thousands and M for millions.
400 Collection identification: the name of the collection of which this entry forms a part. There is a limitation to 10 characters. This field may be input normally or inserted in all records on the file by a parameter card (see below).
410 Inclusive box numbers. This field is mainly used at series level.
900 Abstract (allows a textual note or general abstract).

In the above tabulation, the third character of the tag, which appears as zero in the examples, allows each individual entry to be numbered. If there is more than one entry in any field, they are serially numbered.

However any of these tags may be varied to meet the needs of the particular group, series, sub-series or item of archives being described, if the repository using the system has so determined at the outset and has put in the necessary modification. There is provision for a varying number of fields, not exceeding fifty of varying lengths, and with no general restriction on the form of the input in each. There is an overall restriction that no single field should consist of more than 993 characters, and that the overall length of the total input should not be more than 1981 characters. Since each field requires 14 characters for its identification within the system, this means that input on any one record must not exceed about twenty punched cards (or the equivalent) – rather a generous limit, by comparison with other systems, and probably one that will accommodate most types of input; but still perhaps a limitation to be borne in mind. It would be interesting to know if this limitation has been found troublesome in practice; but on this the literature is silent. Fields may be allocated and controlled by pre-designed parameter cards.

A second limitation to be borne in mind by system designers, of course, is the line length of the IBM line printer, of 132 characters.

SPINDEX's ability to adapt the lengths and number of its fields in this uninhibited way makes it a remarkably flexible instrument.

Permuting Index Terms

SPINDEX was originally devised as an indexing system, and its ability to identify and reproduce index terms from the input material might be expected to be considerable. In practice, this aspect of the system appears less impressive than its flexibility in field construction, which allows very full description of disparate documents in free text. It was not until the development of SPINDEX III during 1978 that the system developed the capability to produce two-level index terms (that is, showing main and qualifying keywords). Index entries are generated by the system, avoiding words in a simple stop-list, and are sorted under primary keywords by any designated field (e.g. by date). The permutation capability allows as many entries as there are indexable words, each keyword being followed in turn by the other terms in the string.

The mode in which the indexing is carried out can be determined for each field by the application of a function code to it. There are five of these: non-indexing field; subject index (field to be permuted word by word); personal-names index (field indexed as a single term); date index (four-character numerical codes); inventory (title fields sorted into alphabetical order).

SPINDEX III extends the indexing capability importantly by making it possible to introduce a qualifying term, which may be a linked and equal term to the original keyword, or else a subordinate qualifier. Thus one may have the following forms:[24]

ARIZONA, Indian affairs
(*reference*)
INDIAN AFFAIRS, Arizona
(*reference*)

and also:

WASHINGTON, GEORGE, Letters to Congress
(*reference*)

in cases where the second term is contingent upon the first; here
the second term does not appear in its own right.

Input format

SPINDEX is as flexible in the mechanics of its operation as it is in its
design. It will take an impressive array of input formats: punched
card, punched paper tape, and magnetic tape. As usual, the
disadvantages of punched paper tape have tended to bring it
unpopularity despite its superficial suitability for work with
variable-length fields. Punched cards are also being discouraged
for large-scale operation, since there is a desire to develop upper-
and lower-case print-out, and the necessary input for this tends to
take up too much of the limited space on 80-character cards,
though there is a procedure for adding continuation cards which
makes their use possible. Magnetic tape, especially in the cassette
format (MT/ST), has all the advantages and none of the
disadvantages of paper tape, and is much more compact.
Such variations as the allocation and length of fields are input by
means of parameter cards, and there are simple procedures for
inputting new records, corrections and deletions. SPINDEX III
incorporates improvements in the technical handling of files in
store during processing, which reduce the need for handling very
large files during each process.

Output formats

Several variations in output formats are possible; these include
altering the print position on the page of an entry; shortening or
lengthening the print lines (within the line printer's capacity);
suppression of particular fields; introduction and alteration of
sub-headings; variations of keyword and secondary sort fields. All
these variations are controlled by input parameter cards.

Recent developments allow electronic photocomposition of up to
twenty-five data field types from each SPINDEX inventory level.
Control of the output format at each level is achieved by codes in
the tag numbers. Many different variations of type are possible, but
hardware limitations generally restrict the size to a range between
6 and 18 points.

The system is fully supported and documented, and has an active
user network. It has been in operation for some years, and there

are a number of practical achievements; but, as noted above, it cannot provide on-line searching.

SELGEM

SELGEM (Self-Generating Master) is a system designed and operated by the Smithsonian Institution, Information Systems Division, and introduced to the Archives of the Institution in 1973. It was an adaptation of the Smithsonian's system for documenting and classifying specimens in the natural history collections. Archives and manuscript holdings are decentralized through the various departments of the Institution, and are related, in many cases, to artefacts held in museum conditions. The aim of the system is both administrative and intellectual control of the archives and manuscript holdings, which consist both of archives transferred from parent organizations and of manuscript collections of individuals or projects.

The system contains two basic divisions, one which produces a Guide Entry (now called SAGE – Smithsonian Archives Guide Entry) for each series or collection, together with internal processing information to assist administrative control; and another which produces a name/subject index to the descriptive finding aids. There is also a guide index, kept on-line in disc storage, for use in searching the corpus of guide entries.[25]

The Guide Entry produces a free text description of the series or collection, together with title (arranged in an alphabetical sequence under the principal keyword) and other standard information. The data are structured under identifying tags as follows:

tag	field description	field limits
.001	Record or serial number of collection	8 characters
.002	Sort number	4 characters
.300	Repository and collection number	variable up to 7 characters
.310	Collection title and description (free text)	variable to 99 lines
.320	Collection dates	variable to 99 lines
.400	Size and type of collection	variable to 99 lines Output appears in italics
.500	First paragraph of text (explanatory and fuller descriptive material: free text)	variable to 99 lines
.501–599	All succeeding paragraphs of text	variable to 99 lines
.600	Arrangement paragraph (for layout control)	variable to 99 lines

In a system based on variable-length fields the tags are needed for field identification, but in SELGEM also function as operators in the photocomposition stage.

An example of a SAGE output is given in Fig. 16, and the subsequent printed version in Fig. 17.

```
30007075    002   01    7607
            300   01    (7075)
            310   01    Henderson Family Papers,
            320   01    1868-1923
            400   01    (2.7 cubic feet).
            500   01    John Brooks Henderson (1826-1913), a lawyer and
                  02    politician, served as United States Senator from
                  03    Missouri from 1862 to 1869.
                  04        In 1869, he returned to St.Louis where he....

                            ........
            501   01    Henderson's wife, Mary Foote Henderson (1841-1931)...
                            ........
            502   01    John Brooks Henderson,Jr, (1870-1923), the son ...
                            ........
            600   01    *arrangement: (1) John Brooks Henderson,Jr, general
                  02    correspondence, 1892-1923; (2) John Brooks....
```

Fig. 16   SAGE entry as arranged in the master list (extracts).
(*Source*: Smithsonian Institute Archives.)

(7075)

Henderson Family Papers, 1868-1923
(2.7 cubic feet).

John Brooks Henderson (1826-1913), a lawyer and politician, served as United States Senator from Missouri from 1862 to 1869. In 1869, he returned to St. Louis where he practiced law and remained active in both local and national politics. In 1889, he retired from practice and moved to Washington, D. C. From 1892 to 1911, he served as a citizen member of the Smithsonian Institution Board of Regents.

Henderson's wife, Mary Foote Henderson (1841-1931), was involved in the suffrage and temperance movements. She was also a well-known socialite in Washington and a devotee of the arts, as well as an author of children's books and books on health.

John Brooks Henderson, Jr. (1870-1923), the son of John Brooks and Mary Foote Henderson, graduated from Harvard University in 1891, and Columbian Law School (now George Washington University) in 1893. From 1896 to 1897, Henderson was secretary

Fig. 17   Final version of a SAGE input, in printed form.
(*Source: Guide to the Smithsonian Archives* (1978), p. 194.)

The *name/subject index* to finding aids is constructed in a similar way, each field being identified by a tag (called a 'category' in the Institution):

tag	field description	field limits
000	Serial number	
001	Record number: identifies level.	32 characters
	Structured as follows:	
	(i) repository and collection code	compulsory entry
	(ii) series within the collection	permitted entry
	(iii) box number	"
	(iv) file or volume number	"
	(v) item or page number, microfilm ref.	"
	(vi) special information on format	"

Example of input
SIA7075 CD1.B1.F20
Record unit   Collection Division 1   Box 1   Folder 20

100	Dates	11 characters
101–199	Name entries. Odd numbers used for names, even numbers for descriptive material relating to the preceding name. Overall limit, 50 names. If more are required, a new record is entered.	192 characters each item
200–299	Subject entries, one entry for each tag number. Overall limit, 100 entries. If more are required, a new record is entered.	192 characters each item

This format, although less flexible than some, allows a variety of outputs, including a general guide. An index by name to archives and manuscripts finding aids is also produced by a separate system. In the early stages some difficulty was experienced in obtaining upper- and lower-case print-out, but this has now been achieved, and a high standard of presentation is maintained, as befits a body of international standing. The layout of the final print is determined by a system of guide locators controlling type size, paragraphs, lines and pages, which are written into the file. The system is capable of further development by the insertion of new sub-fields, if this should become necessary.

STAIRS

STAIRS (Storage And Information Retrieval System) is a program package developed by IBM, which is used by several large documentation services, including that of the IBM Technical Information Retrieval Center, White Plains, New York. Of particular interest to archival users is the system designed for use by the House of Lords Record Office, London, in association with the Parliament Office and the Greater London Council computer

```
                              S. I. A.   INDEX 19
                                 MASTER LIST
DATE: 01/24/78 " "

 SERIAL  CATEG LINE  ....2....V...,3....V....4....V....5....V

00290100    100   01   1921
            101   01   WEEKS, JOHN WINGATE
            103   01   WERBER, GUSTAVUS

00290200    001   01   SIA7075 CD1.B1.F19
            100   01   1897-1902
            101   01   WESLEY AND SON, WILLIAM

00290300    001   01   SIA7075 CD1.B1.F20
            100   01   03/13/1899
            101   01   WETHERBY, A. G.

00290400    001   01   SIA7075 CD4.B6. F13
            100   01   1915
            101   01   WHITE, HENRY

00290500    001   01   SIA7075 CD1.B1.F20
            100   01   1897-1898
            101   01   WILLIAM, ALICE L.
            103   01   WINKLEY, HENRY W.
            105   01   WRIGHT, BERLIN H.

00290600    001   01   SIA7075
            100   01   1890-1923
            200   01   AUSTRIA-HUNGARY:   TRAVEL AND DESCRIPTION
            201   01   BAHAMA ISLANDS:  EXPEDITION
            202   01   BAHAMA ISLANDS:  MOLLUSKS
            203   01   BALKANS:  TRAVEL AND DESCRIPTION
            204   01   CALIFORNIA:  EARTHQUAKES
            205   01   CONCHOLOGY
            206   01   CUBA:  EXPEDITION (1914)
            207   01   CUBA:  FRESH WATER SHELLS
            208   01   CUBA:  LAND SHELLS
            209   01   CUBA:  POLITICAL AFFAIRS
            210   01   EXPEDITIONS TO:  BAHAMA ISLANDS
            211   01   EXPEDITION TO:  CUBA
            212   01   EXPEDITIONS TO:  HAITI
            213   01   EXPEDITIONS TO:  JAMAICA
            214   01   FLORIDA:  DREDGING EXPEDITION
            215   01   FOOD:  RECEIPES
            216   01   FRANCE:  TRAVEL AND DESCRIPTION
            217   01   GREECE:  TRAVEL AND DESCRIPTION
            218   01   HAITI:  MOLLUSKS
            219   01   HAITI:  SNAILS
            220   01   HAITI:  TRAVEL AND DESCRIPTION
            221   01   HAWAII:  TRAVEL
            222   01   ITALY:  TRAVEL AND DESCRIPTION
            223   01   JAMAICA:  SHELLS
            224   01   JAMAICA:  TRAVEL AND DESCRIPTION
            225   01   MAINE:  OFFSHORE DREDGING EXPEDITION (1899)
            226   01   MEMORIAL TO:  PROPOSED TO ABRAHAM LINCOLN ON MERIDIAN HILL
```

**Fig. 18   Name–subject index printed out as master list.
(*Source*: Smithsonian Institution Archives.)**

unit. This aims at a data base which consists of an inventory of Acts of Parliament, with a facility for on-line retrieval and retrospective searching.[26]

The inventory format is as follows:

field	description	example
DATE	year-month-day	1852/07/01.
REGNAL	regnal year	15–16 Victoria.
CHAPTER		167 L&P.
TOWER	location code	275
STITLE	short title	Birkenhead, Lancashire & Cheshire Junction Railway Act.
LTITLE	long title	An Act to Consolidate into One Act and to amend the provisions of the several Acts relating to the Birkenhead, Lancashire and Cheshire Junction Railway Company, to define the Undertaking of the Company and for other purposes.
	[Volume, page, document information]	15–16v1681p DOCUMENT 45 of 45.

subfields

DATE	year-month-day	18520701,
EVDC	evidence, Commons ⎤	*Evidence submitted to either house by*
EVDL	evidence, Lords ⎦	*interested parties during the hearings.*
MAIN 1 ⎤	'main papers'	*Two fields allowing reference to*
MAIN 2 ⎦		*documents.*
PLANC	plans, Commons ⎤	
PLANL	plans, Lords ⎦	*Plans laid before the houses specified.*
SESSC	sessional papers, Commons ⎤	
SESSL	sessional papers, Lords	*Further supporting documentation.*
XREF	local references to sessional papers ⎦	

Searches

STAIRS employs a battery of commands allowing searches on specified paragraphs or on the entire unit, and can be adapted to a variety of formats. Commands include the following:[27]

SEARCH allows the user to search a data base for documents containing the words defined in the enquiry.

SELECT allows the user to formulate an enquiry into one of the fields of a document, e.g. an enquirer could ask for a list of all documents with a particular date.

EXPLAIN asks for details of the fields being used in that data base.

BROWSE (after SEARCH or SELECT) allows the user to browse by getting relevant documents displayed.

SORT provides for the sorting of documents obtained from a SEARCH command.

MAIL instructs the system to print documents selected in a high-speed printer and then send them by post to the user's address.

RANK provides a search which includes a weighting function, so that documents retrieved by the search are ranked in order of their relevance. This is determined by the frequency of occurrence of keywords included in the query.

PRINT used with BROWSE requests that documents displayed be printed out.

The SELECT command can be used with one of a number of operators: EQ (equal to), NE (not equal to); GT (greater than); NG (not greater than); LT (less than); NL (not less than); WL (within the limits); OL (outside the limits).

Thus it would be possible to request the retrieval of all documents between two specified dates, or with a location reference less than a given number, or with a specified characteristic.

The SEARCH command also has a number of operators which are used with it: AND, WITH, SAME, ADJ[acent to], OR, NOT, XOR, SYN:

keyword1 AND keyword2	Search for all documents containing both keywords.
keyword1 SAME keyword2	Search for all documents with keywords occurring within the same field.
keyword1 WITH keyword2	Search for all documents which have both keywords occurring in any sequence within the same sentence.
keyword1 ADJ keyword2	Search for all documents which have these keywords immediately next to each other in the same sequence as specified in the enquiry.
keyword1 OR keyword2	Search for all documents containing either or both keywords.
keyword1 XOR keyword2	Search for documents with either keyword but not both.
keyword1 NOT keyword2	Search for documents which contain the first keyword but not the second.
keyword1 SYN keyword2	Search for documents containing keywords 1 or 2, treating them as synonyms.
keyword1 TITLE	Search for documents containing keyword1 in the field named TITLE.
keyword$	Search for all documents containing the root word ignoring terminations. (e.g. 'survey', 'surveying').
keyword$2	Search for all documents containing the root keyword, followed by up to 2 characters (e.g. 'survey' as a root could be followed by 'surveys' or 'surveyed' but not by 'surveying').

The system automatically records a statistical summary of any search, including the number of occurrences of any keyword specified, and the number of documents found which include it.

The Federal Archives of Western Germany employs two packages, STAIRS and GOLEM2, supplied by IBM and Siemens respectively. Both are for the interactive retrieval of index items from a data base. A description of the GOLEM procedure during an interactive interrogation appears in Bell and Roper.[28] STAIRS is also used by the Italian archives service for an historical project concerning the archives of the Council of Venice.[29]

The federal archives project using STAIRS is of wider interest to archivists in that it attempts to establish and use a data base consisting of administrative histories of government ministries – an analysis of changes of function and areas of responsibility. Both records and archives managements are much affected by the instability of government or public authority chains of responsibility: since both records and archives are stored and described on the basis of their provenance, a transfer of functions from one authority to another may upset the continuity of a records or archives series, and it may also make it difficult to refer back to earlier documents in a subject enquiry. This problem was sidestepped by PROSPEC in the Public Record Office, which removed the historical summaries from the automated field of action. The STAIRS project means that on-line interrogation of the computer will give an answer on queries relating to the state of ministerial competence over any given subject at any given time after the foundation of the West German state in 1945.[30]

PARADIGM

This system was developed at the University of Illinois. It deserves close attention, since it is an operational system for the control of archives introduced by a relatively small institution for its own use, and later extended to other archive accumulations deposited there, such as those of the American Library Association. This development was aided by grants from the National Endowment for the Humanities.

PARADIGM is aimed at administrative and subject control over archives. As with most archival systems, this is established at series level; access to actual documents still relies upon typed inventories available in the searchroom, and the primary finding aids, consisting of typed 5" × 8" cards, are still compiled in the course of sorting the archives for description. Once the archival information is assembled, however, it is input into three data bases. Originally data input was by punched cards, limited to one 80-character card to each record (i.e. corresponding to each archival series), but this has now been transferred to machine-readable discs and tapes for on-line access, and new data or amendments can be input by this means. Print-outs are provided for annual shelf checks and for immediate searchroom reference, and summary tables showing the number, volume and type (publication, official records or personal papers) of series in each group are generated.

Subject control is achieved by inputting subject descriptions with a 6-character code attached to each. The terminal operator enters the numerical subject codes to one data base, and the descriptor term and numerical code to another base (subject descriptor listing). A subject control program combines these two bases and produces lists which include an alphabetical subject index referring to series and a listing of subject descriptors. Another program systematizes data on archive series and subject codes for the publication of selective guides.

Like other small-scale systems which have been developed through the interest and enthusiasm of an individual archivist (in this case Professor Maynard Brichford, the University Archivist), this system displays some minor crudeness, and a tendency to allow hardware or systems limitation to dictate the mode of operation. In view of the methods of work available to the university archives, which include the regular use of student labour in listing, arranging, etc., the resulting system is practical and provides forms of access to the archives which would not otherwise be possible.

MISTRAL

This is a CII package which has been adopted by the national archives of the Ivory Coast for retrospective searching of data bases which consist of bibliographical lists of documents. Consequently the application has been limited to archival series which resemble technical documentation: (a) the official acts of government as recorded in the official gazette, and (b) legal documents of title to land in colonized areas. Input is by punched cards, in batch mode, the input documents having been completed by teams of specially trained clerical workers. Access to the data base is provided on-line; but financial constraints have determined that the VDU is available only for one or two hours in each week, so that enquiries are accumulated batch mode. Print-out can also be delivered from the computer centre.[31]

Each document is described in nine fields:

(*reference number*)	67014902	Number of journal	67
		page	0149
		position on page	02
(*date*)	17/01/1967		
(*nature-acte*)	AR,MAEF	Arrêt, Ministère Afrique Equatoriale Française	
(*table-analytique*)	131–67	Chapter	
(*résumé*)	ARRETE 131 MAEF. CAB.DE. PORTANT		
	DESIGNATION DE CECCALDI DOMINIQUE EN QUALITE		
	DE CONTROLEUR D ETAT AUPRES DE LA SOCIETE POUR		
	LE DEVELOPPEMENT DES PLANTATIONS FORESTIERES		
	SODEFOR		
(*nom-personne*)	CECCALDI DOMINIQUE		
(*nom-commun*)	CONTROLEUR D ETAT, SODEFOR (Name of public body)		
(*mots-matière*)	NOMINATION, SOCIETE D ETAT, REFORESTATION		

(Source: *Journal Officiel de la Republique du Cote d'Ivoire*).

The reaction of an archivist to this is, first, that it is a very limited use of a computer system. The journal entries have the advantage that they are very uniform; they resemble technical (published) documents, and so are apt for treatment by programs designed for documentation services. If one were to move into the main body of the archives, the problems would become much more complex. However, it may well be that this body of official acts, retrieval of which is important in law and administration, is sufficiently important in itself to warrant special treatment; and in any case piecemeal systems are a good way to gain experience.

Secondly, in evaluating the success of this system in its context, one would have to know much about the explicit and implicit aims of the project. These were given by M. Cangah at the Chelwood Gate Conference, but his statement is not entirely clear. It would appear that intellectual control was his objective, and that manual methods of achieving this were proving too slow and defective. One can accept this suggestion, if allowance is made for the circumstances. The official acts are bound into volumes, and would need to be indexed. A manual index would take as long to compile as an automated one, and would not allow on-line searching, the comparison of index terms or the compilation of specialized lists.

Although as far as is known the system has not been subjected to a rigorous evaluation, MISTRAL may well demonstrate the special value of archival data in developing countries which do not have the infrastructure of information services familiar in Europe and America.

The Ivorian national archives also has a parallel project covering deeds of title to land. Here the fields are seven in number: REF (document reference – a security classification code may be used); SSR (sub-series reference); CTP (location code); DTE (date); GEO (geographical names (place names) in the document); PER (principal administrative agent or participant named in the document); MAT (subject keywords).

This simple system has the distinction, as far as is known at the time of writing, of being the only automated system to be operational in any archives service of any country outside the developed world. It should be evaluated by reference to the needs and resources of its country of origin, and not by those of more advanced countries, and its outcome should be studied with interest. It is likely to be of consequence in many places in the developing world.

ARCAIC

ARCAIC (Archives and Records Cataloguing and Indexing by Computer) was the first operational computer system to be put into

operation at a smaller archives office. It is a straightforward
adaptation of an ICL package (NIC:1900 Indexing and Cataloguing),
which is a package for simple bibliographical control; the system
was introduced in 1971–2, but is no longer in use. Credit must be
given to the pioneering efforts of the East Sussex Record Office and
to the County Archivist at the time, S. C. Newton. It is the lot of the
pioneer to suffer the trials of experimental work only to find that
others have benefited from his mistakes. The product of their work,
ARCAIC, was an interesting experiment from which in fact much can
be learnt.[32]

An important argument for the adoption of ARCAIC in 1971 was
that there was at that time a very large amount of unlisted or
inadequately listed archive material accumulated in the East
Sussex Record Office. It was thought possible to solve this problem
of unusable holdings by mounting a computerized listing system,
which would make the basic data available more immediately. The
basic data, naturally, would still have to be captured by skilled
labour in sorting and listing the original archives. It was hoped that
the variety and flexibility of the output material from a computer
system would revolutionize both the method of physically storing
the archives and the ways in which the archives could be publicly
described and retrieved. Where computer listing had been done, it
would be possible to store the original archival documents strictly
by physical format: for the computer could easily produce organic
lists showing the composition of the archival *fonds*, just as it could
produce subject-based lists or indexes of places or persons. It
would be possible to compromise the triple difficulty of the
archivist: the long-term interpretation of his archives depends upon
their being arranged and described in accordance with their
original provenance, but at the same time physical storage is best
done on the basis of shape and size; and all the time most access
to the archives is sought on the basis of subject-based enquiries.
The speed and variety of computerized lists and indexes derived
from a single data base could solve this problem by producing
finding aids in all possible sorts of order.

The problems which prompted the adoption of ARCAIC as a radical
solution for a small archives service are therefore common, and the
reason for the lack of success of the system are also those common
to most archives services.

The East Sussex Record Office did not acquire any hardware in
connexion with the project. The pre-existing package was adapted
in consultation with the County systems analyst, keyboarding to
punched cards was undertaken by County staff, and the County
computer (at that time somewhat under-used) was utilized. There
was therefore adequate available local facilities, both hardware and
software, and even though it was intended to cover backlog

accumulations as well as current entries (to make a clean sweep of the record office's holdings) the whole operation was relatively inexpensive. The cost elements are set out in chapter 1.

Input

Document descriptions were written into four main fields, each with a number of sub-fields. The size and layout of each were rigidly determined by the punched card layout and the package program. Because of the disparity between the lines of the punched card and the line printer, the input forms onto which the data were entered presented rather a complex appearance, and this no doubt had its effect on the attitudes of the staff. The four fields obviously were originally designed for bibliographical description, and their adaptation to archival description was forced. The underlying defect of the system is thus apparent at the start. By using a specific code at the head of field 1, the whole space could be used for a single entry of up to 119 characters. It is not clear to what extent this facility was ever thought useful in practice.

Field 1, originally the author section, was utilized to give persons or place index. Placing an index thus at the head of the description is another strange feature which proved of doubtful utility. This field can cover two punched cards and allows up to six index entries each of 20 characters. The limitation on these entries is strict, and all qualifiers of the index terms must appear within the 20 character space. The problem was how to exploit fully this facility, and it was decided to attach to each name reference the year with which the document was chiefly concerned – a sort of rough and ready qualifier which would at least distinguish the name from similar names at other dates in the general index. It was soon apparent that the number of index terms was insufficient. It is a feature of many archival documents, and particularly legal archives relating to localities in Britain, that many different places are often mentioned in the same document: fields scattered throughout a single township, several villages within a single parish, several parishes within a single hundred, and so forth. Limited to six entries, which were also to include the persons indicated in the text, it was necessary to restrict the number of topographical references.

Field 2 provided the main descriptive entry, and for this seven punched cards could be used, giving six lines in the print-out. There was little difficulty here, except that staff had to bear in mind the point at which the line printer would end its line, as this was not coincident with the end of the punched card line. Print-out in which words were unnaturally broken by line endings helped to alienate or confuse users of the system, which did not provide for machine composition. An additional minor irritation was the need to repeat the full document reference at the start of each line (corresponding to the start of each punched card) of the input document.

Field 3, of four punched cards, provided originally for the bibliographical details of a printed book, and so presented the biggest difficulty in adapting the system for non-print materials. The field was divided into seven sub-fields: format, classification, cumulator, language/miscellaneous, seals/miscellaneous, section mark/miscellaneous, and miscellaneous details. Each requires some explanation, which was provided to the original users by means of a staff manual.[33]

Format (16 characters). A description of the physical character of the document – paper file, parchment deed, three bundles of documents, etc. Abbreviations were often necessary.

Classification (16 characters). This provided an opportunity to explain, in terms of a coded system, the provenance and archival character of the document, and to indicate its relationship to the main series or to other classes of document. It was on the basis of the classifications determined in this section that specifically selected print-outs could be obtained which would reconstruct scattered or obscured archival relationships, draw together documents of a like kind but with different origins, and provide an additional means of retrieval. To achieve this a system of coding was devised, set out in the staff manual. Documents were allocated a code letter in four sectors, and a number provided a fifth sector. Each letter-coded sector needed the archivist to allocate the document to one of many predetermined classes, based on physical form, type of originating authority or body, or broad subject, or a combination of these. For example, a volume of minutes for a nineteenth-century board of guardians would be coded as: (*type*) PL [Public Local records]; (*group*) G [Guardians of the Poor]; (*division*) C [Clerk's office]; (*class*) MI [Minutes]; (*century*) 1933.

The final sector, indicated by a 2-character figure, allocates the document to a particular century. It would thus be possible to identify (if that were thought valuable) all documents held in the archives office which emanated from a particular century. Thus 17 indicated that the document being described belonged to the seventeenth century, its date being, say, 1676.

Cumulator (16 characters). This provided for a subject-index keyword which may be used to compile a subject-index thesaurus. It is not certain how far this facility was in fact used other than as a straight subject-index reference.

All the following sub-fields, in which 'Miscellaneous' appears, may be used for an extended entry describing any aspect of the document. Specific areas were provided to include a note of the document's language (where it was not English), whether it had a seal or not, and other features. In practice, much of this space was not used, although technically it was from this field that most of the information to be retrieved by using the FIND2 package was to be stored.

Field 4, of 2 punched cards, allowed up to five subject index keywords of 20 characters each. These keywords, in the system, were arranged as a chain index – that is, they were arranged in an order which demonstrated the hierarchical links between the terms. They would appear in the final index as a hierarchical chain, where A is the broadest term and E the narrowest:

A–B–C–D–E
B–C–D–E
C–D–E
D–E
E

As there was no thesaurus in the record office, the staff were usually unable to indicate five hierarchically connected keywords for any given document. They did however need to put in at least that many unrelated keywords for places or subjects. Eventually an adaptation was accepted whereby names used as keywords would be prefixed by a terminal square bracket, and subject keywords by an initial one. In this manner the whole of field 4 could to some degree be used as an extension of field 1. The chain index process remained to the extent that the keywords 'subordinate to' (i.e. following) any other keyword would continue to be printed out in the final index, where they could easily be disregarded. Here was another factor tending towards staff and user alienation.

Punching, verification and computer processing were provided centrally.

Output

A weekly line-by-line print-out (general list) allowed proof-reading. One of the minor irritations to the staff of the E.S.R.O. was the cumbersome procedure whereby errors were indicated to the card punchers; this caused unfavourable comparisons with the similar procedure for correcting manual typing mistakes.

Formal output was in six forms:

(i) *Place index*, based upon field 1 in alphabetical order, giving the place name and document reference.
(ii) *Persons index*, also based upon field 1, in alphabetical order.

Personal names were qualified, as noted above, by the addition of a date after the name. This index gave the name and document reference only.

(iii) *Descriptive list* (weekly class list), in order of document reference numbers. This list gave all the information in all four input fields, and is the master list. For the sake of economy these document descriptions were printed out in two columns on line printer paper, and in capitals only. Some difficulty was experienced in overcoming user resistance to the format.

(iv) *Subject index* on 5" × 3" index cards. These cards gave quite a lot of the input information, including not only the document reference but also a version of the full descriptive entry, and format/classification details from field 3. The cards were printed out directly by the line printer, but of course had to be sorted manually into their correct places in the card index cabinets.

This is an interesting instance of a facility which must have looked very attractive to the E.S.R.O. staff at the planning stage, at a time when they were still only accustomed to using traditional formats. The fact that the system would provide them with a full index of all materials must have been seen as a major point in its favour. In practice, however, once the excursion has been made into print-out formats, it is much easier to work with regularly updated and replaced line print-outs than with manually sorted index cards which cannot be easily updated or corrected.

(v–vi) A printed-out *chain index* based on field 4, giving the subject/name keywords followed by their (supposedly) subordinate keywords and the document reference. This was used in effect as an updated simple subject and name index, in which the chain of subordinate keywords was disregarded.

Retrieval by FIND2 was part of the original package, and provided the opportunity for the retrieval of any part of the input data under various labels – for example, by provenance as determined by the classification data in field 3.

A good deal of listing was done under the ARCAIC programme in 1971–4, but at the Chelwood Gate seminar in September 1974, the E.S.R.O. staff were ready to admit that the accumulated defects (each of which was in itself minor) amounted to a decision to abandon it, and that the rigidity of the package on which it was based made it impossible to adapt to meet the criticism of both staff and users. It might be added that an important contributory factor in this failure was the sudden reduction in available staff caused by a combination of illness and external financial or economic constraints in 1974; this reduction would equally of course have damaged manual programmes for listing and control of archives. However in the interim the system had been further adapted for the control of certain classes of document in the county's records management system, and this adaptation, called PARC (Pre-Archival Records Control) was at that time regarded in a much more optimistic light. At the time of the seminar, a total of about 2000 documents had been processed onto ARCAIC, and some 15000 onto PARC.

The adaptations required by PARC were not radical, but since the problems of listing were not so great, the system was found to answer much better. In records management applications, where listing onto the input document was effected mainly by clerical staff, and not by archivists, and where the documents being described conformed very largely to standard formats, there was less resistance both from personnel and from the material; large numbers of documents in standard form, mainly legal documents relating to property title and the correspondence files of the clerk's department, were rapidly listed onto PARC.

In the PARC application the input form was adapted as follows:

Field 1. The whole space was allocated to an index of persons involved in the transaction recorded, place-name references being transferred to field 4.

Field 2 was unchanged as the field for document description, in free text up to the limit of seven cards.

Field 3. The sector for the cumulator keyword was reallocated to give a 'function' keyword. For this a new coding system was developed which would allow a reconstruction of the departmental routine that originated the document. At first it was intended to indicate the committee (of the County Council) under whose authority the transaction occurred; but in the course of local government reorganization in the period 1972–4 the committee structure of most local authorities was much altered. Instability of structure in government has since been recognized as a universal factor in administrative history; in abandoning this in favour of function (which is related to specific specialized departments or sections in local goverment administration) as the feature by which archives may be classified as regards their provenance, E.S.R.O. was following the precedent set by many national archives services. In the circumstances of PARC to determine the function under which a document was produced and held was a relatively easy matter, and retrieval of documents under the functional heading could be provided by the computer package quite simply.

Field 4 now had to provide index entries for both place names and subject keywords. These were distinguished from each other by the use of the symbols] and [to indicate places and subjects; using these symbols, the system can identify and print out keywords in separate lists. It may be noted that there seems to have been a tendency to confuse function in the special sector of field 3 with functions expressed as subject keywords in field 4.

A final evaluation of ARCAIC/PARC must note that a combination of small defects or misfits mounted up to a rather formidable critique, even though no single one of them was sufficient to dismiss the whole system. An important defect was the lack of direct access to the input machinery. The process of submitting input data, checking and verifying punched cards, correcting errors, proof-reading initial print-out, and again correcting errors, proved in practice to be slow and wearisome. Similarly, some of the benefits of rapid and flexible forms of output were lost by lack of immediate contact with the computer facilities. It is probable that by the end of the 1970s these defects could have been much reduced by the adoption of some of the more direct means of access to the computer that are now common, and which render the in-house preparation of data less necessary.

Also important was the system's lack of flexibility or openness to adaptation. Field and record lengths were fixed, and no second-generation system could be developed.

4 Machine-readable Archives

Since computer systems are widely in use for administration and in research projects, many archives produced over the last two decades are (or were) in machine-readable form. This fact poses archivists and records managers with considerable problems. Some of the major national archives have been aware of these problems for some time, and have taken measures to deal with them. Other archives services have chosen to ignore the problems altogether. In this they are often accompanied by the creators of records and archives.

Government agencies in general are not accustomed to thinking of machine-readable records as records at all . . . NARS will have an enormous problem for a long time in educating agencies to assume the same responsibilities with respect to the creation, maintenance and retirement of their machine-readable records as they now customarily have in the case of the more conventional record categories.[34]

Some archives services, like that of Israel at the time of Bautier's survey, resolved not to tackle the problem at all. After all, the media employed by ADP systems are technically difficult to handle and need special equipment. In this they resemble an earlier specialized form of record, cinematographic film; the Grigg report in 1954 recommended that archival film should, as a practical expedient which ran counter to traditional principles, be divorced from paper-based media in public records, and be transferred to the National Film Archive for treatment. The same solution could be considered in the case of machine-readable records, which are generated by ADP units actually or potentially acting as data banks. What is of value in the records would naturally be built up by the units into specialized data archives, and the technical questions posed need not concern the traditional archives services. Finally, there are already established data archives services which have the equipment and the expertise to handle the problem.

It is not the purpose of the present study to suggest that this approach to the problem of machine-readable records is incorrect; indeed it may be the best solution to the problem. However, archival problems in connexion with such records remain, no matter who does the archival processing. Whether or not machine-readable records and archives are accepted or ignored by existing traditional archive services, they must still undergo the archival processes of appraisal, arrangement, description and preservation, and must, if suitable, be made available for access. Someone must carry out these operations, and those persons will naturally be, in relation to these functions, archivists. A professional study of the question must therefore be undertaken by archivists, and the matter must be included in the professional training and experience of new entrants to the profession. Steps should be taken to establish suitable standards, and to press for suitable resources with which to reach and maintain them.

There is certainly a natural tendency for archives services which already have responsibility for the transition of records from current administration into management systems and archives to accept this new technical area of operation and stimulate the necessary developments; this includes most national archives.

Some modern archives centres are certainly being converted into real data banks, the Public Record Office, for instance, and in the longer term its equivalent in France . . . Elsewhere . . . it is considered that a central bank of administrative data should be placed under the control of the directorate of archives, thus reinforcing its commitment in the field of documentation.[35]

Against this view, however, it may be argued that a totally centralized national archives service is not likely to be possible in a developed country: the problems would be too great, and to assemble in one place all the resources necessary to solve them would be both politically unlikely and practically counter-productive. Better, perhaps, to allow separate specialized services to become established and develop. Either solution is acceptable professionally, provided, of course, that proper standards are observed, and that the essential functions of an archives service – functions valuable to a nation – are carried out.

Appraisal

In the present context the term appraisal is intended to subsume the basic processes of records management, which are undertaken, after all, in order to ensure that records undergo an orderly process of appraisal before they are destroyed. Machine-readable records, like any others, must be appraised. In order to arrange for this, there must, as with conventional records, be some system to establish that the various record series exist, what information they contain, what administrative, legal or other function they serve or served, and how much they grow each year. With this information, a records manager, in consultation with the appropriate administrative staff, must suggest a disposal policy for each series, and see that whatever policy is decided is carried out. So far nothing has been suggested here which is not in accordance with traditional records management practice.

There are however several technical difficulties. One of these lies in the physical form of the record. Machine-readable records are usually on magnetic tape, but may be in some other medium such as magnetic discs or drums, punched cards or tape, or on microform. Magnetic tape is the most common form. It is expensive but re-usable, and to make a retention decision involves cost, so that the medium can in effect be replaced.

The other main difficulty lies, of course, in the fact that the archivist must be able, in some way, to read the record. This question should be discussed with the technical staff who administer it. A study of the documentation, and some of the input and output texts may be sufficient; in other cases it may be necessary to rerun part of the program during the appraisal exercise.

For this reason it is important in appraisal to determine and record the system details, ensuring the preservation of the basic documentation with the record. Both the National Archives of the USA and the Public Record Office have evolved systems for doing this. These systems are similar, at least in the technical recording of the machine-readable records series. The NARS form GSA 7036 (magnetic tape record inventory) and the P.R.O.s information review job inventory, reproduced in their manual, *The Selection and Preparation for Transfer of Machine-Readable Records,*[36] are striking in their similarity, the one in fact deriving from the other.

The file of inventory forms will constitute a permanent record of important series of machine-readable records. From it appraisal can be carried out, and those series which are of archival or other long-term value can be singled out at a very early stage.

Appraisal of records is always difficult, and the issues involved have been discussed elsewhere.[37] All the normal difficulties still apply to machine-readable records, but there are also a number of special factors:

(i) It is particularly important that the review leading to the appraisal should be early in the record's life (indeed if it is not, it is likely that the record will no longer exist); ideally perhaps soon after the system has become operational. In practice this means that appraisal must take place during the file's currency, or at a planning stage.

(ii) Not all tapes associated with a system are equally useful. The P.R.O. does not require details of 'scratch tapes, raw data input tapes, working processing tapes, printing tapes, test tapes or interim master tapes.' It does require details of any specially written operating systems program tapes, as well as the tapes containing the master file or main data base.

(iii) Files for appraisal should be considered in the context of other records (both machine-readable and paper), and any relevant

PUBLIC RECORD OFFICE

MACHINE READABLE RECORDS INFORMATION REVIEW JOB INVENTORY	1.		2.	
3. OFFICE CREATING RECORD	4. LOCATION OF INSTALLATION			
5. CONTACT FOR FURTHER DETAILS NAME	6. ADDRESS		7. TELEPHONE NUMBERS	
A.	A.		A.	
B.	B.		B.	
	8. DESCRIPTION OF RECORD			
A JOB TITLE				
B FILE(S) TITLE				
C PURPOSE OF COLLECTING DATA				
D CONTENT AND COVERAGE				
9. SOURCE DOCUMENT(S) USED AS INPUT (ATTACH SAMPLES)				
10. USE OF FILE OUTPUT				
11. DATES OF FILE	12. ONETIME STUDY OF SURVEY(S)		13. PERIODIC UPDATE (Specify period)	
A. FROM				
B. TO				
14. DUPLICATION ELSEWHERE (PHYSICAL OR CONTENT)		15. CURRENT RETENTION PERIOD		
16. RESTRICTIONS ON USE OF TAPE				

Fig. 19 Inventory of machine-readable records (Public Record Office)

Box No.

1 & 2		RESERVED FOR PRO USE
3		DEPARTMENT AND BRANCH WITH ADDRESS
4		ADDRESS OF COMPUTER INSTALLATION
5	A	NAME ADDRESS & TELEPHONE No. of CONTACT RE DATA
6	B	NAME ADDRESS & TELEPHONE No. of CONTACT RE
7		PROCESSING (IF DIFFERENT)
8 A & B		SELF EXPLANATORY
	C	BRIEF STATEMENTS OF MAIN PURPOSE e.g. 'STATISTICS OF TRADE'
	D	INDICATE HERE e.g. SAMPLE %, REGIONAL OR NATIONAL ETC.
9		IF SOURCE OF FILE ANOTHER VALIDATED MAG TAPE MASTER FILE INSERT 'M/T' AND INDICATE PRIMARY SOURCE OF INFORMATION
10		IF MORE THAN ONE OUTPUT INDICATE THE IMPORTANT ITEMS
11		INCLUDE MONTH AND YEAR SHOWING BEGINNING AND ENDING REPRESENTED BY THE DATA ON THE TAPE
12 & 13		ANSWER *EITHER* 12 OR 13
14		INDICATE IF THE SAME INFORMATION APPEARS ON OTHER TAPE SERIES OR IN MANUAL FILES AND RECORDS
15		IF A FIXED PERIOD SET FOR RETENTION INDICATE TIME – IF HOWEVER RETENTION OR DISPOSAL DEPENDS ON OTHER ACTIVITIES e.g. RECEIPT OF NEW REVIEW – SHOW DETAILS
16		SHOW GROUNDS FOR RESTRICTIONS e.g. STATUTORY, DEPARTMENTAL OBLIGATION, DEPARTMENTAL PRACTICE. NOTE: THE RESTRICTION REFERRED TO IS AFTER THE NORMAL 30 YEAR PERIOD. IF EARLIER PUBLICATION IS POSSIBLE PLEASE GIVE DETAILS.

Fig. 20 Instructions for completing inventory (Public Record Office)
(*Source*: Public Record Office, *The selection and preparation for transfer of machine-readable records* 1974)

published material, including reports and statistics. A group of files created for a particular job within a single system should be treated as an entity.
(iv) Routine files and other ephemeral material, and jobs or systems of no permanent value, may of course be disposed of. To allow this there should be an agreed disposal schedule describing these records, which afterwards can be got rid of routinely. This provision parallels records retention schedules in traditional records management, particularly those concerning series of records which are too ephemeral even to be considered for transfer to the records centre.
(v) Files which represent a single transaction, such as a survey, can be appraised directly for their own long-term value to research. Files which are part of a time-series and are

periodically supplemented, such as a census repeated every
few years, should be evaluated in the context of earlier and
later parts of the series. The greatest difficulty, however, and
one which is peculiar to machine-readable records, is
presented by files which carry a continuously updated data
base. With these, the only practicable method seems to be to
record the position at predetermined dates, and accept tapes
which hold the data at those times.

(vi) Software dependency may affect appraisal decisions. Data-base
tapes are often compiled as part of a system which depends
upon a standard package such as SPSS (Statistical Package
for Social Scientists). Some of these packages may go out of
use or be incompatible with particular hardware; tapes
which use them might have to be transcribed into a standard
format.

(vii) Continuous series of records which are selected for retention
constitute series of case files or studies ('particular instance
files', in the terminology of the P.R.O.). In normal
circumstances the bulk of such files is such that it affects the
appraisal process; they tend to be too bulky to keep. In
machine-readable form they are naturally not so bulky
physically, although likely to be expensive; but they are
(subject to the solution of technical problems of access)
much easier to use for research purposes than conventional
records series would have been. This may tend to encourage
records managers to suggest retention more often than in
the past. In any case, it is always good archival practice to
select periodical or other samples from a long series which is
not to be retained as a whole.

The instructions issued by the Public Record Office on the
evaluation of machine-readable records for their long-term use are
given as Appendix B.

Two other alternatives to keeping machine-readable records for
archival purposes may be considered. These are that the input
material, probably on paper, or the output material, or print-out,
might be kept instead. Unfortunately both of these solutions
present problems which are likely to be insuperable in many cases.
The raw input material will be bulky, and will require a great deal of
processing before it can be made useful; this it has already
received, in the course of the project that included it; to propose
that it should all be repeated for purposes of archival access is a
counsel of despair. Secondary input material may exist in the form
of processed input documents, typically punched cards. These also
are bulky and present problems of interpretation. Punched cards
too are machine-readable, but if one is to keep a machine-readable

record, it is better to keep one that is compact and readily accessible to the machine; one that also is easy and quick to copy.

There is a strong case for keeping at least some of the printed output from a system. However here too problems of bulk will be important, and in any case it is not necessarily true that print-out will be any more intelligible than the tape file from which it comes. If the data base is to be kept it is better to keep it in a form which

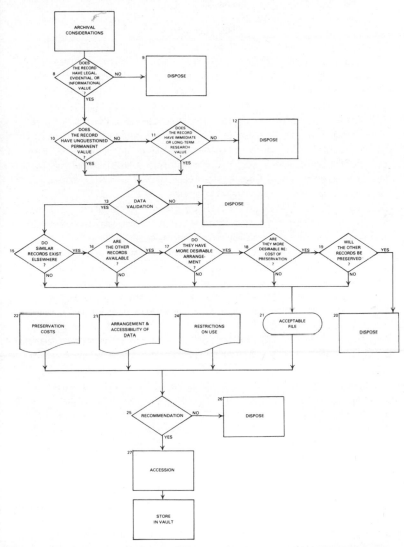

Fig. 21 The process of appraisal (*Source: NARS accessioning procedures handbook*, p. 3)

will (if certain precautions are taken) allow further working of the data to take place. Print-out data cannot be used for this without preparing them once again as input.

Preserving the material as COM or CIM is certainly worth considering, but, in this case, the microfilm merely replaces the magnetic tape as a medium; it is not a way of solving the problem of machine-legibility.

Preservation

After appraisal, some magnetic tapes will be released to go back into service, and others will have been selected for archival retention. These will have to be stored in conditions which will preserve them. Magnetic tape is not regarded as suitable for long-term storage, as it is not as inherently stable as other, more traditional, information media. The physical requirements for its conservation in storage are exacting. These are summarized in the Public Record Office guide referred to above; a much fuller and technically complete description is given in a publication of the National Archives and Records Service of the U.S.A., *Handbook of recommended environmental conditions and handling procedures for magnetic tape*[38] which includes a checklist for environmental conditions in both the active area (computer laboratory store) and in the inactive area (archives store), as well as detailed specifications in the body of the handbook; this is reproduced in Fig. 22. It will be noticed that, as well as stringent conditions for temperature and humidity controls, with emergency backup equipment in case of the failure of air-conditioning plant, there must be protection from magnetic fields, and provision for regular re-spooling of the tape. Even correct tension in rewinding is important. Everything must be kept elaborately dust-free, and the staff, using lint-free gloves, must handle the material with great care.

There is a great variety of formats within the general description of 'magnetic tape'. Most tape archives have decided to concentrate on one standard type based on half-inch industrial tape, usually 9-track using 1600 bits per inch density, and ask that non-standard tapes be transcribed to this format before transfer. Transcription to a standard format may also be needed in some cases where there is software dependency.

Microfilm is an inherently more satisfactory medium and equipment to transcribe magnetic tape to COM would be a desirable addition to the service. However unless there are also CIM (Computer Input by Microfilm) facilities this solution will not be practical except as an interim measure.

Preservation

115

Tape storage rooms and buildings
(i) Rooms should be temperature and humidity controlled, with a
    sufficient internal air pressure to prevent dust intrusion.
    Temperature range: 65°–75°F ±5° in storage areas; 60°–80°F.
    ±10° in working computer laboratories.
(ii) Humidity range 45–55%RH. ± 5%.
(iii) Dust and dirt controls to keep dust particles to 50 microns.
(iv) Tape should be protected from high-intensity magnetic or
    electrical fields, such as power generators, transmission
    lines, radar, bulk degaussers, and magnetic check sorters.
(v) Metal tape racks should be earthed and kept at least two feet
    from any electrical fixture or lead. Tape boxes are heavy, and
    racking should be strong. Tapes should be stored upright,

Active Tape Area
1 Fireproof building —
2 CO_2 extinguishers —
3 No open flames —
4 No smoking —
5 Dust free conditions —
6 No paper chips
   (keypunch and printers) —
7 No food —
8 No waxed floors —
9 Temperature 70°F ± 5° —
10 Humidity 50% ± 5° —
11 No magnetic fields —
12 Positive internal air pressure —

Storage Cabinets or Racks
1 Shelves adequate in strength —
2 Dust free conditions —
3 2' clearance to any electrical
   fixture —
4 Electrically grounded —
5 Vertical stacking of tape —
6 No magnetic door latches —

Tape Containers
1 Cleaned between use —
2 Hub supported —
3 Dust tight —

Inactive Storage Areas
1 Fireproof and protected —
2 No fire hazards —
3 Dust-free conditions —
4 Temp. 70°F ± 5° —
5 Humidity 50% ± 5° —
6 No close magnetic fields —
7 Positive internal air pressure —

In Transit (short period)
1 Fire resistant packaging —
2 Dust protected —
3 Careful handling —
4 No bumping —
5 Temp. 50–90°F ± 10° —
6 Humidity 40–60° + 10% —
7 Inspected before and after
   shipment —

Tape Handling
1 No finger contact —
2 Lint free gloves —
3 Careful handling —
4 Clean transports every shift —
5 'Low-wind tension' —
6 Rewound annually —
7 Certified product —
8 Receiving inspection —

Tape Reels
1 No sharp edges —
2 Undistorted flanges and hub —
3 Labelled properly —

Fig. 22 Checklist of requirements for storage of magnetic tape records
(*Source: NARS Handbook of recommended environmental conditions and
handling procedures for magnetic tape*, July 1972)

and housed in plastic canisters which support the reel at the hub.

(vi) Buildings should have lightning conductors.

Tape preparation

(i) Physical quality of the tape selected for storage should be high, and there should be some certification of its having been tested for storage. A maximum of 5 write skips allowed on the tape prior to storage; none within the first 100 feet or last 200 feet. The tape should not have fully passed the read/write devices fewer than four or more than fifty times.

(ii) Before the tape is stored, it should be read and verified as error free.

(iii) Before storage the tape should be rewound at a constant low tension (6–8 ozs force.) The leader should be secured with vinyl or sponge rubber strips to prevent unwinding; vinyl should not be stretched. The 'write permit' ring should be removed after dismounting from the drive.

(iv) Tapes should be labelled with self-adhesive labels with minimum residue.

(v) Water-soluble felt-tip pens or graphite pencils should not be used to write on labels.

(vi) Containers should be non-magnetic and transparent, labels visible from outside.

(vii) Containers should be clean and dustproof, with a positive-action latch mechanism. Tape should be supported at the hub, not at the rim. Tape should be transported in containers which resist heat, moisture and dirt, and withstand shock. The reel of tape should be more than 3 inches from the outside of the case, to reduce the effect of magnetic fields. The inside of the case may be lined with foil.

Tape maintenance

Tapes may be expected to last 12–20 years under optimal conditions. However errors caused by physical changes on the tape increase rapidly over storage time. The following routines keep the development of errors to a low level:

(i) Annual rewinding and inspection. Rewinding should be on a precision winder and under constant tension.

(ii) Before rewinding, sample tapes should be test read; there should be annual test readings of sample tapes. If there are permanent errors, the whole file should be test read. Defective tapes should be copied.

(iii) Physical examination should note the following:

(*a*) cinching: separation of adjacent layers in the tape with a corresponding crosswise wrinkle in the tape.

(*b*) protruding layers of tape, causing damage to the edge.

Both (a) and (b) can cured by rewinding on a cleaner-rewinder followed by a check.

(*c*) broken flange, hub or canister. Transfer tape to a new reel.

(*d*) chemical reaction between the oxide binder on the tape and some substance in its vicinity, e.g. ink, adhesive, mechanical holders. Evidence of reactions are discolourations or spots in the tape pack as seen from the side. Chemical activity on the tape is generally irremediable.

(*e*) surface contamination by dirt. Remove by frequent cleaning passes.

(*f*) creases and scratches caused by poor winding and handling. Rewind.

(*g*) distortions at the end of the tape, caused by high temperature or humidity or extraneous effects. Rewind.

(*h*) tape torn along the middle, caused by temperature/humidity extremes, leading to loss of some blocks of data. Rewind.

(*i*) adhesion and blocking, caused by static build-up on tape surfaces aggravated by low humidity; high humidity also will cause blocking at the centre of the reel. No remedial procedure is possible. Test examination may reveal a high rate of unreadable or erroneous sections; this may be caused by the effect of strong magnetic fields or by curvature of the tape. Technical help should be sought to deal with these.

In all the above cases remedial action (rewinding) should be accompanied by a period of rest, followed by another rewind, perhaps passing the tape several times over the drive.

Fire precautions

General fire precautions should be those appropriate to the protection of electronic equipment. Tape reels and containers should be fire resistant, and the storage room should conform to general archival standards. No open flame should be permitted in it. The room should be insulated to provide fire resistance up to 150°F. temperature and 85%RH. Combustibles such as paper and cleaning fluids should not be brought in. Carbon dioxide and water extinguishers are appropriate. Wet tapes should be carefully dried within 24 hours.

General working conditions

Tapes should never be touched by human skin; for handling,

lint-free gloves are necessary. Working or storage areas should be completely free from cigarette ash, food, drink, polishes and waxes or dust. Tapes must be handled with great care and not pulled, squeezed, scratched or dropped. Reels should be true, and take-up reels should be inspected before use.

Arrangement and Description

The main difficulty in arranging transfer and retention of archival files is that of investigating and recording the system and its technical processes. In the P.R.O. a systems review is carried out; this is aimed at compiling all the information required to give a complete picture of the processes involved in the system when current. The review must be a continuous process throughout the active life of the file. Documents should show the main function of the system, its main files, input, output and input file maintenance procedures, and other technical characteristics.

To assist in collecting this data an accession form may be useful, this being used to supplement the information given in the data file inventory form. An example is the GSA form 7091 (data archives inventory) of NARS.[39] The purpose of this form is to extract technical details which should include the following (for their explanation of technical terms see the glossary):

Recording Mode Information: Number of tracks, density of bits per inch, character code and frame parity, parity control of blocks, logical record length and blocking factors; logical and physical record length control, with information on file padding characters, last block length and reel padding field.

Recording system information: CPU manufacturer and model, tape drive manufacturer and model.

Operating system used to generate the file, with name, design and level, and file structure information, file ID location, and contents, reel sequence number and location, checkpoint location, logical record-count location, physical record-count location, and hash or control totals.

To complete this highly technical form it will be necessary for the archivist to consult not only the systems documentation but also, inevitably, the operators and programmers who are operating the system. It would be desirable to record their names and addresses.

However completely the above information is collected, it is still necessary to assemble an archive set of the systems documentation, which will be kept in association with the tape files.

The minimum systems documentation would normally consist of general system outline flow charts showing the functions to be performed, detailed system flow charts, program flow charts and listings, input and output layouts, operating instructions and control procedures. The P.R.O. would expect to receive copies of the tape layout in question and of other items necessary to explain the files.[40]

There should also be samples of input data, both raw and processed, and of output in its appropriate formats. The NARS *Accessioning procedures handbook* gives even more detail.

The documentation which results from all this can be made up into a standard package like a code book, which can be kept with the tapes. It can also be microfilmed or fiched, and made available to technical users in an SDI scheme; or it can itself be put into machine-readable form.

The American Library Association has produced a set of cataloguing rules and formats for machine-readable documents, and these are now part of the *Anglo-American cataloguing rules.* In view of this, it would be perverse for archives offices to produce lists at variance with these rules. Listings should be communicated to social science data inventories and to the appropriate abstracting journals or services. Archivists in the machine-readable area will find themselves much more integrated into the research and documentation service industry than archivists operating traditional services.

Access

Difficult as are the problems of appraisal and preservation of machine-readable archives, in some ways the problems of giving access to them are even more troublesome. Users must have access to computer facilities, and possibly also the time of data-processing staff. The user's hardware must be capable of processing the files produced by another, earlier system.

Charles Dollar gives the example of the American census returns of 1960. There are some 6500 tapes held by the census office, but they can only be read by using a make of tape drive that is now out of production. Tape drives are an example of the type of peripheral which is constantly being improved. Alterations in the make and characteristics of peripherals are more likely to be serious obstacles to the archivist than changes in CPUs, since compatibility of systems is an important characteristic in the design of later computer models; but the problem of obsolescence generally is likely to remain a serious one. It may be necessary eventually to construct or maintain archival peripherals which can interface with current hardware.[41]

Confidentiality is also a problem. Most machine-readable archives record statistical, demographic, sociological or personal data. It is likely that there will be a positive research relevance long before the expiry of the traditional closed periods (30 years in general; up to 100 years for information acquired from individuals under seal of confidentiality). It is not easy to restrict access to information about individuals once access to a file has been granted, nor to control or monitor the use of data derived from machine-readable files once it has been tapped through a computer-assisted project.

These and other difficulties have been approached in a pragmatic way by machine-readable archives units. The archives makes its descriptive materials widely available in appropriate quarters. Intending users then approach the archives for further information and work out a suitable plan of access. The archives will supply him either with a full copy tape of the file he requires, or with an edited copy on which specific data are omitted or reworked; in some cases the archives may decide to process the data themselves, and to issue files of worked statistical material. Some users may be content with print-out, direct or edited. In all cases the archives need access to suitable equipment: tape copiers, computers, software and input/output devices. It is not likely that there will be a central searchroom where users may use archive files on the spot, using the archives' own computer; this solution would require too much investment in hardware and technical staff, and would create problems of congestion. To issue – in effect, to sell – copies of the archival data is the most practical approach. It may also be necessary for the archives to make relevant software available with the copied file.

It is customary for users to pay for these services, and the principal MRA units have established a scale of fees. The fees charged by NARS in 1978 were:

Tape-to-tape copy without adaptation $65 per reel.
Extracts from files $65 per output reel plus $150 per hour computer processing time.
Print-out $150 per hour computer processing time.

Computer networking is a possible means for the future of arranging access. A university or research institute could establish by this means close access facilities with the archive which do not involve lengthy visits elsewhere. Ultimately finding-aids to both machine-readable and paper-based archives could be made available in machine-readable form and open to access via a computer network. Users could then get on-line access to indexes, for example.

Glossary of Technical Terms

This glossary contains technical words in the fields of archives administration, computer operations and indexing; all have bodies of literature which will supply and explain many further technical terms. This list is not intended to be an exhaustive dictionary but to help archivists and others making a beginning in the area of automatic data processing who feel they have no relevant background in their previous training or experience. Not all the words in the list appear in the text. The following explanatory symbols are used: A: Term used in an archival context; C: Term used in a computer context; I: Term used in an indexing or information science context.

Access (A)   The opening of archives to public inspection. Facilities for enabling members of the public to inspect archives.

Access (C,I)   Identification and retrieval of data items held in store by a system (often used as a verb).

Administrative control (A)   A set of aims held by an archivist when he sets out to construct finding aids intended primarily to allow him to regulate the physical processes which archives must undergo: they must be accessioned, sorted, described, boxed, stored and retrieved, and to ensure that these processes are carried out in due order demands administrative control instruments. See also *Intellectual control*; the Society of American Archivists' basic manual, *Arrangement and Description*, p. 19, and M. Cook, *Archives Administration*, pp. 117ff.

Algorithm   A computation or procedure broken down into a series of consecutive steps. Although the term is much wider, the relationship of the concept with systems analysis and flow-charting is clear.

Archival description set (A)   An assembly of archival descriptions (see Arad and Bell (1978), p. 3). These descriptions may be at any level; e.g. a guide is a set composed of descriptions of all the series in an archives office; a calendar is a set composed of descriptions of all the individual papers in a volume.

Archival entity (A)   The basic unit of archival description in any particular case.

Assembler (c)   A program, or set of programs, which translates
    programs into machine code so that the computer can translate general
    instructions into specific operations. It is not necessary for the
    non-technical user to understand the construction of assemblers. See
    also *Compilers*.
Backing store (c)   A memory store supplementary to the main memory
    of a computer. Access to it entails a degree of delay as compared with
    access to the main memory, but it allows a large quantity of data to be
    stored which can still be tapped quickly and easily.
Batch mode (c)   A method of preparing input data by which items of data
    (e.g. completed input forms) are allowed to accumulate until there is a
    sufficient quantity of them. They are then passed in a batch to the card
    punchers or other data preparation staff, and from them to the
    computer. Alternatively, batches may be set in at set periods of time,
    such as once a week or month. Contrast on-line mode.
Bit (c)   The smallest unit of data as held in an electronic store. It
    corresponds to the digits used by the binary code (i.e. 0 or 1), and to
    one element of core storage.
Bits per inch (BPI) (c)   The number of bits held on an inch of magnetic
    tape (the 'bit density') in any particular data storage system.
Boolean logic (c,i)   In practice, a feature of a data management system
    which allows the selective linkage of significant items. Possible linkages
    are term1 and term2; term1 or term2; term1 not term2, etc. A
    considerable degree of sophistication is possible where operators such
    as NOT-IF-THEN are employed.
Bug (c)   Mistake or malfunction in the system.
Bureau (c)   A private or commercially run agency which will carry out
    tasks related to computers on behalf of any user. The bureau may or
    may not have its own computer or its own battery of packages.
    Services may vary from the simplest (mechanical data preparation) to
    the most complex (design and running of a whole system).
Byte (c)   A set of bits used as a unit of storage or calculation. Some
    computer systems use the byte as a unit for reckoning storage of data,
    some the 'word', which is equally a set of bits.
Calendar (A)   A method of archival description wherein an attempt is
    made to include in the description all significant data held in the
    original archive, but excluding common form or irrelevant detail. Such
    a description would in most cases be a statisfactory substitute for the
    archive, and most users would not need to have access to the original.
    Also used for a compilation of such descriptions.
Chain index (i)   A method of indexing in which a chain of index terms
    demonstrates a hierarchical relationship running from general
    categories to specific item. In display, these terms all appear in their
    proper places in alphabetical order but the chain is truncated by the
    omission of terms which are more general that the one displayed; more
    specific terms are however displayed, down to the final and most
    specific, which appears alone. The method was used in the ARCAIC
    package, but proved not to be apt for archival indexing in that
    case.
Central Processing Unit (CPU) (c)   The central and quintessential part of
    a computer. It contains a control unit, an internal memory and
    arithmetic unit, which organizes the basic operations to be carried out.
Central processor (c)   See last entry.
Character (c)   One single component of a set which comprises letters,
    figures and puncuation marks (including spaces between words). Each
    character is represented in the computer by a unique code of bits.

Class (A)   In Britain, and especially at the Public Record Office, this term
  replaces the international *'series'* (q.v.).
Compaction (c)   The compression of signals into a smaller space. 'White
  compaction' is the reduction of white areas on the output paper that is,
  the reduction of wasted paper and data store, and the more economical
  working of a data management system.
Compiler (c)   A program for converting computer instructions written by
  a programmer into machine code in the form of an *object program*
  (q.v.). Compilers are more complex than assemblers, but neither need
  to be understood in detail by non-technical users.
Computer Input by Microfilm (CIM) (c)   Microfilm designed to serve as
  the input to a computer system. See next entry.
Computer Output to Microfilm (COM) (c)   An alternative to output on
  paper or to visual display. COM allows very rapid printing, often using
  laser technology, and a high standard of physical record, as well as
  other advantages (access at multiple points, for example) of microform
  systems. It may be a particularly valuable alternative to printed output.
Configuration (c)   The physical arrangement of electronic devices which
  comprise a computer system.
Data archive   An organization which collects, stores and makes
  accessible data of permanent value arising from research conducted
  with the aid of computers. The holdings of a data archive will normally
  be in the form of machine-readable records.
Data bank (c)   Files of data, usually stored in some sort of direct access
  system, so that multiple users may call upon them.
Data base (c)   A file of data, usually rather large, which is structured so
  that it can be used by different sections of the organization which
  controls it. The use made by these sections should not alter the content
  or distort the structure of the data base, which however should be
  readily updated.
Data base management system (c)   A system in which all the operations
  of an organization are based upon one set of data, the common data
  base, which is compiled by capturing data generated by each part of
  the organization as its work proceeds. This type of system can only
  succeed if the data recorded are accurate and the data base suitably
  structured to allow varied uses, including access limitations in
  particular cases; and if there is suitable software.
Data capture (c)   The process whereby raw data are gathered into a
  processing system and thereby fed into a computer system. In an
  archives service data capture is achieved by setting up a process so that
  each department generates information on the archives being handled;
  for example, the accessioning department provides data on
  provenance, physical character, date of accession; the conservation
  department may record its location, method of boxing, state of
  preservation, and so on.
Direct data entry (c)   A method of data preparation which avoids
  intermediate formats. In practice, the term covers devices which allow
  keying of data to magnetic tape, and have a facility for verifying them
  as they are processed.
Disc (c)   A data storage device consisting of a series of magnetic circular
  plates with pick-up heads. This allows the storage of large amounts of
  data, but also provides very rapid access to them.
Entity record (A)   A description of an archival entity as prepared for
  computer input. See Arad and Bell, p. 3.
Error report (c)   A document supplied to an archives service which
  specifies any errors in the last batch of input data. These may include

descriptions in the wrong format, mis-keyings, or simple mistakes in the material; the last can only be rectified by intelligent proofreading.

Facet (I)   Any object which may give its name as an index term can be considered under a number of aspects, representing its function within a category of activities. These are the object's facets. To determine all possible facets of a term, it must be classified into all appropriate major categories. Traditionally, these were: Personality, Material, Energy, Space and Time. In fact a more specific classification is usually necessary in any indexing situation.

Field (c)   A subdivision of a *record* (q.v.) containing a particular kind of information. In a list of file titles, for example, each record might contain the following fields: reference number, file title, date, location number.

File (c)   An assembly of *records* (q.v.). Normally a file will be a structured accumulation of records which have some common feature; e.g. they may be holdings of a particular archive office.

Floppy disc (c)   A small flimsy *disc* (q.v.) for data storage. These discs, with their containers, are small enough to be suitable for use on electronic devices, including micro-computers, which are kept in office space.

Flow-chart   A diagram intended to demonstrate a sequence of events and the logical relationship between them: systems flow-charts demonstrate how data processing or an administrative system works; program flow-charts illustrate the technical steps in a computer program. There are several standards which attempt to regulate the use of symbols.

Free text (c)   The contents of a field written in ordinary language without constraints or restriction by the requirements of the system.

Front-end devices (c)   Devices included in the computer configuration so that they carry out processes on input material. As an example, complex input data may receive preliminary processing by a mini-computer, which by means of an interface program is then able to act as an input device to the main computer.

Guide (A)   An assembly of archival descriptions at group and/or series level, which in the whole amounts to a summary description of the contents of an archives serivce, or at least of a major portion of it; typically a guide is for publication. A more detailed inventory is needed for retrieval.

Go-list (I)   A list of words which are permitted to appear as index terms in an automated index. Incorporated into a computerized system, index references will be generated wherever these terms appear.

Group (A)   The largest quantity, or highest level, of archives which can conveniently be administered and described as a unit. It would be normal for groups to have a common provenance (as with a government ministry), though in some cases they have been formed by bringing together a number of smaller entities (this is particularly so with the American 'record group' application of the concept). In Britain the term 'archive group' is preferred. There is a tendency everywhere to reduce emphasis on the group as a unit for archival description and to increase emphasis on the series; but descriptions of groups remain necessary, in order to preserve the record of provenance at the broadest level.

Handlist (A)   An assembly of archival descriptions which is based upon a subject-oriented selection, or upon a distinct documentary form. Thus, a handlist of archives of interest to social scientists brings together archival descriptions from several different groups or series; a handlist

of enclosure awards brings together descriptions of all such records
held by one or more archives offices.

Hardware (c)   The actual physical equipment in the computer
configuration, as distinguished from the software, the programs, etc.

Housekeeping reports (c)   Output generated by a computer system
which is designed to facilitate the system's working and is not itself an
example of the objectives which the system was set up to reach. Thus
error reports, reports of the numbers of documents requested in a
certain period or of the numbers of amendments recorded, etc., are
housekeeping reports in a system where the main output consists of
archival descriptions and indexes.

Intellectual control (A)   The aims of an archivist when constructing
finding aids intended primarily to retrieve and exploit the information
contained within the text of the archives concerned. This will normally
require very full inventories or even calendars together with an index of
names and subjects. These finding aids may be distinguished from
those aimed at *administrative control* (q.v.), although in practice a good
deal of coincidence is possible between the two. In computer terms
there is a strong distinction, since intellectual control will normally
entail on-line searching and elaboration of indexes, whereas
administrative control may well be content with updated print-out
lists.

Intelligent terminal (c)   A small computer capable of carrying some types
of data processing (perhaps with a local line printer for its output), but
which can also be interfaced with a large computer for more complex
processing. In the latter case it can be regarded as a terminal for the
larger computer, but one which can carry out programmed operations
by itself.

Interactive mode (c)   A method of operation whereby the user is able to
obtain an immediate response from the computer to his input
messages. Also known as 'conversational mode'.

Interface (c)   The connexion between any two units, for example between
a computer and its peripherals. More widely, the connexion between
any two systems, as between a records management and an archival
system. A complex interface, as between two computers, would require
specific programs.

Inventory (A)   An archival finding-aid which consists basically of a list of
entity descriptions with standard fields. The term is applied particularly
to micro-descriptions, that is descriptions of entities below series level.
A typical archival description system might consist of a *guide*
supplemented in the searchroom by a larger number of inventories
(more detailed description of the contents of series) and indexes.

Inverted file (c)   A feature of information retrieval systems in which
characteristics of items listed in the file are given an identifying key.
This key indicates each record which contains that characteristic. The
inverted file may be created from other forms of stored information,
and will be a technical feature in the total system.

K (c)   A common abbreviation for 'kilo', denoting one thousand. It can be
applied to *words* (in the technical computer sense, q.v.) or to *bytes*, or
even to pounds sterling.

Key-address storage (c)   A method of storing data in a machine-readable
medium. In this method particular records or fields are stored randomly
in the medium, but have addresses indicated by keys. The computer is
thereby able to find the data when necessary. An alternative method of
data storage is sequential. In designing a system, it is important to
choose a method of data storage which is appropriate, for, where large

amounts of data are concerned, much computer time can be saved (or wasted) in retrieving data items.

Language (c)   A set of instructions or conventions by which programs are drawn up to control computer operations. High-level languages are adaptations of ordinary speech, but programs written in these have to be translated into more technical forms, assemblers, compilers and machine-codes, before they can be acted upon by the computer. The means whereby this is done usually results in some degree of restriction of the computer's inherent flexibility of operation, and therefore it is important to the success of any system to use the appropriate high-level language.

Level (A)   Archival descriptions are divided into levels which correspond to the position in an analytical hierarchy of the archives being described. There are generally five levels, ranging from the highest (the group) down to the lowest (the individual document); these are discussed on pp. 21ff. It is essential in an archival description system, to be clear about what level is being dealt with, and it is also of importance that index terms can be generated at the appropriate level.

Logical operator (c, ı)   A symbol attached to a data item, or linking data items, to indicate that some function is to be applied to them. For example, in a system where retrospective searching is available, the terms 'greater than', 'less than', 'equal to', or the Boolean terms 'and', 'or', etc., are logical operators which serve to define the aims of any particular search.

Line printer (c)   An output device which prints out output material on continuous stationery, line by line.

Machine language (c)   Instructions to a computer which are written in technical forms so that the computer can operate directly from them without any intermediary. Programs written in high-level languages must be transposed into machine codes before they will work.

Mainframe (c)   The main body of a large computer, especially in distinction from its peripherals or from mini-computers.

Maintenance (c)   Hardware maintenance is the engineering work needed to keep the computer at work. Software maintenance, much more important to the non-technical user, is the work required to keep a system up to date. In practice, systems always require adjustments to their programs as time goes on: new forms of data appear, new variations of output are suggested; there are bugs, or problems with the input/output devices. Resources must therefore be provided for maintenance of the system.

Memory (c)   Normally applied to the main memory, the data store attached directly to a computer and immediately accessible to it. It is usually supplemented by a *backing store*, which may also be thought of as a memory unit, which can be tapped with a slight delay.

Micro-processor (c)   Strictly speaking, the *Central Processing Unit* (q.v.) of a micro-computer. More generally, used as a portmanteau word to describe the whole configuration of a system using micro-computers. A micro-computer is not different in its operation from a *mainframe* computer, except that it is usually smaller. Its distinguishing feature is that it uses very small components, such as silicon chips.

Mini-computer (c)   A small computer, usually with limited capacity and situated in normal working space. There is no hard line of distinction between mini- or micro-computers and *mainframe* computers (or even between them and large programmable calculators).

Modem (c)   A device which connects certain kinds of terminals to the computer installation, so that data can be transmitted to it.

MOP (Multiple On-line Processing) terminal (C) A terminal which is one of a number operating with a computer system. Users can operate these at the same time, and the operating system will arrange things so that each one appears to be in sole direct communication with the computer at any one time.

Network (C, I) Any system which has a number of operating points and an arrangement for connecting them. A user network is a system in which there are several different users, usually in different places, all of whom can use the system and communicate with each other, and the system can utilize the data input of each to provide joint output.

Object program (C) *Programs* written in a source language have to be translated into an object program, which will normally be in machine code and therefore ready for operation.

Off-line (C) Any part of a computer system which is not under the direct control of the central processor. Data preparation by a card puncher is off-line.

On-line (C) On-line devices are directly under the control of the central processor. On-line input/output devices such as a VDU are able to operate in conversational mode because of this relationship.

Operating system (C) A system for controlling the various programs and operations which a computer is to carry out. In effect it takes the place of a human controller as far as any routine operation is concerned.

Package (C) A program written for a particular kind of task, which can be leased or purchased by a user and then adapted to his special needs.

Parameter (C) A quantity or item in a system which can have different values in different records. The algebraic symbol x is a parameter in an equation; in any specific application its numerical value varies. In an archival description system the field 'earliest date' is a parameter in the file; in each record a different value (i.e. year number) is given to it.

Parameter card (C) A punched card which gives a particular value to one of the parameters in a system. Hence a way of adapting or controlling a particular system application.

Parity bit (C) A *bit* (q.v.) added to any group of bits as a check on the group's validity. A parity bit will be even or odd, according to the system in operation, and this must be recorded for archival data tapes, so that the groups of bits can be read.

Peripheral (C) Equipment peripheral to the central processor which operates within the general system, whether or not it is actually linked to the central processor.

Permuted index (I) A method of indexing which allows each of the indexable terms in a text to appear in turn as the principal term in an index entry. There are many different kinds of permuted index, the most elaborate being those in which the syntax of the index sentence is analysed, the resulting analysis being significant in choosing the terms to appear as index entries, and the shape of the qualifying entry which would follow them.

Post-co-ordinate (I) A style of indexing in which a record is indexed under a number of simple terms. A searcher isolates the record he is seeking by combining these terms until he finds a record which contains the appropriate combination, and can reject all other records.

Pre-coordinate (I) A style of indexing in which indexing terms are elaborated to the point where each compound term describes the whole concept expressed in the record. A searcher in this case scans the index display until he finds the most appropriate concept.

Program (C) A set of instructions to the computer with the object of solving a particular problem or carrying out a particular set of operations.

Record (A)   Any media of information which are generated in the course of business by any organization, and kept for reference in connexion with that business. See Cook, *Archives administration*, pp. 1–3.

Record (c)   A unit of data which constitutes one of the units in a file. In an archival description set each description is a record, thus in a *guide* the description of each series is a record; in an inventory of documents, each document is a record. Records are usually divided into *fields* (q.v.).

Schedule (A)   A list of types or forms of record produced in an organization, together with an instruction or recommendation as to the disposal of each. Also called a 'retention' or 'disposal schedule'.

Searching (c, I)   Operations in a system whereby each unit of information is examined for certain characteristics. For example, a data base may be searched for records containing a combination of two (specified) index terms. Searching can only be carried out if the system provides the necessary facilities.

Selective Dissemination of Information (SDI) (I)   Printing out selected records and distributing these in advance of requests to potential users.

Series (A)   A component of an archive group which consists of an organized set of archives with some strong unifying characteristic; also called a class. See Cook, *Archives administration*, p. 110.

Software (c)   Usually used to refer to the assembly of programs and advice given by a computer manufacturer to purchasers of the equipment, to enable them to make the best use of it; or by extension, any set of programs or instructions for solving a problem or setting up a system on a computer.

Source language (c)   The language in which a program is originated, and which requires to be translated into an object language/program before the computer can operate upon it.

Stoplist (I)   A list of words which may not be used as index terms. The stoplist will form part of a system in which index terms are machine-generated, and will prevent the system from choosing as index terms words such as 'the', 'together with', etc.

String (c)   Any connected set of characters or sequence of items.

String (I)   A list of index terms which together give a complete keyword entry to an indexed document. Terms in the string may be single words or compound phrases, they may form a chain of hierarchically related terms, or they may be independent.

Structure (c, I)   The structure of a data base comprises the ways in which the data items are set out in the input formats, the output formats and whatever is stored in the memory. The arrangement of the file, the sequence of records, the restrictions and order of fields, the presence or absence of identifying tags, are all elements in the structure of a data base.

System   A very large general term which may refer to any group of interrelated elements which together act in a co-ordinated way. In the present work the term has been used in the following main senses:
   (i) a set of procedures for the administration of archives within an archives office, or for the management of records within an organization;
   (ii) A set of programs for processing archival data;
   (iii) Coordinated activity between archives offices on a regular basis.

Tag (c, I)   A symbol or code attached to a data item in a record so that it can be recognized and manipulated.

Teletype (c)   A terminal device used for input and output, using a typewriter keyboard which can be operated automatically on impulse from the system.

Transfer/transmittal list (A)   An inventory of records which have been or are to be transferred from a current records system to the records centre or intermediate store. Normally this is a printed form on which individual records are entered manually.

User network (c, ı)   An association of users who are operating a system or network in common, with provision for mutual advice and sharing of resources.

Validation (c)   Checking data input entries to see that they conform with system requirements, that they are valid entries within the terms of the system. Much validation can be done automatically.

Verification (c)   Checking the accuracy of data preparation and entry; proof-reading. Data entries of course can be valid but not accurate. Verification is often done by processing input data twice by independent operators. Discrepancies between the two represent possible errors. A manual element always remains, however.

Visual Display Unit (VDU). (c)   An input/output terminal on which the characters input or output appear on a cathode ray tube. Used interactively, a vdu allows rapid and clear conversational interchanges with the system; but characters displayed on the tube of course are ephemeral. To remedy this, vdus may be used in conjunction with a teletype or line printer.

Word (c)   The basic unit of data within a computer system, consisting of a predetermined number of *bits*. The length of words varies according to the make of the computer or the nature of the system; some systems use *bytes* instead.

Zone bit (c)   In electronic storage, zone bits are included in the set of bits which represents any character. Their function is to identify the character as being a numeral, a letter or a symbol. Like parity bits, the nature, position and number of these must be recorded wherever machine-readable archives are involved.

Appendix A

Select Directory of Archival Systems

This directory is not intended to be exhaustive. In particular it omits most programs or systems which have as their main objective the exploitation of archives as objects of research; it also ignores most systems which have been developed outside Britain or North America. It is intended as a useful guide to system names which may be met with in the literature. A few non-archival systems are mentioned which have been considered for, or adapted to, archival uses. Literature references are given within parentheses.

AIRS; AIPS/CFC (Kurantov (1976), pp. 80–1, lists these systems as operative in Comecon countries and in the U.S.S.R.)

ALPHATEXT (Kurantov.) Operative in Canada.

ASSASSIN (*Agricultural System for Storage and Subsequent Selection of Information*) (A description is in Rowley (1979), pp. 107–15.) Developed by I.C.I. originally for in-house use, the system has become fairly widely used outside and is one of the predecessors of INSPEC. It provides SDI and KWOC indexing, with on-line search facilities.

BLAISE (*British Library Automated Information Service*) A networked facility used by member libraries.

CAIRS (*Computer Assisted Information Retrieval System*) (Rowley, pp. 116–27.) Developed by a private company, the system is now widely used by documentation/information services. The distinctive feature of the system is that it uses mini-computers with linked hard and software. Although reasonably flexible, it depends on a bibliographical-type input to its data base.

FAMULUS (A description appears in Crennell and Marsh (1979).) The system is a package to run on an IBM 360/195. It has been successfully used to computerize the catalogue of the Rutherford Laboratory library, and seems a reasonable choice for smaller archives services. Descriptions are limited to 4000 characters per record, but may be structured into up to twenty fields. Fields are of variable length each one separated from the next by a descriptor symbol. There is a KWIC index facility, with 'stop' and 'go' lists. Interactive interrogation exists with 11 possible commands. It is thought that the system is inefficent for very large amounts of data.

FIND 2 An ICL package. Single or multiple enquiry system. This system provides facilities for searching data bases, and is simple enough for

130

non-specialists to use. It will compare and check fields under AND, OR
NOT, etc., instructions and print out the results.

GOLEM (2) (Bell and Roper, pp. 208, 219–27.) A Siemens package, used by
the Central State Archives of Italy and the Federal Archives of West
Germany. This is a standard documentation system, slightly adapted to
archival circumstances, but for a situation where the national archives
holds series which do not widely deviate from bibliographical records.
Interactive interrogation is possible.

GOS Program package developed by the Museum Documentation Advisory
Unit for handling catalogues. It is capable of dealing with bibliographical
and archival material as well as objects.

HETRINA (Franz.) Operative at the archive school, Marburg.

IDMS One of a group of Data Base Management Systems (DBMS), available on
ICL, IBM and other hardware. (Atkinson (1979), p. 56.)

IRGMA (*Information Retrieval Group, Museums and Art Galleries*) now
superseded by MDA (Roberts (1976)). Developed under the sponsorship
of the Museums Association. Provides standard input cards for
artefacts, photographs, and other special materials. An attempt to
extend the system to archives as such has not progressed at present;
this may be due to its approach by cataloguing discrete items.

ISIS Package developed by the International Labour Organisation, referred to
by Arad and Bell (1978), p. 7, as a permuted indexing system.

KWIC (*Keyword In Context*) (Mathews et al. (1973).) This is an IBM package
which originally was simply a permuted index of titles, but has now
developed some sophisticated features. (See *Catalogue of
Documentation*, compiled by P. Stewart (1975), p. 25.) These include the
following forms of output: bibliography, author index, title index (KWOC
format), permuted title index (KWIC format), assigned descriptor index.

KWOC (*Keyword Out of Context*) A variation of KWIC in which the index term
is extracted from the indexed title and printed in the left-hand margin.
The full title then follows as the term's qualifier. (Kendall (1973)).

MARC A bibliographical system developed in the Library of Congress and
now widely used in the U.S.A. and elsewhere as a means of
disseminating bibliographical information on magnetic tape. There is
an adaptation by the Library of Congress for use with manuscripts
(MARC (1973).) This differs from the standard MARC tape in that it does
not disseminate cataloguing information on manuscripts, but provides
a format which manuscript libraries can use for their unique material.
Though adaptable to local circumstances by the use of tags, indicators
and sub-field codes, the format as used by the library looks rather
bibliographical, and uses the following standard fields for document
description: main entry ('author'); title; physical description; repository
name; scope and contents (free text description); provenance;
subject-topical (string of subject terms); six fields for personal name
index entries.

NRA Indexing systems developed at the National Register of Archives,
London, covering persons/names, and subjects. See the Register's
Subject Indexing Schema and *Wordlist* (1969); it is understood that
these have been updated.

PASSAT (Bell and Roper, p. 209.) A system for automatic generation of
keywords from text which makes allowance for inflective and other
syntactical changes in the form of words. This makes it suitable for
indexing Latin.

PENTAKA (Kurantov.) System in use in East Germany.

PRECIS (Austin (1974).) Permuted indexing system from machine-held
bibliographic data base (MARC) developed at the British National

Bibliography. This index prints out a full statement of the context of its keywords by providing a short abstract or precis under each one. The human indexer is required to classify terms for inclusion in the index by specifying their syntactical function. Its suitability for archival indexing has been investigated by the Public Record Office and by the Devon Record Office (*JSA*, **6** (1978), 116–17).

PROMPT (Bell (1976).) A system for requisitioning archives by members of staff or by users in the searchroom at the Public Record Office.

RECODEX (*Records Management Control and Indexing*) (Bell and Roper, pp. 88–90.) This system was developed by the Public Archives of Canada as a means of controlling its own operations, and was also intended to provide a model for government departments. It was not adopted outside the Public Archives.

ROBOT (*Record Organization Bases on Transposition*) A data base management system devised by a private firm (Software Services Products Ltd). This is a system which allows direct access to data stored on discs. It uses fields rather than records as the basis for file structure and this allows a good deal of flexibility in sorting arrangement and search facilities.

SAGE (*Smithsonian Archives Guide Entries*) A component of SELGEM for producing guide entries for publication and series-level descriptions for in-house reference and control.

SARIAS A Romanian system (Kurantov).

SERAC A French system used to construct a *fichier informatisé* of sub-series of archives from communal (local government) administration over the nineteenth century; really, therefore, a research rather than a management system.

SESAM (Bell and Roper, p. 219.) A Siemens package considered for use at the Federal Archives, West Germany.

SPSS (*Statistical Package for the Social Sciences*) A non-technical computer language developed for social scientists working from data bases and data archives. (Nie, Bent & Hall.)

STARR (*Systematic Tracing and Retrieval of Records*) (Bell and Roper, pp. 90–7.) Package developed at the Canadian Department of Transport. Basically an adaptation of a stock control package, it controls disposal of files from a very large registry system, and can be extended to provide registration, bring-forward dates for review of files, classification of correspondence, and printing of file title labels. Plans to develop it into a fully automated RM system have been suspended.

Appendix B

**Guidelines for Selection of Machine-Readable and Related Records for
Permanent Preservation
(recommended by the Public Record Office)**

In considering which records should be preserved permanently it is
necessary to establish appraisal criteria which are applicable to a particular
department or to particular kinds of records. These criteria should take into
account, not only the value of records for the long-term purposes of
government or of the department but also their value for much wider
research needs. The following general descriptions of the main kinds of
records which should be kept permanently are intended as guidelines for
use in deciding detailed appraisal standards.

(i) Records describing computer-based systems for work processing and
management information. In many cases there will be no need to keep
machine-readable system files or job files (apart possibly from specimens),
but documentation (e.g. manuals, flow-charts, administrative records) may
be worth preserving to show how a department functioned, or how a
particular type of job was handled.
(ii) Files of information and text retrieval systems relating to reports, etc.,
where no acceptable print-out version exists.
(iii) Files of data which have been processed to produce reports which have
had a bearing on departmental or government policy, e.g. for submission to
a minister or a senior official or to the Cabinet or a Cabinet committee.
(iv) Files of data produced for the benefit of royal commissions and
departmental and interdepartmental committees and working parties.
(v) Files of data recording rights or obligations of or against the Crown.
(vi) Files of data relating to issues which were the subject of interest or
controversy on the national or international plane.
(vii) Files which, taken individually or in conjunction with other sources,
record trends or developments in social, economic or other fields,
particularly if they contain unpublished statistical or financial data covering
a long period or a wide area.
(viii) Files of historical or practical importance relating to aspects of
scientific, technical or medical research and development.
(ix) Files containing data of significant regional or local interest on matters
for which it is unreasonable to expect that evidence will be available locally,
or comprising synopses of such information covering the whole country or
a wide area.
(x) Staff personal files held in a machine-readable form constitute a special
case. Routine pay and pensions files will not be preserved, but the
treatment of other personal files should always be discussed with the PRO.

Appendix C

It is the general policy of the Machine Readable Archives to provide as quickly as possible, at a nominal cost, copies or extracts of its files together with supporting documentation, subject to the following conditions:

(i) Under no circumstances will files (regardless of medium) originally transferred to the Machine Readable Archives be sold, loaned or given out. Only copies or extracts of such files will be released.

(ii) Copies or extracts of files (regardless of medium) will not be made available if such access contravenes the conditions or regulations determined by transferring agency or individual.

(ii) Copies or extracts of files (regardless of medium) containing information gathered through questionnnaires, interviews, etc., in which respondents were assured of confidentiality, when they are released by the Archives, will contain as many data elements/variables as possible (or a subset thereof) without jeopardizing the anonymity of individual respondents, interviewees, etc. whether these be companies, organizations or individuals.

(iv) The Archives reserves the right not to release any file copy or extract if it considers such an action to be, or possibly to be, a breach of public trust, detrimental to public welfare, or injurious to one or more individuals.

(v) The purchaser of file copies or extracts sold to him by the Machine Readable Archives will agree that these are for his exclusive use and that the information contained therein must not be sold or otherwise transferred.

(vi) The purchaser will also agree to credit the Machine Readable Archives and the principal investigators in publications which use the files and to indicate that neither bears any responsibility for the analyses or interpretations which appear in such publications.

Notes and References

Where full bibliographical references are not given, they will be found in the Bibliography, section C

(1) *Report of the Committee on Departmental Records.* Cmd 9163 (H.M.S.O. 1954), 6.
(2) Darwin, K., 'The use of the computer in indexing records', *JSA* **4** (1979), 226.
(3) For example, SPINDEX User Network: news note in *AA*, **42** (1979), 110.
(4) Gracy, 1.
(5) Arad, A. and Bell, L., *ADPA* **2** (1978), 2–9.
(6) An interesting reinforcement of the foregoing analysis comes from Iredale, D., 'Organizing Archives', *Library Review*, **26** (1977), 110–13.
(7) Bearman, D. *AA*, **42** (1979), 187.
(8) Ibid., 187.
(9) Ibid., 189.
(10) Society of Archivists, working party on subject indexing. Processed paper, *Subject Indexing Classification Scheme* (Feb. 1975). There are subsequent amendments.
(11) Arad and Bell, 6.
(12) East Sussex County Council, *Systems description: computer indexing and cataloguing for the County Records Office* (County Treasurer's Dept. Lewes, 1970), 33–4.
(13) In a lecture delivered at a Society of Archivists in-service course held at Liverpool University.
(14) Quoted by Bautier, 49–50.
(15) Calmes, A., *AA*, **42** (1979), 168.
(16) Bell and Roper, 85ff.
(17) Ibid., 98–112.
(18) Ibid., 88–9.
(19) National Archives and Records Service, May 1974. Specific reports on aspects of the system are available from NARS on microfilm. I am indebted to Mr S. E. Hannestad for this information. See also Calmes in *AA*, **42**.
(20) Bearman, D., *AA*, **42** (1979), 187.
(21) For an important comment on this see David Bearman's review in *AA*, **42** (1979), 350–1.
(22) From National Association of State Archives and Records

Administrators, *Report on the Conference on Automated Guide
Projects, July 19–20, 1977, St Louis, Missouri*, 72.
(23) *User's introduction to the system*. I am obliged to Mr S. E. Hannestad
of NARS for a copy of this unattributed print.
(24) SPINDEX III instruction paper [1978], kindly provided by Mr Hannestad.
(25) Smithsonian Institution, 1973. I am indebted to Mr Alan L. Bain for
much additional material.
(26) I am indebted to Mr H. S. Cobb of the House of Lords Record Office for
this material.
(27) Rowley, J. E., *Mechanised in-house information systems* (London,
1979), 154–60.
(28) Bell and Roper, 220.
(29) Ibid., 207.
(30) Ibid., 224.
(31) N'Diaye; Direction des Archives Nationales (Côte d'Ivoire), *Guide du
lecteur* (Abidjan, 1972). I am obliged to M. G. Cangah and his staff for
further material.
(32) A progress report to 1974 and a critique appear in Bell and Roper,
176–98.
(33) East Sussex County Council, County Record Office, *Staff Manual* (1970),
appendix III.
(34) Bautier, 90–1.
(35) Ibid., 51.
(36) P.R.O., London, 1974; processed.
(37) Cook, M., *Archives Administration* (Dawson, Folkestone, 1977).
(38) National Archives and Records Service, Washington, D.C., July 1972. I
am grateful to Mr C. M. Dollar for much material.
(39) Alldredge, E. O., 'Inventorying magnetic-media records', *AA*, **35** (1972),
341, gives both forms in full.
(40) Public Record office, *The selection and preparation for transfer of
machine-readable records: a provisional guide* (P.R.O., London, 1974;
processed), section 3/3/3.
(41) *AA*, **41** (1978), 423–30.

Select Bibliography

This bibliography is restricted to books or articles which are reasonably easy of access, and which are judged to be of direct value to archivists who wish to study the questions involved in applying ADP to their discipline or to begin a related systems analysis. It is arranged as follows:

A Bibliographies
B General computer applications, ADP, systems analysis, information science
C Specifically archival ADP
D Records management
E Indexing, both general and in relation to archives work
F Machine-readable archives
G Preservation of machine-readable archives

Abbreviations

AA	*The American Archivist* (This journal carries an annual bibliography of publications in archives science, details of which are not given specifically here.)
Bell and Roper	Public Record Office, *Proceedings of an international seminar on automatic data processing in archives*, ed. L. Bell and M. Roper (H.M.S.O. London, 1975).
JSA	*Journal of the Society of Archivists*

A Bibliographies

Bautier, R. H., 'Archives and automation', *Record of the 13th International Conference of the Archival Round Table, Bonn, 1971* (International Council on Archives, 1975), 82–4.

Evans, F. G., *Modern archives and manuscripts: a select bibliography* (Society of American Archivists, 1975), 13–15 ('Automation and the control of archives and manuscripts').

Fishbein, M. H., 'ADP and archives: selected publications on automatic data processing', *AA*, **38** (1975), 31–42.

Fisher, B., and Evans, F. B., 'Automation, information and the administration of archives and manuscript collections: a bibliographic review', *AA*, **30** (1967), 333–48.

International Council on Archives, 'Mechanisation, automation, data

processing', *Basic international bibliography of archive administration*, ed. M. Duchein, *Archivum*, **25** (1978), 122–7.
Roper, M., 'ADP in archives: a bibliography', *JSA*, **5** (1974), 107–9; (1977), 443–7.

B General computer applications, ADP, Systems Analysis, Information Science.
Annual review of information science and technology, **1–10** (1966–75).
Artandi, S., *An introduction to computers in information science,* 2nd edn (Scarecrow Press, Metuchen (N.J.), 1972).
Atkinson, M. P., 'Progress in documentation: data base systems', *Journal of documentation*, **35** (1979), 49–91.
Bingham, J. E. and Davies, G. W., *A handbook of systems analysis* (Macmillan, London, 1972).
Bisco, R. L. *Data bases, computers and the social sciences* (Wiley International, New York, 1970).
Bishop, P., *Computer programming in BASIC* (Nelson, London, 1978).
Boss, R. W., *The Library manager's guide to automation* (Knowledge Industry Publications, London, 1979).
BS 5408: Glossary of documentation terms (British Standards Institution, 1977).
Chandor, A. (ed.), *A dictionary of computers*, 2nd edn (Penguin Books, Harmondsworth, 1977).
Clough, C. R., and Kilvington, L. C., 'ASSASSIN: the quiet revolution', *Program*, **12** (1978), 35–41.
Coblans, H., *Librarianship and Documentation* (Deutsch, London, 1974). (Grafton Basic Texts)
Cutbill, J. L., *Computer filing systems for museums and research* (Museums Association, London, 1973).
Davis, C. H., *Illustrative computer programming for libraries: selected examples for information specialists* (New Greenwood Press, 1974).
Department of Education and Science, *Automation guidelines for public libraries* (H.M.S.O., London, 1975). (Library Information Series 6)
Department of the Environment, *General review of local authority management information systems* (H.M.S.O., London, 1975).
Eyre, J., and Tonks, P., *Computers and systems: an introduction for librarians* (Bingley, London, 1971).
Finer, R., *A guide to selected computer-based information services* (Aslib, London, 1972).
Fry, T. F., *Further computer appreciation* (Newnes-Butterworths, Sevenoaks, 1977).
Gautier, T. G., 'Automated collection documentation system at the National Museum of Natural History, Smithsonian Institution, Washington D.C.', *Museum* **30** (1978), 160–8.
Grosch, A. N. *Minicomputers in libraries, 1979–80* (Industry Publications, London, 1979).
Harmon, G., *Human memory and knowledge: a systems approach* (New Greenwood Press, 1973).
Holloway, A. H., Ridler, E., and Yates, B., *Information work with unpublished reports* (Deutsch, London, 1976). (Institute of Information Scientists Monograph Series).
Houghton, B., and Convey, J., *On-line information retrieval systems: an introductory manual to principles and practice* (Bingley, London, 1977).

Hunt, R., and Shelley, J., *Computers and commonsense*, 2nd edn (Prentice-Hall International, Englewood Cliffs (N.J.), 1979).

Inman, K., and Swinburne, J., *Introduction to flow charting* (Polytech Publishers, Stockport, 1972).

International Federation for Information Processing, *Guide to concepts and terms in data processing*, ed. I. H. Gould (North-Holland, Amsterdam, 1971).

Jeffreys, A. E., and Wilson, T. D., *The U.K. MARC project* (Oriel Press, Newcastle, 1970).

Kalthoft, R. J., 'Document vs. data based information systems', *Journal of Micrographics*, **10**, 2 (1976), 79–88.

Kent, A., and Galvin, T. J., *The On-line revolution in libraries* (Dekker AG., Basel, 1978).

Lamb, G. H., *Computers in the public service* (Allen and Unwin, London, 1973).

Laver, M., *Introducing computers,* 3rd edn (H.M.S.O., London, 1976).

Malinconico, S. M., and Fasana, P., *The future of the catalogue: the library's choices* (Knowledge Industry Publications, London, 1979).

Mitchell, R. K., *Information science and computer basics* (Bingley, London, 1971).

Monro, D. M. *Interactive computing with BASIC* (Arnold, London, 1979).

Open University, *Computing and computers: course book. An introduction to systems analysis and design*, ed. D. Yates (Open University Press, Milton Keynes, 1973).

Open University, *The digital computer. Unit 1: Computers and their applications* (TM221/1) (Open University Press, Milton Keynes, 1975).

Open University, *Systems performance: human factors and systems failures,* ed. J. Naughton and G. Peters (TD342/1) (Open University Press, Milton Keynes, 1976).

Porter, M. F. 'Establishing a museum documentation system in the U.K.', *Museum*, **30** (1978), 169–78.

Pritchard, A., *A guide to computer literature: an introductory survey of the sources of information*, 2nd edn (Bingley, London, 1972).

Roberts, D. A., Information retrieval group of the Museums Association: *Introduction to the IRGMA documentation system* (Museums Association, London, 1976).

Rosenberg, P. M., and Durr, W. T., *The urban information thesaurus: a vocabulary for social documentation* (New Greenwood Press, 1977).

Rowley, J. E., *Mechanised in-house information systems* (Bingley, London, 1979).

Saffody, W., *Computer-output microfilm: its library applications* (Library Association, London, 1978).

Sher, J. A., 'The use of computers in museums: present situation and problems,' *Museum*, **30** (1978), 132–8.

Sherrod, J. (ed.), *Information systems and networks. 11th annual symposium in information processing* (New Greenwood Press, 1975).

Shorter, E., *The historian and the computer: a practical guide* (Prentice-Hall, Englewood Cliffs (N.J.), 1971).

Tedd, L. A., *An introduction to computer based library systems* (Heyden, London, 1977).

Van Belleghem, G., 'Computer output microfilm', *Archives et Bibliothèques de Belgique*, **46** (1975), 122–6.

Vickery, B. C., *Techniques of information retrieval* (Hamden, 1970).

Vickery, B. C., *Information systems* (London, 1973).

Wooldridge, S., *Data processing made simple* (W. H. Allen, London, 1976).

c Archival ADP

ADPA: Automation, Archives, Information. Bulletin of the Committee on Automation of the International Council on Archives (1972–   ). In progress.

Arad, A., 'The use of computerised systems at the Israel state archives', *ADPA*, **1**, 3 (1975), 2–10.

Arad, A., and Bell, L., 'Archival description–a general system', *ADPA*, **2**, 3 (1978), 2–9.

Atherton, J., 'Mechanization of the manuscript catalogue at the Public Archives of Canada', *AA*, **30** (1967), 303–9.

Atherton, J., 'Automation and the dignity of the archivist', *Canadian Archivist*, **2** (1970), 56–8.

Austin, D., PRECIS: *a manual of concept analysis and subject indexing* (British National Bibliography, London, 1974).

Austin, D., 'Progress in documentation: the development of PRECIS. A theoretical and technical history', *Journal of Documentation*, **30** (1974), 47–102.

Bain, A. L., 'Computer applications to archives and manuscripts at the Smithsonian Institution archives', *ADPA*, **2**, 3 (1978), 13–21.

Bautier, R. H., 'Archives and automation', in *Record of the 13th International Conference of the Archival Round Table, Bonn, 1971* (International Council on Archives, 1975).

Bearman, D., 'Automated access to archival information: assessing systems', *AA*, **42** (1979), 179–90.

Bell, L., 'Public Record Office survey of computer installations', *ADPA*, **1**, 2 (1974), 11–14.

Bell, L., 'An archivists' co-operative?', *JSA*, **5** (1975), 149–57.

Bell, L., 'Survey of archival data processing in Great Britain', *ADPA*, **1**, 3 (1975), 11–26.

Bell, L., 'Document requisitioning at the Public Record Office, Kew', *JSA*, **5** (1976), 327.

Bell, L., and Roper, M. *See* Public Record Office.

Block, I. J., and Hampson, G., 'Use of an ICL 1901 computer for listing archives and manuscripts', *Program*, **3** (1969), 70–4.

Boberach, H., and Buchmann, W., 'Advanced technologies and the expansion of archives access' (report to 8th International Congress on Archives, Washington, 1976). German text in *Archivum*, **26** (1979), 127–36.

Boer, D., 'Business archives in automated information retrieval systems', *Archivum*, **18** (1968), 191–8.

Bond, M., 'Computer applications in the House of Lords Record Office', *JSA*, **5** (1977), 466.

Brichford, M. (ed.), *Guide to the ALA archives* (University of Illinois, 1978). Processed paper.

Buckard, F., 'Les archives et l'informatique en France: perspectives et directions de recherche', *Gazette des Archives*, n.s. **75** (1971), 159–77.

Burke, F. G., 'The application of automated techniques in the management and control of source materials', *AA*, **30** (1967), 255–78.

Burke, F. G., 'Automation in bibliographical control of archives and manuscript collections', in *Bibliography and the historian*, ed. D. H. Perman (1968), 96–102.

Burke, F. G., 'Report on a survey of automation activities in archives and manuscript repositories in the U.S. and Canada', *AA*, **31** (1968), 208–10.

Burke, F. G., 'Computer techniques for the National Archives', *Computers and the Humanities*, **4** (1969), 11–18.

Select bibliography 141

Califano, E., 'L'introduction et l'adaptation des moyens mécanographiques aux archives', *Archivum*, **14** (1964), 147–56.

Califano, E., 'Etude sur la possibilité d'appliquer les moyens électroniques et mécanographiques au traitement de la documentation archivistique et la gestion des services d'archives' (International Council on Archives, 1969). Processed paper.

Calmes, A., 'Practical realities of computer based finding aids: the NARS A–1 experience', *AA*, **42** (1979), 167–77.

Campbell, R. R., 'Automation and information retrieval in archives–the broad concepts', *AA*, **30** (1967), 279–86.

Cangah, G., and Boutillon, G., 'Contribution à une méthodologie de la documentation automatique', *ADPA*, **2**, 1 (1976), 2–6.

Carrington, D. K., and Mangan, E. U., *Data preparation manual for the conversion of map cataloging records to machine-readable form* (Library of Congress, Washington (D.C.), 1971).

Carroll, M. E., 'Public Archives of Canada survey of EDP installations', *ADPA*, **1**, 2 (1974), 15–25.

Clarke, R. L., 'Standardisation and technology', in *Archive–Library Relations*, ed. R. L. Clarke (Bowker, New York/London, 1976), 133–40.

Clough, C. R., and Kilvington, L. C., 'ASSASSIN: the quiet revolution', *Program*, **12** (1978), 35–41.

Cloulas, I., 'Information et archives: un bilan international', *Gazette des Archives*, **91** (1975), 249–57.

Crennell, K. M., and Marsh, E., 'Computerisation of the Rutherford Laboratory Catalogue', *Program*, **13** (1979), 73–84.

de Tribolet, M., 'Archivistique et informatique: maladie sénile ou bain de jouvence?', Vereinigung Schweizerische Archivare, *Mitteilungen*, **27** (1976), 26–37.

Dewhitt, B., 'Archival uses of computers in the U.S. and Canada', *AA*, **42** (1979), 152–7.

Direction des Archives de France, *Informatique et archives contemporaines* (Service de l'Informatique note d'information 5, 1974). Processed.

Direction des Archives de France, *Notes d'information. Service de l'informatique*. Periodical.

Elliot, A., and Jones, B., 'Recent work at Newcastle University on the cataloguing and indexing of manuscripts', *Program*, **7** (1973), 60–6.

Etor, J. R., 'Computers and accounting archives', *Business Archives*, **40**, (1974), 8–16.

Franz, E. G., 'Projekt HETRINA: elektronische Datenverarbeitung an der Archivschule Marburg', *Der Archivar*, 24 Jg (1971), 381–90.

Gandilhon, R., 'Montant des dépenses entraînées par le classement d'un fonds d'archives', *Archives et Bibliothèques de Belgique*, **46** (1975), 489–96.

Gracy, D. B., II (ed.), *Archives and manuscripts: arrangement and description* (Society of American Archivists, Chicago, 1977).

Hackman, L. J., Sahli, N., and Burton, D. A., 'The NHPRC and a guide to manuscript and archival materials in the United States', *AA*, **40** (1977), 201–5.

Hannestad, S. E., 'SPINDEX II: a computerised approach to preparing guides to archives and manuscripts', *Computing in the Humanities: proceedings of the 3rd international conference on computing in the humanities*, eds. S. Lusignan and J. S. North (University of Waterloo Press, 1977).

Hickerson, H. T., Winters, J., and Beale, V., *SPINDEX II at Cornell University and a review of archival automation in the United States* (Dept. of Manuscripts and University Archives, Cornell University Libraries, Ithaca (N.Y.), 1976).

Holland, C. G., 'Indexes, computers and public service', *JSA*, **4** (1972), 428–31.

International Council on Archives, 'Report on archives with punched card or electronic facilities for the processing of data and the special documents involved', *Proceedings of the 8th and 9th international conferences of the Round Table on Archives* (London, 1965), 164–89.

International Council on Archives, 'Minutes and agenda of the working party on the implications of automatic data processing for archival management held in Spoleto, Italy, May 1972, *ADPA*, **1**, 1 (1972).

Kurantov, A. P., 'Progrès dans la science administrative des archives' (in Proceedings of the 8th International Congress on Archives, Washington, 1976), *Archivum*, **26** (1979), 73–83.

Lamberti, A., 'Management of computer records', *Records Management Journal*, **6** (1968), 2–13.

Library of Congress *Manuscripts: a* MARC *format. Specifications for magnetic tapes containing catalog records for single manuscripts or manuscript collections*, by L. S. Maruyama (Washington (D.C.), 1973).

Mukula, P. M., 'Problems of using computers in developing countries' archival institutions', ECARBICA *Journal*, **2** (1974), 38–42.

National Archives and Records Service (U.S.A.), NARS A–1 *general systems study report. Control and description of records in the National Archives: a summary* (Washington (D.C.), 1974).

National Archives and Records Service (U.S.A.), *Managing information retrieval. Computer output microfilm* (Washington (D.C.), 1975. (Records Management Handbooks)

National Association of State Archives and Records Administrators, *Report on the conference on automated guide projects, St Louis, Missouri, July, 1977.*

N'Diaye, A., *Archives nationales: manuel de codification à l'intention des archivistes* (Archives Nationales, Abidjan, 1975).

Newton, S. C., Review of *Proceedings of an international seminar on ADP in archives, Journal of Librarianship,* **8** (1976), 212–14.

O'Toole, J. M., 'The use of computers in archival institutions', *Information Revolution*: Proceedings of American Society of Information Scientists, 38th annual meeting, Boston (Mass.), 1975 (ASIS, Washington (1975)), 89–90.

Pieyns, J., 'L'informatique aux archives de l'état en Belgique: outil de travail et moyen de conservation', *Miscellanea Archivistica* (Brussels), no. 10 (1975), 27–39.

Public Record Office, *Proceedings of an international seminar on Automatic Data Processing in Archives*, eds. L. Bell and M. Roper (H.M.S.O., London, 1975).

Public Record Office, *PROSPEC Manual*, ed. F. McCall (London, n.d.).

Reed, M. A., 'Archives', *British library and information science, 1971–5*, ed. H. A. Whatley (Library Association, London, 1977), 325–31.

Rhoads, J. B., 'New archival techniques', *Archivum*, **24** (1974), 77–134.

Rieger, M., 'Archives and automation', *AA*, **29** (1966), 109–11.

Roper, M., 'Computer applications committee: a consultation document', *JSA,* **5** (1974), 101–9.

Roper, M., 'PROSPEC-SA. A case study in setting up a co-operative computer project', *ADPA*, **2**, 2 (1977), 9–14.

Saclier, M., 'Computer applications at the Australian National University Archives of Business and Labour', *ADPA*, **2**, 1 (1976), 16–18.

Shaw, J., 'Archives and automation', *Archives and Manuscripts*, **5** (1974), 147–50.

Simmons, P., Bell, L., and Roper, M., 'PROSPEC: a computer application for the Public Record Office', *JSA*, **4** (1972), 423–7.

Smithsonian Institution, *A proposal for the computerised control of Smithsonian Institution archival resources*. Processed paper, Sept. 1973.

Society of American Archivists, *Inventories and registers: a handbook of techniques and examples* (1976).

Society of Archivists, *PROSPEC–SA pilot project. The development of PROSPEC for wider use in providing guides to record offices*, ed M. Roper (processed paper, Sept. 1978).

Wilson, P. D., 'Computers and archives: some random thoughts', *Archives and Manuscripts*, **4** (1972), 11–18.

D Records Management

Butler, D. J., 'Computer based records management at Tyne and Wear County Council', *Local Government Chronicle*, 28 July 1978.

Butler, D. J., and Nicholson, W. H., 'ARMS: a computer-based records management system developed by Tyne and Wear County Council', *JSA*, **6** (1979), 200–8.

Diers, F. V., 'Computer indexing for a records retention center', *Records Management Quarterly*, **12** (1978), 21–4.

East Sussex Record Office, *Pre-archival records control: operation manual* (East Sussex County Council, Lewes, 1973) (Technical Memoranda 4).

Kilmer, I. L., 'ADP documentation and records management', *Records Management Journal*, **10** (1972), 9–14.

Patch, M., 'Records management in Dyfed', *JSA* 6 (1979), 209–13.

E Indexing

Aitchison, J. and Gilchrist, A., *Thesaurus construction: a practical manual*. (Aslib, London, 1972).

Alexander, D., 'A description of indexing procedures for the "Agreement on Account of Crew"', *Archives*, **11** (1973), 86–93.

Bakewell, K. G. B., 'The PRECIS indexing system' in *Indexers on Indexing*, ed. L. M. Harrod (Bowker, New York/London, 1978).

Bell, L., 'Controlled vocabulary subject indexing of archives', *JSA*, **4** (1971), 285–99.

Campey, L. H., *Generating and printing indexes by computer* (Aslib, London, 1972).

Campey, L. H., 'Costs of producing KWIC/KWOC indexes', *Information Storage and Retrieval*, **10** (1974), 293–307.

Cox, N. S. M., and Davies, R. S., *The indexing of records in the Public Record Office* (University, Newcastle-upon-Tyne, 1970). Privately circulated.

Darwin, K., 'The use of the computer in indexing records', *JSA*, **4** (1971), 218–29.

Field, B. J., 'A thesaurus-based indexing and classification system developed for INSPEC products and services', *Journal of Documentation*, **30** (1974), 1–17.

Gross, R., 'The application of thesauri in the State archives of GDR', *ADPA* **2**, 1 (1976), 11–15.

Jones, K. S., *Automatic keyword classification for information retrieval* (Butterworths, London, 1971).

Kendall, P. F., 'A note on the use of KWOC indexes for weeding a records repository', *Program*, **7** (1973), 145–6.

Kuch, T. D. C., 'Computer supported indexing', *The Indexer*, **9** (1974), 16–17.
Lancaster, F. W., 'Vocabulary control in information retrieval systems', in M.
   J. Voigt and M. H. Harris (eds.) *Advances in Librarianship*, **7** (1977),
   2–41.
Liebesny, F., *A state-of the-art survey of automatic indexing* (UNESCO,
   Paris, 1974). Processed.
Lynch, M. F., 'Computer-organised display of subject information', *The
   Indexer*, **7** (1971), 94–100.
Matthews, F. W., et al., 'Variations on KWIC', *Aslib Proceedings*, **25** (1973),
   140–52.
Mills, J., 'Chain indexing and the classified catalogue', *Library Association
   Record*, **57** (1955), 141–8.
Ramsden, M. J., *An introduction to index language construction: a
   programmed text* (Bingley, London, 1974).
Ryan, V. J., and Dearing, V. A., 'Computerized manuscript and index
   processing', *Scholarly Publications*, **4** (1973), 333–50.
Townley, H. M., 'Computers and indexes', in *Indexers on Indexing: a
   selection of articles published in The Indexer*, ed. L. M. Harrod (Bowker,
   New York/London, 1978).
Underwood, M. G., 'A computer index for the archives of St John's College,
   Cambridge: a progress report', *JSA*, **6** (1979), 214–18.

F Machine-readable archives

Alldredge, E. O., 'Inventorying magnetic-media records', *AA*, **35** (1972),
   337–45.
Bell, L., 'The archival implications of machine-readable records', *Archivum*,
   26 (1979), 85–92.
Carroll, M. E., 'A perspective of machine-readable archives and public
   service', *ADPA*, **2**, 1 (1976), 7–10.
Dollar, C. M., 'Documentation of machine-readable records and research: a
   historian's view', *Prologue*, **3** (1971), 27–31.
Dollar, C. M., 'Problems and procedures for preservation and dissemination
   of computer readable and process produced data', in
   *QUANTUM–SSHA Conference. Quantification and methods in social
   science research: possibilities and problems with the use of historical
   and process-produced data* (University of Cologne, 1977). Processed.
Dollar, C. M., 'Appraising machine-readable records', *AA*, **41** (1978),
   423–30.
Evans, F. H., *Modern archives and manuscripts: a select bibliography*
   (Society of American Archivists, 1975), 82–6 ('Machine-readable records
   and archives').
Fishbein, M. H., 'Appraising information in machine-language form', *AA*, **35**
   (1972), 35–43.
Fishbein, M. H., 'Report of the ICA committee on ADP. Report of the
   committee on data archives and machine-readable records', *ADPA*, **1**, 2
   (1974), 3–10.
Fullmon, F. A., Jr, 'Legal aspects of computer records problems',
   Information and Records Management, **7** (1973), 38–9.
Geda, C. L., 'Social science data archives', *AA*, **42** (1979), 158–66.
Marquant, R., and Perotin, Y., 'Les documents utilisés ou produits par les
   machines mécanographiques et électroniques' in *Manuel
   d'archivistique* (Direction des Archives de France, Paris, 1970), 555–62.
National Archives and Records Service, Machine-readable Archives Division,
   Accessioning procedures handbook (Washington (D.C.), n.d.). Processed.
National Archives and Records Service, *Catalog of machine readable*

records in the National Archives of the U.S.A. (Washington (D.C.), 1975).

National Archives and statistical research, ed. M. H. Fishbein (Ohio University Press, Athens (Ohio 1973). (NARS Conferences No 2)

Naugler, H.. 'FOCUS: the machine-readable archives division of the Public Archives of Canada', *Archivaria*, **6** (1978), 176–80.

Public Record Office, *The selection and preparation for transfer of machine-readable records: a provisional guide* (London, 1974). Processed.

Public Record Office, 'Analysis of replies to questionnaire on machine-readable records' (appendix to 17th Report of the Advisory Council on Public Records) in *Seventeenth Annual Report of the Keeper of Public Records* (H.M.S.O., London, 1976), 36–42.

Rosenkrantz, G. J., 'Data automation program records: general records (retention) schedules No. 20', *Records Management Journal*, **11** (1973), 2–18.

Ruggles, R., 'The preservation and use of machine-readable records', in *The National Archives and Statistical Research* (1973), 29–38.

Tomberg, A. (ed.), *Data Bases in Europe: a directory to machine-readable data bases and data banks in Europe* (Aslib, London, 1976).

Whiteside, N., *New uses for public records* (P.R.O., London, 1975). (RAD Occasional Papers 3). Processed.

G Preservation of machine-readable archives

Alldredge, E. O., 'Preservation of documentation for conventional and automated systems', *Computer studies in the humanities and verbal behavior*, **2** (1969), 39–44.

Billige, S., 'The environment and its effects on tape', *Computer Weekly*, **459** (1975), 15.

Davison, P. S., Giles, P., and Matthews, D. A. R., 'Ageing of magnetic tape: a critical bibliography and comparison of literature sources', *Computer Journal*, **2** (1968), 241–6.

National Archives and Records Service, *Preservation of machine readable records*, by L. E. Davis (Washington (D.C.), 1969). Processed.

National Archives and Records Service, *Handbook of recommended environmental conditions and handling procedures for magnetic tape* (Processed paper, July 1972).

Recommended procedures for the care and maintenance of magnetic tape (Civil Service Department, London, 1976). (Central Government Code of Practice 14). Processed.

Shapley, B., 'The care and storage of magnetic tape', *Data Processing Magazine*, **10** (1968), 80–1.

Index